The Dance of Lost Souls

KELLI CALL

SMASH BEAR
-PUBLISHING-

First published in Great Britain in 2021 by SMASHBEAR PUBLISHING.

Office 6945, London, W1A 6US, United Kingdom

www.smashbearpublishing.com

This paperback edition published 2022

ISBN: 978-1-915636-09-6

Also available as an ebook.

To my husband, Shawn. Just you and me babe.

The Dance of Lost Souls

Prologue

Rogan

One last gust of wind whipped Rogan's hair as he ended the mournful melody on his duduk pipe. Breathless and exhausted, Rogan wiped the grave dirt off his hands. He pushed himself upright after the force of gathering souls had knocked him to his knees. The wind dropped, and the crashing cliffside waves calmed while the fog lifted to a thin haze. It was as if the island sighed in relief at the release of the dead.

The fist-sized trident brand on his chest no longer burned. The mesmerizing white light had faded back to its usual black, now looking like any other sailor tattoo. He could feel the souls inside him, fluttering, restless to be released on his ship.

Now that he was finished, he looked over his cursed domain. The moon shone in the parted clouds, placing the cemetery in darkened shadows and white fire. There were no animals scurrying in the undergrowth. Parties that accompanied the Festival of Souls had ended early for the night.

Rogan took one last calming breath. The air was muggy and heavy in its silence. Since the jungle was so close to the cemetery it should have smelled like rotting wood and wet earth. Instead, there was a stinging of salt and thick brine that tickled the Captain's nose, like a building sneeze. Magic was still in the air.

After placing his pipe into his back pocket and putting his shirt back on, he readied himself to return to his ship, *Calypso's Voyage*, when a movement caught his eye. Squinting into the dark cemetery, he made out a human-shaped silhouette rising between two large tombstones.

Standing where only the dead should be was a young woman, clearing sleep from her eyes. He froze, like a child caught stealing sweets, foolishly hoping that if he didn't move the young maiden wouldn't see him. If he hadn't been so surprised he would have just vanished back to his ship, but his shock kept him from acting fast enough. Now it was too late. She had seen him, and would remember him. He was going to have to stay and fix it.

The young woman should have been tucked tight in her hut, like the rest of the islanders. However, the very superstitious culture of the island hadn't deterred her. Rogan gave an irritated sigh, breaking their frozen shock at the reality of each other. She ran a hand through her mess of black hair as he jerked his shirt collar straight.

About once a generation, someone on the island disregarded the rules and snuck into the cemetery to prove if the soul collector was real. When they went missing without a trace by the next day, speculation and fear provided all the proof the rest of the island needed. It was insisted that they had been taken as punishment for their disobedience and disrespect. That fear usually kept mortals out of the cemetery on collection night for the next couple of decades. It looked as though this young woman was the current daredevil of her generation.

Rogan expected her eyes to widen in surprise or terror once

she realized who was staring back at her. However, her expression didn't change. She looked earnest. His chest felt as tight as her fists that rested atop the headstones she was behind. The hand-holding couple that had emerged from there only a few minutes earlier took quite a bit of convincing to come to him. She looked like an avenging angel statue standing over their graves. Her brows scowled as he gritted her teeth like the Captain had somehow hurt her feelings. Rogan registered that his mouth was gaping open, forgetting how to speak. He closed it with a clop.

If she wasn't there to prove he existed, maybe he wouldn't have to take her with him and remind the rest of the island of the rules. A mortal's motivation seemed to be a gray area that perhaps Rogan could exploit. He didn't like taking life to keep his existence a mystery, that wasn't supposed to be his job, so he tried to find as many loop holes in the rules as he could. Rogan had to make her forget him. Only, erasing memories was tricky, they couldn't simply be taken, they had to be given, and he had never done it before. The thought of erasing her memory made him sad for reasons he didn't fully understand.

'Captain!' came a stubborn shout. He refocused at her call, his intrigue overruling his anxiety at being seen by a human.

The young woman raced around the headstones, but halted to a stop two rows away from him, carefully keeping her distance with a dirty shawl still gripped in her hand.

Rogan hadn't talked to a living mortal since his branding. None of them had ever wanted to have a conversation. Now that she was closer, he looked her over while trying to calm his sudden nerves. Her cotton dress was soiled and dirty from laying on the ground. Her hair hung in damp, limp waves. This maiden, with a determined set to her shoulders, sparked something inside his own rebellious spirit, something he didn't know was still there to ignite: respect. His mouth felt dry.

'Yes?' he asked, his voice raspy from disuse.

Lifting her chin, she stood a little taller. Rogan's grin widened. He liked this girl. She was brave. He couldn't recall the last time he liked something.

'I need you to bring my parents back. Please.'

Rogan's brows lifted in astonishment as his head tilted like he couldn't have possibly heard this mortal correctly. If he had heard her right, he was a little worried about her sanity. He asked, 'You're willing to make a deal with Death? Without even asking the price?'

'Whatever the cost is, I'll pay it,' she said, not the least bit apprehensive.

Rogan sighed. 'I'm sorry. Truly. But no. I don't do that.' His sympathetic manner made her grit her teeth. Her anger only intensified her beauty. Rogan cleared his throat, hard.

'Don't or won't?'

'Can't,' he replied. She huffed through her nose, frustrated that an immortal being had such limitations.

'There is no reversing death, love. Besides, would your parents want you to exchange anything for them? I highly doubt it. They would want you to live.' The souls thrummed in his chest, like her parents were agreeing with him.

'What they would want is to be alive,' she fired back.

The Captain nodded, patiently. 'True. No arguing that. Unfortunately, the gods don't ask us what we want.'

'Aren't you one of them? A god, I mean?'

He chuckled ironically. 'No. I most certainly am not.'

'Then, what are you?'

'Something in between. Think of me as a being with an indenture of servitude. I'm endowed with enough power to do what I must, nothing more.' Rogan answered.

Her full lips thinned into a frustrated line. Standing there clenching her fists, the Captain wasn't sure if she was going to punch him or run away.

He found himself in uncharted lands and needed to act fast.

Technically, he had until sunrise to be back on the ship, but he had never dallied on land before. If he wasn't back soon, the Goddess would notice and she would ask questions. Yet, he didn't feel compelled to leave.

'But, perhaps I can do something else?'

'What's that?' she asked, guarded.

'A deal of sorts. I can make you forget you ever met me, along with your disappointment, giving you peace to move on with your life.'

'In exchange for what?'

The Captain shrugged. 'A kiss.'

'Why do I have to kiss you?' she asked, highly suspicious of the handsome stranger in the cemetery asking for a piece of virtue.

'Let's just say, it is a kind of magical currency. A kiss holds a lot of power. Without a brand,' he gestured to his trident tattoo just visible by his open collar, 'it's the way magic is transferred. It was how I became a collector, after all. '

'It was?' she asked, now sounding dutifully frightened while taking a step back.

'Don't worry, love, that won't happen to you. I promise, only your memory of me, and the sorrow you are feeling, will be taken in exchange.'

She stood there, distrust etched in her furrowed brows. Rogan tried not to fidget by running his hands through his hair. But, the longer he was gone, the more the Goddess of Death was sure to notice. It bothered him that telling her about the alternative, death, would scare her into a decision. He didn't want to scare her. For some reason, that he would study later, he wanted her to trust him. He really needed her to take the deal. The Goddess, Angelos, had strict rules about the need for humans to get to Paradise or Hell based on their own merits, which meant he had to stay a legend. There was no wiggle room. The Goddess wasn't known for her understanding.

There was a pause before she said, 'Deal.'

'That's it? That fast? No questions asked?' he asked, the words out before he could stop them. What was he doing? He needed this done quickly.

'Desperate times.' Now it was her turn to look uncomfortable by shifting her weight. 'If you can't bring them back, this seems like my next best option.' She tossed aside her wild hair from her face, again. 'My brother,' her voice broke. She took a deep breath, the oxygen pushing down whatever emotion had been bubbling to the surface. In an instant she was resolute again. 'I won't live like this anymore,' she gestured to the open air around her, like the Captain knew what she was talking about.

Rogan's sigh of relief was hidden by his forced nonchalant shrug and the girl's own shaky gulp.

He stepped lightly around the two rows of headstones separating them. The young woman was tall, with her arms frozen at her sides, one fist full of fabric from her shawl. Lightning flashed above them, brightening the sky enough to see the goosebumps run down her bare arms and across her collarbone.

Thunder sounded in the distance, drowning out the deafening roar of blood rushing in his ears. He hadn't touched a mortal in a lifetime, let alone kissed one. The desire to kiss her was so strong, Rogan felt shaky. The smell of jasmine coming from her cleared out the sting of magic that still hung in the air. He took in his own steadying breath, placing his palms on either side of the girl's face. His hands quivered, nervous and excited to touch such soft, warm flesh under his fingertips. She didn't seem to notice. She was also trembling.

Her round eyes met his, and he tilted her face slightly.

'Will it hurt?' she whispered.

'No, I wouldn't hurt you,' he said, surprising himself at the honesty of his answer.

He drew her closer.

'Wait,' she said, gripping his wrists, but not pulling them away.

'Have you changed your mind?'

She swallowed, 'No. I just— can I at least know your name?'

'Why, you won't remember?' He certainly would, though. There was no way his immortal memory would let him forget how she looked at him with warmth and hope in her brown eyes instead of fear or disdain.

'Just, please? Kissing a stranger in a cemetery who is about to take my memories might be less scary if I at least pretended like we knew each other.'

He smiled at that. Her grip on his wrists eased.

'Rogan,' he whispered. 'Yours?'

'Malia.'

'It's a pleasure to make your acquaintance, Malia.'

She gave him a small, calmer smile back and exhaled through her mouth.

'Have you done this before?'

'Malia, stop stalling,' he said with a grin, loving the way her name felt in his mouth. She gave him her own "caught in the act" smirk and nodded. He hadn't done this before, taking memories, but the process wasn't complicated. The kissing, however...

He slowly bent down, giving her all the time she needed to protest again, but she didn't. Her lips parted, expectant. Rogan grasped her heavy tresses, keeping them out of their faces as the wind blew. Something else echoed through him that hadn't in centuries – loneliness mingled with longing. The absence of his apathy made his chest ache. The scent of her, jasmine flowers, filled his senses. She closed her eyes first. He was grateful for the small moment to settle his own anxiety.

Rogan wondered, only for a second, if she had ever been kissed before, but decided it didn't matter. He closed the distance between them.

Their lips met, gentle. Her mouth was unsure, turning stiff. It almost made him pull back, until the thundering of souls in his chest reminded him he had a job to do. Her tight lips finally softened as he patiently nudged them ever so slightly open with his own. A delicate hand clasped the opening of his shirt collar as the kiss deepened. The Captain planted his feet to steady them while his free hand cupped her waist.

She moved closer against him. The curves of her pressed against the hardness of him. Their breaths mingled. Malia gave a delicate moan from the back of her throat, causing an unexpected explosion of fervor to burst in his chest. Rogan's grip tightened in response to her hand gripping the back of his neck. Thunder boomed, and the souls inside him wrestled, jarring him back to the moment, like they were beating their fists against his skin in an effort to get out. He couldn't stay any longer. Careful to only release the right amount of magic in their breaths, Rogan exhaled and pulled back.

Then, in a gust of wind, before her eyes opened, he was gone.

CHAPTER 1

One Year Later

MONDAY

Malia

'F or sale! Blessed cemetery dirt!' shouted an islander along the wooden pier.

'Fortune telling tonight on the beach!' cried another from where the pier met the sand.

'Come and see a piece of sail from the soul ship. One coin for one touch and stave off death for a whole year, guaranteed!'

Vendors kept shouting enticements at the hundreds of foreigners who were embarking onto the island for the week-long festival. Malia fought her way through the sweating crowd to the neighboring beach. A small, overdressed, sweaty man jostled her aside, causing her to bump into a falling basket full of smelly fish. She jumped off the wood planks onto the hot sand, barely dodging the pouring of dead fish. Instead, the lantern and paint supplies she was carrying clattered to the ground.

She was already struggling to keep her white lace dress pristine for the first day of the festival, a basket of slimy fish would have ruined it for sure. She didn't have another to replace it, and tradition dictated that everyone wear white with their red sashes.

'Watch it, girl,' said the old fisherman as he placed his fish back into his stick basket.

'Girl,' she muttered through tight lips, like he didn't know her name, like he hadn't used to work for her father.

Malia apologized as she scrambled to gather the supplies before either she or her things were trampled.

'Try to keep your bad luck curse to yourself,' Sam, the man who was shouting about the blessed graveyard dirt sneered down at her. 'No one wants to catch your family's bad fortune!' He said this as though ruination was a disease that was spread by getting too close.

Half a dozen rude responses bounced inside Malia's head, but before she could spit them out her name was shouted by someone else and Sam went back to bellowing enticements.

'Malia!' came another angry shout.

Malia groaned and hustled through the swarming throng, hoping to lose whomever was calling her. There wasn't time for this. She was running behind as it was. Her trip back to the house to fetch the paint she'd forgotten had put her behind schedule. She and her best friend, Cora, who was waiting down the beach, needed to get a good spot and set up their palmistry booth before sunset and it was already mid-afternoon.

'Malia, don't ignore me, girl. You are too tall to lose in a crowd anyway,' the breathless voice had caught up with her. She wished people would stop shouting at her like she was a piece of disobedient livestock ... wished her brother's messes would remain his own.

'Yes, Toa. What can I do for you?' She did her best to sound relaxed as the rotund man lumbered through the sand beside her. Malia kept her eyes forward.

'Tell your brother after this week, time's up! He needs to pay the money he owes me.' Malia would have been more fearful of his threatening tone if they hadn't grown up together, daring each other to eat mud.

Malia spotted Cora next to the sideboard table they had brought down from the house that morning. She quickened her step and said, 'Sure, Toa. I'll put you on the list, how's that?'

Toa didn't seem inclined to let the conversation drop. He put his broad hand down upon her shoulder, stopping her. 'You know, you're awfully mouthy for someone who is in debt to almost everyone on this island.'

'I don't owe anyone anything.' Malia shook off his hand.

'No, but your brother does. And since he is your guardian, that includes you.' Toa said, pointing a pudgy finger at her.

'I'm not my brother's property,' she said, standing eye-to-eye with him, ignoring the growing number of stares from onlookers. She could have sworn her near-shout caught the attention of everyone on the island, even those from their huts in the village or homes above their shops at the market. Islanders were waiting to pounce on the gossip like piranhas to flesh in the water.

He chortled. 'You are until you're married.'

'That is an outdated custom, and you know it, Toa.'

'Not on Blisse it isn't. You want new customs, go to Starzea.'

Malia was about to tell Toa where he could stick his debt and his podgy fingers when Cora sprang in between them.

'How about you let us set up and work in peace so we can get your money back?' Cora said calmly, hand on her hip. Cora might have only been as tall as Toa's chest, but her attitude more than made up for her lack of height. With the festival starting in a few hours, no one had time for this kind of nonsense.

Toa looked down his wide nose at them, even though Malia was nearly as tall as him. Visible sweat stains were soaking through his shirt. The sun was growing hot. When his shoulders relaxed, she knew they had won – for now.

'You might want to get rid of your companion,' he said to Cora, jerking his double chin at Malia. 'No one will want to come to your booth if they are told you work with a family of charlatans.' He turned to leave.

Malia whispered after him, 'I'm pretty sure they will feel the same way when they find out your blessed cemetery dirt actually came from your flower garden, Toa.'

He waved off her last jab and walked closer to the shore, where his booth sat in the hot sand.

Malia felt her mango breakfast stir in her gut. She couldn't go one afternoon in the village without someone harassing her over Brandt's debts and stupid mistakes. Even going to the market had become too embarrassing as villagers refused to trade anything for her mangos, claiming they were cursed. Cora went by herself instead.

'Don't worry about Toa,' Cora said, giving Malia a bump with her hip and bringing Malia's focus back to the task at hand. 'Is he what took you so long?' Cora asked as they arrived at their table which Malia promptly dumped her armful of booth supplies onto. The red sash around Malia's waist had come loose and she huffed, tying it impatiently.

'Toa? No. The harbor was a jungle to get through. And Brandt stumbled in, right as I was about to come back, so I had to deal with that.'

'How was your brother this afternoon?' Cora asked.

Malia began organizing their supplies with a little too much force against the table surface as she remembered the exchange she had just had with her brother.

She had come from her room and down the stairs to find the front door wide open and her brother passed out on the floor at the bottom step, again. She looked around the entryway, disgusted. The rugs were encrusted with old sand, the marble floor was caked with noticeable traces of dirt and there was sand by the doors that never really left the house. Cobwebs hung from the crystal chandeliers, making her shudder. After taking one look at him, she marched to collect a bucket and then dumped icy water all over him.

Brandt had bolted upright, gasping. His eyes were wild and glassy as water dripped from his hair onto his face, but after a few moments, he seemed somewhat coherent.

'Good morning,' Malia said even though it was the middle of the afternoon. She carefully stepped around him on the slippery surface, and slammed the empty metal bucket on the marble floor. The clang echoed painfully off the barren walls and vaulted ceiling.

Brandt put his face in his hands and moaned. He laid back down on the bottom step, his hangover bothering him more than the frigid water.

'Go away, Bug,' he mumbled behind the wall of fingers. Bug, the nickname he used to call Malia when she was little because she always danced around him like a swarming gnat. Now, he said it like she was vermin.

'Oh, Brandt,' she said in a pout, inching closer, 'Don't be that way.' She picked up the bucket.

'Malia, do you have to be so obnoxious?' asked the drunkard, his face still in his hands.

'Oh, I'm obnoxious?' she asked, trying to sound innocent, but her voice rose. She threw the bucket down next to his head.

With more speed than she thought he was capable of, Brandt shot to his feet. Malia jumped back as he slipped on the floor and grabbed a hold of the banister to keep his balance. The hand that, before, had always held a violin, but now held glass bottles.

'Yes! You are an obnoxious, spoiled brat!' he shouted.

'And you are a useless, drunken fool!' she fired back.

Brandt looked like he wanted to retaliate, only once on his feet, he swayed. Squeezing his eyes shut, his right hand held onto the

13

banister with a white-knuckled grip. His left arm was kept tucked to his chest.

'Have you ever considered,' Brandt slurred, 'that you are the reason I drink, Malia?' Brandt gingerly sat down on the bottom stair, holding his head with his right hand like it weighed as much as a cannonball. Malia looked at his nearly-useless left arm resting on his lap and felt her chest ache. Would he ever stop blaming her? It wasn't like she had asked him to cover her body with his during the accident. If she could have switched places with him, or either of her parents on that day, she would have.

'Have you ever considered that you are the reason you drink?' she asked, her cheeks burning hot. Her sadness quickly turned into her own resentful anger.

'Where are Mother's pearl earrings?' she asked. When there was no response she said louder, 'You know, the very last of our mother's jewelry, what was supposed to be my inheritance. Where are they, Brandt? You gambled them away to Eldon Haych, again, didn't you?'

'Leave me alone, Malia. It was a bad night, the cards were cold.'

'In other words, yes. Just like everything else. Didn't you?'

'I'll win them back, don't worry,' he gave a wave of his hand, his eyes already closed as he laid his head on the step above him and seconds later, began to snore.

'My brother was asleep when I left,' was all she told her friend, but a knowing look passed between them. Since Cora still lived at the once-grand house, she was no stranger to Malia's troubles – and neither was the rest of the island.

'Let's set up your palmistry booth over there, by the sandy tree line. That way you won't be in the way of the dancing, but people will still see you,' she suggested as Cora bundled her mass of black curls into a tight ribbon, ready to work. Careful not to tumble their supplies off of the table, they gingerly lifted it before they climbed up the sandy hill.

'I'm not sure this is worth it,' Cora said between grunts.

'It will be, trust me,' Malia said.

The smell of rotting fish from the harbor and sweaty islanders abated the further up the hill and away from the harbor they went, replaced by sweet fruit and the ocean breeze.

'Perfect,' Malia declared as they finally put down their table. Cora's warm toned skin had started to glisten, but she gave Malia a satisfied smile as they studied their perfect spot.

'Do you want to talk about it? Your brother, I mean,' Cora asked as she began to untangle a piece of rope.

'What's there to talk about that we haven't already discussed?' Malia shook out their sail canvas. 'He gambled away the last piece of my mother's jewelry last night. As far as he knows, we have nothing left, and he seemed to care more about sleeping off his hangover than paying his debts.'

'Shameful,' Cora said, shaking her head, while taking a hold of the other side of the sail canvas. She drew close to Malia and began to whisper, her brown eyes nervously looking around for anyone that might be close enough to overhear, 'After this week, it won't matter, right?'

Malia gave her friend an unsure small smile. 'Right. Escaping to Starzea is going to be incredible.'

'You're not having second thoughts, are you?' Cora asked in a worried whisper, brushing a wild curl behind her ear as Malia jumped on top of the table, sail and rope in hand.

Malia shook her head. 'No, of course not. We have to get off this island. It's just . . .' Malia noticed that she was rolling her sash at her waist in her hands, wrinkling it. She immediately dropped it and began securing their sign, earning her some scowls from the islanders along the beach. Sure she was in her festival dress that was a little shorter than normal, and jumping on the table wasn't exactly proper, but what else was she supposed to do? She didn't see any of them volunteering to help.

So, Malia resumed her task of tying their sail-canvas-turned-sign between two trees, regardless of their stares.

'I keep hoping for some kind of a miracle,' Malia said.

'Who needs a miracle?' Startled, her bare feet almost slipped off the table. Malia turned on the balls of her feet, muscle memory of hours of dance lessons taking over, keeping her securely on the table. The sound of Eldon Haych's voice sent a shiver of revulsion down her spine. He smiled up at her, his gray hair reflecting the bright sun. He was the last person in the world who needed to hear about her plans for escape. The older man was flanked by two burly guards, whom he kept around for additional intimidation, or when he didn't want to get his own hands dirty. No one had ever had the guts to physically assault Haych, even in self-defense when he assaulted them first.

The guards turned their backs toward them, becoming a wall of muscle, securing unwanted privacy for her and Haych, with Cora getting stuck on the other side of the human wall. Malia's breathing hitched, feeling suddenly claustrophobic, despite the open air from her perch. She walked across the table to the other side, further away, taking a deep breath in.

From on top of the table, she saw the whole beach, looking pointedly away from the couple. Cora's petite form was the only one standing her ground, even if it was from the other side of the two men. Meanwhile, the islanders whispered to their neighbors as they stole snide glances toward her. She was sure that half the island suspected that she was already his lover with his incessant attention, not to mention her brother's known financial troubles. Why else would Haych, now the island's richest, and socially dominant figure, show interest in the island pariah? The answer, she was sleeping with him in exchange for forgiveness of her brother's debts? The other half was resentful that Malia was ungrateful over Haych's favor. Rumors swarmed through the island, like bloodthirsty mosquitoes in the jungle, that Haych planned on making Malia his next wife. Nevermind that his first two had died mysteriously. Nevermind that last year, before her father had died, he refused Haych's intentions to court Malia because of his temper, suspected shady dealings, and questionable past. However, according to her brother and certain islanders, beggars shouldn't be picky about where their next meal comes from, even if that meal would eventually poison them.

'Perhaps I could provide one, a miracle that is,' he continued, clasping his wrinkled hands together in self-importance. Malia glanced down and noticed they were bruised at the knuckles, like he had just been in a barefisted boxing match. She had no doubt some poor urchin, who had displeased him, was laid in a heap somewhere. Haych liked hitting things. He might have been older than her own father, but he still had the physique of a hard-muscled islander, even if that muscle was under a comfortable layer of fat now. A life of heavy fishnets and rowing boats gave the man muscle that hadn't disappeared with age.

'Performing miracles? Are you a deity now?' Malia asked, tightening a knot that was already so tight it creaked around the palm tree.

He licked his lips while studying her exposed brown legs. She fought the urge to kick him in the face. Carefully, but quickly, Malia got down from the table, pointedly ignoring his outstretched hand. She regretted that decision as he instead placed his large palm on the small of her back. Her fists curled tightly onto her dress to stop herself from swinging them into the man's beady eye. He had no right to act so familiar. Her knuckles began to shake with the effort of self-control. She only had to make it to Sunday.

Six more days until all the traveling ships left, with her and Cora safely and secretly aboard one of them. She focused on her potential future and the feeling of excitement to start a new life on Starzea, rather than her intolerable present. They could do it, they just had to be smart and careful, which meant she couldn't hit the old walrus in his face. She had to act like nothing was wrong or suspicious.

'I'm afraid I'm not a god. Not yet, anyway.' Finally, he removed his hand, and the fabric at Malia's back stuck to her skin, like an invisible mark of disgust. 'But, as the newly elected governor of Blisse, I don't think I need to be a deity to help the island's most beautiful damsel. What can I do for you?'

His demeanor was flirtatious as he faced her, but Malia knew better. The lines around his eyes were too tight for his smile to be genuine. Everyone knew better than to think Haych was some sort of lovesick fool. He didn't give something for nothing, even in the form of a flirtatious gesture. In the end, he wanted something, whether it was marriage, or a lover, Malia would be dead before she became either to him.

'We were just saying this sign is only going to stay up with a miracle.' The lie came easily. 'The only help I require is for someone to control the wind,' Malia said lightly as she grabbed the last flapping corner of the palmistry sign, and secured it with a little too much force to the palm tree. Normally, Malia would love the cooling wind coming off the ocean and the promise of fast sails in a few days, but at that moment, it was just one more sign of defiance from the gods at her attempt to have any control over her fate.

'For you, my dear,' he said, sweat beading down his brows as he stood there in a ridiculously layered suit, high collar, and shiny leather boots, 'anything.' The breeze no longer smelled fresh, but like sour onions, as she stood downwind from him..

Malia was spared from further conversation when a Starzea cabin boy came running up. One of Haych's guards stopped him from getting too close with a trunk-sized arm.

'Sir Haych?'

'What is it, boy?' Haych's pretense of kindness disappeared in a flash with his harsh tone and sharp turn. The boy flinched back, fidgeting with the dirty hat in his hands. 'Beg your pardon sir, but my capt'n be wantin' to speak to ya. Capt'n Marques of the *Emilien*. He said he would be in the fruit fields, sir.'

Haych straightened a little at this news. It looked like the boy's ears would go without being boxed.

'Excuse me, my dear. This is a meeting I cannot miss. I look forward to dancing with you on the beach later this evening.' Without another gesture or word, he marched off through the sandy divots toward the harbor, his men and the boy in tow.

'I wasn't sure he would ever leave.' Cora said, as they watched them disappear into the parted crowd.

'The old man has some nerve assuming I'll dance with him tonight,' Malia grumbled through gritted teeth.

'Oh really? Who do you plan on dancing with instead?' Cora asked, raising her eyebrows up and down. Malia appreciated her friend's attempt at playful distraction, and felt her shoulders ease a bit in response. Cora always tried to see the bright side of things. Even when she lost her mother at fourteen and came to work for Malia's family, she told Malia that at least she got a best friend out of the worst thing that had ever happened to her.

'Well, since my preferred partner will be reading the palms of travelers all night. . .' Malia trailed off, gesturing to her friend who bowed her head remorsefully, 'I guess I will go with the next best person. Myself.'

'What a wonderful choice,' Cora conceded.

'We better hurry and finish up. It will be sunset before we know it.' Malia said.

'Yes. We don't want to offend the Captain by being late with his invitation. An offended god is a nasty business.'

'He isn't a god.' The words came out of Malia's mouth before she even thought about how it would sound like hearsay.

Cora gasped.

'I'm sorry,' Malia said to her deeply religious friend. 'I don't know where that came from. You don't think he heard, do you?' Malia said conspiratorially to lighten the mood.

Cora gave her friend a side-long glance as she began unfolding the table cloth. 'The last thing you need is for more odds to be stacked against you. So, for your sake, I hope not.'

Chapter Two

Rogan

L and! She was both beautiful and exhausting. As the ship heaved and sank beneath Rogan's feet, he could see the entire rocky cliffs of the west coast of the island. The white, sandy beach backed-up to a palm tree line where the jungle awaited. The jungle foliage rose up the hill in the center of the island and to the west, creating the cliffs along the western coast.

On the opposite side the island sloped back down to small fields. The green foliage of the jungle trees on the hill swayed in the wind, like the island was waving hello, welcoming him. He sailed around the coast. Firelight from lanterns in the harbor, and windows from the village huts were appearing, like Blisse was winking at him. Flirtatious and inviting.

He ignored the lying invitation that the island was soft and welcoming and made his way to the cliffs, where the island was honest. The cliffs were menacing and sharp, like jagged teeth threatening to chew up any ship seeking port. That part of the coast was isolated, serving Rogan's purpose perfectly. The brooding lighthouse sat there, dark and quiet, like the cemetery it lauded over. Rogan thought it was odd that the light wasn't lit, but waved it off. It didn't matter for him and his ship anyway. He steered the bow toward Cliff's Teeth where he would anchor the soul ship, *Calypso's Voyage*.

The brand on his chest started to give off a slow burn as the ship neared the island.

Rogan's power soared in his veins, like wind leading the sails. The control of the ship, sea, and even life and death itself made his veins hot and body warm. The sounds of laughter and revelry could be heard wafting on the waves, minutes before sunset, when the party would start. Anyone that saw his ship after sunset would think he was one of dozens of ships arriving for the Festival of Souls: Rogan's festival.

None of the other soul collectors got a full week of celebrations just for them. The people of Blisse held their costumes and superstitions tight, and practically worshiped the soul collector as much as the Goddess of Death herself. Places like Starzea had their celebrations; parades and other holidays for other collectors, maybe, but not a full festival.

He was lucky, really. The Goddess had decided to gift him with a rare mercy and let him participate in the festival that year. Not once had he been late, or missed a pick up. With the exception of the year before, namely Malia, anyone else that had ever seen him over the decades had been dealt with swiftly. Now, because of his perfect record, instead of only stepping on land on collection night, he was being allowed on land every night during the week-long festival.

Rogan thought it funny; when he was alive and escaped the fate of the workhouses for that of a ship's cabin boy, he had never wanted to see land again. Now that land was mostly forbidden, he found that he missed it. Or was it something else he longed for? A young woman with wild dark hair and eyes flashed in his memory.

The thought of seeing her again stirred something inside him that he couldn't name. It was a feeling that matched the look Malia's mother had given her husband as they clasped hands to meet their eternal fate when he dropped them off at Paradise. Longing? Hope? He wasn't really sure, but it was like a mirror of himself.

The desire to see Malia again, just to see if she was alright of course, had his feet itching to touch land. The memory of the young woman he had kissed, touched, had repeated in his mind in a constant loop. The possibility of seeing her again in only another hour sent a tremor of excitement to Rogan's hands. He shook them out, hoping the surge of anticipation that made his fingers tingle would leave.

Rogan knew he was being foolish. Running into her again could only bring disaster, even if she didn't remember him. He shook his head this time, determined to focus, but anticipation, it seemed, was not something he could easily shake away. Clearly. He sailed to recover souls, deposited them at either Hell or Paradise, and sailed back to collect more. There was no difference between years and hours on the ship, nothing to look forward to, or anticipate. Now, with the promise of going ashore for the week, Rogan rushed along his deck and released his anchor.

It had been a year since he had taken that maiden's first kiss, and he hadn't stopped thinking about how warm her mortal lips had been. How those few minutes weren't nearly enough time with her. He paced the deck, watching the sunset. He could have sworn the sun was now deliberately slowing down, drawing out Rogan's restlessness, just to teach him the value of time. As soon as night came, he was transporting himself onto that beach and finding Malia.

'Hello, Pet.'

On instinct, he reached behind his back for the hidden knife he used to keep on his belt. Years of reflective habit for survival hadn't broken with immortality. He didn't need such a crude piece of protection now, not when he was more powerful than any weapon. It only took him a moment, and he recognized the voice. He calmed and turned, his hand knifeless.

'Angelos, my lady,' Rogan said in a casual greeting. The Goddess of Death was leaning against the railing of the ship. Waves sprayed water against the haul, but the Goddess and the ship deck stayed dry, as if they were in their own elemental protective bubble.

She looked relaxed and comfortable as she leaned back. Her white dress flapped in the wind, loosely covering the intimate parts of her, the bangles at her wrists and ankles glowing a warm orange as they reflected the setting sun. Her feet were bare, like she was about to enjoy an evening on the beach. Waist-length black hair was tightly pulled back from her face with a black tiara of ten spires made from finger bones, with gold chains and black pearls interlaced in the space between each finger. She had an eerie vanity down to an art form.

'Rogan, how nice to see you,' she said, like he was a rude dinner guest that showed up late to the party. Rogan tried to gauge just how annoyed she was while she studied him with an intense gaze, meeting his blue eyes with her unnatural gold ones. She looked at ease while she studied him with a raised eyebrow, and not at all like the storm of power that she was.

'You weren't about to leave the ship early, were you?' If the sun was up, Rogan was to be on the ship. No excuses. Since he was a being of the night, he could not be among the living during the day. Daytime that week was his isolated time to sit and think about what he had done on that ship all those years ago when he was just a mortal. When he left the festival on Sunday, he would go back to his permanent dark seclusion.

'Of course not, Goddess,' he said, fidgeting with a rope.

'Anxious to get to the festival? To enjoy yourself?' Her fairy-like voice sounded nonchalant. It was a lie. The Goddess was never indifferent. This was some sort of test. The woman was like a fox, beautiful and sly, and waiting to tear his head off at the first wrong move.

Rogan placed the rope on top of a barrel. If he looked busy, maybe he could get out of having to answer any questions. Enjoyment would mean admitting his feelings, and he didn't want to do that, not even to himself.

'Come now, Rogan,' she said, her voice twinkling as she approached. 'Don't pretend that you aren't. You're restless and I can hear the excitement as your heart races. There must be a reason why you are so excited to join the mortals on the beach. Something more than just a night of dancing around like chattering monkeys.'

She stopped beside him and playfully swept her fingers through his long hair as she would have a small child she was trying to coax the truth from. Rogan felt his teeth clench and the muscles in his forearms grow taught, on edge. The Goddess' emotions could flip from calm to a hurricane in a matter of seconds. All it would take would be to give her an answer she didn't want to hear. He knew better than to think this was a simple question.

Rogan decided changing the subject would be the best course of action and asked, 'Is there another reason why you're here? Do you need something, Goddess?' She moved away and began a leisurely stroll around the deck. Rogan felt a muscle in his neck twinge. If he had been mortal, he would have felt a headache coming on.

Angelos wasn't the type for routine house calls unless a collector did something wrong. With the exception of being spotted by a mortal last year, which he fixed, Rogan had a perfect collection record. Rogan hadn't told Angelos anything, and he didn't think she could possibly know about his repressed feelings for the cemetery maiden. At least, he hoped she didn't. It was hard to tell what the Goddess did and didn't know for sure, so Rogan played it safe and stayed quiet.

After a minute of her being cryptically silent while walking around the deck, she looked back over her shoulder and said, 'Wednesday is the night that you gather the souls. Is it not?' Her fingers trailed along the ship's balustrade. She knew the answer, but the Goddess loved to play games.

'Yes,' he answered carefully, 'but this is hardly my first time, Goddess.'

'Yes, of course. However, I am a busy woman. Reaping the souls of humanity and all that. So, I need you to do your job efficiently. Since this is the first time that I am allowing you to participate in the festival, I just wanted to remind you of the rules.'

Rogan tensed his shoulders, preparing for a blow. What would make her have cause to remind him of the rules? The thought made Rogan fight the urge to clear the dryness in his throat.

'Sometimes Captains need reminding, especially if they risk becoming ... unfocused.' She gave him a knowing look while tugging on a sail rigging when she walked by. 'You're not going to lose your focus, are you, Rogan?' She said his name like he was her favorite pet. Maybe he was.

'Of course not,' Rogan said, insulted. The constant burn of the trident on his chest, like an itch he couldn't scratch while he was on the island, wasn't something he could just turn off. It wasn't as though he could ignore who he was.

'So there really is no need to remind you,' she drummed her fingers along the wood, 'that no living being is allowed on this ship? If you bring anyone with life in their veins onboard, I'm afraid the price you or that person would pay would be greater than either of you could afford.' She had started circling him. A shark ready to strike.

'Why would I bring a living person on this death ship?' Rogan asked incredulously.

The Goddess shrugged her exposed shoulders. 'There are many reasons why people do foolish things.'

'I'm not a fool,' he defended.

'No, you're not.' The Goddess stopped her wandering to look at him. 'But, things do happen.' Then, without missing a beat, she continued like checking off a list, 'The souls must make it onto the ship for their voyage, and you must be the one that collects them and brings them here before sunrise.'

'Goddess,' Rogan interrupted, which she took good-naturedly as she looked on with patience. 'Really, I don't need to be reminded of all this. I've done this hundreds of times. I'm focused and on task. Nothing will happen to the souls or the ship.' Rogan hoped that his bravado was enough to cover his nervousness. She made him feel uneasy, like a coward, and he hated it.

'I hope not, Rogan, for your sake,' she said, arching a perfectly shaped eyebrow.

'For my sake?' he said, his eyebrows shooting up in surprise. 'You know I don't care about what you do with the collateral you have on me.'

'You mean the fate of your own soul?' she asked, reminding Rogan that she thought it was important.

Rogan only gave her an emotionless shrug.

He knew what he had done in life and what he had to do now. He wasn't sure if his indifference came from his curse, or if that was just how a person endured.

'I know you are apathetic,' she conceded again, sounding disappointed. 'But I'm hoping that one day, soon, you will have an awakening. What if I decided to keep you on this ship forever, Rogan? Forever in limbo? Forever is a long time.'

'Forever's no time at all on a ship where time means nothing,' he countered.

'Yes,' the Goddess said eagerly, 'but once you have tasted time and its meaning this week, I'll want you to ask yourself if forever on this ship is what you really want. Not everyone gets a second chance at redemption.'

'I want nothing,' Rogan said, indifferent as a statue. Angelos' eyes glowed gold like a deep flame, and Rogan knew the winds of her internal hurricane were shifting, straight towards him. The Goddess' eyes always changed shades according to her mood, or he should say, the restraint of her power.

'Why do you care, Goddess?' Rogan asked, exasperated while carefully avoiding answering her sticky questions.

'I'm the Goddess of Death, dear,' she said brightly, her eyes turning back to lovely gold as though she hadn't been annoyed with him a moment ago. 'It's my job to care. Every person, every soul, contributes to an eternal cosmic power struggle, a balance, a game, if you will. And I don't like to lose.'

'Mortal souls are just pieces of a game to you?'

Angelos waved off-handedly, 'No, of course not. Not to me, anyway. To other gods you are worth much less. So be grateful I am your ally.'

Rogan gave her a confused look. It was the first time she had talked to him about any other gods or goddesses and he didn't like to think that Angelos was the best he could do as an ally.

'What kind of power struggle?'

'Souls are power, Pet. I thought you knew that. Anyway,' she said, dismissing any further questions with a wave of her hand as she sat on the anchor shackle, 'Don't worry yourself about the affairs of scary gods and goddesses. Just remember that you're lucky it was I who took an interest in your particular situation and not one of my sisters. They aren't as understanding or as patient as I am. Most of them would have dismissed your soul straight to Hell. But I saw the potential in what you could have been when you were alive, and it's fascinating. With some education you could have been brilliant, with some advantages you could have been successful. With some care, you could have been capable of a love people cross oceans for. You could have been so much more had you been given just one of these opportunities. I would suggest that you not squander this one.'

Rogan suppressed an eye roll. She even admitted that cursing him as Captain was just part of a sport that the gods liked to play. However, Rogan wasn't stupid enough to say this aloud. Just because he didn't care about the fate of his soul didn't mean that he enjoyed pain. And he knew she could inflict plenty of it if she so wished. If Rogan's life had taught him anything, it was that there were worse things than death. A life of beatings, and the crack from the lash of a whip echoed in his ears. The surprise of his memories from his mortal life, which he tried very hard not to think of and hadn't in a long time, caught him off guard. He held his breath for a long pause until the phantom sting disappeared from his back.

Almost like she read his mind, she sighed, 'You still haven't learned what it's like to trust, have you, Rogan?'

'I've never trusted anyone other than myself, why start now?'

The Goddess gave him a pitying look that he chose to ignore.

Since it seemed like she wasn't going to leave until she finished, he gestured for her to continue, then crossed his arms over his chest and leaned against the mast, waiting.

She gave a small smile, which he didn't believe, before saying, 'Good luck Wednesday night, Rogan.'

'I don't need luck,' he said almost rudely. Rogan hadn't enjoyed this visit at all. Angelos had made him feel small, petulant, and incapable, having to check in on him like an unruly child. It was insulting. And if he dared to admit it, he felt uneasy about the kiss a year ago and the Goddess' possible knowledge of it. All of this had made him edgy, even on the ship where he had never felt anything. Somehow that made everything worse. 'The souls will come,' Rogan said confidently.

Angelos grinned, flashing her perfect white teeth which looked more dangerous in her smile than if they had been sunk into Rogan's arm. 'I wasn't talking about the souls, Pet.' was all she said before she turned, and with the next gust of wind disappeared, like the spray of sea water against the ship.

Chapter Three

Malia

The eastern beach bustled with activity by the time Malia and Cora finished their setup. Men and women had constructed their stalls and booths running parallel between the water and the treeline, providing a sort of avenue for the main-landers. Woodpiles were ready to be turned into massive bonfires down by the breaking water, allowing plenty of space for dancing and mingling. Imported roasting pigs, and peacocks, were already cooking over smaller flames beside the usual island food of fish, clams, and crabs. The smell of cooked meat mixed with the sweetness of baked sugary fruit breads made Malia's mouth water. She was going to eat her weight in food. No mangos for her that night.

For as many fortune tellers on the beach, there were twice as many food stalls dotted down the coast, stopping only where the bonfires and dancing would start.

Their palmistry stall wasn't as fancy as others', with their lush rugs, private tents, and canopies, but it looked respectable and affordable. The lace tablecloth gave their booth class, while Cora's artistic talents made their sign of swirling letters and a painted feminie hand looked inviting.

Cora settled onto her stool, ready for customers as soon as the festival officially started at sundown. Malia took one last look at their hanging sign and was pleased it had stayed straight throughout the afternoon.

'You should let me read your palm before the crowd forms a line. My gift is strongest during the festival,' Cora said. Malia's friend claimed, along with most islanders, that the magic of the festival made them supernaturally gifted. It was mostly for entertainment for all the travelers, or a way to swindle coins from people without a pesky thing like accountability getting in the way. Cora, however, truly believed she had the ability to read a person's palm. Especially after she predicted Toa's wife would have twins, and she did. Her confidence only grew when she just knew old man Tupu was going to die and two days later a coconut, of all things, randomly fell on his head and killed him.

'No thanks. I want my future to be a surprise.' Malia winked down at her friend. That was partially true. The other part was terrified of what Cora would say. 'I don't need a clock constantly ticking in my head, counting down,' she said, and placed both palms on the table, leaned forward and gave a conspiratory whisper. 'You just save all your wisdom for those paying customers. Maybe I'll have you read my palm on our way to Starzea. It will give us something to do on the ship.'

As Cora smiled back, she lit a small lamp and anxiously drummed her fingers against the lace tablecloth. They were going to need all the money they could get.

Promising to check on her later, Malia wandered a little ways down the beach and away from the rows of booths and stalls. With the sun setting and the ocean breeze clearing away the stuffy humidity, the beach was cooling fast. The white sand was already cold as it played around her feet and filled the crevices of her toes. She squeezed her way through the crowd of waiting islanders.

Every space of the beach surrounding the island was covered with people finding their spots to watch the sunset. As the sun dropped down further behind the waves, everyone stilled and became quiet. It felt like the island was holding its breath too as it waited for the living to light up the beach fires and invite the Captain of Souls to the island.

When only distant dying orange streaks were left in the sky, a sigh could almost be heard around the island, the calm before the storm of revelry now over. The shouting and music began an instant later, lifting Malia's spirits. She rushed toward the closest food stall. Malia's stomach rumbled as she swiped a piece of sweet bread from the food stall run by her old cook, Samora.

Samora saw it and handed her another one and said with a smile, 'For Cora. You girls are all skin and bone.' Malia took it thankfully, but didn't stay to chat as a small crowd was starting to form a line behind her. She ran the sweet cake up to Cora, who already had several people in line, waiting to see what their palms foretold.

Malia continued to pluck free samples from stalls as she strolled down the line. They hadn't been able to afford meat or sugar in a long time, and she wasn't going to waste the opportunity to eat something besides mangos.

Malia licked her fingers nearly raw of any sugar residue by the time she drew closer to the wood piles that were being lit. Men and women sat in groups of four around each large pile of wood with their drums, flutes, pipes, violins, and cellos, and began playing rapidly, giving the beach a hungry, haunting atmosphere. The very sand beneath them vibrated with the music and shifted to the turning of feet. It was changing the island into something otherworldly.

'Sacred cemetery dirt sold here!' Toa's voice boomed as Malia walked by him. He squinted his eyes and she gave him a small nod. A truce, if only for a few days. He nodded back in acceptance and continued shouting. Everyone, including herself, was willing to be a little nicer during the opening of the festival. For one night she wasn't the orphan with the disgraced brother. She was just another islander, just another girl on the beach.

The atmosphere was electric with eagerness, as if it was everyone's wedding day. The whole island was celebrating life as shouts and whoops of excitement filled the air.

As she walked around greeting people, she stuck close to the fires and breaking water. Looking up the coast at the crowd of people made her question the wisdom of where Cora's booth was set up. Maybe they should have set it up further from the trees and closer to the fires? The amount of people filled with confusion, abandonment, and alcohol could easily result in trouble. Malia's number one safety rule was to stay on the beach. It was important to remember the cautionary tales of what happened to young girls that didn't keep their wits about them. With all the noise, tree cover, and ships that never returned, it was smart to keep in the open. However, islanders did look out for each other, and Cora was near plenty of neighboring stalls that would keep an eye out for her.

Bonfires erupted, becoming beacons to guide the Captain to the beach. The heat from the flames seeped through the lace of her dress, warming Malia against the cool ocean breeze.

The fires made skin and cloth glow with red and orange as shadows played on the crowd's features. Everyone appeared mysterious and wild. But it was the growing music that captivated Malia. She heard the beat and felt the rhythm flow through her fingers down to her toes. She could feel it, the pulsing just under her skin – the urge to dance with abandon.

Malia had been one of the best young dancers on the island. She always hoped that the islanders would vote for her to be the performer for the Dance of the Lost Soul on Wednesday night.

That was until Brandt had lost all their money and the respect of the islanders the year before. Now, she didn't know who would have the most sacred honor of performing the role of the Lost Soul, but she was certain it wasn't going to be her. The Lost Soul dance was the single most honorary tribute an islander could bestow on the Captain of Souls and the memories of loved ones past. It was done on the night of the collecting and reminded everyone of the true purpose of the festival: death was inevitable, and so made life worth celebrating.

As the crowd swarmed around, Malia spotted Eldon Haych and Brandt talking not far down the beach. Malia's stomach roiled. The fact that Haych insisted that people call him "Sir", like a gentleman, only made Malia more aware of how much he was not. The pair of them walked close together looking through the crowd. Haych said something in Brandt's ear that turned his head. Both men focused on an unaware young woman as she passed by. Haych said something else in Brandt's ear that had both men laughing.

Brandt looked to be relatively sober – he walked without stumbling into the sand divots, anyway. Malia gave that a few more hours. He seemed in good spirits, though, as he surveyed the beach, noticing the pretty girls. Malia wasn't sure how Brandt would be, his first festival where he had to act as a spectator and not a musician, where he had been the most comfortable. Maybe all the food and pretty girls would be a distraction for him, that he wasn't playing the violin with the rest of the musicians on the beach, like he had before. Haych, however, was alert as his beady bird eyes fleeted from one person to the next, eager to miss nothing. Not wanting to get caught in his gaze, she looked for refuge and spotted an ally.

'Come on, Malia!' Samora's daughter, Arieta, pulled her toward one of the bonfires as the music started again. Arieta was closer to Brandt's age, so they had never really been good friends, but like her mother, she continued to be one of the few that was regularly kind to Malia. Within the first three notes, everyone knew that the musicians were going to play the Invitation Song, the first official dance of the festival; one to welcome the Captain to reap the resting souls. The dance steps were simple but powerful, just like death. It was one of Malia's favorites. All the islanders, for those three minutes, were united in celebration and anticipation.

They reached the fire with a group of others and the heat blasted her face like a furnace, while the ocean breeze sent chills down her back. The large circle around the bonfire alternated between boy and girl for partner work. Malia didn't even look at who was beside her as she immediately began stomping her feet; sending sprays of white sand from her bare feet up her legs, while clapping over her head. It only took two beats before she was carried away into the dance. Music filled her ears and body. The thundering drum beats thumped into her while the cellos' haunting strings sent a thrilling feeling of being watched by something mystical.

Just on beat, Malia's hand was taken by a young man. His hair was light blond and his skin pale, clearly not someone native to Blisse, but likely lived further north on Starzea where it was colder and the weather didn't allow for much sun. He knew the dance, so it probably wasn't his first time at the festival. He offered Malia a wide confident smile as they clasped hands and closed the space between them. She found his smile sweet and politely smiled back. As they separated and returned, he winked, and she had to suppress rolling her eyes.

It was a well-known fact that the single (and sometimes married) men that came alone to the festival came to be scoundrels. Just like the island merchants who swindled coins, they swindled virtue without a pesky thing like consequence getting in their way. Many girls were whisked away on a week of romance and lamented unkept promises of return. By doing so, being a bastard was almost a rite of passage. Cora was one such child, which was one of the reasons why she believed in her gift so much. She, and the rest of the islanders, believed if a baby was conceived during the festival then they were magic blessed.

Malia had no intention of ever being one of those poor women that swooned and fell in love. Who was there to fall in love with anyway? The travelers wouldn't take her with them without payment, and love was not a currency they accepted. Plus, the locals all knew of Brandt's money problems and Haych's infatuation, so she was as useless to them as they were to her. It was a mutual understanding of disdain.

He reached for her hand again and gave it a little knowing squeeze. Malia almost missed a step in agitation. She jerked her hand from his grasp. Better let him know now that she was not the kind of girl he would find pleasurable company with that week. The music was too loud for her to tell him she was the wrong girl to try to go for a row in the sand with. Instead she opted for a rude hand gesture and glowered at him. He flinched back, missing a beat or two before moving on to Arieta beside him, who returned his smile with all eagerness.

Just as Malia was getting over her irritation, the drums stopped, and the first dance was over. She clapped and cheered along with the rest of the surrounding crowd. Turning to face the ocean breeze to gather her wild hair and cool her cheeks, she spotted lover boy and Arieta disappearing together into the crowd. Typical.

As Malia waited for the next song to begin, she turned back toward the fire. Shadows, like ghosts, played in the background around the fires. That's when she saw blue eyes on the edge of the sea of people. Unshakable, devilish, familiar sea-blue eyes.

Chapter Four

Malia

Malia did a double take at the young man staring at her. A strong wave of déjà-vu hit her gut. He seemed familiar, she just couldn't place from where. He was handsome in his loose black shirt, pants, and tall boots, like he just stepped off a ship. The man contrasted greatly against everyone else's pristine white, and red sashes, blending into the fiery shadows. His hair was long and as black as his clothes, but his eyes, his eyes were what she recognized the most. They were such a brilliant sea blue they could be seen twenty yards away in the dark. He looked back at her, with round startled eyes.

A firm but weak grip took her arm and spun her around, away from the stranger.

'Bug!' Brandt said cheerfully. Malia took a second to study his hazel eyes, surprised to find them still clear. His dark hair was combed, his face shaved, and his clothes a stark white. It was the nicest she had seen him look in recent memory. He almost seemed like his old pleasant self.

'Brandt,' she replied, looking back into the crowd. He wasn't aware of her distraction as she searched for the familiar blue eyes that had disappeared.

'Sir Haych wishes to dance with you,' Brandt boasted, loud enough for those in their vicinity to hear, like dancing with the old walrus was some great honor.

Malia quickly twisted her arm out of his grip and said through gritted teeth, 'Brandt, I'm not dancing the Soulmate Dance with him.'

Brandt looked confused. 'Why ever not?'

'Because it would be embarrassing for both of us. He just wants an excuse to put his hands all over me.' Malia glanced over Brandt's shoulder to where Haych was a few paces back with one of his bodyguards. He looked Malia up and down like he wanted to do more than touch her with more than just his hands. Malia gritted her teeth in firm disgust.

'Don't be ridiculous, Malia. You should be flattered that the richest and most powerful man on the island fancies you.'

Malia backed away a step in revulsion. Brandt took her arm again and pulled her closer, his face wincing in pain as he fought to keep a hold of her. 'If you insist on being ridiculous, at least keep from being rude. Rejecting him will have consequences.' Brandt's warning was just below a whisper, but Malia heard him clearly. She knew Brandt wouldn't hurt her – not physically, anyway – but he spoke like he was afraid for their safety.

The violinists played the first strings, a signal: the song was about to start.

Malia looked again at the older man and blanched when he licked his smiling lips.

'I suddenly feel nauseous. Please give Haych my apologies.' Malia easily pulled her arm free from Brandt's weakened grip, and fought her way into the fray of the bonfires.

Bodies bumped into Malia as she pushed her way through the throng. Everyone was hustling to gain a new partner and find a spot by a fire.

Finally, her salvation appeared, the treeline just beyond the last bonfire. Malia didn't like the thought of using the treeline as cover. It violated her safety rule to stay on the beach, but dancing with Haych might have been just as dangerous. Stopping to risk a glance over her shoulder, Haych was easy to spot as people bolted out of his way. Brandt, whose neck and ears were now red with embarrassment, followed. As the gap between them lessened, someone grabbed her hand and pulled her into a formed circle around a fire.

She whirled and stared at the familiar stranger. His eyes were dancing and his luscious mouth gave her a rakish smile. She could almost place him but as soon as she thought she had it, the memory was gone. It was like the feeling of just waking up from a delicious dream, only to forget the details a moment later. All the details except his face. She had to look up to see his eyes since he was a good head taller than her, and she wasn't short. He looked younger than Brandt, but older than Malia, maybe twenty. The midnight hue of his hair and the scruff on his face contrasted with his alabaster pallor.

'Hello, love. Fancy a dance?'

Love? A memory flitted. She saw his smirk, his eyes. A fluttering tapped across her chest as she remembered his cool breath tickling her cheek. The feeling of lips on hers, when she had never even been kissed.

It was like a memory, but not one she recognized. His wide eyes and waiting smile spoke only of mischief as he stared back at her, giving nothing else away.

She had just rejected a scoundrel for being too forward, but this felt different. The man looking at her didn't feel like a stranger.

The moment was broken when he looked over her shoulder.

Malia followed his gaze. Brandt and Haych had caught up with her and waited on the other side of the bonfire with arms crossed tightly over their chests, cutting off her escape into the trees. Neither of them could pull her away now that the song was starting without causing a scene. And Brandt knew his sister well enough to know that she would make one.

When it was clear that Malia wasn't going to pull away, the roguish man's cold grip became strong in hers. Raising her chin and planting her feet, she relaxed her arms and swallowed the dry lump in her throat. The stranger sent a smirk of triumph over her shoulder, driving Haych into a blustering fit. He waved his arms towards Brandt, expecting him to somehow control his sister. Like a scolded child, Brandt sulked, with his arms still crossed while shifting his weight side to side. Haych's forehead vein thrummed with surpassed anger. This stranger clearly didn't know who he was dealing with.

Slowly, she turned into position, her shoulders against his back. The other half a dozen pairs of dancers at their bonfire were ready, their backs against each other.

The bows played across the violin strings, their rhythm slow and heady, like the beginning of a tango. The six men around the fire took the first slow half-turn. He was still directly behind her, but now his chest touched her shoulders. He felt like a stone wall against her back. All muscle and stability. Malia took a calming breath.

Sweat prickled on the back of her neck. Half a beat later, his sturdy hands encircled the red sash on her hips. Malia reminded herself to breathe.

The cold from his touch seeped through the fabric to her skin, sending a delicious shiver up her spine. Steadying her hands, she placed them over his, and without missing another beat, he lifted her feet off the sand. Staying straight, he turned them in a full circle before placing her back on the soft ground.

They made a turn away from each other when he caught her

eye and winked. Thankfully, her cheeks were already flushed from the fire, nicely hiding her blush.

Again, he lifted her easily off the ground by her hips. They circled, like unwinding a clock. Strong arms lowered Malia, sliding her down his chest, back onto the sand, she felt every taut groove of muscle under his shirt. He was holding her too close.

He turned her to face him. She had never been so intimately close to a man before. The stares of onlookers burned on the back of her neck. It was oddly satisfying to finally give all the gossips on the island something true to talk about, instead of the whispers that she was Haych's mistress.

'We have an audience,' he pointed out, their lips only inches from each other now.

Malia looked around them and saw that they did indeed have a collection of bystanders watching them.

'It seems we do.'

'Does that bother you?' He brought their arms up and guided her under them before bringing her back against his chest.

She looked over again to her brother and Haych. Islanders were looking between the four of them, like they were watching characters in some play and couldn't wait to see what happened next.

'Not in the slightest,' she replied. In less than a week, who she danced with on the beach that night wouldn't matter. She would be gone, forever. Let it be known, good and fast, that she didn't belong to Haych, and would dance with whomever she wanted, however she wanted.

The beat picked up. The stranger arched a brow as he looked down at Malia, his arm encircling her back, pulling their embrace tighter, their chests touching. His breath was sweet, like he had enjoyed some sweet bread too. She noticed that his eyes kept lowering to look at her lips. She smiled.

'Are you ready to really give them something to watch?' he

asked.

Paying both Brandt and Haych back for the humiliation they had caused her would be intoxicating. A smile broke across her face and her eyebrows rose, 'Absolutely.'

The night, the fire, and the music had all changed like the festival had released its magic, calling Malia to something more than just a dance on the beach. Some people looked scandalized as her partner's hand roamed freely over her thigh, others smiled and cheered at their display.

This man was trouble, and Malia liked it. It was the first time Malia hadn't been looked at with either pity, scorn, or lust since her parents' deaths. He gave her an extra twirl and kissed her hand, making her laugh. He was truly seeing her for who she was. And she hadn't been seen for a long time.

His fingers traced her fire-kissed collar bone. Despite the heat, goosebumps danced along her arms and down her back as he shifted Malia's hair off her shoulder down to one side. His hands were still cold.

She hooked a leg to his hip as he dipped her so low that her hair brushed the sand. Who was he? She did her best to study him as his body pressed tight against her own, trying her damndest to seem subtle. His blue eyes caught her and he winked again.

Her mouth felt dry as he lifted her upright to his chest, their lips, again, hovering only inches from each other. The music ended, their heavy breathing mingling. If dancing with him left her feeling this passionate, she couldn't imagine what kissing him would do.

Her hands had become entangled at his open collar, pulling him closer. Malia felt his thighs strain as his heels dug into the sand, holding them steady. One of his hands twisted in her hair that swung at her hip, the other at the nape of her neck, sending familiar goosebumps down her spine. She was hit with another memory, of both of them standing together just like they were now and she gasped. She looked at his chest, already knowing, somehow, what she would see there. The top of three prongs from a trident tattoo touching his collar bone. His dark brows furrowed as his jaw tightened, like he was gritting his teeth to keep his mouth from coming down on hers. Malia looked away and straightened, confused and embarrassed that she had momentarily felt hopeful that he would kiss her. Letting go of his shirt, her hands came to rest on his arms, providing her some much needed breathing room.

He took a deep steadying breath. 'I'm Rogan,' he whispered, his voice hoarse.

'Malia!' In those few blessed minutes, she had forgotten all about her brother and Haych. They were both still on the far side of the fire, the swarming crowd keeping them in place until the next dance started. Brandt's shout was like the village bell that warned of an incoming storm. When you first hear it, you freeze, then you run to safety.

Looking around her, Malia spotted the treeline. The escape was worth the risk. She wagered she could make it to Cora's booth safely if she was quiet and fast. Letting go of Rogan's arms, she ducked low behind a few tall sailors and ran. She didn't know what Rogan thought of her sudden departure, but she hoped to see him again.

The air was oppressively humid in the trees, with the only light being provided by the fires that bled through the space between the foliage. Malia dashed between palm trees; the sand was now irritating on her bare feet with vines entangling her path. Impatiently, she swiped her arm across them. She nearly screamed when her hand blindly brushed the slick scales of a tree snake instead of a vine. Harmless tree snakes were as common as coconuts on the island. She placed a hand on her chest and took a few deep breaths. The last thing she needed was to scream when she was trying to sneak away. Edging forward, Malia stopped behind every couple of trunks, looking back and holding her breath. She could just make out that Brandt and Haych had split up, looking around opposite sides of the bonfire crowd. She watched as they met near the treeline and began to argue, each gesturing in different directions. They were probably debating which way she took. They finally agreed she had given them the slip through the crowded beach, and started back in that direction. They had underestimated her desperation.

Malia exhaled and made a rush to the cover of another tree. Resting her back against a trunk, she listened. Jungle frogs croaked and insects chirped. No footsteps, though. Sweat started to form between her shoulder blades. The jungle was steamier than the beach.

The music had picked up again; this time a lively tune which didn't require a partner. Of course, she would miss that one.

Now that Malia had a second, the implications of what it meant to dance that way with a stranger was starting to hit her. For a man that had grown accustomed to getting what he wanted, either through threat or payment, was refusing to dance with Haych in front of the whole island really the smartest thing? Would Haych really take revenge against her for refusing him? But the foremost question in her mind was: who had been the mysterious stranger, and would she see him again?

Malia crept along, listening for pursuit. She only heard giggles from hidden girls, and the smack of kissing and sighs coming from the darkness. Squinting into the black jungle to get her bearings, Malia noticed that she was getting further and further from the light of the fires. The jungle in the dark wasn't somewhere she wanted to stay long. The warm sand and soil mixed over her feet, making her steps heavy. She ran faster, now loud, ducking through the brush until she spotted Toa's cemetery dirt stand between the trees. Malia recognized the small clearing, thankfully she was not far from Cora's booth.

She was about to run off again when a familiar voice startled her.

Chapter Five

Malia

Malia had evaded her brother and Haych, but she forgot to account for the man's guards.

'Where are you off to?' The voice belonged to one of Haych's goons that had formed the muscle wall on the beach that afternoon. He appeared in front of her from behind a thick palm tree. She believed this one's name was Brom.

'Home. I'm not feeling well,' she said, taking a step back further in the trees. The short, balding man took slow, deliberate steps forward. Her pulse quickened as sweat ran down her back.

'Sir Eldon Haych requests you return to the beach,' he said. The man didn't look like he was going to take no for an answer as he inched closer.

Malia's eyes darted around for an escape. It was to either get beyond the treeline to the beach, or further into the jungle. His legs were so short compared to his bulky muscled torso that he looked like a disproportionate minotaur. Hopefully, he would be as slow as he was ugly. There was a wicked slash scar on his neck. His taunting sneer suggested that he would enjoy a chase. However, since she was a full head taller and much slimmer, chances were she would be fast enough to get past him, but he looked persistent.

She didn't have anymore time to think through a plan as he lunged. She dodged and spun, her arm barely missing his hand. But he snatched a handful of her dress instead, and pulled her back. Malia heard the delicate lace rip. Rage flew hot from her hand as she slapped the man's face. That was her mother's dress, one of the few she still had, and this monster had damaged it.

'Let go of my dress and leave me alone!' she said through gritted teeth.

Brom moved his jaw around just before he yanked on the dress again, furthering the rip up her thigh and twisting her away, throwing her off balance. Her foot tripped over a fallen palm branch and Malia stumbled toward rough ground.

Before she collided with the ground, someone else caught her waist and heaved her to his chest. Malia was about to scream in protest, thinking she was being attacked by Haych's other guard, Ku, but saw the three prongs of a trident tattoo through the open collar of a black shirt.

Rogan.

A protective arm went around her hips until she caught her balance.

'Are you alright?' he asked, his voice was gentle, but his eyes had a glint of fiery fury.

'Yes. I'm fine.'

'I believe the young lady told you to go,' Rogan said, Malia still in his arms. Now that she was steadily on her feet, he gently nudged her behind him and stepped in between her and the man.

'Move along, sailor, this doesn't concern you,' the brute said.

'The welfare of this young lady is my concern.'

KELLI CALL

Rogan stepped closer to him. The smaller man didn't give an inch.

'I have been hired by this young lady's intended to make sure she—'

'Make sure that she what?' he interrupted. Rogan came within inches of Brom, forcing him to either take a step back or be stepped on. 'Goes back to the beach wearing a torn dress and is humiliated? Traumatized? I don't think so. You are going to leave her alone. Now.'

Brom snickered at Rogan's threat and casually took out a long knife from his belt. Rogan looked down at the man's threat, unimpressed.

'I'm not worried about that,' Rogan said.

Brom gave a bark of a laugh just before he slashed the blade at Rogan's chest. Rogan easily deflected the knife with a forearm and brought his other elbow down on Brom's wrist, forcing him to lose his grip on the weapon. Rogan kicked it away. The glint of the knife flew into the brush, lost to the jungle. Brom growled in frustration and barreled toward Rogan.

Wrapping his arms around Rogan's torso, he heaved to no avail. It must have felt like hitting a ship's haul when Rogan didn't move or so much as lift his feet off the ground. Quickly realizing his tactic was getting him nowhere, Brom let go and scattered back. Malia saw his stunned round eyes. His massive muscles were nothing against the cocky sailor.

'Who are you?' Brom asked as Rogan took him by his shirt collar with one hand and pulled him up on his toes.

'I will be your reaper if you touch her again. And, I will collect. Do you understand?' he whispered so quietly Malia almost didn't hear him, even facing Rogan's back.

Brom stood there dumbfounded, as if Rogan truly did have the power to suck the soul out of Haych's guard.

When he didn't answer, Rogan gave him a shake so hard the man's teeth rattled.

'Understand?'

Brom gave a terrified nod.

'Good,' Rogan said, shoving the man away. Brom tripped over the same branch Malia had and fell straight on his backside.

Scrambling back, Brom got to his feet and made a run for it back up the path.

'You're his reaper, huh?' Malia asked, leaning back against a palm tree trunk and crossing her arms in humor over her chest, hiding how her hands shook. There was no way she was going to show just how terrified she had been before Rogan showed up. Rogan turned around.

'I will be if he comes near you again.' Malia was suddenly grateful for the darkness hiding the heat that inched up her chest and to her neck. 'Anyway,' Rogan said after clearing his throat, 'The threat worked.' He shrugged. 'Poor simpleton almost wet himself. Must be hard to realize all those muscles are meaningless if you don't know what to do with them. Let's move fast before he comes back with friends. Hopefully he is too humiliated to relay what really happened to anyone.'

Rogan took a few steps back to her, his arm extended out in invitation to leave the trees. Malia shoved off the palm tree. He put a hand on the small of her back to rush her along.

They easily weaved their way through the trees, the path becoming sandy again. There was an occasional pleasurable sigh just audible through the sounds of bugs in the bushes, making the silence that had settled between them feel awkward.

'Thank you,' she managed to say as they walked side-by-side, almost reaching the break in the treeline.

'You're welcome.'

Rogan's eyes flashed down to her and quickly back up, before moving aside several large leaves reaching like hands to stop them on the path. Malia looked down and noticed the amount of thigh flashing from her torn dress. She clasped a fistful of fabric and held it together. They walked a little further, Rogan looking everywhere but at Malia's exposed leg.

'What were you doing in the trees, alone?' he asked.

'Sometimes, the risk is worth the reward,' she said.

'Ah, you mean the escape from those two men on the beach?' He didn't wait for confirmation as he stopped walking and relaxed against the closest tree trunk. 'Who are they, exactly?' After crossing his arms over his chest, there was a comfortable air to him, as if he could stand there all night.

'Who are you?' Malia countered.

He met her gaze. 'You really don't remember me?' he asked. Malia hesitated but eventually shook her head. Rogan gave a sigh that sounded like relief. Why wouldn't he want her to remember him?

'Should I? You do seem familiar, but I can't place where. Have you been to Blisse before?'

The man scratched the back of his neck. 'I'm a ship captain. I've been ashore before, but never for very long. I remember seeing you, briefly, last year.'

'You remember seeing me?'

He gave a chuckle as he rubbed his reddening neck, 'Yeah. You're hard to forget'.

Again, she felt her palms begin to sweat. She had never felt so flustered in her life.

'So, why are you on the beach tonight?' she asked, brushing her hair forward over her shoulder, making a curtain between them until she pulled herself together.

'That's two questions in a row, seems unfair,' he said, wagging a finger at her like she was disobeying the rules of a game. 'One question at a time.'

'Fine,' Malia huffed. 'The younger man is my older brother Brandt.'

'And the walrus?' he asked.

Malia broke into a smile; she used the same nickname for Haych.

'The walrus is the man Brandt keeps trying to convince me to court. But I am not interested.'

Rogan nodded while looking down at a scuff on his boot.

'So, why are you in the trees tonight?' she asked again, hoping he would give her answers to settle her curiosity. Had he been concerned for her when she ran off?

He looked up like the answer should be obvious. 'It's my first time spending the evening on the beach during the Festival of Souls. I got a little lost.'

'Lost? You're a sea captain. Shouldn't you have an innate sense of direction?'

'I do, at sea. Getting through the jungle at night is a different story.'

'Right.' Malia fought the urge to fidget with her fingers. His stare was unnerving.

'You don't believe me?' he asked when she began to walk again.

'Of course not. You were following me. Why?' Malia wanted to trust him, sadly, she wasn't as optimistic as she used to be.

'Fine. You're right. I did follow you, but only because I knew you were running from those men on the beach, and I wanted to make sure you got to wherever you were going safely.'

'But why?'

'Why? Isn't that what any gentleman would do?'

'Not on Blisse. Single women are always someone else's problem.'

'Well, I'm not from Blisse.'

'Where are you from?'

'Nowhere, anymore. My ship is my home.'

Malia was outside the treeline now. Her friend was visible, sitting at the table reading the palm of a young, well-dressed gentleman with glasses. She turned back when her rescuer didn't follow her out. The silence between them grew awkward, again, as the distant music and the pleasurable noises of nearby lovers hidden in the trees filled the void.

'Thank you, again, for what you did,' she said.

'You're welcome,' he said. His grin widened in a self-satisfying way.

That smile brought a feeling that she couldn't label starting in her chest and ending in her gut. Was it trust? It had been a long time since Malia trusted anyone other than Cora.

'I should be getting home before more men come looking for me.' Malia turned to see her friend still talking and laughing with the man at her booth.

'Do you think anymore will?' A protective concern in his voice made Malia's head turn back. Rogan was studying his nails again, but his tight jaw matched his tone.

'I don't think so. The start of the festival is too much fun to miss out on by chasing me around the island. Even for Haych. He will find a substitute for his attention, I'm sure,' Malia said.

The Captain nodded. 'Well, it looks like it is time for me to find a substitute, too. Goodnight.'

And before Malia could respond, her familiar stranger abruptly disappeared back into the trees.

Chapter Six

Rogan

R*ogan,* he chided himself. *I know it's been a long time since you've had human interaction, but try to be less awkward.*

Rogan watched Malia slowly kick sand up with her toes as she walked to a palmistry booth. The last customer was leaving to join the roaring party.

Not wanting her to know or see him still watching her, he disappeared and materialized a few yards away from the palmist, hidden nicely in the shadows of the trees, but now within hearing distance.

'Hello, Malia,' the palmist greeted as Malia sat on the empty stool beside her friend with wild black curls and a petite frame.

'Why aren't you out there dancing?' the palmist asked, putting away the last of her coins inside a small leather pouch.

Malia simply shrugged. 'No one worth dancing with. How did the crowd pay out this evening?'

'Oh, pretty well. Enough to feed us something other than mangos for a few days. It's always the best on the first night, when the excitement for magic is in the air and those that are willing to pay are more obliging to do so.'

'How about that last customer? He seemed rather interested in you reading his future.' Malia teased.

The palmist looked down shyly before glancing at the retreating figure. 'He is a doctor on one of the ships. His name is Duncan.'

'First names already, Cora?' Malia asked, smiling, only making her friend straighten her shoulders before swiping imaginary sand off the lace tablecloth.

'Well, we will see if I happen to run into him again,' Cora played off.

'It is a small island,' Malia pointed out.

Cora began to place her things in the center of the table.

'Miss, you really should let me read your palm while I'm all set up here.' Cora skillfully changed the subject but continued stealing glances at the doctor's back.

When Malia didn't answer right away, Cora finally looked at her. Malia shook her head in a polite refusal.

'It might be helpful,' Cora persisted.

Malia was still shaking her head when her eyes bulged, and she dove under the covered table. Her unexpected disappearance had Rogan straightening and whipping his head around looking for danger.

Has the man with the neck scar come back?

'What in the world?' Cora asked before lifting up the tablecloth. Malia shushed her, pulling the white cover back down to hide once more.

A staggering figure approached the stall.

'Hello, Cora,' Malia's brother said. He had lost his older companion and looked rather unstable on his feet.

'Hello,' Cora replied, standing in alarm.

'Haven't s-seen my s-sis-sister, have you?' he slurred, like he was full in his cups, a bottle of brown liquid sloshed in his hand.

Malia's hand slipped from under the cover and gave Cora's ankle a pinch, making the little woman jump. Rogan couldn't help but smile.

Brandt looked a little alarmed at her startled hop.

'Crab!' she said, recovering well as Cora stomped her foot on Malia's hand until it disappeared back into its hiding place. Rogan bit the inside of his cheek to keep from laughing out loud. 'No, Sir. No, Sir, I haven't. I imagine she is on the beach somewhere. Good luck finding her in that crowd.'

He only nodded and stumbled off.

When he was no longer in sight, Cora lifted the sheet. 'Mind telling me what that was all about?' she demanded as Malia made her way out from under the table, brushing the sand from her legs and hands. 'I would hate to be homeless because I was caught lying,' Cora said, putting a hand on her hip.

Malia gave her a condescending look to rival one of the Captain's own.

'Oh please, Cora, like Brandt would ever banish you from the house, and do you honestly believe I would allow it?'

'He is still the legal master, not you,' Cora said sternly, wagging a finger at her. 'You would do well to remember it.'

'I remember it,' Malia muttered as she slumped on the stool. Rogan felt something expand under his ribs. A feeling he had almost let come uncaged when he fought off the man with the scar. He was feeling it again. He couldn't name it, but it also had him balling up his fists, like he was instinctually waiting to punch something for Malia's sake, not his own.

Cora gave her friend's shoulder a squeeze.

'Sorry,' Cora apologized.

'He wanted me to dance with Haych,' Malia confessed,

looking down at her crossed arms like they would be enough to protect her from the old man's advances.

Cora nodded her head, understanding.

'Dangerous man he is,' Cora surmised.

This new knowledge made Rogan's ears perk just as his fists had begun to loosen. Now, his knuckles were clenched and white again.

Dangerous? How? He had noticed how the crowd at the beach avoided him, like a fish avoiding a shark. But, Rogan hadn't considered how the man in the trees might have been under orders to harm Malia if she didn't comply, rather than just acting in his own stupidity.

Malia nodded, but she looked like her thoughts were already far away before replying, 'It would be more dangerous to encourage him. Hopefully, I can keep dodging him until Sunday when we leave this place.'

Understanding dawned as Rogan's stomach dropped, loosening the hold his emotions had on his fists. Malia was going to try and run away at the end of the festival. He felt both protective and panicked. Panic over her leaving. If she left the island, he would, in all likelihood, never see her again, not even when she was dead. If she left Blisse another collector would reap her soul. Protective, because the thought of harm coming to her burned something inside his chest stronger than his soul brand.

'You need to be careful playing that game with Sir Eldon Haych,' Cora whispered barely loud enough for Rogan to hear over the echo of the party and the singing of insects behind him.

'Sir?' Malia snorted. 'The last time I checked, a gentleman wouldn't send goons to drag a young lady back into his company. Besides, my father didn't trust him, and neither do I.'

'What do you mean? You never told me that Mr. Limoze and Haych didn't get along,' Cora said.

Malia exhaled and gathered her memories. 'Several years ago,

I overheard a conversation between my parents. They were talking together in the study. My father mentioned how twenty years ago, Haych had been suspected of war crimes against a village in the nomadic conflicts on Starzea. Father hadn't moved to Blisse yet, and remembered the stories in the papers. Haych was apparently acquitted of any charges, but had returned to Blisse very rich and favored by powerful people on Starzea. Father hadn't trusted him. People on Blisse completely ignore the continent and what happens there, so no one here knew about the nomadic conflict, let alone the accusations against Haych. They just saw the money he brought here, never questioning how he got it.'

Cora looked appalled, and put her hand to her chest like her heart was racing.

'What was he accused of?' Cora asked her friend in a whisper. Almost like she was afraid to know the answer.

Malia looked at her friend steadily, 'Mother asked my father that, but I was spotted eavesdropping and that cut their conversation short. I never heard the answer.'

Malia took an angry huff, looking out at the distant waves with a longing Rogan recognized.

'What happened tonight?' Cora asked with a look that suggested she would take a club to anyone that would try and hurt her friend.

'Nothing.' Malia waved off. 'I'm just ranting. Haych is a monster, not a gentleman.'

Cora sighed. 'Well, that wasn't Haych you were talking to in the trees over there,' Cora pointed out.

Malia looked as surprised as Rogan felt about being seen while conversing together. He thought he had stayed further in the shadow of the trees.

'No, it wasn't,' Malia said. The blush that rose to her cheeks made Rogan lean forward, hanging onto every word she said .

'So, who was he?' Cora pushed, nudging her in the ribs with her elbow again. 'He was handsome.'

'How did you even see us? We were in the shadows, yards away.'

Rogan's mouth felt dry. His feelings were so conflicted, it was like his insides were in a heap of knots. He shouldn't have wanted her to blush when she thought of him. He shouldn't have danced with her the way he did. He shouldn't have gotten involved in her life at all. And he certainly shouldn't have been hanging onto every word she said to her friend, hoping that the mention of his name turned her cheeks that perfect shade of pink again. But, there he was, hanging like a worm on a hook. Fool.

The Goddess would not be pleased if he began meddling in mortal lives. Having a bit of freedom and fun one night on the beach was one thing; fighting off suitors and their guards in a jealous rage was another. Not to mention their history, even if Malia didn't remember it. No, the Goddess would surely think of a deeply unpleasant punishment for him if any mortal's integrity was compromised.

'It's my gift, dearie. I *see* more than you do,' Cora said in a spooky voice with dancing fingers. She sounded like she was teasing, but Rogan wondered if she was telling a bit of truth. Maybe if the little palmist was conceived during the soul collection during a festival and was magic born? Such a thing was rare, more rare than the islanders liked to boast of, but had happened in the past. Magic of the Goddess penetrating the air and soil of the people on Blisse giving a conceived child mortal seerer gifts. If she were, it would account for her claim of having a gift and the success of her booth when she showed Malia her heavy coin purse. Just another reason for him to steer clear of Malia that week. Her friend could be gifted enough to figure out who he was.

'He was nobody,' Malia told her, sweeping hair from her face and straightening her spine.

He exhaled, but the relief was a double-edged sword of frustration. Her nonchalance had him fighting the urge to run toward her and kiss her again in a way she was sure to remember. Instead, he roughly raked his fingers through his hair.

Get a hold of yourself.

There were too many emotions rolling through him for one evening. He missed the comfortable indifference that the purgatory of his ship provided.

'He didn't look like a nobody,' Cora pushed.

'Honestly, Cora.' Malia rolled her eyes and stood as she began to fold up the table cloth. 'It was just another lusty ship captain looking for a good time. No different than the rest of the living and breathing men everywhere. By the end of the week it won't matter who he was. Come on.' She stood from her stool. 'I'll help you pack up and we can head home.'

'Ship captain you say?' Cora said with a raised brow. 'I would argue that he could make a great deal of difference.'

Malia only shrugged a shoulder, clearly wanting the subject to drop.

'Are you sure you don't want to stay? The night is young,' Cora asked, placing the folded lace under her arm.

Malia shook her head. 'No, I've had my fill of dancing for the dead and putting up with the living for one evening.'

'If you say so,' Cora relented as she grabbed their lanturn. They left the rest of the stall, ready to return tomorrow.

Rogan retreated deeper into the jungle brush. Bugs buzzed in his ear, and something slithered near his foot, unhappy at the intrusion, but none of those things drew the Captain's gaze from Malia as she started up the jungle path.

Without spotting Rogan, they left the beach.

He was tempted to follow them home, just to make sure Malia got there safely, he told himself; but he didn't want his status as a member of the undead to be the least creepy thing about him.

Rogan looked out over the raging party contemplating if he should return to his festival. Only the beach no longer held any interest for him. Suddenly feeling exhausted from all the emotions, he went back to his ship: his numb sanctuary and prison.

Chapter Seven

TUESDAY

Malia

'Malia!' Brandt shouted from the marble foyer. The echo reverberated through the mostly-empty house, startling her and Cora. Malia rolled her eyes playfully at Cora's concerned frown. She hadn't expected anything less than dramatic theatrics from her brother. Malia continued to eat her breakfast of mangos from the floor cushions in silence. He would find her soon enough. Even though the dining table and chairs had been sold weeks ago, Malia still felt compelled to eat in the large room, as though her mother had ordered new furniture and it was simply late in arriving.

Another curse and clack of boots on marble flooring came from Brandt in the foyer.

'He must be really worked up yelling like that with a hangover,' Malia said casually. Cora, on the other hand, fiddled awkwardly with her fork and bowl.

Malia squinted at the only wall decor left in the long room: a small clock, barely making out the hands that pointed to six-thirty in the morning. The last remnants of music on the beach had ended only half an hour ago, the last of drum beats waking her up with the sun.

Brandt spotted them in the dining room from the foyer and staggered towards them, stopping once he reached the doorway, red-eyed and sweaty.

It took a long moment for Brandt to gain his equilibrium, his back braced against the doorframe.

'YOU!' Brandt pointed an accusing finger as he lurched into the room and tripped over a vacant floor cushion. He leaned against the wall to collect himself.

'What can I do for you?' Malia asked before taking a long swallow of water.

'You! You little bug, where have you been?' he shouted, waving a shaky finger in her face, his voice still echoing loudly.

'I came home early with Cora.'

'Why did you come home? You were supposed to s-spend the evening with Sir Haych,' he accused, slurring through his speech.

'I think I'll be heading down to the market,' Cora said and quickly exited through the serving doors towards the kitchen.

'I s-pent all night looking for you on the beach!' Brandt continued to yell like he had cotton balls in his ears as he came further into the room. He didn't make it far before he backed himself into a corner, saving his backside from toppling to the ground.

'Your concern is touching,' Malia said, before putting her last bite of mango in her mouth.

'You s-stupid girl!' Brandt said, his eyes round more from fear than anger. 'Don't you understand that he could take everything?' He swiped his good arm across the room, finally knocking himself off his own feet, hitting the floor hard.

'So, you aren't upset that you couldn't find me on the beach for fear that I was kidnapped by pirates, or my virtue being stolen. You are upset because it might have offended Haych?'

'Don't twist my words,' Brandt said.

'There is no twisting Brandt. It is very clear what I am to you. A meal ticket.' After a moment Malia realized something else Brandt had said. 'What do you mean by "everything", Brandt?' Malia drew herself up to her feet. The cold marble bit into her toes.

'I mean if I don't win everything back by Wednesday night, the last day of the month,' he said, struggling to keep himself sitting upright, sweat dripping down his brow, 'We will have nothing left! My debts will be called in, leaving us bankrupt. Sir Haych will take everything! You are the last thing there is to leverage! You are our salvation!'

Thing? Her brother just referred to her as a *thing*. When had she become an object to be used for his gain? Malia felt like she had just been slapped with the cold hand of reality. *Wednesday?* That wasn't enough time. Anything could happen between tomorrow night and Sunday morning.

'You can't use me as your wager, Brandt! I'm not some piece of furniture.' She threw a seat cushion at him. Seeing his bewildered face when it hit him only made her angier. 'I am a human being!' she pleaded. 'I am your sister!'

'Exactly. My sister. Haych is the richest and most powerful man on the island. He is the absolute best match for you. If you would stop letting your anger at me rule your judgment, you would see that this is the best plan for you.'

'No, it is the best plan for *you*.' She pointed an accusing finger at him. 'It is your carelessness that led to our situation, and now you think you can escape accountability for it by marrying me off to that monster, who owns everything that you lost. Why don't you ask Haych's previous two wives what they think of him?'

'One died in childbirth and the other was an accident.' Brandt defended.

'Brandt, how are you so blind?'

'And how are you so judgemental? You should know better than anyone that rumors and gossip about a person's character on this blasted island aren't always true.'

Malia felt his words hit her chest like a fist. He knew what people were saying about her, and still he did nothing to defend her honor.

'You think you are making things right, when really, you are making them worse.' The longer Brandt sat on the floor blurry eyed and confused, the angrier Malia was becoming. It was like he wasn't hearing her at all. 'I would never do something like this to you! How can you treat me this way? You are the only family I have left.' Malia was out of breath and near tears. She inhaled deeply, composing herself as Brandt's blood shot eyes widened as he sat in stunned silence.

'I *will not* pay for your ruin! You dug your own grave; lie in it!'

'You don't understand,' Brandt whispered. 'You are in this, Malia. Even if you refuse to go along with Haych's interest, do you think you will be free? No one will hire you – what do you think will happen when Haych forbids it? You won't even get pieces of scraps off their tables. If you ever tried to leave, Haych would hunt you down, and threaten the merchant ship captains with boycott or violence. Don't forget, he has powerful friends on Starzea, he will own everything here – the fields, the ships, *and* he will have the people's fearful obedience. No one will stand against him for fear of losing their jobs or homes. We will starve, be made an example of. He is the one in charge of this island and the rest of us are his pawns.' Brandt gave Malia a moment to absorb everything he said before he kept going,

'Would it really be so bad if you married him? You would want for nothing and I would run the fishing business, just like before. You would even get all of our mother's jewelry back. He has looked out for us since our parents died.'

'What are you talking about, Brandt?'

'The man took me under his wing. Tried to teach me about the business and how to keep it running. He gave me medicine for my shoulder.'

'He is also the one that introduced you to gambling, and not to mention drinking. He is the one that bought all of your debts. The man has literally convinced you to dig your own grave. Manipulating you from the start.' Brandt looked at her with incredulity. Even with the truth right in front of him, he didn't believe it. She threw another pillow at him. On instinct he lifted his left arm to block. He gave out a hurt yelp as the pillow hit his raised arm.

'Oh Brandt, I'm so sorry,' she began but was cut off as Brandt threw the cushion aside, his face a grimace of pain. Malia held her breath. She just hurt him, again. Anger, regret, and guilt all beat against her chest. She was a horrible sister. She owed him so much, but could not bend to Haych. Brandt was right, marrying Haych would be the easiest solution, but one that would eventually destroy her.

After the spasm of pain left his face, he swiped a hand through his dark tangled hair and stood. He turned to leave, pausing just inside the doorway.

'Since you seem determined in your course to reject Sir Haych's interests, it seems like there is only one other course of action. Sir Haych will be at the Dinner of the Dead tonight. He requested that you sit by him. I suggest that you consent. For your own sake, if not for both of ours. Thwarting him twice, two nights in a row, would not be wise.' Malia was about to protest when Brandt held up his hand in a miserable plea. 'It will buy me some time. Just give me until Wednesday, Malia. I'll make this right. I can make this right.' Malia wanted to believe him, but hope in Brandt came at too high a price.

'You better be careful, Brandt,' she warned, stopping him in the doorway, 'because you will be selling your soul next.'

He looked back at her dismally, like a lost puppy. 'If that's what it takes,' he said before retreating up to his own room.

Malia's chest ached and she still felt out of breath. Hurt and disgust swirled in her stomach like acid. How he had let things go this far was heartbreaking. She knew this had been coming, but the reality of the pain was still surprising enough to knock the wind from her. If he knew her plans to leave now he would probably chain her up and throw away the key. Maybe that was what she deserved for being so disloyal to someone who had saved her life. But, like Cora had told her before, just because someone saves your life, that doesn't give them the power to own it. .

All she had to do was survive the week. Even if Brandt lost everything by Wednesday night, she could still escape by Sunday. It wasn't like she would be forced to marry Haych within three days. He was too vain and elaborate. He would want a big wedding, and that meant invitations to Starzea, and importing food and guests from there as well. She would have at least three months from the time Brandt lost everything to the time she would be forced to marry Haych.

Once she was sure Brandt was sleeping, Malia bolted up the gritty stairs, and to the wardrobe in her room. Brandt hadn't sold her wardrobe or bed yet, probably because he had forgotten she had one. He hadn't been to her room since their parents' deaths.

Grabbing the small key she kept under the leg of her settee, she moved aside the few clothes she had left and reached into the back corner. The key turned easily and sprang the false bottom. Malia reached in and gingerly pulled out a linen wrapping.

Unexpected tears sprang to Malia's eyes as she unfolded the

cloth. Inside her palm were two pearl earrings, an emerald ring, a pair of small pearl combs, and a diamond bracelet with a matching solitaire princess cut diamond jewel on a silver chain. Her inheritance, or what was left of it anyway. Inheritance she was going to have to sell to gain her freedom. Brandt thought that she had given him the rest of the heirloom jewels months ago. The truth, he had no idea about the amount of jewelry their father had given their mother over the years. Their mother had hardly ever worn the expensive jewels. There was very little occasion for wearing such finery on the island. Also, Malia remembered her mother claiming that since she had been raised a fisherman's daughter on the island there was no need to rub the family's fortune in the faces of her peers and husband's workers. So, when Brandt said he needed funds to pay the bank for the house a few months back, Malia had handed over only half of the jewels. The rest she kept safely tucked away.

From what Brandt just told her, she would have to sell more jewels than planned to pay for hers and Cora's passage – to bribe anyone that might see them leave.

She had no choice now, and could no longer wait for Brandt to become the man and brother she knew he could be. Only yesterday, she held onto the small hope of a miracle for Brandt and the financial mess he had got them in. Not anymore. Hope, it seemed, was coming at too high a price.

She and Cora had to start their plans of escape today.

Suddenly afraid that Brandt would burst in and catch her holding her salvation, she tucked them safely away back in the false bottom of the wardrobe. Malia knew Cora was scouting for possible ships right now before she started reading more palms that afternoon, instead of at the market. What would be the best vessel to escape on? Who would take her and Cora the furthest from the island and be quiet about it?

Without meaning to, the handsome stranger popped into

her head. He had said he was a captain. If she ever saw him again, perhaps it would be possible to gain passage on his ship.

Why had he just left? She remembered the teasing twinkle in his eyes and how they had lit up with mischief one moment, and iced with cold fury when Brom had assaulted her. The fact that she still couldn't place him or the flashes of memories was maddening. She chewed on her thumbnail, searching through her hazy memories of last year's festival. The deaths of her parents had happened only weeks before the festival, causing a haze of grief to cover all her memories from the year before. She might have seen him at one point, but had been too distracted by grief to remember him properly.

She wanted to see him and somehow figure out how she knew him. The flashes of memory filled her with longing and warmth. Her frustration kept her from sitting still. Unable to stand the echoing quiet of the house, Malia left in hopes of running into a certain dark-haired ship captain.

* * *

Malia didn't see Rogan or his ship as she and Cora searched the harbor and island for possible means of escape. Luckily, she didn't see Brandt either, until it was time to leave the house for the Dinner of the Dead.

The stroll over to the cliffside pavilion was tense and gloomy as distant dark clouds rolled by. Malia didn't speak one word to her brother, and he looked like he wanted to avoid conversation like he would the pox. He trudged beside her, kicking stones in his nicest boots. The rocks almost knocked over several ground lanterns before he stopped. The delicate parchment paper glowed pathways throughout the island, so the dead could find their way to their last family meal.

The siblings took the long way, far from the shorter cliff path, up to the pavilion. The stone path was becoming more crowded with familiar faces. The pavilion was to the east of the northern lighthouse that was set up on the cliffs.

Malia's toes were numb in her tight, black boots by the time they reached the top of the hill. Trying to wiggle them only resulted in more toe-binding suffocation. She detested shoes; boots most of all, but wearing them was worth the free dinner.

Honestly, she hated the whole Dinner of the Dead event. She understood the respect concept of the dinner. However, that didn't mean she wanted to symbolically eat with ghosts. She felt like she already did that most days in the echoing ruin of her house. Her father had hated the Dinner of the Dead tradition too. He wasn't from Blisse, like her mother, who observed the festival traditions religiously. For many years, Malia remembered her father and mother coming home early.

Children weren't allowed at the dinner. They were considered too loud and irreverent. The siblings had spent many Tuesday festival evenings with Brandt playing the violin and Malia pretending to dance with spirits throughout their house, too busy to ever want to sit still and silent with a bunch of grown ups. Neither of them had ever argued to be included inthe Tuesday night tradition. But now, as an adult, she was going to be forced to sit stiff as pins, in all black, with pinched hair as her feet blistered in her boots. As if that wasn't bad enough, eating a meal where the only noise was the clanking of forks on plates and smacking of mouths while everyone stared at each other was torturous. If she were dead, she would want a meal in her honor to be filled with music, dancing, and bare feet on the beach.

All over the island, variations of the feast were being held, but only the locals and their guests were allowed into the pavilion. Having strangers would offend lost loved ones at their last dinner with their family. But that didn't mean others didn't try. Tried and failed, a stranger could be spotted a mile away with their pale skin and nicer silk spun clothes.

The sky was growing more overcast, promising rain. It felt more like a funeral procession than a party. A funeral. That's exactly what Malia felt like she was attending in her dead mother's dress, gloves, and boots.

As the siblings climbed the few stone steps to the open doorway, the smell of the ocean waves greeted them. The low hum of conversation could just about be heard through the open doorway. The pavilion walls were covered in canvas, like a tent, for privacy.

'Hello, Malia, Brandt,' greeted Noah Murdoch with a smile. He was the local butcher and one of the few people Brandt didn't owe money to. The older man would occasionally slip her and Cora cuts of meat that no one else wanted. She focused on the annoying clicking of her heels to keep her emotions in check. Everything and everyone she knew was soon to be as good as dead to her if her escape was successful. People she had grown up with, old teachers, dance instructors, men that yelled at her to be careful in her father's fishing boats, and women that helped her mother pull fruit from the trees, they were all part of her home that she would never see again. She was half spiteful at the island and half nostalgic. Both feelings brought a sting behind her eyes that encouraged tears to spill. She blinked them back with sheer determination. She would not let anyone see her cry. Islanders weren't big on pity.

'Hello Noah,' Malia said and smiled in greeting.

Noah ushered them in. They were one of the last to arrive. As everyone walked around in the large open tent, greeting one another and arranging who would sit with whom, Malia looked around in search of Cora. She came earlier to bring their meager contribution of mangos to the meal. All households that attended brought something to eat, so no one had to cook or serve anyone else.

She surveyed the room and couldn't hear Cora's distinct pounding walk on the bamboo floor. Cora walked like she was always marching into some kind of battle. She also couldn't make out anyone's individual voice from the throng of chatter in the large open space.

With no sign of her friend, Malia's shoulders deflated. It wasn't plausible for her to have gone home. Maybe the man she met last night, Duncan, had visited her booth on the beach again and convinced her to have the dinner on his ship where many of the sailors were dining for the night. Malia certainly hoped not. She needed her as a buffer from her brother and Haych. She had silently agreed to sit by Eldon Haych, hoping to gain more freedom from their scrutiny until Sunday. Being forbidden to speak to him as soon as the dinner started was going to be the greatest blessing of the evening. Almost anyone could be tolerated for a few hours if they didn't have to communicate. The only problem was, silence was only required during the actual meal. Which meant she was going to have to endure at least some semblance of a distasteful conversation with him beforehand.

'Miss Malia.' Haych's voice came from behind, like he had been waiting until her back was turned so he could pounce. She gritted her teeth and put on a polite smile as she faced him.

Only a few more days, she reminded herself.

'Hello, Sir Haych,' Malia said so politely she surprised herself. Calling him "Sir" made her want to gag. Brandt stood beside him, looking agitated as he fidgeted with bloody hangnails. He licked his lips and glanced around, probably in search of the liquor bar.

Haych bent and took her black-gloved hand. She hadn't offered it. As he kissed it, his face disappeared behind the bushes of his graying eyebrows. She felt the eyes of the islanders turn and hungrily analyze the gesture. Malia's other hand became a fist so tight behind her back that the delicate material threatened to split at her knuckles. His lips were rough and coarse as they scraped against the smooth fabric.

'I'm sorry we didn't have a chance to dance last night,' Haych said after he lifted his snake-like lips off her hand and stood upright. Malia jerked her hand back and put it behind her, delicately wiping it on the silky folds of her dress. The man had kissed her mother's glove!

She gave another small smile; she couldn't bring herself to blatantly lie and apologize in return.

Only a few more days. Just keep repeating it Malia. You can do this.

'Your brother said that you had fallen a bit faint and had gone home early to rest.' Haych's beady eyes narrowed as his disbelieving tone suggested an excuse like that would not be accepted again.

She nodded in agreement and looked around desperately for Cora or any other opportunity to leave that wouldn't come across as rude.

When she still couldn't spot her friend she replied, 'Yes. I'm afraid all the excitement of the dancing and the heat had me feeling quite dizzy.' It wasn't a total lie. Dancing with Rogan had left her very much excited and full of vigorous heat. She bit back her incident with Brom. Better to keep how she escaped his guard until he brought it up. Hopefully Brom was humiliated enough that he kept his mouth shut about her rescuer. Luckily, he and Ku were seen as foreigners and were not welcome at the dinner. Malia was sure by the next festival Haych would have so much power that it wouldn't matter what tradition dictated, he would do what he wanted, including having his henchmen at a sacred dinner.

'Well, it is a good thing we are here, where a feast awaits us. No dancing for you tonight,' Haych said wagging a teasing finger at her, but his still-bruised knuckles held darker threats.

'Of course,' she said lightly in return, with a smile as stiff as her hair. Their short conversation was like a glimpse into her future if she failed this week. Empty, and always full of veiled threats.

Haych opened his mouth to say something else but was interrupted by a growing commotion at the entrance.

Malia saw a head of long raven hair, pulled into a ponytail at the nape, talking to Noah, who was still standing at the doorway, keeping all foreigners out. Her stomach clenched.

There was a break in heads and she saw that it was *him*. His bright eyes looked irrationally annoyed as he talked to the butcher. He was dressed all in black, like he had been the night before, only now he blended in.

Noah wasn't going to let him through unless he could prove he was a family member of an islander.

Malia made a hurried excuse to Haych and rushed over.

'Excuse me, maybe I can help?' Malia said, keeping her eyes averted from the sea captain. She still wasn't sure how she could help him get in. There was no way Malia could say he was her guest. Even implying that he was with her would destroy all the complacent illusion she was crafting for Brandt and Haych.

'Do you know this man?' Noah asked, pointing an accusing finger at the Captain's chest.

She looked appraisingly at the Captain. The whispers were already buzzing as phrases like, 'her dance partner last night,' 'scandalous,' 'handsome,' and 'slut,' roamed through the air. When he looked down at her, there was an excitement that replaced his annoyance. But the longer she took to answer, the more he began to shift his weight, anxious. She didn't know how to get him in. The smart thing to do would be to send him away, showing everyone on the island that he meant nothing to her. That would stop the rumors before they reached Haych, endangering both of them. She had been so foolish the night before. Only, she couldn't bring herself to send him away. Not when he was the only one in the building that looked genuinely happy to see her. His smile made her toes tingle for a whole different reason than her shoes. What had come over her?

'Well?' Noah asked, interrupting their wordless conversation. 'Do you know him or not?'

'Yes, I do,' she finally said, a lie now forming. The Captain unfolded his arms and gave a satisfied grin.

'You know the rules, Miss Malia. There aren't supposed to be any travelers. How will our late family members enjoy their last meal with us if there are interlopers present?' Noah chided.

'I know, but he is a guest—family. I believe he is a. . .' She gave the Captain a searching look but received no help from him. He stood there grinning at her like an idiot who was interested in seeing what she would come up with. So, she went with the most believable lie, 'A cousin of my maid, Cora. We met last night. He is her guest.' She exhaled when Noah gave a reluctant nod. Since Cora was on the island with no blood family, there was no one that could refute it.

'What's your name, guest?' Noah asked, just as the Captain walked into the room.

'Rogan. Captain Rogan,' Rogan answered pleasantly, giving the smaller man a little bow that Malia suspected held a hint of mockery, before he walked toward her.

Chapter Eight

Rogan

I f Rogan had known there was a guard posted for such a boring dinner, he would have just appeared in the building instead of using the door. Being this close to the sea, no one would have thought twice about the salt and brine smell of magic that would have followed him into the canvas walls. But instead, he went for the full mortal experience and used the door.

He had spent all day on the *Calypso's Voyage,* away from everything that could make him feel any emotion other than apathy, just how he liked it. But a few seconds arguing with a random man who was threatening to ruin his evening with Malia had all kinds of emotions rolling through him.

Damn him.

Rogan took a deep breath as he stepped closer to Malia. The pleasure of seeing her again helped replace his anger, making him grin as big as an idiot. Maybe he should have avoided the dinner?

After all, if seeing her made him happy, she could potentially make him miserable.

The Captain continued advancing toward her, a happy swagger coming from his knees. He thought maybe she would be wary of him, with the abrupt way he left her last night. But her eyes looked welcoming. However, her two wardens from the night before stood in disapproval behind her.

She looked stuffy and uncomfortable in her high-collar, ankle-length, black dress. Her hair was up and forced into a severe knot at the back of her head. She looked as serious as the black boots she wore. He almost didn't recognize her, which gave him the urge to pull the pins from her hair and let the black waves cascade down where they belonged. He wouldn't have minded releasing her from her dress either. Suddenly, an image of his lips on her neck instead of the collar had Rogan choking on desire. He coughed into a fist before clasping his hands tightly behind him.

'What are you doing here?' she asked, a gloved fist by her mouth, like she was used to biting her nails when she was anxious.

'Hello love, it's nice to see you too,' Rogan said. He felt bold as he took her hand in his. Her eyes rounded in surprise before darting around the room. She hadn't offered it, but he had never cared for rules. Her gloved hands were warm.

When Rogan looked up at her, he had expected Malia to swoon or at least blush. Instead, she was still looking around the room until his lips met her glove. That caught her full attention and her cheeks grew a lovely shade of pink.

Jerking her hand back, Rogan straightened and took a safe, small step away. She asked in an urgent whisper, 'What are you doing here? Really?'

He answered back with a simple shrug.

Malia scowled.

'It's the Festival of Souls', he answered a bit more seriously. 'I want to see everything this celebration has to offer.'

Malia placed a fluttering hand like a nervous, caged bird to her severe bun.

'Malia,' a voice said behind her. She started a little, but recovered quickly by the time she turned. The older man from the night before was approaching. 'Would you mind introducing us?' he asked, his smile as sharp as a shark that smelled blood in the water.

'Of course,' Malia said, staying stiff and proper. Rogan suddenly saw what she could be like twenty years down the road. Dull and bitter, and it made his jaw clench. 'Sir Eldon Haych, Brandt, this is Captain Rogan. Cora's cousin,' she said, formally gesturing with her hands as her eyes burned holes of warning that Rogan decided to ignore, 'This is my brother Brandt, and his good friend, and Blisse's newly appointed governor, Sir Eldon Haych.'

They both nodded to Rogan; Haych's eyes squinted in calculation and Brandt's shifted to find distraction, wandering around the room.

'Gentlemen,' Rogan said jovially.

'Where is Cora?' asked Brandt. 'Surely if she had a guest coming, she would be here.' With the scrutiny in his voice, he obviously didn't believe the lie.

Malia gave her brother a dark glare before her eyes brightened, looking over his shoulder.

'There she is!' Malia nearly shouted, waving in the air.

They all looked behind Brandt. Rogan heard stomping steps before he saw the petite woman's wild curls break through the crowd.

'Cora,' she said sounding relieved, 'I'm so glad we spotted you.' The little palmist from the beach stopped mid-step. Her eyes grew large in either horror or surprise, or maybe both, when she saw Rogan standing there, like she was facing her death. She quickly snapped out of it and put a smile on her face.

'Cora, your *cousin* Captain Rogan has arrived.'

Cora caught on in an instant and greeted Rogan as if they really were old relatives.

'Oh, cousin Rogan!' she gripped both of his cold hands and squeezed them hard enough that she either wanted to hurt or warn him. The smell of the ocean whiffed strongly off her. She smelled like magic and didn't even know it. Definitely magic born. 'I'm so glad you could make it!' she said, latching onto his arm and lightly nudging him toward the round dining tables that were set up throughout the hall. 'How is Aunt Mora?' she asked. Rogan assumed Mora was supposed to be his mother. The woman could be an actress.

'Thank you for the warm welcome, cousin, she is splendid and sends her regards,' he said, turning his back on the two men and Malia. Cora and Rogan continued their pretend catch-up about aunts who didn't exist. 'Your friend helped with the guard, otherwise I don't think they would have let me in.'

'Thank you, Miss Malia, for taking care of him.' She said it so casually that no one would guess at her bruising grip. 'I was careless not to meet him at the door and greet him. You would think I had the manners of the dead.'

Her knowing glare caught him by surprise. Rogan did a double take and studied Cora hard. Had the palmist caught onto there being something not quite right with him? The look was gone in an instant before she returned to her role as the devoted cousin, but not before Rogan got a strong whiff of salty air from Cora. Was she using magic just now? Did she even know it? Rogan studied her quickly from the corner of his eye. The corner of her mouth was upturned, in a partial private, knowing smile. Maybe she did know what she was doing?

'Of course,' Malia said, sounding distracted.

The edginess in Malia's voice had Rogan glancing over his

shoulder. Sir Haych had a possessive hand over Malia's arm as he escorted her to the table.

Rogan began to turn on his heel, wanting to confront this Haych person. His right hand curled into a fist. Cora gave his arm a subtle but stern jerk, turning him back towards her. Rogan looked down at her, surprised. The small woman was stronger than she looked. Cora gave a small shake of her head. She knew what was wrong, but doing something about it was going to require patience. Reigning in his temper, he took a deep calming breath. The sudden burst of anger behind his eyes had almost made him lose his senses. These explosions of emotions were exhausting.

'Shall we all sit together?' Malia asked casually as she and Haych came up beside them. She was either ignoring or ignorant of Rogan's and Cora's silent exchange. 'After all, I don't think there is assigned seating,' she gave a high pitched laugh.

'That sounds fabulous,' Cora said innocently, but her eyes lingered on the older man's hold of her friend and gave Rogan's arm another encouraging squeeze. Cora waited for Rogan to pull out the nearest chair for her.

He obliged as Sir Haych skipped a place setting for Malia. Brandt was about to grab the back of the open chair when Rogan let go of Cora's seat a little early and took the spot for himself. There was a little "humph" from Brandt having lost his seat beside his sister.

'I'm sorry,' Rogan said with wide innocent eyes, 'Don't escorts sit beside their charges at these things? Or are customs different on Blisse?'

'Of course they do,' Malia said, her mouth thinning into an angry line as she glared daggers at her brother.

Brandt ignored his sister and took a tiny step closer. A strong sweetness filled Rogan's nose: alcohol. Brandt's fuming, blood-shot eyes squinted as he sized Rogan up. His fists curled at his sides, his shoulders stiff. Rogan recognized that stance, it usually preceded a punch to the jaw. Although he was shorter than Rogan, he had broader shoulders, like a wrestler. Rogan's fingers tingled and itched at the memory of a good fight. He remembered what it was like to be an angry mortal and loved the pain as much as the release of a good punch. Rogan was about to bounce on the balls of his feet, excited, until he noticed how Brandt's left arm hung at his side, lame. Sense and shock returned to him like a bucket of water. Had he really wanted to go toe to toe with Malia's brother, right there in the pavilion? He needed to get a handle on his emotions.

Just then, the dinner bell rang throughout the hall and the official silence began. Rogan smirked in response to Brandt's threatening stance. He couldn't help it. Something about the guy's petulant manner just made Rogan want to push buttons. Unless Brandt wanted to bring unforgivable shame upon him and his family he had to take another seat and be quiet about it. Brandt's jaw stayed tight, but he slowly moved around and sat on the other side of Cora.

Rogan took his seat with a deep satisfied sigh. Beating him at his game was far more satisfying than a punch would have been.

Malia's dark eyes burned into his skull. Rogan turned to look at her, his triumphant grin still on his face. She stared back like she thought he was crazy, but fought a smile of her own with a small head shake of disbelief. Still trying to hide her smile, she looked down, fidgeting with the black lace on the wrist of her gown.

Everyone else found their seats quickly, causing the clicking of shoes and scraping of chairs to surge, then disappear into an echoing silence. The room was mute. The only sounds were the flapping of the canvas walls that were secured for privacy around the pavilion, the distant buzzing of bugs from the jungle and the clashing of waves against the cliff side.

Rogan looked around, intrigued by the tradition of a silent dinner as he studied the mortals around him. The night was coming fast as lanterns were lit on the tables and throughout the pavilion. With all the people sober and dressed in black, the hilltop looked filled with dark souls. If Rogan were still mortal, the sight would have been creepy, but the fact was, he had seen worse. If anyone else was bothered by the gloomy environment, they didn't give any indication as people patiently waited in their seats for whatever was to come next. Except Malia. Rogan studied her from the corner of his eye as Cora lit their table's lamp and saw her roll her eyes to herself before plastering on a stiff smile.

When the room became awkwardly silent, Sir Haych rose and went to stand on a raised platform at the head of the room. Rogan noticed Malia visibly relax her hunched shoulders when he left.

Everyone's attention turned to the only standing person in the room as he simply gestured to the first rounded table near the back. The people took his queue, stood up, and made their way to the large buffet table. Moving wordlessly, they scooped food onto their delicate plates and made their way back to their seats. Once the line was formed and people were moving smoothly, Haych came back to his place beside Malia.

The next table to go was Rogan's small party.

Following Cora in line, Rogan turned while they waited and caught Malia's eye. In that moment, he saw the same look from the night before when he called her love. Her eyes narrowed, with a determined set to her jaw, like she was studying him. It was a look of confused recognition and it made him nervous. He gave her a winning smile, but it didn't shake her glare. He knew he had put in the right amount of magic in their kiss, so why did she always look like she was trying to figure out where she knew him from? Rogan felt the first pang of regret that she didn't remember him and the kiss they shared. He remembered it well.

Finally, they made it to the long smorgasbord and Malia blessedly became distracted by the feast in front of her. The tables were overflowing with island delights – roasted pig, peacock, and fish. Further up, a cornucopia of bananas, mangos, pineapples, and ackee burst into color against the bleak dinner crowd.

As he stood in front of all the food, he found himself a little overwhelmed. It all looked nice enough, but he didn't have an appetite. Food was for energy to keep a person alive. His body never lacked energy. Besides the bit of fruit bread he had tried the night before just to see if he could still eat, he hadn't eaten or drank anything since his branding. There was no reason to eat, so he hadn't, in a long time. Looking over to Cora for a hint of help, he found her paying zero attention to him as she stood, smiling down at her food, like it was a holiday morning surprise.

His hesitation held up the flowing line. He cast a quick glance to Malia, who was smiling and tapping her boot with impatience behind him. He piled food at random on his plate. He wasn't even sure what some of it was, but it didn't matter so long as he looked like he knew what he was doing.

As they moved down, keeping silent was harder than Rogan thought it would be. Malia was putting small amounts of island fare on her plate behind him, like she wanted to sample everything. Anytime Rogan looked at her and opened his mouth to speak, she raised her eyebrows, daring him to break the tradition of the silent feast.

Rogan was used to long periods of silence. He was Captain of a soul ship, after all; silence and brooding were something he was good at. But he found that he was grinding his teeth in frustration at not being able to talk to her. He wanted to say something about the food, or the people, or ask why she kept rotating her feet and switching from foot to foot with a painful expression on her face, but he couldn't. He just kept peeking at her from the corner of his eye. By the time they were both at the end of the buffet, Malia was close to laughing at his discomfort, enjoying herself immensely at his expense. He was agitated.

There was only so much time given to him before being confined back to his ship. He felt like he was wasting it.

Eventually, they sat back down. As everyone around Rogan dug in, he simply stared at the lumps of meat and fruit on his plate. No one seemed to notice how he hesitated, except, of course, Malia, who was sipping her drink, watching him. Rogan decided to start small and drink something first. He lifted the glass of water to his lips and sipped it. It was cold and clear, just how he remembered it. It felt—good.

Feeling the cool liquid coat his throat without having some kind of physical rejection from his immortal body gave him the confidence to down the whole glass of clear liquid, like he had just finished rowing through high tide. He refilled his glass and downed that just as quickly. If water could be this satisfying, he decided to try the food. The smell of the pork made his mouth unexpectedly water as he brought a bite to his lips. Rogan groaned in appreciation as the tender pork gave a burst of salt on his tongue. He didn't remember food being so delicious. Malia snorted; she quickly covered up her laughter by coughing. Rogan proceeded to stuff his face and make little pleasurable sounds after each bite. Luckily, Cora and Malia were the only ones that heard him. Part of his purgatory on the ship was the absence of the joy food could bring.

The clanking of silverware on plates muffled his inappropriate noises to everyone else. After a particularly loud moan, Malia kicked his foot. While smiling, she gave him an insistent look and put a finger to her mouth, reminding him to be silent. Their exchange received several threatening scowls from others in the room, including Sir Haych beside her. Malia ignored them, like she was used to it, straightened her shoulders and took another gulp of her wine.

It was then that Rogan realized everyone else was somber and drawn, reminding him too much of the company he was used to. He, Malia, and Cora looked to be the only ones enjoying themselves. The party was completely dead, which was the point, but it was boring. The dead were boring. All they did was stand around and evaluate their life choices. They didn't talk to him. They didn't even so much as blink in his direction while on the ship. Being surrounded by people, but still being lonely, wasn't something he wanted to feel that week. Boredom, he realized, was an emotion he knew very well and was sick of. He hadn't snuck into the "party" to be dull; he could be that on the comfort of his ship.

Rogan grew restless at the silly tradition. Restless – that was a new feeling and not one that he particularly liked. The eating part of the meal didn't last long. Were they going to have to sit there for another half an hour? A half an hour he would never get back? The evening was going to take forever. The dead didn't care if you ate a meal in their honor; they were dead.

Sighing, he shifted in his seat, his stomach feeling very full and not entirely happy with him. The large space was filled with flapping canvases, the clanging of forks against plates, the slurping sounds of people swallowing, and nothing else. The silence was starting to grate on Rogan's nerves. He looked around for a distraction and noticed Haych's brooding stare, a threat, clearly, by the way he had a white knuckled grip on his cutting knife. Rogan pointedly ignored him, and looked over to Malia. Her pinched brows and tight straight lips suggested that she was just as uncomfortable as he was as she pulled at her high collar. Then, realizing Rogan was watching her, she put her hand down and moved her food around with her fork without eating.

Rogan wanted to say something witty, like how he would be happy to remove her collar and anything else if it made her more comfortable, and risk being rewarded with either a slap or a laugh, but he couldn't. His restlessness was turning into frustration. Without permission from his brain his hand curled into a fist, again. Precious time was being wasted at the dinner.

But Malia was there, and she certainly intrigued him. He needed to devise a plan that got them both out of the remainder of the evening. He swallowed down his irritation by refilling his cup with some more water and taking careful sips of the chilled beverage.

As he put his cup down, he saw Brandt leaning forward on the other side of Cora giving him an evil glare. Rogan thought about giving him the same rude hand gesture he had seen Malia give a young man the night before, but decided against it. A fight with Brandt wouldn't result in him spending the rest of the evening with Malia. So, he decided to simply ignore him.

As he replaced the pitcher of water, he noticed that he could only see one of Haych's hands. He paused, wondering where Haych's other hand was. The old man was sitting much closer to Malia than necessary. With the large folds of her dress and the long black table cloth, he could be touching anywhere! Rogan was seized with a fierce and sharp piercing in his stomach that didn't come from his overeating. He couldn't stand the thought of another man, even a decrepit old one, touching Malia. He felt his stomach pitch, like he was on the deck of a ship just as a storm hit. He wanted to grip and squeeze something to steady himself, like Haych's neck.

Rogan, you've wanted to punch two different men in the last half hour. Get a hold of yourself! he chidded himself.

He took several deep breaths, hoping no one would notice how his leg had started shaking with the effort of restraint. He needed to think smarter, not stronger. He ran a hand over his smooth hair in its band at the nape of his neck and calmly cleared his throat while adjusting his seat. As casually as possible, he moved his knee until it was touching some part of Malia's dress-covered leg. It seemed to be shaking. Rogan took a closer look at Malia. Above the table she was calm and straightforward but under the surface there was a fight to control what was happening to her. Her wine glass was empty, again. Her plate of food that she had looked at adoringly in line hadn't been touched. She wasn't eating.

She pretended not to notice Rogan's touch or questioning look, but he saw the tension in her fingers as they tightened around her fork. The fork looked like it was becoming dangerously close to being used as a weapon. Rogan wasn't sure if she was planning on stabbing him or the old man. Her other hand made a tight fist on the table like she was holding onto an invisible lifeline.

Seeing her fork gave Rogan an idea. He fumbled and dropped his own to the bamboo floor. The clanging was so loud it was as though Rogan rang a church bell in the hall. He smiled an apology to the attendants that turned to glare at him before bending down to the floor.

While Rogan searched for his fork, he poked his head under the black table cloth where he saw Sir Haych's missing hand. It was gripped tightly onto Malia's dress-covered thigh. Rogan's jaw clenched as he slowly sat back up. Malia's closed fist at the table was probably itching to meet Sir Haych's face.

Malia went to pour herself another large glass of wine. He understood why she needed that too. *There* was his opportunity. He snatched the wine bottle before she touched it, filled his glass, then gestured wordlessly to Malia's empty glass – offering to fill hers.

She nodded eagerly. Their eyes locked for a moment. She looked at him, like she was lost, her breathing shallow, like in a panic. Rogan gritted his jaw and gave her a small reassuring nod.

As Rogan finished pouring her wine, his elbow shoved the goblet and spilled it into his lap. Acting surprised, he fumbled then dropped the rest of the bottle down the front of Malia's dress and lap.

Shrieking in surprise, she threw herself to her feet, breaking Haych's hold, as the chair fell hard behind her, just as the bottle shattered on the floor.

Once the clattering finished, Rogan looked up and saw the room full of spectators silently screaming with their eyes for them to get out. Cora was the only one not looking up at them with pure mortification, but instead was turning purple from containing her laughter.

He looked around, dumbfounded at how he could have done something so clumsy. Malia stood with her arms spread, red wine dripping on the floor from her dress. There was elation in her face as their eyes met. She understood; now she could leave.

Someone was already on the floor picking up the broken pieces of dark glass and mopping up what little wine hadn't been soaked into Malia's clothes.

She quickly changed her expression to horror as she gestured to her ruined dress. She gave Rogan one last withering glance, before looking helplessly at her dinner party. It was obvious she couldn't stay there in a soiled dress, and no one could speak a word of objection. She was drenched. Haych wouldn't be able to leave since he was the main authority figure of the meal. And Brandt, although he didn't want to let Malia out of his sight at the beginning of dinner, looked rather relaxed now that he had a few more drinks in him.

Responding to Malia's gesturing tirade, Rogan bowed his deepest apology and gestured to the door, willing to escort her out. Since his shirt and pants were clinging to him, he would have to change too.

Malia gave him a stiff nod and strode away, her dress leaving a trail of purple wine in her wake.

He gave all the glaring islanders an apologetic bow and followed her outside. By the time he caught up with her, she was already fanning out part of her dress in the cool night air. Her hair had lost its pins as it blew in the wind. As he approached her back she was placing her gloves in her pockets.

Rogan made sure the cliff gravel crunched under his boots,

so as not to frighten her with his natural silence. She ignored him and began unfastening the top collar of her dress as if releasing a noose.

'You're welcome,' Rogan said in her ear.

She whirled around, looking like she wanted to protest, only she couldn't. After a moment of studying his shadowed face, she gave him her first real smile.

'I was about to rescue myself,' she said.

'Oh, I believe you. I meant, you are welcome for me saving your dress from getting Haych's blood on it. I saw that fork in your hand. Now, your dress only has wine to worry about.'

His explanation and conspiratorial grin made her smile bigger.

'Well then, on behalf of my wine and stainless dress, thank you,' she said, conceding a nod and a small curtsey.

Malia's gaze shifted to the open doorway, at the same time Rogan looked back. Eldon Haych had risen from his table and was marching his way out to them.

Rogan rolled his eyes. The man was being way too obvious.

When he turned back to Malia, he expected to see annoyance, but instead, there was— fear. She had dealt with enough of that man for one evening, and so had he.

Grabbing her hot hand in his cold one he said, 'Let's get out of here.' Without waiting for a response, he pulled her off into the night.

Chapter Nine

Malia

Malia didn't know where they were going. She didn't care. Anywhere with anyone was better than the pavilion and Haych.

Rogan's hand in hers was cold, like an ocean breeze, and she squeezed it harder as she jerked him towards the jungle and away from the cliffside path and the deserted village huts. She knew better than anyone, one wrong move and they'd plummet, but maybe she already had. Rogan easily changed direction and led the way through the buzzing trees.

Thinking of Haych and his bruised fingers clutching her thigh had Malia easily keeping up with Rogan's fast pace. Rogan's plan to free her and himself from that dreadful dinner was genius. Her chest warmed despite her cold wet dress. She wasn't ready for Rogan to leave her yet. Malia was glad he was by her side, which was scary. He made her laugh, and she hadn't laughed in a long time.

Despite Haych's vulgarity, she had been enjoying herself in Rogan's presence. Granted he couldn't talk, at the dinner, but his eye rolling and fidgeting hand gestures spoke more than words ever could. Clearly, he had been as bored and aggravated by the dinner as she had been. Watching him squirm had been entertaining.

They were just outside the little market square when Rogan stepped into an alleyway.

'How persistent do you think your beau will be?' he asked in a whisper, like Haych might have been right around the corner, waiting. Their hands were still clasped together, and she didn't pull away.

'You saw him at dinner, right? He is probably sending for his guards right now. Haych doesn't like when his plans go awry.'

He nodded. 'Right. Just let me get my bearings here.' He began looking around the alleyway, clearly lost. Malia laughed.

'What?' he asked, baffled.

'Aren't captains supposed to have a great sense of direction?' she teased.

'I know where I am,' Rogan countered, but was still looking around him, 'I just don't know where I'm going.'

She gave a very unlady-like snort. 'Come on, I know a place,' she said, and pulled him down the alley between stone buildings with thatched roofs.

Rogan followed so silently behind that if his chilled fingers hadn't been intertwined with her own, she wouldn't have known he was there. For a sailor, his hands didn't have any calluses. In fact, they were as smooth and cold as a river stone.

They skirted around dark shops down the street. The painted wood walls and posts that were once bright turquoise, yellow, orange, and blue were now chipped and faded. The evening air smelled strongly of old fish. They kept to the shadows provided by the balconies above the businesses, steering clear of the ground lanterns that peppered the path in single rows and lit the streets up like dots on a map.

Avoiding others and staying out of sight wasn't hard, the streets were mostly empty. All the travelers were trying their best to partake in the death dinner either on their ships or lodgings and most of the island's natives were still in the cliffside pavilion. They hurried along as she guided him up to the lighthouse.

As Rogan shadowed Malia deeper into the island, they followed the well-worn path that ran up through the jungle center, past Malia's home and further up to the cemetery. She noticed that his breathing never changed, and his footing never wavered on the unfamiliar paths, not even as they marched uphill to the highest level of the island. When they cleared the jungle trees and found themselves at the top of the island, Malia welcomed the cool wind against her swampy skin. Mosquitoes buzzed in her ear. While swiping them away, she noticed they didn't seem to be bothering Rogan, just her.

Humid sweat dripped from her brow. The moonlight beamed down on Rogan— he was bone dry. She hadn't realized she was making a list of his peculiarities until that moment when he looked just as comfortable after hiking through the jungle as he did on the beach.

The more she was around him the more she noticed peculiar quirks. Odd things, like his smooth hands, his silent movements, his alabaster skin tone unseen in a seasoned sailor, or like the most recent example, he wasn't sweating through the jungle humidity. Not even his palms felt hot, and they had been holding hands for fifteen minutes.

Malia pulled at her loosened collar, trying to ease the vase of strangulation in the dress that the humidity and sweat intensified.

'Are you alright?' Rogan asked, grabbing her elbow.

'Fine,' she said, shaking him off. 'It's just the climb in this confining dress. I'm fine.' She straightened.

'The cemetery?' he asked, a note of dread in his voice when he noticed they were standing by the iron fence.

Headstones were sporadically placed, reaching up like fingers from the ground. No rows, no family plots, everyone just thrown in together, like planners of the cemetery hadn't actually expected there to be so many dead in it. Turning back at his hesitation she saw that he looked uncomfortable. Was it the cemetery close by that made him squirm or the lighthouse?

'No, we are going to the lighthouse,' she said, indicating the looming structure with her chin. 'Haych won't find us up there.' It was probably the safest place, and she certainly wasn't going to take him home with her.

She noticed he kept clear of the fence and gave it a disdainful look.

'Come on.' Rogan nodded and gave a last edgy look to the cemetery as they went around it. 'Don't tell me you are one of those superstitious sailors who are always worried about disturbing the dead. It isn't like the dead are going to pop out of the ground and grab your ankles.' She snickered at his wide eyes. He rubbed a hand on the left side of his chest, pulling down a corner of his opened collar shirt just before he moved it back up. Her memory flashed again, recognizing the trident tattoo hidden under his shirt.

'Won't the lighthouse keeper object?' Rogan asked.

Malia shook her head. 'There is no lighthouse keeper anymore. When the old keeper died, no one volunteered to replace him. The lighthouse has been dark for months. Most islanders think this place is haunted, with it being so close to the cemetery.' A new expansion of memory flashed and she no longer just saw Rogan's shadowed face, but saw that he had been standing in a cemetery, the same cemetery, shirtless. She gave her head a little shake. Her imagination must have been running wild.

The lighthouse towered in front of them, dark, imposing,

and firm, daring the world's elements to do their worst as the waves crashed against the cliff faces below. She smiled.

There were no other islands around Blisse that had cliffs like theirs. They were mostly sandbars or jungle. Blisse, with its cliffs of defiance, was one of a kind. It was just one more thing that made Blisse different. Much like what she saw in Rogan.

'Does your brother know where you spend your free time?'

Malia shrugged, 'It's not like I keep it a secret; the door is always left unlocked. Unless it involves him, he doesn't care. And Haych will be too busy with business tonight to look for me personally.'

'Let's go,' she urged after staring up at the tower for a moment. The lighthouse was made of the same rock as the cliff that it stood on, having been whitewashed years ago. The paint was now chipped and beaten. If it were alive, Malia thought the lighthouse would have approved of its exterior condition. It made it look tough, unmovable, certain.

Pushing open the door, the smell of cold stone and salt mixed with the iron stairs stirred in her nose.

Rogan froze inside the doorway. Letting go of his hand, Malia lit an oil lantern kept on a side table. There wasn't an actual house attached to the lighthouse. Just the formidable tower and supplies.

Rogan carefully stepped over the threshold, pausing inside the small circular room. Their shadows melded together on the wall, looking intimate and haunted. Malia lifted the lamp and saw Rogan staring up, up, up at the iron spiral stairs.

'Ready?' she asked, her voice echoing. One foot settled on the first step as she held the lantern aloft. She offered her free hand to Rogan.

He only nodded and accepted it. His eyes were even wider than they had been at the cemetery as he looked up to the top of the stairs, lost to the darkness.

The stairs were dizzying. The warm lantern light made their

shadows sway and dance as they ascended higher and higher in circles. Moonlight shone on Rogan's features as they passed small, round windows in the wall. The iron stairs clanged under her boots. Rogan's steps, Malia noticed, sounded heavier inside the tower and his grip was stiff in her fingers.

Finally, they reached the door that led to the rotating light outside. Without hesitating, Malia let go of Rogan's hand, unlatched the door, and walked out onto the windy ledge. She inhaled deeply, embracing the freedom the lighthouse gifted her.

Wind and patches of the starry sky behind the clouds greeted the couple. Malia smiled.

When Rogan didn't follow her outside, she glanced back over her shoulder. He stood frozen, at the edge of the threshold. It occurred to her then that maybe he was afraid.

'Are you coming?' she asked, sincerely wondering if he was going to turn around and run back down the steps.

He nodded in the shadows and took a cautious step forward. Once he was outside, he stayed close to the tower wall, while Malia practically leaned over the rusty railing. The distant sound of the crashing waves below lulled her into comfort.

'Are you afraid of heights?' she enquired.

'I'm not afraid of heights,' Rogan said, apparently insulted. She was certain he hadn't blinked since coming to the outer ledge of the lighthouse. His dark hair that matched the night sky had come loose from the band at the nape of his neck and whipped into his face. He wouldn't let go of the wall at his back, so he just kept thrashing his head around in an attempt to move it out of his eyes.

Malia laughed. He was obviously terrified.

'How can you be afraid of heights?' she asked, still giggling as she reached her hands around Rogan's neck and released the ribbon in order to comb all his hair back. 'How can a sailor be afraid of heights and wind? Don't you climb the mast on your ship?'

'Of course', Rogan said shortly, his back still glued to the wall behind him. Malia ran her hands through Rogan's hair as she gathered it. She noticed a subtle hitch to his breathing on her cheek as she tied it back with his band. She fought back a smile. It was nice to know that she had the same effect on him as he did on her. Rogan placed his hands on her hips, his touch slowing her progress. Once finished, Malia went to step back but stopped when she saw how close his lips were to hers. She stayed there a moment, her hands on the back of his neck, his hands still on her hips.

'Better?' she asked.

'Much.' His voice was hoarse. She waited to see if he was going to pull her closer, maybe give her her first kiss. But he didn't. Instead, he cleared his throat and dropped his hands. The moment had gone.

She released him with a shaky smile, trying to find some room in the less-than-three-feet of ledge between the lighthouse wall and the iron railing. Malia stood back against the railing, and admired her work. He looked good. Unnervingly good.

'How do you overcome your nerves on your ship?' she asked to change the subject.

'Well, it's my ship. It's familiar. This is just. . .' he didn't finish as he gasped. 'Could you come away from the railing, please?'

'Why, captain? Does this make you nervous?' she asked as she leaned back, her hair flapping in the wind over the railing.

'Stop that, Malia.' Rogan gritted, reaching for her but not quite ready to leave the security of the lighthouse wall. 'Please,' he finished. The quiver in his voice madeMalia relent, but still smiling as she went back to lean against the wall with him.

'I'm sorry,' she said. Malia knew fear could be irrational. 'If it makes you feel better, I have a paralyzing fear of enclosed spaces.' Rogan raised his brows at the confession. Malia shook her head at the whisper of memory. The suffocating weight of being crushed underneath Brandt, as he tried to protect her from the rocks raining down on them.

'You're handling this better than I would if I were locked in a closet. I've actually been fighting claustrophobia all night in this suffocating dress and shoes. In fact...' she didn't finish as she bent down, unlaced her pinching boots, and threw the wretched things through the door of the lighthouse. They made wonderful clunking sounds as they clattered to the stone floor. Malia swung around, feeling triumphant.

Rogan still hadn't stepped away from the wall.

'Here, sit down,' she encouraged, afraid he would collapse. *Would he faint?* She took his steady hand, which she thought was odd. If he was as terrified as he acted, why wasn't he shaking? Another oddity to add to her growing list.

Not daring to give their little perch an inch of space that was more than required, Rogan slid down the curved wall. He looked like a cat afraid to fall from its tree branch.

Another giggle escaped Malia. She couldn't help it.

He gave her a hard glare.

'I don't mean to laugh, honest. It's just, you faced a man threatening you with a knife last night and didn't blink an eye. Now, you climb some stairs and you are paralyzed. I was starting to think that you weren't afraid of anything.'

'Fear isn't always rational,' he said as he seated himself.

'Fair enough.' She gave him an apologetic look in return. Once sitting, he breathed a little easier. He rolled his tense shoulders and stretched out his long dark-clad legs before resting his head back against the wall.

'Better?' she asked, while gathering her own blown hair and tied it in a side knot to keep it out of her face.

She leaned her head against the wall and stared at the stars. All around them was the smell of the ocean. The salty air called to her and spoke of freedom and adventure. Or was that just the strong smell of Rogan beside her? He smelled of wind, the sea, and the unknown.

The water shimmered below them, moving with a life of its own. The large full moon gave everything light only to pitch them in darkness when a thick, soulless cloud covered it.

'Have you always been afraid. . .' Rogan gave her a sharp look, 'Cautious,' she corrected, 'Of heights?'

Rogan shrugged. 'Not as a young boy. I didn't have a problem with buildings. I have no problem with my ship or any of the other ships I've been on,' he admitted, now looking comfortable, raising a knee up and resting an arm on it. 'But I've never been on top of a lighthouse before.'

'Other ships?'

Rogan nodded, caught up in a memory. 'I haven't always been the Captain of my current ship, you know. I actually lived and worked on ships in one way or another the majority of my life,' he said, settling into position, his thigh now touching hers. The feel and thrill of it was the exact opposite of the experience with Haych earlier.

'You were a child when you started ship work?'

He nodded, again, lost in a lifetime she was completely ignorant of.

'That's pretty young to start a life at sea, isn't it?'

Rogan shrugged again, but the flex of his fist resting on his knee told her that remembering his old life wasn't as easy as he was pretending.

'It was either that or go back to the orphanage or workhouse. I wasn't going to do either. So I did what I had to do to get myself the position of a cabin boy. And since I didn't cause any trouble and did my work quietly, they didn't throw me overboard.'

Throw a little boy overboard? If he was working for a merchant ship, they wouldn't have just thrown him over the side for slacking in his chores. Which meant one thing—pirates.

Malia was dying to know more, she figured asking a pirate about his business wasn't the best way to go about possibly asking for passage on his ship at the end of the week.

'Have you always enjoyed the top of lighthouses and haunted cemeteries?'

She shrugged in the same false collected manner that he had. 'They're good places to get away.'

Instead of explaining, she focused on the miniature looking ship just beyond the rocks of the cliffs. The ship looked like a small, abandoned toy that should have been in a glass bottle somewhere. Rogan's focus shifted to the ship below them too.

Seeing an opportunity to change the subject, she asked, 'Who would anchor their ship in Cliff's Teeth?'

Rogan made a contemplative face. 'Probably someone who doesn't want it disturbed or noticed.'

'Someone with a death wish is more like it,' she corrected. 'No one sane would anchor their ship in the Teeth.' His pregnant silence brought about an enlightening realization.

'That's your ship, isn't it?' she asked.

Rogan looked at her with his too innocent mocking way she was becoming all too familiar with.

'My ship?' He looked to make sure they were still talking about the same vessel. 'Why, I suppose it is. Huh, interesting.' She rolled her eyes. She did that a lot around him. He didn't seem to take anything too seriously.

Malia looked down at it in wonder.

Of course he would anchor there. A pirate wouldn't want his ship noticed, or boarded.

The moonlight glinted off the dark wood, and reflected off the white sails from the two masts. The Fluyt, pear-shape design was very common for the merchant ships Malia saw coming in and out of the Blisse's harbor for trade. However, this ship was unmoving in the rough water.

It was still, like an anchor, sitting and waiting for the

Captain's return. Its stillness was as unnerving as Rogan's silent movements. Looking down at it made her wonder: who or what was he really?

'Is your crew on shore?' she asked, staring at the dark ship. Not even a glow from a candle could be seen.

'I don't have a crew. It's a ship I can sail by myself,' he said.

'You man that ship all by yourself?' she asked incredulously. Malia had been around ships her whole life. That ship needed a crew of at least half a dozen to sail into a port safely. He nodded, not looking down at it, but up at the stars. He was lying, he had to be. But, if he was a pirate it was understandable why he wouldn't be telling anyone the numbers of his crew.

'What's her name?' Malia asked, peeved that he wasn't being honest, but what did she really know of him?

For a moment Malia thought he might not have heard her since he didn't answer right away.

'*Calypso's Voyage*,' Rogan said with a secret kind of smile.

After another moment of silence, Malia said, 'It looks lonely.'

'Not any more lonely than spending nights in a lighthouse,' he rebutted.

He had her there. She nodded in an unspoken truce, she would stop asking questions about his ship and he wouldn't bring up her home life.

Malia stared up at the night sky, watching the stars and trying to think of a tactful way of asking about payment for passage on his ship when he nudged her with his leg and asked, 'Do you like watching the stars?'

She nodded, keeping her eyes fixed on the night sky. 'My mother said, love was in the stars. Childish I know, but it helps.' She shrugged.

'Helps with what?'

'The loneliness of having a cemetery and lighthouse for a family,' she answered in what she hoped was nonchalance.

Inside, she couldn't believe she had said something so private out loud to this near-stranger beside her.

Rogan looked down from the stars and met her eyes. There was a sad understanding in his smile as he grabbed her hand. When she didn't pull away, he cleared his throat and changed the subject about how he detested the taste of fish.

They spent the rest of the night carefully avoiding issues of loneliness and phobias and talked of things that didn't matter. Like, if he was sitting in seagull poop, would he ever get the stain out of his pants, and how the wine stain would never come out of her dress.

'Yes, but are you really sorry about that?' he asked with an eyebrow raised.

'No. Thank you for getting me out of that dinner. And for ruining this hideous dress. Now I never have to wear it again.'

Rogan nodded his head, like it had been the least he could do.

'If you need me to get you out of a dress tomorrow, let me know,' he said with a teasing wink.

She pretended to debate a moment, holding out her palms as if she were weighing the options. 'Let's see, ask *you* to help me out of a dress,' she raised one hand, 'or spend another evening with Eldon Haych?' she raised the other. 'I can't decide which I'd enjoy more,' she ended with her hands remaining balanced in the air.

Rogan's face cracked a genuine smile. 'Trust me, love,' he said devilishly, 'I would win that competition, no contest.'

She answered back in a flirtatious whisper, 'Too bad we'll never know.'

Rogan's smile grew wider, making his eyes dance in the graying light. The night was giving way to morning.

Rogan must have noticed the same thing because he looked at the sky, suddenly surprised.

'It's amazing how fast time passes when it means something,' he muttered, almost like he was talking to himself. 'I'm sure your brother is looking for you.'

Malia's face twisted in disgust. She was exhausted and the night wasn't over yet. She would still have Brandt's and Haych's wrath to contend with. She couldn't avoid reality forever. The morning had won.

'Come on, I'll walk you to the edge of the cemetery,' Rogan said, taking her arm as they stood. He was either acting the gentleman or masking his fear with the pretense of helping her. She let him, and found his little quirk cute and vulnerable.

'Wow! All the way to the cemetery? What a gentleman,' she joked.

'I'm afraid that is all I have time for,' was all he said. They made their way down the circling iron stairs. The cold bit into Malia's stockinged feet. He helped her pick up her discarded boots at the bottom of the stairs, his hand once again brushing hers.

They walked in silence to the far side of the cemetery, the night sky gradually changing to sunrise. She could feel Rogan's restless energy as he hurried along the path, like he was late for something.

'Well, thank you for ruining my dress,' she said formally.

'It was my pleasure.' He bowed, took her hand again, and kissed it.

The soft pressure of his cool lips warmed her entire body. She could feel a blush rise up her throat and was, for once, grateful for the high collar of her dress.

Rogan returned her hand slowly, reluctantly. The blush was rising higher and she quickly turned away.

After a few steps, Rogan called after her, 'I'll see you tonight.'

She turned around smiling, but he was nowhere to be seen.

'Maybe.'

She turned and hurried down the rocky hill.

Chapter Ten

WEDNESDAY

Malia

The sun was peeking over the horizon by the time Malia reached her front door. The chirping of insects and parrot whistles greeted her from the neighboring jungle as she climbed the dirty front steps.

Her hopes of sneaking into the house unnoticed were dashed as soon as she shut the large creaking door behind her. Glass crashed from the room that used to be her father's office, but was now Brandt's cave of debauchery. The whoosh of papers being thrown and stomped on muffled the crunch of glass on the marble floor.

Cora was at the foot of the stairs of the once-grand entryway, now littered with dirt, sand, and cobwebs.

'Miss!' she whispered in surprise and relief, back in her old maid accent, which she only fell into when she was anxious. She padded over.

'Cora, what's going on?' she asked, not bothering to whisper.

'Miss,' Cora hissed, 'your brother is in an awful state. I suggest that you avoid him and get straight to bed.'

'What happened now?' Couldn't Brandt wait to ruin the rest of their lives until after she left?

'You disappeared last night! With a strange man. That's what happened! When people started whispering about your questionable virtue after the dinner, Brandt flew into a rage. He yelled at everyone in sight, defending you. Got himself a black eye and bruised jaw for his trouble.'

'Brandt defended me?'

'I guess that disagreement you had with him yesterday morning stuck,' Cora said.

Just then, Brandt burst into the entryway, staggering and slurring, stopping only when he fell into the stair banister. Cora gave her friend a pitying look before disappearing into the connecting dining room.

Brandt looked miserable. His clothes were dirty, rumpled like he had spent the night in a gutter. One of his eyes looked like it was turning black and the right side of his jaw was swollen.

'You ran away last night,' he pointed an accusing finger at her chest. 'Again!'

'Captain Rogan spilled wine all over my dress and ruined it. I couldn't stay there in a soaking wet gown.'

Brandt gave a smile that said he was neither tricked nor amused. He began to walk forward on unsteady feet. He got so close that she could smell the liquor on his breath and the moldy jungle water on his clothes. 'If the dress was ruined and you left to change, then why are you still in it?' He paused for a minute.

'Would you rather I be without it? I only have so many dresses.'

'Where have you been all night in a ruined dress? Or maybe everyone on the island is right, and you haven't been in it at all.'

'Please, you're drunk, and I'm not going to listen to this.' Malia roughly pushed past him, making her way to the stairs, furious at his insinuation. She hadn't so much as had her first kiss, meanwhile her brother likely had a communal disease. She would have liked to slap him, if his face wasn't already bruised from defending her against others.

Using his right hand, he grabbed her arm in a painful grip, forcing her to face him.

'Don't turn your back on me when I'm talking to you. You need to listen to what I have to say,' his voice was angry with desperation.

'Or what?' she shouted in his face. 'You'll lose everything we own? Well, you've already done that. Humiliate and destroy our family name and everything our father built? You can mark that off your list too. Enslave me to a monster like Haych while using guilt to keep me compliant? You are already doing it! I don't have much left to lose!'

'We still have plenty to lose!' he shouted.

His grip had turned painful.

'Brandt, let me go,' she said through gritted teeth. He had never laid a hand on her before, but as he proved over and over again, things had changed.

The gravity of her words as he looked down at his bruising, white knuckled grip on her arm shocked him into reality. He roughly dropped his hand from its hold as if the guilt burned him. Brandt staggered back a step and took a swig from the bottle of brown liquid she hadn't even noticed was in his other hand. It was so commonplace it was like an extra limb.

'What are you talking about, Brandt? What did you do?' She straightened, the first real feeling of alarm striking her.

He only waved her off and pulled at his hair in desperation.

'Answer me, Brandt! What did you do?' It felt like a rock had been dropped in her stomach as she looked into his lost hazel eyes. Looking at him in the dim light she could tell something was different. This wasn't his usual pathetic manner; he had dropped down to an even lower level.

'Everything,' he whispered.

'Everything? The house is the only thing left,' her voice echoed through the empty entrance hall . 'Furniture, rugs, silver-ware, paintings, everything else is gone.'.

Brandt shook his head, keeping his gaze from meeting hers. However, he couldn't hide the tears of shame brimming in his eyes.

'When you say everything, you don't just mean the house, do you? You mean me.'

Brandt didn't say anything as he stood there, guilty.

'You sold me?' Her voice caught in her throat. She swung without thinking. Her hand made a satisfying slap against Brandt's cheek. Her fingers stung as Brandt took a startled step back.

'No!' he shouted. But he couldn't look at her. 'But, Sir Haych, he is willing to bargain my debts in exchange for your hand in marriage. He made the formal proposal to me last night. He would want the marriage to happen soon.'

A proposal made to her brother, but not to her. She felt sick all the way to her soul. She remembered her mother saying once, when Cora's mother died, that a person could feel soul sick with grief. Malia felt this way after her parents died, and now she was feeling it again. This weight in her chest felt so heavy it could pull her to the bottom of the sea.

'Our father, your namesake, would be disgusted,' she said, shaking out her hand.

Brandt still wouldn't meet her eyes, even as he lashed out.'You think I don't know that? You think the shame and guilt that swallows me whole doesn't know exactly what our parents are thinking as they wait in Paradise for their son who will never make it?'

'How soon?' she asked, ignoring his self-pity. Surely, it wouldn't be before the festival was over.

'I still have some time,' he said. 'I can win everything back tonight. . .' He didn't finish. He didn't have to. She knew what would happen. She was going to be forced into some kind of monstrous relationship with Haych before the end of the week in order to survive. Malia needed to act fast. Why didn't she ask Rogan about passage on his ship last night? She felt stupid for being so easily distracted by his blue eyes and relatable phobias.

Brandt ran his hand through his thick hair, leaving it looking wild and up at all angles.

Even if he won their freedom back tonight, he would just lose it again in the future. Now it was hers and Cora's survival that mattered, and theirs alone.

There was no use talking to him anymore, she had plans to make. Swallowing down her horror and disgust, she made her way up the stairs.

Brandt didn't say anything, but she heard his shuffling steps back to their father's office echoing off the bare walls.

Once in her room, the bare walls began to close in, like she lived in a mausoleum and was being buried alive. She threw the hateful boots against the wall and ripped off her suffocating dress, kicking it across the room for good measure. Now in her thin shift, she crumpled on the floor and tried to breathe.

Exhaustion seeped into her bones, but she wouldn't be able to sleep. Laying on the floor, with the rising sun coming in through her terrace doors, Malia calmed herself down as she thought of her next steps. She needed to get down to the docks without being recognized. The risk of word getting back to Brandt or Haych about a possible escape attempt was too great. If Rogan wasn't anchored in Cliff's Teeth she could have possibly got a message to him. But now, that wouldn't go unnoticed.

'Malia?' Cora's voice squeaked from the cracked doorway. 'Are you alright?' Cora poked her head through the gap in the door and when she saw Malia lying on the bare wood, she went and lay beside her, waiting patiently for her to speak. Her presence alone was a comfort and let Malia know that she was not all alone in the world, like she had a sister.

After a few minutes, Malia's voice had a new determination behind it. 'I'm fine.' After a moment more she sat up and whispered, 'We have to leave.'

'Leave, now?' Cora rose to her elbows. 'It's not even six in the morning. Where are you planning on going?'

The absurdity of her questions shook her out of her haze.

'No, not right now. I mean we might not be able to wait until the end of the week. The sooner we can sneak off the island the better. We need to buy passage today.' Malia jumped up from the floor and walked over to the armoire, opening it as quietly as she could. As irrational as it was, she was afraid Brandt would barge in and see her with the last of the family jewels that she had kept hidden from him. She released the false bottom and pulled out her heirlooms.

'Brandt isn't the only one in this family that's sneaky,' she muttered. A brief, foggy memory of her mother wearing the pearls to a dinner party wafted through her mind. She pushed down her sentiment.

'With these, Cora, we will buy our freedom.' She showed Cora the twinkling pebbles and plucked up the pearl combs.

Cora gasped.

'Where did you get those? Those aren't your momma's?' she asked, aghast.

'They are,' Malia confessed, caressing them lovingly. She told herself again, for the hundredth time, that her mother would want her to use them to escape. She gingerly put the rest of the jewelry back in its secret spot, locked it, and put everything back the way it had been. 'And these, combined with the money you have saved, will be more than enough to buy our passage off the island and a fresh start somewhere far from here. You can't sell them on the island, as the risk of word getting back to Brandt or Haych that you are selling jewelry is too great. See if any ship will take them as direct payment. Cora, I need you to get to the docks and confirm passage for us. If you can't find anyone in the harbor, Captain Rogan has a ship anchored at Cliff's Teeth. We can try him too. I can't do it. Haych is likely having me watched, especially after last night. But those that know you won't blame you for thinking about leaving your current situation here.'

'Yes, of course,' Cora said. 'Where are you wanting to sail?'

'It doesn't matter where, right now. We can make anywhere on Starzea work, and figure out the rest later.'

Cora nodded. 'Yes. I can do that. You know I can bargain better than anyone. I can get us passage.' She was right. She was shrewd and stubborn; those were the qualities that had kept them fed the last few weeks when she went to trade mangos for food.

'Excellent!' Malia said with guarded optimism. This might actually work.

She sighed and plopped onto her bed.

'What about your brother?' Cora asked. Malia didn't answer right away. 'If he is in as deep as he says he is with Haych, and you disappear. . .' She didn't have to finish. Malia knew what she was saying. If Brandt couldn't figure a way out of his mess, he might end up in prison or dead. Her running away would seal his fate.

Malia sat up slowly, the weight of her decision heavy on her shoulders. 'He can't come with us, Cora. I wish he could, but I can't risk his behavior. This has to stay between the two of us. Understand? Brandt will have to figure out his own fate.'

'What if he fixes everything like he thinks he can?' Cora asked, taking a seat next to Malia on the edge of the bed.

'If he did by some miracle save everything tonight, it would only be for another day, or week, or if we were lucky, a month. I have to leave while the harbor is brimming with chaos, making it impossible to track where we went. I won't be his bargaining chip anymore.'

Cora nodded sadly, but she didn't say anything more about Brandt.

The realization of Brandt's ugly fate made her sick to her stomach. She hated it, but she could not change it, and she couldn't wait around and suffer because of it. He was going to have to fix it himself. The only thing she could do was save herself and Cora from the consequences of Brandt's actions. To stay would bring on a fate worse than death: a life with Eldon Haych.

Chapter Eleven

Malia

The terrace doors were open, filling Malia's room with the scent of jasmine flowers. Cora had been gone all day, and now the sun was beginning to sink lower behind the clouds. The terrace provided the perfect view of the distant western shore and lighthouse to the south, peeking above the jungle tree tops. The lighthouse reminded her of the night before spent with Rogan. Thoughts of him and his promise to see her tonight filled her stomach with butterflies.

Could it be possible that she liked him? And what was scarier, that he might like her too? Remembering the way his hands lingered on her hips, and how his thigh rested against hers for most of the night had filled Malia with anticipation of what he might try and touch next. The thought brought a blush to her cheeks.

'Malia!' Cora exclaimed, bursting through the bedroom to the terrace. 'Great news! There is a Captain Dixon from the

Serenity that is willing to discreetly take two paying female passengers on board Saturday night. I believe he will be at the market square tonight to make the final arrangements with us.'

Malia's fear of failing to find safe passage on a ship had plagued her greatly and prevented her from sleeping much. Relief poured from her.

'Cora, you've saved us!' she said, hugging her tightly. Her fear was replaced with a fragile sort of hope. Could this actually work?

Malia glanced at one of her father's old pocket watches that she kept on the bedside table. It was almost six. The night's dinner and games would begin in an hour; and the dancing started at nine at the market square.

Wednesday's evening events would be held early so everyone would be home and off the streets by midnight when the Captain collected his souls. Tradition stated that if you were out after midnight on the night of the soul reaping, the Captain would claim you out of sheer spite for your disrespect. Malia had tried that, it wasn't true.

'Let's get you ready,' Cora insisted.

As Malia and Cora brushed through their recently-washed hair, Cora cleared her throat.

'There is a sailor that has gone missing,' Cora mentioned.

'Really?'

'A young man, sandy blonde hair, dimples in his smile, so they say. Aerita is beside herself with worry. Apparently, he had made all sorts of promises to her as they shared one another's company.'

'That sounds a lot like the young man I briefly danced with on the beach just before spotting Haych and Rogan.'

'Oh?'

'Yeah. He wanted what all the sailors that come here want, and when it was clear I wasn't selling that particular ware he moved on to Aerita beside him. He is probably just hung over in the hull of a ship somewhere.'

'Normally, I would agree with you. But it seems his shipmates are looking for him too. Rumor has it he was last seen winning at a game of cards, against Haych,' Cora's tone clearly implied that Haych had something to do with the sailor's disappearance.

Malia paused, her brush in mid-stroke.

'What does Haych say?'

'Oh he has an alibi of course. Haych insisted that after the sailor beat him in cards, he said he was going to go celebrate, left, and no one has seen him since. Haych said he went home to bed. Claiming to be too old to be up at all hours of the night. Ku and Brom, of course, vouched for him. The end.'

Malia's panic, that she spent all her energy suppressing, was starting to surface. Haych was getting bolder in his crimes and what was worse, the islanders were allowing it by looking the other way.

'So, now that we have a minute, are you going to tell me about my long-lost, non-Blisse cousin?'

'There is nothing to tell, really.' Malia knew this question had been coming. Cora deserved an explanation, but wasn't sure how much to confide in her. Cora was the most understanding person she knew, but even she might be worried about Malia's mental state if she told her about her flashes of memories that had never really happened, or his list of oddities.

'That's not what I would say if I had danced with him on the beach one night only to disappear with him the next.' Cora slipped her dress over her head.

Malia blushed, 'You heard about the beach, huh?'

Cora gave a playful eye roll as her head popped out of the ruffles of fabric. 'Malia, everyone heard about the dance on the beach, and last night. He must like you a lot to crash the dinner,' she commented with a pin clenched between her teeth. Malia wondered what her friend really wanted to say while Cora carefully brushed Malia's dark waves of hair down to her hips. Cora paused, taking a moment as she continued to pin up half of Malia's dark hair so it cascaded elegantly down her back. 'It looked like he might have done you a favor by spilling that wine in your lap,' she said.

'Yes,' Malia agreed. She owed him one. 'Haych was getting rather too familiar.'

'Besides the missing sailor, you two were all anyone was talking about this afternoon in the village and down at the market. "Malia Limoze found herself a mysterious, handsome beau, giving Sir Haych a challenge". Well?'

'That's ridiculous.'

'Is it? Surely, you've noticed how that man watches you. He is completely infatuated.'

'I think you mean the village is infatuated with this nonsense.'

'So, are you going to tell me what happened last night or not?'

With her back to Cora, Malia bit her lip.

'Fine. We went to the lighthouse,' she said, turning around.

'And?' Cora pushed.

'And nothing. We talked until the sun came up and I came home. Alone.'

Cora frowned in disappointment until her eyes widened in realization. 'Just as well, I suppose.'

'Why do you say that?'

'Well, there was no ship anchored off Cliff's Teeth this morning. And there was no Captain Rogan in the harbor. He might have already left.'

Malia suppressed a moment of sharp panic.

'He didn't leave, not for good anyway,' Malia said confidently, ignoring the nagging voice of doubt as she got up to dress.

'How can you be sure?'

Malia gave a little smile, despite herself. 'Well, he did tell me he would see me tonight. Maybe he just took his ship out on the open water today. He never really talked about what sort of shipping he did or what he does all day. But, I have a feeling he deals in trade that isn't openly discussed.'

'A pirate?' Cora asked, appearing both intrigued and scared, looking at herself in the mirror as she pulled pins out from a wardrobe drawer.

'Possibly. Which is why I won't be getting too familiar with his company.'

'That's probably for the best. I got one of my forebodings when I saw him last night. I know you don't believe in my gift, but I do. And I'm telling you, there is something off about that man despite how handsome he is.'

Cora looked fiercely at her friend.

Placing a hand over Cora's, Malia gave it a reassuring pat. 'Alright, Cora, I'll be careful. I have enough danger in my life right now. I don't need to add a cocky pirate in the mix.' Except she already had.

Malia slipped her dark blue dress over her head. Like all of her festival dresses, this one used to be her mother's. Luckily, she and Cora were skilled enough with a needle and thread to make it work. They had livened it up by hiking up the hem at her right knee, making the dress sassy without being scandalous. She also replaced the white lace by dyeing it an inky black instead. The colors of the day were blue for the ocean and sky with white, representing a ship's sails. She couldn't stand being another sheep blending into the crowd, and knew it would bother a certain older man that was determined to force her to conform. The neckline left her shoulders bare, exposing her glowing skin, and she wore perfect little black slippers. No more pinching boots.

Cora braided white jasmine flowers inside the dark strands

of Malia's hair. Her warning of danger still rang in Malia's ears as she continued to talk about the evening.

An hour later, Malia and Brandt were on their way.

Cora left earlier to meet someone, but she hadn't mentioned whom. Although, Malia suspected a certain ship's doctor had caught her attention.

A carriage passed by the siblings on the path as they walked. Brandt was so jittery, his hands kept moving between his blue jacket and shirt, and his pants. The combination of a sober mind, stress, and the excitement in believing he was on the brink of successfully winning back all they had lost manifested itself in destroying his clothes.

'Brandt!' Malia said, agitated at Brandt's optimistic restlessness. 'Stop! You're starting to give me a headache.' The drunken surly Brandt was preferable to this hyper-energetic one. She wasn't sure what to do with him. Was he really that confident in his poker skills, or did his denial run too deep?

'I'm going to save everything, Malia. I am,' he declared, with a determined set to his jaw and a smile on his lips.

Malia granted him a faint nod, allowing him to keep his hope.

'Brandt,' she said. He glanced toward her, their eyes locked. 'Don't lose.'

Please, for your sake. A childhood memory of the person Brandt used to be hit Malia hard. There was a time when he would playfully throw her across the room onto the furniture. Malia would laugh until she was breathless, asking Brandt to do it over and over until their mother caught them. The older brother she once knew wafted through her memories behind her closed eyes, leaving a harsh burn behind.

As they approached, the lantern lights from the market square shone in Brandt's hazel eyes, brightening their usual bleakness.

'I won't,' he said with his back straight and head held high as he strode ahead.

'Right,' she muttered.

'Did you say something?' Cora asked, suddenly beside her.

'No,' Malia began to answer but stopped when she noticed Cora's cheeks were a deep shade of rouge. She had been blushing, and there was a single flower now placed in her hair.

'That is a nice violet lily in your hair, Cora. Very flattering,' Malia said.

Cora's cheeks were as red as a parrot's feathers. 'Thank you.'

They walked down the dirt path, quickly changing the subject and talked about how this would be Malia's first year to see the Dance of Lost Souls performed. She'd been too young to attend when her parents were alive, and missed the dance last year because she had chosen to wait for the Captain in the cemetery. As it turned out, she had waited for hours in the cold rain for nothing. He hadn't showed. There was a tickling at the back of her mind, again, as she recalled waking up, already standing several rows away from her parents' graves in the cemetery, like she had been sleep walking. She remembered feeling desperate enough to risk the Captain's wrath if it meant she could at least see her parents again. None of those things had happened. She had missed the dance for nothing after all, so Malia was excited to finally experience it. The Dance of Lost Souls was one everyone on the island had been taught in school, but was only ever performed on the third night of the festival. One man and one lady were selected and voted on by the attendees to perform it. It was a huge honor to be chosen, and she was eager to finally see it performed outside a classroom. Another childhood memory of Brandt practicing the song on the violin with their mother entranced her thoughts. The memory of Malia forcing Brandt to practice with her when she was little produced a small ache in her chest. So, she shook the thought away. Sentiment wouldn't save her. As they came into the large square, people were already bustling in and out of store fronts and casting their votes at a large table which was placed on a raised platform in the middle of the square. People rushed to cast their vote before their time was up. Feather pens scratched excitedly across parchment paper, and villagers of all ages hurriedly made their way to the table with its list of names.

As Malia scanned the names, she came up short. The festival council had already hung up the list of six names of the nominated men and women for the Dance of Souls.

'What is it?' Cora asked, a little too innocently.

'My name?' Malia said, not sure she was seeing things right. Was it some kind of cruel jest? Her name was written on the list of potential dancers. She honestly didn't think anyone remembered that she danced, or that they would even want her to perform something so significant. She swallowed hard, the onset of nerves bubbling inside her.

Cora squinted at the paper on the wooden table, checking the list of names. 'Oh, well I suppose that is your name.' Cora picked up two small slips of paper and began to write two names on the papers to cast her vote for the dancing pair.

'Did you know about this?' Malia asked accusingly. Cora continued to look at her own two slips of paper.

'Well, yes.'

'And you didn't tell me?'

Finally meeting Malia's gaze, Cora said, 'Samora is on the festival council, as you know. She was part of the planning, and when she was asked for suggestions on who should dance, she felt it obvious that it should be you.'

'Samora? Other than Monday night, I haven't talked to her in weeks,' Malia said, thinking of the family's old cook that Brandt could no longer afford to employ.

'Like I said, she thought it was obvious.'

The dance was dark and heartbreaking. She also wasn't sure she wanted to do it. Depicting the story of the Captain of Souls

117

awakening a girl who refuses to leave, so he tricks her into falling in love with him just to get her to go with him, felt like just another way that the gods delighted in their ruthlessness. And, unlike a few days ago when she would have loved to do this dance, Malia had lost her desire to honor cruel fates. The dance reminded everyone that death and judgment were the two things in life that were unavoidable.

Terror overshadowed her shock. The reality of her dancing the Lost Soul dance had never occurred to her! It had to be practiced if it were to be performed right, which she hadn't done since stopping her lessons last year.

'Begging your pardon, but if your parents were still alive you wouldn't be in your current troubles, your dance lessons would have continued, and you would already be the obvious choice for this honor. The islanders wouldn't even bother with a vote. Just because they are gone, and your brother is a heathen, doesn't make you any less worthy of the honor,' Cora explained.

'Cora,' Malia whispered, urgently pulling her from the table before she could cast her ballot. 'What if I can't do this?'

'What if you can't do this?' Cora repeated as though she hadn't heard her correctly, then, putting a hand on her hip, 'Have you forgotten how?' Malia shook her head. She knew every step and movement. 'Malia, you were born to perform this dance. If you are chosen, it will be beautiful and perfect, just the way it's supposed to be.'

She nodded after a moment, feeling her hands shake as more and more people stared at her before they filled in their candidates on their voting slips.

'What are you supposed to do?' Rogan asked, his voice startling Malia out of her skin. She whirled around and saw him standing only inches behind. He looked handsome in his blue shirt and black pants. She smiled at the sight of him, and at the fact that he chose to wear black instead of white too. Their similarities were becoming harder to ignore.

Rogan's hair fell down in waves past his neck, highlighting the sharp angles of his face in shadow and light. Just like the night in her mysterious memory. She smiled again—warm relief spreading through her chest. He hadn't left the festival. After Cora's report that he was gone, there was a growing part of her that was afraid that she would never see him again. But, he was there. With a smile that suggested he was as happy to see her as she was to see him.

'Oh, have you heard of the Lost Soul dance?' Rogan nodded his head. Of course he had. 'Apparently, I've been nominated to perform as the Lost Soul and someone else the Captain,' she explained, waving it off, afraid she'd lose her lunch of mangoes just thinking about having to dance this sacred tradition in front of a man she was growing to like.

Malia felt a nudge against her shoulder, and forgot about Cora standing next to her. The small woman was pale as she looked up between Rogan and Malia. Despite being so civil and nice to him the night before, Cora looked at him now as if he was the bringer of death. Malia elbowed her friend, bringing Cora out of her rude stare, and managed to give Malia and Rogan a little quivering smile. Without saying anything, she turned back toward the table, dropped Malia's name in the female box and another in the male partner box before quickly scuttling her way into the growing crowd.

'Is my cousin feeling alright?' Rogan asked after Cora's back.

'I'm sure she is fine. She just gets a little leery of strangers, like a lot of girls on the island. Not all of us want magic blessed offspring,' Malia lied with a teasing wink. She wasn't about to say that Cora was scared of him because she had one of her foreboding feelings.

'You don't want a magic blessed child?' he asked a little too loudly. Several people, including Toa, turned and stared at them, others snickered.

'No, thank you,' Malia said between giggles.

119

'I guess I will have to keep acting like a gentleman,' he said, straightening his shirt collar.

'Absolutely. I have a reputation to worry about.'

Toa gave a derisive snort as he walked by, but Rogan didn't seem to hear. She would let it go, for now.

'Who would be your partner?' Rogan enquired.

'Why? Are you interested?'

He arched an eyebrow in a dare suggesting that he might be. Malia could feel her smile widening until her cheeks ached. Dancing with him on the beach was scandalous and fun. Escaping with him the night before had been more exciting than anything she had experienced in a long time. If she danced the Lost Soul dance with him— she almost swooned thinking about it.

'It will most likely be one of the dance instructors, they are usually the only islanders nominated. But, it's really whoever gets voted for. No one knows who that will be until just before the dance is performed, including the dancers.'

'Oh, so no pressure, huh?' he said with a twinkle in his blue eyes.

'Tradition doesn't care about pressure.'

'Come on,' he encouraged, placing a hand at the small of her back, 'let's go find something fun.'

'You don't want to put in your vote?' she teased.

'No need.' He shrugged and offered his arm.

Malia hesitated.

'What? Do I have something on my sleeve?' he asked, examining his arm.

'No. It's just,' she stumbled on her words, 'are you familiar with Blisse's courting traditions?'

Rogan gave her a confused look.

'No?' His arm still extended.

'If I take your arm, you are ... You will be ... How do I put this? You will be declaring solidarity courtship. In other words, staking a claim for my attention tonight.'

'That sounds a little outdated, not to mention possessive.'

Malia shrugged as he lowered his arm, 'As I've been told before, if I want progressive traditions, I need to live on Starzea.'

'Alright.' Rogan studied her for a moment. 'But, what if I *want* to ask to lay claim to your attention for the evening?' He raised his arm, again.

Malia smiled, feeling suddenly shy. She took his arm, and loved the feeling of his corded muscle beneath her palm. He drew his arm in, drawing her closer to his side. Everywhere Malia looked, eyes were darting between hers and Rogan's connection. Frantic whispers followed.

She took in a steadying breath.

So much for being careful.

Malia led him over to the appetizer table near a food tent entrance.

'Hungry?' she asked, holding up a plate of clams.

Rogan looked at the food like it was as appetizing as a plate of rocks. 'For that? No, thank you. However, I will take some of these,' he said, heading for Samora's table full of small cakes and fruit breads. Samora looked at the couple's connecting arms and gave Malia a wide smile. Malia could feel color rise to her cheeks. Feeling shy and blushing was new for her.

The smell of sugar and fruit made her mouth water and stomach growl. Rogan heard and laughed. 'Are you as hungry as I am?'

She was starving, but her stomach wouldn't unclench, and she didn't have any coins.

'Once you have Samroa's sweets you'll always be starving for them,' Malia said.

Rogan loaded a plate of sweets. Once the plate was nearly overflowing, Rogan handed over a handful of coins.

'Excuse me, sir. This is too much,' Samora protested.

'Oh, excuse me. That is for the whole evening. I'm sure we will be back here tonight,' Rogan explained with a wink.

Malia shamelessly plucked her own helping of banana bread from his plate. Rogan didn't object to her thievery. It was as if it were only natural that they would share food. Comfortable.

'So, Captain, are you the gaming sort?' she asked, gesturing toward the multiple gaming tables set up throughout the square. Haych's home was also connected to the square. The bottom floor he used as a gambling den, his private residence on the second floor, giving him the perfect view of the square and harbor – his growing kingdom. Malia certainly hoped Rogan wasn't interested in the gaming tables.

'Gambling was never my temptation,' he said. Malia exhaled in relief.

She noted the past tense he used, but didn't say anything, just simply added it to the growing list of oddities.

'What is your temptation?'

'I would think it was obvious.' Their eyes locked for a heart-stopping moment. Heat rose, again to Malia's cheeks. 'Sweets,' he said, raising his plate. 'Obviously.'

'Obviously,' she repeated with a playful eye roll before stealing a small fruit tart.

However, Rogan was no longer paying attention to her or the food. He was scanning the crowd, like he was looking for someone.

Rogan's eyes looked frantic as he searched.

'What is it? Did you see someone you know?' she asked.

'I thought I did, but I must have been mistaken.' his shoulders relaxed, but his eyes still looked unsettled.

The square was filled with islanders and travelers alike, as they filtered in and out of the buildings and smaller booths. Others were gathering on rooftops and balconies. She couldn't tell who he was looking for, but she saw someone who caught her attention—Haych.

She dashed behind Rogan, pulling his broad shoulder like a shield in front of her.

'Don't move!'

'You know, if you wanted to get a look at me from behind, all you had to do was ask,' Rogan said over his shoulder.

'Shhhh, you idiot,' Malia said. 'Don't flatter yourself. I most certainly am not staring at your backside.' She most certainly was.

'What are you doing back there then?' Rogan whispered, turning to the side.

'Just the usual, hiding,' she said, placing her hands on his wide shoulder blades and slightly turning them in the direction of her pursuer. Haych was talking with several older men too close to their wall for comfort.

'Right,' he said, straightening to his full height and widening his shoulders, willing to be her protector. He took a small backward step, tucking her into the alleyway corner behind a barrel. Rogan stood there happily eating from his plate. 'You know,' he said over his shoulder, 'after the last two nights, if he sees me, he is going to be looking around for you.'

'Shhh,' Malia said as she pinched a back rib.

'Ouch,' he whispered through all the dessert in his mouth. He relaxed, put his plate down on a nearby barrel and folded his arms across his chest as he leaned against the building's outer wall, leaving Malia nicely hidden in the small alley opening.

Malia held her breath. Rogan stayed relaxed while Haych passed by them, caught up in a conversation with an islander. Suddenly, Rogan's knees and back went rigid. Malia decided to peek around to see if maybe Haych, or Brandt was closing in. But Haych had moved further away. She moved from behind him. Rogan's eyes were darting around, again, his arms held stiffly at his sides.

'Are you alright?' she asked.

Rogan kept looking in the crowd when he said, 'I'll be right back.' Leaving Malia completely baffled.

Once Rogan had left, Sir Haych spotted Rogan's tall stature in the crowd and watched him like a vulture. Malia ducked back into the shadows of the alley, until Haych's gaze passed by her hiding spot. Watching Haych made her lose sight of Rogan. Malia's search for him was cut short when an unfamiliar woman walked toward her.

The crowd parted for her without realizing it, like a ship cutting through water. Everyone was moving in slow motion. An ice-cold chill ran down Malia's back and up her arms as goosebumps shivered across her shoulders. The brine smell of the ocean tickled her nose.

This woman had gold-green eyes and a sly smile that said she could bite you at any moment. Her white dress looked like its own sail, wrapped around her long lithe body like a ship figurehead in the shape of an avenging angel. Terrifying and beautiful.

The woman stopped in front of Malia, sweeping a stray hair away from her face. Malia instantly felt shabby in her dark blue dress with black lace.

'Malia, is it?' the woman asked, as if they had met before and she was barely able to recall her name.

Malia nodded. 'Have we met?' Only, Malia knew she had never seen this creature before in her life. How did she know her? The thought was as unsettling as Rogan's sudden disappearance.

The woman released a laugh that sounded as enchanting as magic. 'Not yet, my darling.'

What is that supposed to mean?

The woman stood, without blinking, studying Malia, as if eager to understand the very depths of her soul. Malia straightened and dared the woman with the cat-like eyes to find her wanting. The woman cocked her head to the side in response, a secret smile playing on her lips.

'Beautiful,' she said. It was her tone that unsettled Malia the most. What should have been a compliment sounded like a tragic warning instead. 'I can see why he is so enamored with you.'

Malia swallowed, as if the fruit bread from earlier was stuck in her throat.

The strange woman clicked her tongue. 'Be careful with broken things, my dear. Although they might be fun and challenging to try and put back together, they can also cut you. Make you bleed.' Malia straightened her spine, a beautiful woman warning her away from Rogan only made her feel more determined, defiant. The woman smiled condescendingly and turned her back to leave.

The crowd parted for her once more, leaving Malia standing alone and tongue-tied. She couldn't even pull it together in time to ask the woman's name. Let alone ask what had just happened as people began to move around at a normal pace. No one else had noticed the strange, beautiful woman. No one else even looked at her. The square was full of people, surely she hadn't been the only one to have seen her? But, no one acted like anything out of the ordinary had occurred. People sipped their drinks and sampled their fruit. Everyone acted like fish in a reef. Swimming through a sea of people, with no one remembering the shark they just swam past.

The sudden smell of salt and smoke stung her nose, overpowering the delicious food nearby. Malia grabbed a cup of wine from a table. Just when she felt like screaming to see if that would force the people to open their eyes to their surroundings, Rogan came back and everything returned to normal. The chatter of conversation, the clanking of mugs and roars of laughter were almost deafening. Malia was starting to wonder if she had imagined the whole thing. Except, Rogan looked as spooked as she felt. His eyes were wide while constantly glancing behind him, like he was watching out for anyone that would stick a knife in his back.

'Did you see that woman?' she asked.

'What woman?' Rogan asked, his eyes never settling.

Her gut told her that he and the woman were linked. Why had Rogan suddenly disappeared just as the mystery woman singled her out? It was all so odd.

'Are you alright?' he asked, looking at Malia for the first time since he came back. Concern etched his brows when he took her hand and felt it shaking.

She shook her head. She didn't know what was happening, but something still felt wrong—off.

'Some woman just came over here, and it was like I was the only one that could see or hear her. It was...strange,' she explained, soothing the lingering goosebumps from her arms.

'What did she look like?' he asked in earnest, as he gently grabbed her shoulders.

'She looked, I don't know, gorgeous, but also like she would enjoy eating me for dinner.'

'Did she speak to you?' he asked. His eyes grew darker with every syllable.

'Yes,' she answered, unsure of what to make of his sudden serious shift of behavior. The lines in his forehead spoke of his worry, but the tightness around his mouth hinted anger.

How many emotions can one person have at once?

'What did she say?' He covered the lower half of his face with a large hand, deep anxious lines etched by his eyes.

'She asked me if I was Malia. I said yes. Then, all she said was the word "beautiful" and left.' Malia didn't want to tell Rogan they had discussed him and the implied warning that he would hurt her in the end. 'Only, I don't know her. And while we talked, the square was in a trance, like a bunch of windup toys set in motion. I've never seen anything like it.' The feeling of being watched still hadn't left. 'Rogan?' she asked, when he hadn't responded.

He looked at her with troubled eyes but kept the lower half of his face hidden behind his hand.

'Who was she?'

He sighed and dropped his hand. 'Someone from my past looking for trouble, that's all.'

'Your past? That's it? What kind of trouble? Is she ... are you...' She didn't know how to finish asking her question. Were this woman and Rogan somehow matched or together?

'Something like that. It's complicated. Don't worry about her. She's gone,' he said through gritted teeth. Then, like striking a match, his mood shifted, and he gave her a smile. 'Come on, this square is starting to feel dead. Let's see what else there is to do.'

Chapter Twelve

Rogan

None of it felt right to Rogan. It felt like a trap. Why would Angelos talk to Malia, if not to make him anxious?

While escorting Malia around the square, he had felt the Goddess' lingering presence, like a prickling on your neck before someone tried to stab a knife in it. She hadn't left yet, but he couldn't spot her. What did she want?

Luckily, he was spared from making up some lie or excuse to leave Malia's side when Cora found them.

'Malia?' she asked, after giving the Captain a wide berth. He could tell by the way she had greeted him when he first arrived that Malia's magic blessed friend really could sense something otherworldly about him. Cora avoided looking directly at the Captain. 'I have someone that would like to talk to you for a moment.' A strange look passed between the two women. Malia's eyebrows shot up in excitement.

'Of course,' she agreed, sounding eager. 'Rogan, will you excuse me for a moment?'

Not trusting himself to say anything, and afraid he would insist that she never leave his side again, he gave a reluctant bow. With Angelos running around the island, he didn't want Malia to leave his side, while at the same time, he didn't want her within a mile of his person. He wasn't sure which would be the best way to keep her safe.

Once the girls were inside the bakery, he made his way through the crowd in search of his master. Unable to stop himself from checking on Malia, he turned and saw both of them talking to a younger gentleman in the doorway. Rogan recognized him as being the same man that Cora had been palm reading the first night. A ship's physician, he recalled.

They looked safe enough for the time being, so he made his way deeper into the square. Strings of music started as musicians began tuning their cellos, readying themselves for the dancing and Lost Soul performance that would soon take place.

'Hello, Captain,' an unwelcome gravelly voice said beside him –Haych. Rogan really didn't need this right now. He had bigger problems to worry about than standing there in a pissing contest with this guy. Seeing the old man's strict, ugly face, Rogan slapped on his favorite irritating smile. Self-important men were easy to read and even easier to annoy.

'Mr. Haych, was it?' Rogan said. The older man's eyes narrowed. His buttons were so easy to push; Rogan might actually enjoy keeping him around. He couldn't help the delight the little rebellion brought him.

'Yes,' Haych said abruptly as he jerked his arms and pulled on the sleeve of his jacket. 'I believe you ruined my fiancée's dress last night.'

'Your fiancée?' Rogan asked. 'Does Miss Malia know she is under such a contract?'

Haych merely shrugged in an unapologetic way and uncaringly fiddled with his jacket cuffs. 'It will become official soon enough.' The older man rocked on his heels, sending his jowls flapping. 'So, I suggest unless you want to stay permanently embedded in the island, you had better stay away from my property.'

Property?

'Is that a threat?' he asked, his smile still firmly in place. The fact that this old man thought he could do anything to the Captain was comical.

'Oh, you and I both know I'm too smart for open threats.' He gave Rogan a hard pat on the back that made Rogan want to snap off his wrist. But he wasn't allowed to harm mortals while on land, only in self-defense. His ship, however ... 'No, this isn't a threat, dear boy, just a promise. Laws are a little different here on the island.'

'You mean different for you.'

'I thought you knew. I'm the only one that really matters.' Haych gave Rogan's shoulder another firm pat and walked away.

'What interesting people you know on this island, Rogan,' the Goddess said, suddenly over his shoulder.

'Angelos.' He turned. She was staring after Haych with an angry crease between her brows, her eyes burning from gold to orange with rage. The sight of her set Rogan's teeth on edge. Out of all the emotions that had been rekindled in him that week, anxiety was the one he hated the most. It twisted inside him like a snake making every other emotion connected to it stronger, including fear and jealousy.

He took his eyes off Haych, who was approaching Malia from behind like a jungle cat just outside the bakery. She and Cora were talking to one another, the ship doctor now gone. He turned to see the Goddess beside him. He needed to look anywhere but at Malia. Angelos couldn't be led to believe that Rogan had any real interest in her. 'I'm surprised to see you here among all these mortals.'

Angelos laughed, her voice sounding like a fairy's chime while taking his arm, leading them toward another narrow alley opening between shops. People parted around them without realizing it.

'That was Sir Eldon Haych,' Rogan pointed out. He had no problem bringing him to the Goddess of Death's attention.

'Ah yes, I know of Eldon Haych and some of his work,' she said darkly.

'Some of his work?' he asked, curious. If the Goddess was aware of someone's work it could only mean a few things.

She nodded, still looking at him with squinted eyes. 'That man has made several premature deposits into my account.'

'Deposits?'

Angelos nodded, 'He has had two marriages. None of them lasted long. Although, they did last longer than his numerous business partners.' Understanding dawned on Rogan as Angelos turned from him to stare at Haych's retreating back. The black-guard had almost reached Malia now and it had Rogan fighting the impulse to go to her .

So, he was on her bad side. Good. Murderers disrupted the natural balance of life and death. It wasn't something the Goddess took kindly to. But his happiness was short-lived as Rogan's suspicions were confirmed. Haych was more than just annoying, he was a murderer and dangerous, and was now talking to Malia. Heat like fire spread from his chest, angry and hot.

'Well if that's the case, why don't you right his wrongs? Take him and his worthless soul away from here?' Rogan asked.

'I'm the Goddess of Death, dear. Not fairness. There are certain rules that even I have to abide by in order to maintain balance. I cannot overstep what the mortals call boundaries.'

Rogan wanted to roll his eyes, but kept them firmly set on Malia, who was looking around the crowd like she was trying to find an escape route.

'Then, what brings you here, Goddess?' Rogan asked, trying to be cautious. His turmoil of emotions were becoming exhausting.

'Well,' Angelos brightened, 'Your interest in the festival and the island's inhabitants caught my attention, and I wanted to see what all the fuss was about.'

Rogan had never said anything about being interested in the inhabitants of the island; in fact, he had deliberately not said anything. Rogan felt his nerves spike, like hackles on a dog. He pushed down the instinct to protect Malia and tried to appear calm as he stood stiffly with Angelos on his arm.

'So that's it? You wanted to attend a mortal party?' he prodded, as they looked out over the crowd. Everyone was laughing, mingling, as they slipped in and out of the stores. Others were sitting on their small balconies or on their window sills above the square, enjoying their view and readying themselves to watch the dance. The whole island was oblivious to the immortal creatures that stood to the side and watched them.

She shrugged. 'It's an important night, Rogan . . .' she left her sentence unfinished.

'Why? I don't feel like this night is any different from all the other countless times I have collected.'

Angelos sighed sadly, like she was tired of waiting for a toddler to learn his lesson. 'I can't tell you why, darling. It's something you are going to have to figure out yourself.'

He really did roll his eyes now, barely able to pass off his genuine fear as playful annoyance. Angelos laughed and patted his arm like she was flirting instead of patronizing.

She leaned in close to his ear. If anyone could see them they would think that they were lovers sharing a secret.

'She is beautiful; I can't wait to see her dance,' the Goddess said.

'Who is?' Rogan asked innocently, looking anywhere but in Malia's direction.

Angelos laughed again. She gently took a hold of his chin and turned his face to look directly at Malia. Her fingers were too firm to be gentle. 'Why, your lady love, of course. She is fetching.' The Goddess' grip went from firm to bruising on his jaw. He fought the urge to flinch. 'But still breakable.' Her tone turned from light flirtation to a warning that sent a chill through to his bones. Rogan swallowed a lump forming in his throat as she let go of his chin in a caress.

'What do you want?' he asked. There was no use pretending that Angelos didn't have an agenda in place anymore. Her flashing gold eyes turned fiery. Rogan's stomach dropped.

Then, she whispered in his ear right as Malia made eye contact with him. Her eyes went round with shock. He didn't think that she could see them, as no one else had acknowledged their presence. Haych was saying something to her, but she didn't notice. Her eyes held Rogan's. Angelos turned his chin to face her.

'Remember, I do not like sharing the attention of my collectors. Remember also that you are nothing but a player in my game. All of you are small, simple pieces for me to move around as I will.' Her cold breath hissed in his ear, harsh and brutal, but still quiet, calm.

Rogan's jaw clenched as he swallowed down something he hadn't ever remembered feeling—fear. And not the kind he had experienced the night before at the lighthouse. This felt sickening and desperate. A fear that he had never felt before. It made his mind go blank in panic and his body froze. It was the fear for someone else.

'Don't hurt her, please,' Rogan said through gritted teeth, trying to reign in his fear. His fists shook with the effort.

'Oh my Pet, my love, sometimes pain is good. Like pulling a tooth, or blade from a chest.' The image of Malia bleeding from a blade seared into Rogan's mind. He felt like he might go mad from it. The image was so real, and Angelos' smile so sly that he knew she had put the image in his head, and kept it there. All he could see was red, an ocean of it spilling out of Malia.

Rogan wanted to whimper as the image in his head progressed, watching Malia bleed out and die right in front of him.

'If you do what you are told.' Without warning the image was gone and he was back in the village square with Angelos. His chest hurt like it had been gutted, he was finding it hard to breathe. The illusion had been so real. 'There will be no reason for such upsetting events for Malia. I want you to do your job, Rogan. Nothing else matters. The souls are all that concern you. I allowed you this little vacation for past good behavior in hopes of you wanting to redeem yourself. But if I find you careless, or distracted, I will remove the distraction. Are we clear?'

He remembered now why feeling anything for anyone was always a bad idea. As soon as emotions grew, they were twisted and used against you. Hadn't his life of being an orphan and pirate taught him that? Emotions were a weakness that others exploited.

Her hand released his chin and settled lovingly on his cheek.

'Do we understand one another, Pet?' Rogan nodded slowly as he looked into her dangerous eyes, not trusting himself to speak without his voice shaking.

'Good. Now enjoy the dance, and remember...I'm watching,' she said, then smacked his cheek just a little too hard to be considered playful. The Goddess of Death drifted off Rogan's arm and was instantly lost in the crowd, as though she had never been there.

Chapter Thirteen

Malia

W homever this former lover of Rogan's was, she had obviously done something to him, because he stayed as far away from Malia as was possible once she left.

As the night wore on, Malia was half-tempted to just leave, but she wanted to be there when Brandt and Haych were done playing for her life at one of the game tables in the tavern. Plus, this was her last chance to see the Lost Soul dance performed.

Besides, Cora was enjoying herself, especially with Duncan, and Malia didn't want to dampen her friend's mood by having them leave early. After the run-in with the neck scar goon, Brom, on the beach the first night, Malia was determined to always have someone with her, unless it was an emergency. The doctor and Cora even had matching violet lilies; one in Cora's hair, the other pinned to his breast pocket. He assured them, earlier, that acquiring safe passage for both of them to Starzea could be done discreetly. They were to give his captain payment the following night.

Rogan stayed mostly out of sight. By eleven o'clock, Malia hoped to never see him again. She was fuming at him for abandoning her like everyone else. He had been the one pursuing her. Then, just talking with another woman was enough for him to avoid her like she had the plague.

When she hadn't seen him at all for the last hour, she decided enough was enough and that she was going home. Staying wasn't worth the humiliation. What had she been thinking? That he was different from all the other men she knew? That he would sail away with her at the end of the week? What did she even know about him, really?

'Ladies and gentlemen,' Noah said from the small musical stage in the center of the square, just as Malia was making her way towards the street home. She stopped in her tracks. 'We are ready to announce the dancers of this festival's Lost Soul dance.' He gestured to an envelope in his hands.

Noah unfolded the piece of parchment, squinting at the names.

He licked his lips before announcing 'The Lost Soul will be danced by Miss Malia Limoze.' Malia was too surprised to even gasp as hundreds of eyes suddenly swiveled to find and focus on her

Noah didn't miss a beat as he smiled into the crowd before proceeding to announce her partner. 'The Captain of Souls will be performed by. . .' he squinted harder. Malia would have liked to think he just needed glasses, but the confusion on his face suggested he might be unfamiliar with the name. A strong breeze, carrying with it the salty brine smell of the sea, blew into the square. Noah's features relaxed. 'The Captain of Souls will be,' he started again, 'Captain Rogan, of the *Calypso's Voyage*.'

Everyone peered eagerly around the square in search of the Captain. There was no murmuring or whispering. It was baffling that no one appeared confused that a total stranger, not an islander, was going to dance the island's most sacred tribute. Was this someone's idea of a joke? Why weren't the islanders outraged at this break of tradition? Finally, she spotted him leaning up against a building wall by the wine table looking as surprised as she felt.

Her palms began sweating as her heart hammered, sending a tingling sensation to her fingers and down to the tips of her toes. Every little girl dreamed of performing this most prestigious of dances, and she was living that dream, or was it a nightmare? Malia inhaled slowly through her nose and out through her mouth. She shook out the tingles in her hands, feeling calmer. She could do this, no matter who her partner was. It was only a dance.

Four minutes of dancing. No problem, she told herself. Too bad her trembling knees weren't listening.

The crowd parted for Malia as she walked to the side of the stage where the dance was to be performed. She took off her slippers and stretched.

She hadn't touched her toes for more than two seconds when Cora rushed to her side.

'Oh, Miss, I'm so sorry,' she said, wringing her hands together like there was an invisible dish towel between them. 'I didn't know he was going to be your partner. If I had, I never would have... He wasn't even on the list!' Cora looked close to tears.

'It's alright, Cora.' She hoped it would be anyway. If someone had told her at the beginning of the night that she would be dancing the Dance of Souls with Rogan, she would have delighted in it. They would have shared in banter and scandalous touches. It would have been fun. But now, something had changed. She didn't know what to expect.

'Stop fretting,' she said, lightly swatting Cora's wringing hands. 'You better go find a good spot. I'll probably only do this once,' Malia teased. Cora nodded, looking helpless but resigned.

The square's chatter had started up again as people started moving towards their viewing places on balconies, roofs, or toward the raised platform to watch the dance. Rogan, however, hadn't moved. He was planted, motionless on the far side of the square, a hand resting over the bottom half of his face, hiding most of his expression.

Does he know the dance? Malia wondered.

As Malia stretched, it gave her a chance to focus on the story behind the dance and get into character. She had to channel the character of a bitter young woman scorned in love and life. She could do that. The Lost Soul begrudgingly fell in love with a man she couldn't keep. It seemed like Malia could do that too. In the end, the mortal believed the Captain loved her and boarded the ship. The dance was the telling of the story of how there is worth in every soul, even the lost ones. It's supposed to fill a person with hope. She wasn't sure she could do that. Being chosen was an honor. Since she would be leaving the island and all the people she had ever known in a few days, she felt it was her duty to perform the dance well, even if it brought her suppressed feelings of loneliness to the surface.

All at once, the cellist and pipers were set up and the crowd was waiting.

Malia rose to her feet, ignoring the temptation of hesitation that flared within her. The hard cold surface of the cobblestone square prickled her toes and traveled up her legs as she walked to the elevated round stage.

Out of the corner of her eye, she saw that Rogan hadn't moved from his spot at the far corner of the square.

Is he going to do this, or not? she wondered, placing a foot on the smooth wooden stage.

All the lamps around the square were put out. Lightning flashed in the distance from the sea. Complete silence befell the audience waiting to see the most anticipated dance of the festival. Others had noticed that Rogan was still on the other side of the room as they looked from Malia to him. Glowing light from the game rooms reminded her that Brandt and Haych were absent. It was considered very rude not to view the dance, but Haych could do what he wanted. And right now, he wanted to play and beat Brandt out of her freedom.

Dim lanterns were lit near the floor of the platform, providing it with a soft glow while plunging everything else in moonlit shadows. Malia saw the whites of hundreds of eyes; mortal spectators waiting to judge her dancing, her soul. Looking at the shadowed eyes only magnified the feeling of being a lost soul.

Rogan was lost to the soft light. Malia could only hope that by the time it was his turn he would come and join her for the dance, but if not, she would do it herself, just like she always did. Why should that night be any different? She straightened her shoulders, took a deep breath and lifted her chin. She could do this.

Sitting on the edge of the circular stage, she laid down and waited for the whistling of the pipes to start. Just like the Captain was said to use a pipe to awaken his souls, it was how the musicians would begin the dance. She closed her eyes and waited. Distant thunder rumbled once more. The sound of the growing waves grew louder.

The first pipe started low like a whispered secret. The next joined seconds later, growing louder in the surrounding silence. Malia could feel the music vibrating the stage beneath her. Slowly, she opened her eyes and sat up. As the pipes continued their awakening notes, Malia looked at her arms, hands, and legs in awe, pretending to marvel at the miracle of being alive again. Her arms waved and flowed, like she was just learning how to reuse them.

The strumming of cello strings began. She stood, looking

down. Malia tiptoed, lightly, jumping as if trying to balance on lily pads on a pond. Pirouetting on the balls of her feet, she hopped on the lower half of the stage. Her back faced Rogan's section of the stage, not knowing if he'd shown up yet. But she kept on, just the way the dance was supposed to go.

The strumming stopped as the first bow went mournfully over the strings low and sad, doomed. Rogan should be there by now.

Please be there.

As Malia turned, to her surprise, he was there. His dark blue shirt looked completely black in the orange glow of the lanterns. His face was hesitant but somehow still determined like he too had something to prove. He truly looked like the ghost of tradition: beautiful, *other*, and a little terrifying. Her heart pumped harder while lightning danced across the sky behind him.

As the Captain stood there, on the other side of the circle, looking exactly how the Captain of Souls should, she remembered her anger. Her emotions mirrored the bleakness of the dance perfectly. And she wasn't just angry at Rogan, but at almost everyone. Her parents for dying, Brandt, all these people that were supposed to help and protect her, all of them had failed. Rogan had shown, with his earlier abandonment, that he also couldn't be trusted. Malia clenched her jaw as the strings continued low and despondent. Remembering that she was in the middle of a dance with hundreds of eyes watching, Malia pulled herself together and sidestepped at Rogan's advance, keeping her distance from this man unworthy of her trust. He retreated and she did the same. Their feet carefully placed, like they were balancing on the edge of the world.

He took a large step closer, in challenge. She accepted his dare and stepped closer as well, until they were within arm's length of each other.

She glowered at him, and he stared stoically back at her. Were they dancing for the observing audience, or was it real? Did it matter?

The music called to her. But she stayed rooted. How could she trust him? Whirling around, in an attempt to flee, Rogan's strong hands caught her waist. Freezing both of them, as his icy fingers clasped her hips, wrinkling the blue material. Gingerly, he enfolded her in his arms, and she allowed it, his touch thawing her resolve. She hadn't realized she was holding her breath until she felt Rogan's fanning the hair at her neck. Malia exhaled, shaky. At his touch, the anger and resentment that had risen melted, despite her determination to hold onto it. No one else had ever touched her like he had. Leaning back into his chest, they swayed twice.

She wanted so desperately not to be alone anymore even if only for a few minutes.

Wherever he was, that's where she wanted to be.

He lifted her off the floor in an intimate embrace. Her body crushed to his as they circled back to where they had been. Malia's hand found the back of his neck as they spun, her fingers easily lacing through his waves of dark hair. Her feet were placed back on the ground. A hand feathered across her collar bone, pushing her hair that blocked the path of his fingers, exposing the tender spot behind her ear. She felt his restraint leave as the cool, soft pressure of his lips landed on her neck. Gasps could be heard all around them. Malia turned and backed away in surprise. She had completely forgotten that they had an audience, the entire island, watching.

Locking eyes with Rogan, the audience disappeared again. The Captain of Souls and the Lost One, but perhaps now, not forgotten.

They moved across the floor. He picked her up and placed her back down on the smooth surface. The Captain manipulating the Lost Soul to fall in love with him, so he could get her on the ship. Thus, preventing her from becoming one of the eternally forgotten, a ghost. She had felt like a ghost since her parents died. But Rogan, for however brief a moment, had made her feel remembered.

Rogan had just lifted her nearly above his head, twirling as she extended her leg for the last lift, when Malia saw Brandt and Haych come to the front of the enthralled audience.

She caught sight of Brandt's glazed over eyes and a bottle in his hand. Reality crashed back, and she knew. He had lost. Haych's eyes were devouring her exposed thigh.

Malia swung back to the floor, early, surprising Rogan, but his steady grasp on her waist kept her from crashing. Malia began to shake in Rogan's hands. All of the terrible things Haych had planned for her were evident in his cruel eyes and lustful sneer. He wasn't going to wait very long to start inflicting the terror. She wasn't going to make it to the end of the week; she wasn't even sure if she was going to make it to the end of the night, so dark were the promises in his eyes and popping knuckles. Haych's hold would be so tight, she might never see Rogan after that dance. She would be watched, confined, claimed. Strong trembles overwhelmed her body as Malia struggled to breathe; the suffocation had begun. Rogan held her up when her knees buckled. Gasps of surprise came from the audience. Oxygen wasn't reaching her lungs as she fought the instinct of fight or flight. The dance was almost finished. All of it was finished. Her soul was judged and life condemned.

Rogan still held her, the closing musical notes forgotten.

'Malia?' he whispered. She looked at him briefly before looking back at Haych and her future. He followed her gaze. Haych's victorious smile. Unable to stand the sight of him, she looked away.

Looking at Rogan's eyes reminded her of what he really was, a stranger. She backed away out of Rogan's reach. Her hand pressed against his chest as she tried and failed to calm the panic swirling there. If she could just breathe. The last notes were playing. Rogan offered his hand, a life line for her to take. The dance dictated she take it and have him escort her off the stage onto his ship, figuratively speaking. But she hesitated and stood there staring at his hand, his strong capable hand that could not help her. If she were to go with him, Haych might go after him too. Lightning flashed, closer.

Only the pipes played now, isolated in their sound. Everyone held their breath, just like her, waiting to see if she would take his hand. She didn't. Another step back, forcing a greater expanse of space between them and Haych.

A look of determination crossed Rogan's face. A look that said he would change the ending to their story, no matter the cost.

Rogan stepped forward, catching Malia before she fell backward off the stage. Just as the last note of the pipes played, his lips met hers. Thunder clapped, and the square erupted in applause.

Chapter Fourteen

Malia

L ike a dam being broken, memories flooded Malia, leaving her drowning in its wake. She gasped for air as she pulled back from Rogan's lips.

He was the real Captain of Souls. She had met him in the cemetery the year before. They had kissed. He was her first and only kiss. Malia's head was no longer drowning, grasping for purpose, but was swimming in confusion, like being stuck in a whirlpool. There was too much to take in. The kiss from that night, exactly one year ago, the feeling of his lips gently pressed to hers just now, in front of the whole island. His tenderness as he held and kissed her, sparked a fire within Malia that had been snuffed out, along with her memory of him. The ocean blue of his eyes, the recognition of them on the beach, her flashes of memory that she thought weren't real, all made sense. It all made sense! Malia had just caught her breath when the recollection of who Rogan was returned. The crushing reality was that he would never be hers.

Rogan's eyes were wide with vulnerability and a little panic. He still held her in his arms, but easily let go when the first raindrops hit their cheeks. Malia backed away. She couldn't focus on the hurt that crossed his face, she had to think. She needed space and air. With another clap of thunder, the rain poured down like a pitcher being poured. Rogan looked up, temporarily distracted by the elements.

Malia jumped from the stage and practically landed on Cora's feet.

'Malia!' Cora said, sounding startled as she steadied her friend. People swarmed in a hurry to get out of the deluge.

'I have to go,' Malia said. She looked back and saw that Haych hadn't moved. Like a cat letting a mouse go for a minute before it pounced. Rogan also stood where she left him on the stage. With his straight spine and clenched jaw, Rogan looked like he wanted to follow after her, but didn't.

'I'll come with you,' Cora said as they pushed through the dispersing crowd. Everyone had to get home before midnight. Only ... she couldn't go home. They would be waiting for her there. Haych would be waiting, ready to do whatever it was he wanted to her. Brandt had just given him that power.

'No,' she told her friend as they neared an alleyway. 'I can't go home. No yet. Distract Haych and Brandt. There is something I must do.'

'But the collecting? You can't be out after midnight, that doesn't leave you much time. What are you going to do?'

'I can't go home, Cora. Not tonight. Please. I'll be fine, I promise.'

A moment of clarity passed over Cora. She looked back at Haych and Brandt. Neither had moved, waiting for the crowd to clear. Brandt took a long swig from the bottle in his hand, while his hair plastered to his forehead from the rain. Haych was now under an umbrella, held by Ku. Malia no longer saw Rogan.

'Of course. I'll distract them. They won't know which way you went.'

Cora fought her way back through the crowd, earning her more than one yelp of protest and dirty looks. Malia tore through the last couple of islanders that were in the way.

People might have been trying to congratulate her on her performance, but Malia didn't hear them. All she focused on was her escape.

Finally, she was out of the square and on the jungle path. A wall of thunder clouds covered the distant night sky, making the world look like it was being covered in a black blanket on its way to snuff out the moonlight.

As she stood behind the trees and watched people pour out of the square, Malia didn't spot Brandt, Haych, or even Cora as everyone blended together in the sea of faces down the lantern lit paths. Haych wouldn't go after her, not that night. He would count on her going home. Scared of the captain like everyone else, like he was. Everyone but her.

She knew where she had to go. Malia had to see it for herself, just so she knew she wasn't losing her mind. At the time, the bombardment of memories and panic over her future had left her too shocked to ask questions. But now, as she made her way through the jungle path, alone, her mind buzzed like a wild bee unable to settle on just one question before her thoughts flew off to another. Had Rogan meant to give her the memories back? Why would he do that? It was part of their bargain. Was he going to leave the island as soon as his collection was done? All of his cryptic and vague answers throughout the week now made sense.

Lightning flashed again, cutting a silver crack through the sky. The clouds were directly over her now. The rain turned the path to heavy mud. She needed to reach the cemetery before the moonlight was gone, or worse, before Rogan finished collecting and maybe left forever. He couldn't leave, not now that she remembered him. Not now that she would miss him if he left.

The one thing Malia could count on tonight was that Haych couldn't leave a building after midnight. He was bound by this law like everyone else. The islanders would turn a blind eye to most things, but sacrilege wasn't one of them. For this one night, he could not break tradition.

Ku and Brum, she was sure, would be on the jungle paths until the last possible minute, waiting to escort Malia home. She ducked into the cover of trees, the muddy jungle floor swallowing her toes as she climbed the incline, using vines to help with her muddy ascent. The cliff paths were dangerous and rarely used anymore, especially after her parents fell to their deaths last year, as did one of her father's former ship captains only last month. The islanders had started saying that the cliffs were haunted and cursed. No one would be taking the cliff paths on the night of the collecting, she was sure. Her way would be clear.

Malia stayed in the tree line parallel to the cliff path until she could no longer see the glowing lights of the lanterns dotting the landscape. The building crash of the waves on the cliffs muffled her curse when a sharp rock jabbed into her bare foot. She had forgotten her slippers by the stage. Memory and dancing lightning bolts lit her way to the cemetery. The wind was blowing stronger by the minute, like hands that were pushing her back, urging her home instead of towards the Captain. Malia's hair whipped in her face, making it hard to see where her feet were. She slipped and scraped her knees and palms, but it was better that than falling to the rocks below. She slowed. Malia had fallen down the rock face before, she had no wish to do it again.

Finally, the lighthouse was there, only a few yards in front of her, like a pillar of hope. It must have been midnight by then, but when she came upon the cemetery it didn't look like anything extraordinary was happening – yet. Malia weaved and ducked through snarling branches, moving her feet carefully off the rocky terrain and into the spongy mud of the jungle brush, right where she and Rogan had been the night before. Pebbles were sticking to the balls of her feet and between her toes. Malia welcomed the sharp pierces of reality that the tiny rocks brought, reminding her that she was not in a dream, but that what she felt and saw was real.

The Captain had entered the cemetery.

Chapter Fifteen

Rogan

Rogan was still thinking of Malia when he entered the cemetery. Her gasp of shock and confusion after Rogan had kissed her ached in his own burning chest.

He had seen her pain, felt the horror in her shaking limbs when she looked toward Haych and her brother. The panic on her face had gutted him. He had to let her know that whatever had just happened with Haych and Brandt, she wasn't alone anymore. Letting her know that he cared for her in a way that she would never forget was all he could do. The only way to do that was to kiss her, to give back what she had given him. He had to let her know that she was kissed, again, by the Captain of Souls.

Rogan had stared into her brown eyes hoping to reassure her, but all he saw was confusion, a crease in between her brows making her look both vulnerable and terrified. Her hand had, once again, fisted his shirt, holding tight. His hands still held her waist, keeping her from falling off the platform. Applause echoed off the shop walls in the square.

Thunder clapped again as Rogan eased her forward so both feet were securely on the ground. She let go of his shirt like it had burned her, leaving it wrinkled. Malia shook her head once as Rogan held his breath. What would she do, now that she knew the truth?

A large raindrop splattered down on his cheek, pulling both of them back to reality. The storm had arrived. He was the Captain, and he had souls to collect. Malia looked from Rogan's torn expression to Haych's triumphant one.

A moment later, water poured from the sky. The crowd scattered for the shelter of their homes. Rogan looked around him. He had to leave. Why wasn't there enough time? How could he just bombard Malia with her memories, then leave her? At that moment he hadn't considered how bad his timing was. He couldn't pull her aside to explain. He didn't even have time to stand there like he was.

Thunder clapped again as Malia took the moment of Rogan's distraction to leap off the platform.

'Malia!' Rogan pointlessly called after her. Malia had landed right next to Cora and both were swept up in the crowd. His brand gave a painful burn in his chest. He had to leave. Now.

Leaping from the platform, he ran toward the closest alleyway out of the populace. The jungle path was devoid of mortals as they all ran toward their homes in the opposite direction. It only took him a minute to reach the edge of the jungle where he could disappear and reappear in the cemetery without witnesses.

When he arrived the only sounds to be heard were the rain and wind rustling the nearby palm trees and the waves crashing against the cliffs. The iron gate creaked as Rogan entered the cemetery. The trident brand seared, but instead of bringing pain it brought him release, like he'd stretched a muscle.

Now, with a break in the rain, lightning flashed in the distance, and waves crashed louder. A clap of thunder reverberated, like a warning. Rogan's breath came in short spurts in preparation. He was behind a small, new mausoleum. Lightning cracked in a furious pulsing light that illuminated the graveyard.

Even though it had only been a few short seconds since the lightning, Rogan saw everything clearly. He felt the souls stir in their tombs and graves, like they were being awakened from their sleep. His blue shirt was now on the ground by his feet. His trident brand, that stretched over his heart, burned and began to brighten. No longer looking like an ordinary tattoo, it shimmered at the edges, like the sight of moonlit waves. White knuckles gripped the short duduk pipe in his hand as he fought the familiar revulsion of being the vessel of the dead. The souls would float around inside him unable to attach to him like they would their own bodies. Everytime all the different spirits swarming and swimming inside his chest left him reeling– it felt like there were crabs crawling under his skin. It was in those brief moments before he collected that he felt the loss and comfort of his own soul and body, the loss of never feeling whole. The burning intensified and the blue white glow brightened as the seconds grew closer to midnight. His brand was ready. Rogan licked his lips as the rain started again. He thrummed the pipe against his thigh, like a nervous tic, counting down the seconds.

Another crack of thunder brought the storm right on top of him. From the corner of his eye, he thought he saw movement just outside the iron fence, but he ignored the animal that scurried to safety. His breathing became harder, like he was gearing up for a blow to the gut. The pressure inside his chest was suffocating, driving him to his knees. The time had come.

Rogan staggered back to his feet. He lifted his pipe to his lips with shaking fingers. The air was charged, and his trident covered the cemetery in a pulsing white light. The wind bent the tall trees; only to stop for half a moment, like the island inhaled and held its breath just as Rogan blew into his pipe. The first mournful notes sent Rogan's tattoo from pulsing to an intense brilliance, illuminating the whole cemetery in a light so bright it would have blinded any mortal. This was a ritual solely for beings of the night and the dead.

He stood there amongst the sleeping dead with his pipe gaining strength.

Now, if Malia could see me, she would finally realize. Finally see.

Rogan looked like the stone angel headstone beside him. Beautiful and sorrowful as he played the notes and pulled the souls from their resting places. The rain started to splatter against his bare skin, soaking into his hair.

Thunder became a deafening beat as lightning struck the lighthouse, exploding and shrouding the rest of the island in flashing light, then nothing. The angel beside Rogan began to weep with rainwater. His hair was slicked to his cheeks and neck as water ran down his skin. Rogan ignored the elements. What were they to him?

As he continued to play, a thick fog began to rise from the ground, despite the rain pouring down on top of it. The restless souls were awakening, finding their way to the surface.

The fog completely covered the ground, as thick as carpet, and rose to his thighs. Lightning flashed. Thunder drowned out the sound of the pipe, but the dead still heard him.

Finally, the fog stopped rising and began moving, taking shape. It looked as though figures were standing under the cover of sheets.

Rogan played fervently now; his fingers moving over the holes in the pipes so quickly they almost blurred. His trident tattoo was like a flame attracting moths.

The souls shook off the veil, revealing white and gray people underneath. Features visible, the outline of clothes over limbs took shape and body heights and widths formed before Rogan's eyes.

There were more, much more, than the last time Rogan had been to collect in years past. Too many for an island of Blisse's size, unless something had happened like a plague, war, or just plain unchecked cruelty. Souls were untarnished when he called them. All of them looked perfect and untainted, so it was hard to tell what exactly killed each person. He had never cared before, but he noted that it was strange that he found himself caring now.

The earth at Rogan's feet was quickly turning into sandy mud, but he played on. The spirits began moving toward him. Some were unsure and hesitant; others were so eager that they ran like they were late and afraid they would miss the ship if they didn't hurry.

Rogan never stopped playing as they entered his body. All his efforts, both physically and mentally, centered on accomplishing his task. He didn't notice the pair of living eyes watching him outside the iron fence.

As the collection notes called to all the dead of the island, not just those in the cemetery, an eager, young male spirit emerged from the jungle. As he came closer, Rogan recognized him. He was the young man who danced with Malia on the beach. The sailor that everyone in the square had mentioned at least once earlier that evening. The sailor that was missing after winning a game of cards against Haych.

Haych. This must have been what the Goddess was talking about when she mentioned he had been making too many deposits. Rogan wondered, briefly, if Haych was responsible for the numerous spirits being collected. Deciding he would examine that later, he refocused on the task at hand.

All at once, the sailor's eyes went from being aware to glazed and hypnotized at the sight of the glowing ink. The once fervent spirit was now slack-jawed as it walked closer and closer until he walked straight into Rogan and disappeared inside his chest. The tattoo flared as it swallowed the soul then dimmed before flaring again as a woman copied the sailor's example, stumbling into Rogan, disappearing. The rest followed. As the dozens of spirits began to dwindle to only a few, Rogan grew haggard and weary. His lips never left the pipe, but they were grim and hard as he gritted his teeth against the instrument.

Finally, the last reluctant spirit, a child, approached Rogan. The Captain kept playing, giving the boy a reassuring nod. The soul gave one last look over his shoulder before he, too, vanished into Rogan's bare chest.

With one last burst of light from the tattoo, the brand dimmed and cooled, leaving the cemetery in heavy darkness. The fog instantly disappeared, leaving only the wet murky ground and the smell of magic in the air.

Out of breath, Rogan released the pipe and fell to his hands and knees on the thick mud.

The rain continued to pour, but the wind and lightning were moving on. Rogan took in a few shaky breaths as he felt the souls swim inside his skin before settling. When he first collected, the sensation made him want to scratch his skin off like there were worms crawling underneath his flesh. Now, countless years later, he still hated it, but had learned to deal with the discomfort.

Using the aid of a tombstone, Rogan rose, put his pipe in his pocket, and re-donned his shirt.

A scuttle in the bushes caught his attention again. He slowly turned, mud now splattered on his pants and arms, as his dead eyes met hers, again.

Chapter Sixteen

Rogan

There she was, again. Rogan could tell by Malia's wide eyes and the drop of her speechless mouth that this time she had witnessed everything.

Great. Serves me right for only checking the inside of the cemetery. She is unbelievable.

He didn't understand it. Was she trying to destroy her life? Was she suicidal? The Goddess surely knew about this. Did this woman have any idea the kind of wrath that she had just unleashed upon herself? He had found a loophole to save her last year– now what was he going to do? He had acted impulsively, something he never did. It was strange to realize that the emotions of panic or fear could make someone act without thinking.

The rain continued to drench both of them. Malia's hair was a heavy strangling curtain around her body. Her shoulders were bare, dress soaked, legs clad with mud splattering up her calves.

She just stood there staring at him, looking ... concerned. Not scared, or terrified, or confused, but worried.

Worried for me? Rogan sighed and rolled his eyes toward the heavens; this girl made no sense at all. She should have run away screaming, but instead, she stood there looking beautifully vulnerable and concerned.

Lightning flashed, momentarily blinding Rogan. When his eyes readjusted, Malia was gone.

Lurching forward, unsteady on his feet, he hit the iron fence. As much as Rogan wanted to stay detached and ignore the consequences of what the night would bring to both of them, things had changed. And not just by her witnessing the calling forth of souls, but it had started when they danced. It started a year ago.

Feeling some strength returning, he climbed clumsily over the iron.

'Malia!' he yelled against the wind and thunder that returned.

A shriek came in reply.

He burst into the trees.

'Malia!' he yelled again as he tripped over sticks and stones in the dark, his body weakened and unsteady.

As Rogan's feet gave out from under him, it took a second too long to realize he hadn't tripped but was instead falling.

'Whoa!' he yelled and cursed as he slid down an embankment. Muddy sand and loose rocks were swept away with his tumbling body. He knew he could have just dissolved and appeared at the bottom of the hill, but he was too weak. He needed that kind of magical strength to get himself back to the ship with his cargo. If his power was wasted, he would be unable to return to the ship and that was unacceptable. But he couldn't just leave Malia, so down he tumbled.

Rogan hadn't fallen long before he slammed into something.

'Ouch!' Malia yelled into his shoulder that had just slammed into her face.

Slushy sand and sticks were everywhere, including places that would take months of intense washing to remove thoroughly. Malia's and Rogan's bodies were completely entangled.

'Are you alright?' he asked loudly in an attempt to be heard, wiping his muddy hair out of his eyes.

'Oh, I'm brilliant,' she hollered back, pushing him away from her. She stood, looking herself over at her ruined dress and muck-covered skin.

Rogan slowly rose to his feet, sinking ankle-deep in mud. Sandy soot squished and slid over his boots, scratching his legs.

'Here, let me help you,' he offered, catching her elbow and keeping her from falling back. Malia surprised Rogan when she didn't resist, but allowed him to hoist her out of the suctioning mud.

'What are you doing here?' he asked, sharper than intended.

'Same thing you are. I fell and slid down the hill in the mud,' she explained, pulling her elbow from his grip now that she was on more solid footing.

'You know that's not what I meant,' he said, sounding angrier by the second.

Malia flung a long strand of sludge-caked hair out of her face, almost whipping him, then stood indignantly with her hands on her hips. Her squinty eyes made it impossible to take her seriously since she looked like a half-drowned cat. As he watched her hands rest on her hips, he remembered gripping those same hips in between his fingers, the curve of her bones fitting perfectly in his palms, and had to mentally pull himself back to the present.

'I was heading towards the lighthouse . . .' she began.

'When all of a sudden,' he prompted.

'When I saw you,' she exclaimed, pointing at him accusingly. 'I didn't think it was possible to see you collecting! And before I realized it, I was watching you call up the dead!' Her eyes were wide. She was starting to sound a little hysterical, like everything was hitting her all at once.

'Say something!' she demanded.

'What do you want me to say? I mean, you know who I am, right? You remember now? It is what it is. The magic worked within the iron. I've never had any experience with anyone outside it. No one else has ever been around. It's that way for a reason.' Rogan realized that he was angry. She shouldn't have been there, again. Mortals weren't supposed to know about judgment after death. It disrupted their choices and therefore, the course their souls took. He had played a huge risk with giving back her memories, and now this? The Goddess would be furious. She already suspected that Malia had become more than just a distraction for Rogan. And she was right. Instead of bringing the souls directly to the ship, where was he? With Malia. She knew of his existence. He had taken mortal souls early for less in the past.

Rogan ignored her look of hurt, but couldn't ignore the sting it left in his chest. A flashing glint behind Malia caught his attention. Underneath fallen tree trunks and sand was a ruin made of iron and glass .

As Rogan got closer, he realized it was an old, glass gazebo. What used to be white marble, was now a cracked and broken dirty floor which encircled the bottom. Iron rods, shaped like vines and flowers, encompassed the rest of the custom-made glass on the top. The walls were open like invisible windows. Everywhere around them, the trees and bushes were overgrown. The jungle was taking back what was built there, the stone walkway barely visible underneath the tall grass.

'Come on, we need to talk,' he said, taking her elbow again. She didn't resist his assistance as they made to remove themselves from the thickening mud.

'Yes, we do.'

He escorted her to the abandoned fountain a few yards away from the gazebo where they washed off some of the mud.

Her dress looked like it weighed as much as she did as she began to wring it out. Not that it was doing much good with the rain still pouring down on them. Despite the storm having brought warm air, she was shivering.

'We'll go in there, at least until the rain stops,' he insisted. Rogan went to touch her again, but she pulled away. He could see her side-eyeing him. Now that there had been a minute it was clear that touching him made her uncomfortable. He tried not to feel hurt, but it seemed as though he had no control over his emotions anymore. They were simply swaying him to and fro like the waves did to a ship.

Malia led the way through the broken stone path and into the ruined gazebo.

'Where are we?' he asked to ease the awkward tension that encompassed them. Most of the glass ceiling was still intact except for a jagged opening through which a branch had fought its way in and now leaned haphazardly against the far corner. There was a steady drip of water through the hole in the ceiling and from Malia's dress. The rain continued to fall outside, sounding like coins being dropped on the glass above them.

Malia easily hopped over broken holes and growing weeds that were determined to take back the earth the gazebo was sitting on.

'It's an old garden. Hasn't been used in a while,' she said in a stiff voice that suggested she was keeping tight control of her emotions.

Answering Rogan's questioning look she said, 'We aren't too far from my home. This garden,' she swallowed, 'it's on - Or, it used to be on...'

Rogan nodded. He understood. This was yet another piece of Malia's lost history.

'This was my mother's favorite place,' she managed to

whisper to herself before falling into silence. The clouds were starting to break above them, allowing bright moonbeams to encase the island in light. The rain softened, appearing as shadowed vines gliding down the glass roof.

Malia stood in the gazebo, familiar but not quite comfortable. Rogan stuck to the dark corners of the ruin, feeling more confident in the shadows.

'Are you alright?' he asked. 'You aren't hurt? From when you fell?'

Realization dawned on her face, 'Oh, no,' she said as she put a strand of hair behind her ear and ducked her head, self-conscious. He hadn't seen her like that before. She was full of surprises. 'I'm fine. Are you alright?'

'I'm fine.'

'Are you?' she asked again in wonder, 'Because in the cemetery you looked like you were suffering . . .'

'I was fine,' he replied, shortly.

She raised her arms, signaling she was sorry for asking. This wasn't how Rogan wanted this conversation to go at all.

But what am I supposed to say? Just ignore the glowing tattoo, it does that sometimes? Oh, the sucking in of souls, it's nothing to worry about. It's not like I feel all of them individually inside me, making me feel like an overstuffed wardrobe. Or should I tell you how you might have just evoked the Goddess of Death's wrath by being too curious and too stupid to just walk away from things beyond your understanding?

No, he was safer focusing on her and how she was doing, because if the conversation turned to him, he thought he would prefer the cemetery or the Goddess.

He switched to humor.

'Sure, I feel a little crowded.' That made her smile. He enjoyed seeing her smile. 'But I'll be alright.'

The rain had slowed to a pitter-patter on the glass roof.

'It takes a lot out of me physically. It is intense and no easy task to call forth the dead and keep them—contained. But I'm feeling better now,' he lied. He was dead tired but at the same time, a resurgence of energy filtered through him now that he was around Malia.

'Are you having to keep them contained?' Her voice was somewhere between fascination and terror.

'They won't leave me until I release them on the ship, but yes, keeping the energy under control takes effort.'

'Can that kill you?' she asked, now fidgeting with her fingernails.

He chortled. 'No. Collecting is my purpose. Besides, I'm not exactly alive to be killed.'

This revelation caused her to tilt her head to one side, studying his dark figure.

'The way you kiss suggests that you are very alive,' she said. A second later her eyes bulged, like she was surprised she had said that out loud. Even in the dark, he could see the perfect shade of pink on her cheeks which he was becoming addicted to seeing on her.

'You kissed me,' she said first in wonder then again, 'You kissed me,' like an accusation. 'Why, why would you...' she seemed to be having trouble forming her words. Rogan wondered if her head was spinning at the memories of their kisses like his was.

'My memories ... they're back. Why? Why would you come back into my life? Were you just playing me for a fool for the past couple of days? I don't understand it,' she rambled, throwing her hair back and scratching her head in agitation.

'I gave them back, not because I was making a fool out of you,' Rogan left the shadows and hesitantly put his hands on her bare arms, hoping to reassure her. 'But after I saw you panicking, I knew you needed something, anything that could maybe keep you afloat in hope. I needed you to know that there was someone out there that saw you, knew you, and knew about the loneliness that consumes you.' Malia looked frozen, the pool of tears in her eyes spilling over.

'I had no idea that you would take the return of your memories as permission to spy on the collecting,' Rogan said, dropping his hands and taking a step back. He still didn't know what he was going to do. The Goddess never mentioned that she knew about what he had done for Malia last year, maybe he could just blindly hope that Angelos trusted him enough not to ask any questions about this year either. However, that grew more and more unlikely the longer he was gone. He would have to think of some excuse for his tardiness. Anything but the truth.

'I had to see for myself. One moment, despite having flashes of you in unfamiliar memories, I didn't know who you really were, the next I was bombarded with memories that left me breathless. I had to know that I wasn't losing my mind and that the memories were real.'

'Wait, you remembered me? Before the kiss tonight?'

'Not exactly. Now that I remember you fully, it makes sense. I would get flashes of memory of seeing you in the cemetery, of our kiss, but I couldn't place them. I really felt like I was losing my mind.'

'You shouldn't have been able to remember anything at all.'

'Well, I did. I just didn't understand it. Now I do.'

It was Rogan's turn to be confused. He knew he had done the magic right. Just as sure as he knew there were souls in his body swarming within him. What had happened to cause the crack in the magic? He would have to study it later.

'Now that I remember, what will happen? My memories were part of a deal to comfort my emotions, after all,' she said.

'I gave the memories back, but that doesn't mean you are forced to return the feeling of peace that I gave to you. That is yours to keep.'

Malia thought about that for a moment. It was because of Rogan and their emotional exchange that she had been functional and able to go on with life that past year. 'Poor Brandt,' she said. 'I have been such a brat to him. Granted, he has been awful in his own right. But I guess I understand a little more. My hopelessness was taken away, his just seemed to grow. Who knows what choices I would have made if you hadn't...' she trailed off, like her own thoughts grew too heavy and sorrowful to share out loud.

'We never know what could have been. I know that better than anyone. What's done is done. It's best not to dwell on it.'

'How were you able to do that? You told me once that you weren't a god?

'Yes, but I also told you I was equipped with adequate abilities to do my job successfully. If taking your emotions is what was needed to make our deal successful, then that's what I could do. I'm not limitless, but I have found, recently, that my limits are more of a gray area.'

The rain continued its pattering music on the glass ceiling. As the couple stood silently, a breeze of air that had fought its way through the jungle leaves warmed them. Malia was lost in thought. Whereas Rogan was lost in Malia's presence, still unsure of what he was going to do. How was he going to fix her knowledge of him now, without taking her soul early and leaving her body to a death in her mother's old forgotten garden? Just then, another gray area appeared in his mind. He had told Malia and given her the memories back. Malia knew who he was because of his own actions. He might pay for it, but it could be argued that Malia was still innocent and didn't need to be taken on *Calypso's Voyage* early.

'How did you . . .' she started again. 'What happened to you?' She took a seat on the stone bench, waiting patiently, her back as straight as an iron rod.

Rogan ran his fingers through his damp hair. He looked around the gazebo like he could find an excuse not to explain his past, but he couldn't. There was no reason now not to tell her everything. She already knew his forbidden truth, what did it matter if she knew about how it happened? Maybe if she knew, she would beg for him to take her memories again. Maybe, if she knew the kind of being he truly was and had been as a mortal, she would run away screaming, like she should have that first night a year ago.

'I was on the verge of death and technically did die when the Goddess cursed me to become the bearer and transporter of souls. So, I am alive, in a way, but immortal.'

'That woman tonight at the party? That was the Goddess of Death, wasn't it?' she asked, as if she had pieced it together a long time ago, but was afraid to confirm the truth.

'The Daughter of Death herself.' Rogan didn't mention the Goddess' interest in her, or the potential danger she could be in. He would deal with it.

Malia seemed to accept the answer easily enough. After everything she had seen that night it probably wasn't that hard to believe.

'So, if you almost always have other people's souls in there,' she pointed to where his tattoo lay hidden underneath his soaking shirt, 'do you have room for your own?' She sounded like she was teasing, but she wasn't far from the truth.

'Funny thing about souls,' he started, pushing away from the wall, and began to pace, uncomfortable. 'Even though the soul is individualistic, after death, the vessel in which it is held can be interchangeable.'

'What does that mean?'

'It means that I'm in possession of many souls, none of which are mine at the moment.'

Malia looked confused and more than a little disturbed by this revelation.

'Where is yours?'

Rogan paused, searching for the right words. 'The Goddess

has possession of it. If I'm a good boy,' he said with a devilish smile, 'I might earn it back one day.'

Malia digested this information as Rogan began to causally pace around the cramped space, again.

'What will you do now?'

'I will return to my ship and release them. I'm only the vessel between their resting place and their eternal place. They must all be present for their judgment voyage. While on the voyage, every soul remembers their lives and their actions, at the end of which they will be judged.'

As Rogan paused, thinking of his own potential judgment voyage, all the wrongs he committed in his mortal life flooded his memory, reminding him of why he didn't deserve Malia. Why he could never have her.

Standing now, she began to circle around the gazebo too, still fidgeting with her fingers and carefully avoiding glass.

'So, Hell and Paradise actually exist? They aren't just legends, like *you're* supposed to be?'

'They are as real as I am.' He was in so much trouble. But he felt like he couldn't stop answering her questions, even if he wanted to. The desire for her to know about him, in hopes that she would care for him, was stronger than his fear of the Goddess.

'Gods are real too?'

'Angelos is real enough. I've never met any of the others.'

'Others?'

'You know, the very old gods. The others that you have studied as myth or legend are probably real too.'

Malia soaked in these new revelations for a minute.

'What else can you do?' she asked, still pacing. Rogan, too tired to keep walking around, now took her place on the gazebo bench.

'What do you mean?'

'Well, do you live forever? Do you hold power and sway over

life and death itself? What about the way you suddenly appear and disappear? Can the living be on your ship?'

'That's a lot of questions,' Rogan answered, evasive as he scratched his jaw.

'Do you really have a reason to hide anything from me anymore?' she asked, lifting one eyebrow in challenge. Rogan knew he didn't.

Running a hand through the drying strands of his hair, he answered, 'I can disappear and reappear where I want at will. It's really so I can get straight to the souls and back without any complications. I've lost track of how many mortal years I've been doing this, but it's easy to say it's been a long time, which might be why the Goddess allowed me to come on land and participate in the festival this week. She seems to like to remind me that my second chance at redemption, as she puts it, is running out of time. I can't get sick. I don't know if I'll live forever. I will keep doing this until Angelos sees fit to release me.'

'When will that be?'

'Whenever she feels like I have learned my lesson, or will never learn it. Either way, my fate is up to her. I have no control over it.'

Malia's eyes grew sad.

'And to keep answering your questions, no, I do not have power or sway over life or death, unless it is in protection of the souls. That must be one of your local legends that grew too big.' He withheld the part that discovery of his existence by a mortal fell under the protection of souls and how she had violated that rule, twice. 'Generally, that is out of my hands. I can't save a human life or take it just because I want to. But, the Goddess made sure to endow me with all that could be required to see my job through successfully. Neither mortals, nor nature, can stop me from getting to my destinations. While on the ship, I can be unrestrained in my power, therefore capable of doing whatever is necessary to get the souls on their judgment voyage and to their destination. And lastly, there has never been a living mortal on my ship.'

Her eyes were wide and finally looked properly spooked.

'Can . . .' she started, but hesitated and licked her lips. She was building up her courage. 'You said no mortal has stepped foot on your ship?' He nodded, not sure in what direction she was headed. 'But, *can* the living travel on the ship? Or just stay on it for a while?' she asked. Rogan was a little surprised by her last question. Malia must be more desperate than he realized about escaping if she was asking him about traveling on his ship.

'A person could, I suppose. But it would come with a price,' he said carefully. 'A price the Goddess would make very steep.' He remembered the last notes of the dance when she was terrified and looked like a desperate animal in need of escape. 'Malia, what happened at the end of the dance tonight?'

She ignored his question, substituting it with one of her own. Her pacing increased.

'What's the price?' she asked, looking at the dirty floor. Malia tapped a fingernail on her front teeth, carefully considering something.

'I don't know. I've never asked, and the Goddess has never told me. But if a god says you will have to pay for something, it is never simple, or replaceable.'

She ignored his warning and asked, 'Do you think you could find out for me?' She finally met Rogan's gaze, almost pleading.

'Why? What's all this really about? Why would any sane person want to know the price for a voyage on a soul ship?'

'I need off the island, Rogan. And I might need you and your ship in order to do it.'

Chapter Seventeen

Rogan

Rogan looked at her like she had suddenly grown a pig snout.

'Are you serious?' he asked incredulously.

Malia put her hands on her hips like he was the ridiculous one.

'The Goddess doesn't even want you knowing for sure that I or the ship exist, and now you want to ask her for a favor?' Rogan studied Malia and the stubborn set to her jaw. 'What made you so upset tonight during the dance?' he asked again.

'What does that have to do with anything?' she asked, crossing her arms. It had everything to do with everything.

Light bounced off his eyes and he crossed his arms, too, waiting for her to give him a real answer. It was clear he wouldn't be fooled or distracted. He had answered all her questions, the least she could do was answer his.

'Fine,' she said, throwing up her hands. She explained the

night's events and their consequences to him. How Brandt had lost everything. How they planned to escape, but she wasn't sure if that could happen now. How Haych would most certainly make it impossible for his prize to go anywhere without him knowing it. She explained how avoiding the house was the real reason she had ended up at the cemetery. She needed a place to hide, and if she could beg for just a night and a day on his ship, then she could escape with Cora on the *Serenity* on Saturday.

Rogan listened in silence, his features cast in shadow. His fists clenched tight while she gave her list of grievances. The longer her list grew, the more agitated he became. He started pacing, and swiping his hands through his wet hair. When Malia finished, she waited. It took Rogan longer than Malia would have liked for him to answer.

'I can't let you on the ship, Malia,' he said, the regret in his voice thick and choking as he continued to move from one side of the gazebo to the other. 'Only the dead are allowed. If I did...' he stopped beside Malia and finally looked at her. His face had the look of someone that had just been punched in the gut, his eyes full of fire at not being able to punch back. 'Who knows what the Goddess would do? She isn't in the business of being charitable,' he finished ominously. Rogan's lips dropped into a thin frustrated line, his blue eyes saddened and his brow furrowed like he was fighting for control of his emotions. A shadow danced along his jaw, and he gritted his teeth so hard that if he were mortal they would be in danger of cracking.

Fighting off the threatening sting of infuriating tears, Malia shrugged a shoulder as though she understood, and it was no big deal, but at least she tried. She hoped he didn't see past her façade. The crushing disappointment almost blocked the paralyzing fear that kept climbing up her throat, making her want to scream, and it was getting harder and harder to hold back. It was more than just the knowledge that she didn't have a place to hide for the rest of the week, but the abrupt reality that the man that she was starting to fall in love with could never be hers.

He would be leaving at the end of the week on his ship and she wouldn't be on it. If Malia somehow escaped the island, she wouldn't see him again. She would never see him again in this life or the next. He wasn't of her world and was completely beyond her reach. They had until the end of the week before Rogan was gone, taking Malia's future and hopes with him.

She turned away from him, not wanting him to see the quiver of her chin and the tears threatening to flow. She had to stay calm and think rationally.

All those thoughts went out the window when she felt his cold hand on her arm, gentle and unsure. He moved so silently. Malia whirled on him, taking him by surprise. She was furious. Fate was cruel, and she was tired of it. He dropped his hand and took a cautious step back.

'What did you do?' she yelled at him. 'Why now are you choosing to torment me? Why did you fix the dance, so that it was you that I danced with?' Her voice echoed in the gazebo as she gave his tattooed chest a hard shove. That had as much of an effect on him as if she had been pushing a statue. The Dance of Lost Soulshad changed everything. That kiss at the end of it had changed everything. She needed to know why he did it.

'I didn't do that,' he defended himself. She gave him a doubtful arch of her eyebrow. He rolled his eyes. 'Alright, I did it at first, because I thought it would be funny. But I took it back after. . .' he clamped his mouth shut to keep his tongue from saying more.

'After what?'

'After Angelos talked to you. When I realized that she knew about you and would use you against me somehow, I backed off. It's why I tried to ignore you for the rest of the evening. But Angelos is persistent,' he said, moving his shoulders like his wet shirt had suddenly become uncomfortable. 'She changed the voting results. She wanted to see if I would dance with you or leave you to do it by yourself like every other person in your life has. Either decision would condemn me, and she knew that.'

'Condemn you? Is dancing with me really that offensive to you?'

'Of course not. Don't you see? If I didn't dance with you, she would know I was purposefully trying to fool her into thinking I didn't care about you. And if I did, well then it would be obvious how I feel about you. Anytime I touch you, I lose all rational thought. Either way, I knew I would lose. So, I chose the more enjoyable of the two and danced with you. Plus, I couldn't stand the thought of being yet another person that let you down.'

Rogan's eyes became as big as saucers as Malia's jaw dropped when the implication of what he just admitted to sank in. She impatiently raked the clinging hair from her face.

'You care for me?'

Thunder rumbled in the background, growing closer as the storm prepared for its second wave. The rain was still tapping on the glass and dripping onto the marble floor from a hole in the ceiling. Malia shivered as she waited for Rogan to clarify what he meant. Surely, she had misunderstood or was reading too much into the situation.

He took a few large strides before taking Malia's trembling shoulders in his hands. She had just enough time to gasp in surprise before Rogan's lips met hers, intense and yearning. The cold sleek material of his shirt pressed against her, proving to Malia that it was real. She gripped his wet collar, pulling him closer. His fingers moved from her shoulders to tangle in her hair, and she wrapped her arms around his neck, clinging to him like he was the lifeline thrown to her as she drowned.

Malia couldn't seem to keep her hands in one spot as she felt the strain of muscles in his neck, chest, and shoulders. Rogan had both arms around her now, pressing his chest to hers, leaving her even more breathless. His lips were as restless as Malia's hands as they roamed and explored her neck, shoulders and chest. Malia shivered again, and not just because he was as cold as marble. The heat between them made up for the cold as it spread everywhere, right through her own skin, growing like a tide.

Without knowing when or how, they were on the ruined gazebo floor. Malia sat on Rogan's lap, his strong arms bracing her back as he kissed her neck. Her legs wrapped around his waist. Malia felt Rogan's hand brush her thigh and climb up.

A loud clap of thunder had Rogan jerk away so fast she nearly fell backward. His hands steadied her, but he was shaking.

'What's wrong?' she asked.

He was about to answer when his trident tattoo burst with light. Rogan released Malia and scrambled back. Terrified.

What's happening?

Rogan, now on his hands and knees, was choking, unable to breathe. Malia was on the ground beside him, unsure how to help.

Finally, the light from the tattoo lessened to a dull pulse, allowing him to take in large, grateful breaths.

'Rogan?'

'I'm alright, just give me a moment,' he said in a hoarse voice, like he still didn't have enough air in his lungs.

After another minute, the light disappeared completely and Rogan sighed in relief, as though a tremendous pressure was released from his chest.

'What was that?' she asked.

'That was a warning. A very loud warning.' Rogan sat back against the iron bench, gaining his breath. 'I was distracted from keeping the souls encompassed. The souls should have been on the ship by now. That was Angelos' way of keeping me on schedule. Technically, I have until sunrise, but I wouldn't put down patience as one of her admirable qualities.'

'Damn,' Malia whispered in both shock, awe, and fear at what she just witnessed. The Captain was supposed to be invincible, but one flash of light and he had been brought to his knees.

Rogan gave a humorless laugh. 'It's worse than it looks, believe me.' He looked even more pale than usual, stark in the dark night, weak, closing his eyes and leaning his head against the wood behind him, but his ironic smile told her that he felt better.

'Why are you like this? What happened to you?'

Why can't you be a regular captain that I can just sail away with?

Rogan was silent for so long that she wasn't sure if he intended on answering her at all. Finally, his shadowed head nodded in acceptance. He would have to explain.

He sighed, resigned, his forearms resting on his knees. Malia sat beside him, bringing her knees to her chin, settling in for him to explain his story.

'As I told you the other night, I was orphaned and in order to escape a fate worse than death I begged to work on a ship: a pirate ship. Where I was from, pirate ships weren't hard to come by if you knew where to look. From then on, I worked on the ship to earn my meals and bed. Eventually, as I grew older, I began to grow in the ranks. It wasn't uncommon for young men to be in leadership positions on pirate ships, after all, the life expectancy isn't very high. Surviving a pirate's life isn't easy. There are certain things a person has to sacrifice in order to be alright with what needs to be done. And the older I got, the easier those sacrifices became. Eventually, apathy was the safest and strongest trait I had going for me. The only thing that mattered was survival. I didn't even care about the money and things we stole,' he explained. He looked into the wall of flowing rain, becoming lost in his memories and his story. Raindrop shadows grooved down his face.

'By the time I was twenty, I was the second mate. The captain and first mate of the ship had planned to kidnap the daughter of a wealthy merchant that we hadn't been able to raid yet. They figured the ransom would more than pay for the merchants eluding us.

'I wasn't comfortable with kidnapping, not because of how it is morally wrong, but because it seemed like an unnecessary risk and hassle. We had enough loot to live comfortably for the rest of our lives, but greed and wounded pride aren't so easily convinced. Besides, their plan was well thought out, and I didn't really care in the end. I would get my cut and that was that.' He raked his hand through his almost-dry raven waves.

'Well, we didn't know it, but the plan was flawed in a big way. The daughter of the merchant was a rare beauty who happened to be engaged to a Starzea noble. A noble who was well-connected within the navy. We weren't two days away from the girl's home when a whole armada caught up to us.

'After they blew the ship to smithereens and took back the girl, I found myself shot and dying on the deck of the sinking ship. All my crewmates, including the captain and first mate, were nothing but mangled bodies. As I was gasping my last breath, I saw this beautiful woman appear. I thought I was hallucinating, a side-effect from dying. But I wasn't. You saw her tonight, how she can't possibly be real, but is. She didn't say anything as she smiled down at me; the seawater came to the bottom of her dress but remained dry. She wore a crown of finger bones and sea pearls. When she bent down, she tutted her tongue like I was a naughty child. Then, without warning, she kissed me, touched my chest, and branded me with the Captain Mark, the trident tattoo. I've been one of her Soul Captains ever since. She says I will be this way until I learn my lesson, or until she loses hope that I will. Until then, she holds my own soul and its fate as collateral.'

When he was done explaining, his eyes looked unbearably sad and resigned.

'I deserve this limbo...this purgatory,' he said, sounding surprised at his own realization. 'The crime of denying and trading my humanity for apathy was a worse crime than the ones I was complacent in. I didn't feel much of anything but the instinct for survival when I was alive, and I have felt even less since I've been Captain. That is, until I met you,' he said, turning his face to look at Malia for the first time since their kiss. Vine shadows ran over his features.

Malia uncurled herself and scooted over beside him. She lifted his arm, draped it over her shoulder and leaned into him—comfortable.

'I'm starting to understand the agony of my punishment,' he said, pulling her onto his lap. For the first time in her life, Malia couldn't think of a witty retort or something to say. His features turned sad; his eyes speaking of a lifetime of hopelessness.

His hand came up and pushed back strands of wild hair, leaving Malia's shoulder and neck bare. His hand rested on the curve of her neck, tickling and fascinating.

'What are we going to do?' Malia whispered.

Rogan didn't have an answer.

Not knowing if she would ever get another opportunity, Malia brought her lips to his. He kissed her back, gently this time. It was still all-consuming, but no longer desperately drowning.

They wanted to forget the tragedy and impossibility of their stories and be lost together in this moment. Being lost was working, and it felt good.

His lips were cold, but soft as he pressed her closer to him. His hand went from her neck and slid down to her hip where they encircled her waist. She kept her arms around his neck playing with his long hair as his tongue played with her lower lip. A groan escaped his throat like she was exacting her own form of pleasurable torture. Under her palm she felt the grooves and strain of his naked muscles over his quickening heartbeat. The rain softly falling on the roof was in rhythm with her breathing.

Malia felt a cold hard surface against her back and realized she was laying down with Rogan's lips never leaving hers and his arms wrapped around her hips. The air smelled heavy with jungle mildew but his smell was sharp and bit into her nose. Inhaling the scent of him cleared her lungs. She could breathe.

A bright light flashed under her closed eyes before the immediate BOOM echoed so powerful it shook the ground underneath them and the glass above them. Rogan pulled back looking defeated and angry.

'How is there never enough time? I have to go,' he said in a hoarse voice, his forehead resting on hers.

'Are you sure?' she asked. His flushed face argued otherwise.

'I'm sorry, Malia, but I'm out of time tonight.'

Rogan looked like he could be blushing in the moonlight. 'Are you trying to be noble?' she teased, hoping her tone would free him of any such notion. She wasn't interested in nobility just then.

He didn't look at her, but continued to stare at the floor like he was confused by it.

He *was* being noble, and she had a good feeling it was a new concept for him, something he had probably never experienced. Once he sat both of them up, he lifted Malia off of his lap and gently set her down beside him.

'I need to return to my ship,' he said with a resigned set to his shoulders. 'The souls. I've been warned once. . .' he trailed off, putting a hand to his chest like he had completely forgotten about the dozens of souls that were encrusted in his body. 'And they aren't exactly a distraction I want while kissing you.'

He stood and looked up through the glass ceiling with a scowl in the direction of his ship. Malia looked too and noticed that the gazebo was a little brighter now. She could even make out the mud splatters on his black pants. The rain had stopped. The second wave of the storm never materialized. How long had they actually been in the gazebo?

'Of course,' Malia said as he helped her up, trying to sound understanding, but she was disappointed. He kept a hold of her hand, and she felt a small thrill run through her arm only to be replaced with panic in her chest. What if she never saw him again? What if he didn't come back the next night? After all, he had his souls. He accomplished what he came to do.

They walked out of the gazebo into the clear morning. He let go of her hand and began to walk away. The grass was still wet, the mud thick on the ground. Rogan's boots squished as he walked away while Malia's feet sank.

'Rogan,' she called after him. He stopped and turned around. She inhaled deeply. *Here goes nothing.*

'See you tonight?'

His arrogant smile was back when he answered, 'Of course. It's my festival.'

'No other reason?' she asked, a smile clear in her voice as he began to turn around.

'I wouldn't want to make a lady blush,' he said over his shoulder.

He left her laughing and before she should have lost sight of him, he disappeared.

Chapter Eighteen

THURSDAY

Rogan

Rogan hadn't fully materialized on the deck before Angelos had him on his knees. Her voice, interlaced with the last thunderclap, screamed his name. Since he had ignored the magical tether that usually pulled him back to the ship, now came his punishment for such insolence. However, when the trident had blasted Malia off of him, warning him of the Goddess' fury, Rogan knew whatever she dealt him would be worth it. Feeling Malia's skin between his fingers and lips against his own would always be worth it.

The pain and pressure in his head increased, like his skull had turned into a vise and was crushing his brain. He crumpled completely face-down, cringing on the deck as black spots filled his vision.

'Rogan,' Angelos cooed sweetly, like she wasn't torturing

him but simply filing her nails, 'Pet, where are my souls?' Her voice was inches from his ear, sending vibrations through his skull and down his spine. He recoiled, wanting to disappear between the crevices of the wooden deck. An axe to the head would have been a reprieve from the torture she was soliciting. His throat strained to keep from screaming, fighting against the urge so strongly that he couldn't answer. A grunted sob was all Rogan could muster. His eyes stang and water sprang from them as he felt the distant memories of dizzying nausea strike him.

'Speak up, darling. I'm afraid I can't hear you,' she whispered. He choked out a garbled answer, but Angelos had closed his windpipe too. He knew he couldn't die, but that didn't stop the panic from building when he could no longer breathe. The potential for never-ending panic and pain was true Hell.

The pressure on his throat released slightly, allowing a few choked gasps of air to infiltrate his lungs, but Rogan remained as still as possible on the deck floor. A warm trickle ran from his ears down his neck. His ears were bleeding. *Bleeding.* It was a strange sensation, an unfamiliar feeling. Granted, he hadn't bled once since becoming Captain. In fact, Rogan wasn't even aware that he still could.

'I have them, Goddess,' Rogan croaked, rolling onto his back, gulping and gasping for air. The tattoo brightened once again, anxious to let the souls out now that they were aboard the ship. Still unable to see straight from the lingering pain, his vision blurred. Rogan tried to focus on the middle Goddess in front of him and ignored the other two. It was like recovering from a night of drinking rum that left him seeing triple.

Angelos smiled dangerously above him. Clearly she wasn't done yet. Pale pink light was turning orange on the horizon.

'I know you have them, love, but it is nearly sunrise and I don't see a single soul on the deck of this ship. Would you care to explain?' she asked so sweetly that Rogan tasted her sour condescension in his mouth.

Angelos released enough of the pressure in his head so that Rogan could rise to his hands and knees. His limbs shook from the strain, but her power continued to ebb away from him, his own returning. Angelos patiently observed as Rogan slowly climbed to his feet.

He was out of breath by the time he straightened, leaning against the railing of the ship for support. 'There was a complication,' he explained, as evasively as he dared.

'A complication?' she asked with a raised eyebrow. 'What kind of complication could possibly keep you from your very purpose?' Her sweet, sing-song voice had Rogan desperate to cower. He knew the sweeter she sounded, the angrier she was. There was no way he was going to tell her that he had just explained the entire curse to Malia, then proceeded to stick his tongue down her throat.

'It's nothing,' he rushed, 'I took care of it.' Even though his shoulders were slumped in exhaustion, his feet were no longer unsteady beneath him. His chest burned uncomfortably as the trident began to glow. The scratchy burning sensation grew stronger, feeling like the spirits were trying to claw their way out of his skin.

Angelos didn't look satisfied with Rogan's weak explanation. 'I did tell you that last night's collection was important, didn't I? I warned you against distractions.'

'Yes,' he answered, doing his best to sound repentant. 'But you haven't told me why.'

'In fact,' she continued, ignoring Rogan as she put a thoughtful finger to her chin in feigned contemplation, 'I would say that the events of last night's collection might have permanently altered your future.'

'What does that even mean?' he asked, no longer bothering to hide his exasperation.

'All in good time, dear.'

His pain was gone, but Rogan still felt like his teeth were on edge. It happens when you have just experienced agonizing pain and the aggressor acted like she had already forgotten that she had dished it out.

'Malia wouldn't have anything to do with this complication, would she?' Angelos asked, stepping away from the mast to walk innocently towards him. Her crown of bones and pearls glowed orange, reflecting the brightening sky, like the crown itself was fire.

There was no point in lying. If she didn't already know the truth, she would find out soon enough, but he wasn't going to confess to anything either. She took his silence as affirmation.

She clicked her tongue as she had in their first encounter all those years ago. Like Rogan still hadn't learned a thing.

'Rogan,' she said, sounding both annoyed and disappointed, coming within inches of his face. Her poreless skin and cold breath had him fighting to repress a shiver that desperately wanted to escape down his spine. 'Out of all my collectors,' she ran a hand through his muddy hair, 'You were the one that had always been the most focused, most reliable.'

She grabbed hold of his hair and looked straight into his eyes, holding his gaze with the raw power she held behind her golden orbs, wild and untamed. Waves of water slammed against the sides of the ship. So much power. He stiffened, readying himself for another dose of pain.

'And now,' her voice stayed sickly sweet as it echoed through his skull. 'You have betrayed me.' Pain seeped through his eyes, sending his knees crashing to the deck once more. 'I saw you dance with her. I saw you hold her. I saw you touch her, *kiss her!*' she spat the words like a curse through gritted teeth. The feeling of pounding nails being driven through his scalp where she held a fistful of his hair became so intense that if he possessed the ability to throw up, he would have. If he could have passed out, he would have. If he could have died, he would have welcomed the release. The fresh blood leaked from his nose and dripped down to his bare throat and collar bone.

As quickly as the pain invaded his every cell, leaving him clutching for breath, Angelos released him, and once again the Captain found himself lying on the deck barely able to move.

'Goddess, please,' Rogan gasped, hating himself for begging. 'She gave me her memories last year in a bargain. But somehow she still remembered me. I don't know why the magic didn't completely erase me. Her full memory seemed like it was slowly coming back to her anyway.'

'It isn't that the magic didn't work, you fool,' Angelos said, her lips thin, 'It is because that kind of magic wasn't strong enough to cover the consequences. Do you think a girl, a little virgin like her,' she said in a mockingly high voice, 'Would, or even could, forget her first kiss? There are rules and a balance to human nature. Love, it seems, is the strongest weapon humans have in their weak arsenal. Too bad they don't have any idea.'

Rogan was stunned for a moment, absorbing what the Goddess had just revealed. Did that mean that Malia loved him? Even if she didn't fully comprehend it herself?

'Now, Rogan, since you are my favorite Pet, I'm going to make you a deal.' The waves that had been crashing against the ship in time with her fury were calming. He inhaled deeply, hoping the worst was over with. With a flick of her wrist, his body twisted unnaturally to face her. Rogan groaned as his back and head hit the deck. He choked on the blood now streaming down his throat.

Angelos knelt beside him and cleared a strand of hair from his eyes - like they were lovers. 'You know I don't like hurting you. But you force my hand.' she said, sounding like every abuser of power. 'I won't kill Malia, for now. I know if she wanted to tell people who you were, she would have run from the cemetery last year, or even tonight, which has been the only thing that has kept me from tearing her to pieces.' Rogan gulped and wished, for the first time, that he had a drink of water. 'She has her own reasons for keeping you a secret. As it turns out, her knowledge of you doesn't change her fate. However, if she were to tell anyone of your real identity, well, that would change things for her, and not for the better.'

'But –' Her voice turned sinister once more as she gripped Rogan's jaw and brought him up to face her, his feet dangling just inches above the deck of the ship. He could feel the bruises forming under her fingers as she squeezed tighter, 'as I told you before, *I will not share you.*' She dropped his jaw, jerking his head to the side so she could talk directly into his ear. 'So, if you behave yourself for the remainder of the week, you can stay, and no harm will come to her or you by my hand. But, Pet, if you do not heed this final warning, you will learn the true meaning of pain. After all, the worst pain isn't physical, it's mental. It's an emotional gouging. Do you understand what I'm saying?'

Rogan nodded and Angelos dropped him to his feet. Rogan's knees gave out and crumpled, exhausted, to the deck floor. Physical pain would be nothing compared to what Malia would endure and he knew Angelos would make him watch.

'I think that sounds more than fair, don't you?' she asked, backing away.

As he laid there, a deeper understanding of what she actually meant dawned on him. The game where Malia and him were the main pieces was still in motion, and she didn't feel like putting them away yet.

'Why don't you just make me leave?' he asked, struggling to sit up. 'What's the point of this game?' She could threaten him all she wanted, but he couldn't imagine giving up Malia for even a second as long as he was still there. But, if she was going to harm her, he would leave now to keep her safe. Angelos smiled at him over her shoulder and released a manic giggle.

'Because it has to be your choice, dear. People are hurt or saved by the consequences of another's actions all the time.

Malia's no exception. Or did you not get that from the sad little sob story of her life?'

After pausing for a moment to collect his thoughts he asked, 'So what exactly do you want from me? Why are you forcing me to stay here now? What exactly are you threatening?'

All his hopes of keeping the Goddess unaware of Malia were obviously gone. He wasn't allowed to leave the island yet, but he had to "behave". His instinct to protect Malia from everything and anything flared, making him irrational. The fact that he was on his apathetic ship, being a smartass to a goddess was evidence enough that a change was developing within him, somewhere deep and unknown. Every feeling he possessed for Malia an hour ago still burned red hot through him, even as the Goddess of Death threatened her life and his soul.

Angelos' lips pouted. 'Oh no, no, no, darling,' she crooned, 'You misunderstand me. *I* am not threatening anything. You see, I do not have to. I'm warning you. I'm trying to protect you both. Disappointment is hard to recover from, my dear. You two continue on with your little affair and all I have to do is stand by and watch the consequences unfold on their own. This has developed into a delightful little game.'

Well, Rogan didn't like the sound of that either.

'Great, that sounds promising,' he muttered.

Angelos laughed, sounding for all the world like they were once again the best of friends. And granted, he didn't know much about friendship, but he knew plenty about enemies. He was pretty sure friends didn't manipulate, threaten, torture, and make the other person's ears bleed. That was the work of an enemy. He looked at her scathingly. She ignored it.

'So, what's going to happen?' Rogan questioned, feeling confident that Angelos was done physically torturing him for the moment. They had moved onto the emotional aspect of the torture session.

She shrugged a pale slender shoulder. Orange light was

starting to reflect off her dress, making it too bright and too hard to look directly at her.

'Again, dear, that's your choice. I just hope for you and your besotted's sake, it's the right one.'

Cryptic, but at least it's not a total death sentence.

'Go ahead, woo the little brat. Fill her and yourself full of foolish and selfish dreams. The punishment of natural consequences will be more painful than anything I plan on giving.'

'And the fact that she knows and remembers who I am?' he asked.

Angelos waved it off. 'She will keep your secret. I'm sure of it. Like I said before, her knowledge of you does not change her fate, for now. We will all see where her soul's integrity stands by the end of the week.'

Now that Rogan's head no longer felt like it was on the verge of implosion, he climbed to his feet. The trident tattoo was really beginning to burn, shining brighter as he straightened. The souls were anxious and restless; Rogan knew the feeling. It was clear that the magic of the ship was calling to them, and he was more than happy to oblige.

'If we are done here, can I release them now?' he asked, feigning nonchalance over their recent antics.

She gestured impatiently with a flap of her hand to go ahead. 'By all means.'

Rogan headed below deck, where the souls were kept for their journey. Taking a deep breath, he relaxed his shoulders. He inhaled again and pulled the air deep down like he was getting ready for a long underwater swim and pushed it out in a gust. All at once, the souls rushed from his body, like a stampede, and glided into the ship. Each individual soul formed and took a silent seat, like they were prepared to row to Paradise or Hell. They sat, complacent but alert, like each person was watching something only their eyes could see. They were watching their life and all the choices that they did or could have made, good and bad. Once each soul was settled and silent, Rogan went back above deck.

Angelos had disappeared.

As soon as Rogan noticed she was gone, he remembered the question about the price of carrying a living person on the ship. But after what he had just been through, he was glad he had forgotten. No way would he allow Malia to be indebted to Angelos, no matter the cost or pay-off.

Chapter Nineteen

Malia

Malia jumped through puddles and sloshed through the mud as she made her way to the house. She felt giddy as she remembered Rogan's lips on hers. Her face was hurting from the constant smile that wouldn't leave her face. The memory of his skin touching her made her cheeks burn, filling her with the courage to face whatever awaited her in the house.

Rogan had made Malia feel invincible. She was going to see Rogan again tonight. She had to. She could still smell his breath and see the goosebumps on his chest and arms that her touch had wrought.

Malia reached her front door, and as quietly as the rusty hinges would allow, she entered. Her dress sodden and dripping mud would leave a trail through the house, alerting anyone that cared that she was home. She would ask for Cora's help in cleaning it, as soon as she cleaned herself up.

'Miss!' Came Cora's harsh whisper from the dining room doorway. Cora had slipped back into her servant's dialect. She was nervous. Cora's curls had formed into one frizzy ball around her shoulders, but smashed on one side, like she had been in a chair all night. The dark circles under her eyes, and the fact that she was still in her dress from the night before, made it clear that she hadn't slept.

'Oh, I know,' Malia said apologetically, looking at the mess around her feet. She picked up the skirt as best she could to stop the dripping while tiptoeing toward the stairs. 'I'll clean it up as soon as I've. . .' She didn't finish as Cora rushed to her and grabbed her friend's arms tight, eyes wide with panic.

'Cora? What is it?' she asked.

'Miss,' she said, tears brimming in her red eyes, 'Why are you here?'

'I live here, Cora, at least for another couple days, and stop calling me Miss,' she whispered back.

Cora shook her head vigorously, like that answer was nowhere near good enough, 'I thought you left with your Captain. After last night, I thought you would have left with him. You should have left with him! Why are you back?'

'Cora, I would never just leave you. Ever. Besides, you are terrified of Rogan, remember? You said your gift told you that he was dangerous because only death followed him, or something,' Malia tried playing it off, but Cora was really making her worried. 'I can't leave with him anyway. Not yet.' The bitter memory replayed over and over in her head. Even if they wanted to leave together, they couldn't. She pushed down the sudden weight on her chest.

'You can't be here!' Cora whispered urgently, looking around, afraid that they were being overheard or watched from the brightening shadows in the corners. Cora began to tug Malia back toward the dining room door.

'Cora, what is going on?' Malia asked, resisting only a little.

'Don't you remember what happened at the end of the dance?'

Boy did she ever, but Malia had a feeling Cora wasn't talking about what had transpired between her and Rogan.

'Brandt lost everything. Including your freedom.' It felt like she had been punched in the stomach. 'Brandt is in your father's old study signing papers right now. The house, everything is being turned over to Sir Haych as part of your dowry. Malia, they are signing a marriage agreement too.'

Brandt had lost everything and that included Malia. That familiar panic rose in Malia's throat. Haych practically owned her now, or would very soon. With this new ownership, what would she be expected or demanded to do? What horrors awaited her in the near future? Cora's explanation nearly blew her over with memories and emotions that Rogan had briefly distracted her from having to deal with. She thought maybe that she would have a few hours to gather herself. Perhaps a day or two before everything was official. But she had sorely underestimated Haych's eagerness to take over her life.

'Sir Haych has been here all night waiting for you. When you didn't arrive before curfew and no one could leave to look for you...he has been raging and drinking all night long in your father's study. Brandt is in there with him, in case you didn't show up.'

They had reached the dining room door. The fear in Cora's eyes was clear, if she hadn't come back home, Haych would either kill or do something horrible to Brandt as a vengeful payment for being slighted by her.

Like fate wanted to emphasize the danger, glass crashed, echoing through the smooth walls. Both girls jumped.

If she stayed, the chances of being able to escape on Saturday were almost impossible. She would be watched and imprisoned.

Cora was right. Malia couldn't be at the house, not now. But Cora lived there too and she knew where the jewels were hidden. She would just have to do her best to stay undetected until she could get onto the *Serenity*. With any luck, he would think she had already left, like Cora had hoped for. If she hid, she would be hunted, but at least she would have a chance of stowing away on a ship. Only...no one on the island wanted to get on Haych's bad side and meddle in his affairs. Where could she possibly go on the island that he wouldn't eventually find her, and punish anyone he thought was guilty of helping to hide her?

'Cora, I have nowhere to go,' Malia whispered, panic and desperation leaking into her voice and through the tears beginning to sting her eyes. They were practically out the back door now.

'Anywhere is better than here.'

'Is that so?' Haych's cruel voice asked from the doorway just as the kitchen door behind him crashed against the wall.

Cora grabbed Malia's arm in a tight grip that suggested she was ready to throw Malia out the door if she had to. Haych gave Cora an icy glare for only a moment before his gaze turned to Malia, freezing her in place. Ku and Brom came in through the back door, blocking the exit.

'Hello, Miss Malia,' Haych said, restraint barely contained in his voice. Malia noticed his knuckles were bruised and bloody as he clenched them.

If his hands look that bad, what does Brandt's face look like? What is mine about to look like?

Malia nodded politely. Maybe if she played this right, she could get out of whatever punishment he had thought up for her.

'Sir Haych,' she said so evenly she surprised herself. 'If you will excuse me, I'm afraid I wasn't expecting you this early in the morning. I'm a mess. I got caught outside last night when the storm hit,' she said, gesturing to her obviously ruined dress like she was just a simpleton girl.

'Malia, come into the study for a moment. Your brother and I would like to have a word with you.' Sir Haych swung his arm out in an invitation, but it came through gritted teeth. She nodded, unable to see any other options. Not with Haych's men standing behind them, and her brother and Cora being used as hostages.

Malia felt Cora's grip tighten, unwilling to let her friend go. Malia gave Cora's hand a light pat, still playing up her illusion of being a silly girl. 'It's okay, Cora. I know you are upset about the floor, but I'll be sure to help you clean it up.' Malia unhooked Cora's fingers from around her arm, trying to be as reassuring as possible.

As Malia passed Haych, his hand balled into a fist. She hoped that fist wasn't going to meet her face as soon as she stepped inside the room.

Malia squared her shoulders and went toward what used to be her father's study, her dress sloshing mud along the way.

She didn't go into the study very often anymore. It reminded her too much of her father. From the smell of books and tobacco, combined with leather from the large chair sitting behind the big wooden desk and books on the shelves. It symbolized everything she had lost: comfort, security, love. Brandt had made it his office, but the only thing he ever did in there was wallow and drink in his cave of memories.

But as she entered the room, it looked nothing like it used to. The walls were bare from all the art sold long ago. The books were gone too. In fact, the only thing left of the books were the thousands of papers littered all over the room. This, above all else that had transpired, left her swallowing back her tears.

All the figurines were sold. The glass containers that used to hold her father's barely-used alcohol had been thrown and broken against the walls, staining the once off-white paint with streaks of brown and yellow. The floor was now a carpet of papers, glass, and pieces of broken furniture. The only furniture left in the room was her father's desk, probably because it was too big to throw and smash against something, and the ruins of what used to be her father's overstuffed leather chair, now shredded to the springs. The sad thing was that she wasn't sure if Haych had done this, or if Brandt had over the past few months.

Malia stepped gingerly with her bare feet as she walked further into the destroyed room.

'Where's Brandt?' she asked, her breathing hitched. Brandt was her only buffer. Haych closed the door behind him. The crunching of glass and tearing of papers followed the door, cutting her off from the rest of the world. She looked around the room briefly, to see if Brandt was hidden in the rubble somewhere.

Just then, a slight groan came from behind the desk.

'Brandt?' she said. Haych and about a million pieces of broken glass stood between Malia and her brother.

'Malia?' he asked, muffled by all the papers that were covering his face.

'Your brother,' Haych said, grabbing her arm to keep her from running to her brother's aid, 'lost consciousness an hour ago when he hit his head on the corner of the table. Sloppy drunk he is.'

It was obviously a lie, but one so believable no one would question it. It was clear that Haych, or one of his men, had had a hand in all of this since Brandt was buried underneath pages of torn books. Haych smiled. He knew Brandt's weakness, and reputation was one of the strongest cards he had to play. He was the devil who bought Brandt's soul and he wanted Malia to know it.

'Interesting party last night,' Haych continued, releasing her arm, as he took a step back. Glass and broken splinters of wood crunched under his feet, making Malia's nerves twitch as he walked to the desk like he was talking about the weather. Dangerous weather. A hurricane.

Malia figured it was smartest not to say anything. Haych wasn't actually there for conversation so much as intimidation. Only Malia wasn't intimated. Everything was happening exactly as she feared it would happen. No...she wasn't intimidated; she was terrified.

'That captain you danced with? Who is he?' Haych asked, sitting back against the desk, arms folded over his suited chest.

Malia shrugged innocently. 'Just a sea captain here for the festival. Cora's distant cousin. She never even met him until the first night of the festival.'

'Really, cousins?' Haych asked, unfooled.

Play stupid. If he knows you're smart, you're done for.

Malia shrugged. 'I suppose. I don't exactly have Cora's family tree handy to see how that happened.' She laughed, light and airy.

'He has taken quite the interest in you,' Haych observed with a tone that implied that it was her fault.

She shrugged a bare mudded shoulder, again. It seemed like her safest innocent gesture.

'What do you know about him?' he asked, studying the cuticles on his nails and bruises on his knuckles.

'Not much,' she lied.

Good luck intimidating him, she wanted to say but kept her mouth firmly shut.

'Were you with him last night?' he asked.

'Of course not,' she said, lying through her chattering teeth, but she managed to sound greatly insulted. 'As I said, I got caught in the storm and couldn't get back by curfew, so I stayed in my family's old gazebo in the garden all night, by myself.'

Haych ignored her fib and went on like she hadn't said anything, 'There are rumors going around about a mysterious captain on the island with his ship anchored off Cliff's Teeth. A ship that has only been seen at night.'

'A disappearing ship is ridiculous,' she said, hoping to sound convincing. Haych looked at her with an arched brow. 'No ship can anchor there, everyone knows that. People just like to make up stories, especially around the festival. That's all it is – ghost stories. The ship that was seen was probably just taking a pleasure cruise around the island. You know it doesn't take much for people here to start making up rumors.'

Faster than she had ever seen him move, Haych launched himself the few feet left between them, stopping inches from her face. He had gone from calm to murderous as fast as a match being lit. Malia only had time to recoil. As she stepped back, she felt the slice of glass on the side of her foot. She gave a yelp of pain and surprise as Haych pushed her, painfully slamming her back into the empty bookshelf behind her.

'DON'T LIE TO ME!' Haych shouted, his spittle landing on her cheek. One hand was gripping her hair as the other forearm slammed into her neck, choking her slowly as he started applying pressure.

Panic engulfed her, and suddenly she was no longer in her father's office, but in a carriage with a creaking wheel, like a clock ticking down.

Haych let up slightly, allowing Malia air, and pulled her out of her memories and into coherent thought.

She coughed and wheezed, struggling against Haych's forearm, trying to keep him from strangling her. No sound of movement came from the pile of papers that hid her brother.

'I'm not lying!' she tried shouting back, but her voice hitched, showing Haych her real fear.

'No one knows anything about this mysterious captain. Not his cargo, his crew, or what his ship is called. It's like he just appears at night out of thin air. It's like he is the bloody Captain of Souls!'

Even through her muddled, oxygen-deprived brain, his guess shocked her.

'What?' her tone implied that he was crazy. 'Of course not! I know you are a devout believer, but think about what you are saying.' She knew that revealing Rogan's secret would bring on faster and more severe consequences than whatever Haych could do to her.

'No? I know every ship and every Captain anchored here, but not him. Don't you think that is strange?' he asked through gritted teeth. He pushed on her throat. 'You know what?' he asked, tightening his grip on her hair. Despite Malia's best efforts, she winced and knew he got satisfaction out of it when he licked his lips, the sour smell of old rum lingered on his breath. 'It doesn't matter. I'll find out all about this Captain Rogan and dispose of him. If you don't mind your manners, I'll cut him up so small that not even the fish would be able to feed off his rotting corpse.' He gave her a jolting shake before slamming her against the shelf again, forcing it into her bruised back.

'Meanwhile, you will not see him again. I own you now.' With each word his voice became lower, darker and manic. 'You will do what I say. Or I will make your life miserable beyond your comprehension. Do you understand?' Malia raised her chin in defiance, forgetting her plan to appear submissive. 'You might think that you don't have much left to lose,' he got close to her ear and whispered, 'but trust me, you still have plenty.' He pulled back. 'You are practically my wife, and will be by law come Sunday evening, so you better start acting like it. I could carve my name into your back by taking you right here on this dirty, broken floor and no one would stop me, no one would interfere. No one would *care*. Do you understand that?'

Try it. There is glass big enough for me to carve my name on you too.

When she didn't respond, Haych twisted her hair so tight she felt strands being ripped out. It took everything Malia had to keep quiet. She was no good to herself or Cora beaten, bruised and cut. If she killed Haych, even in self-defense, she would be locked in a cell until after the ships left, or hung before. She focused on a brandy stain on the wall. She would live through this morning, and she would do it with her dignity intact. 'But I won't...yet. I'll save that for Sunday when we are married. It'll give us both something to look forward to. To savor.' Haych sneered, his hot breath coated on her neck as his tongue carved a line up to her jaw. Bile rose in her throat. His breath smelled like whiskey and fish. If Malia had any food in her stomach, she would have enjoyed vomiting all over his nice, crisp jacket and pants. 'I will not be embarrassed, I will not be laughed at! So, you will do as you're told. Do we understand one another, my dear?'

She clenched her jaw shut, meeting his eyes. She hated him. He looked at her searchingly, like he hoped for defiance, a fight. He wanted a wild horse to break and break again.

She nodded, but kept silent.

'Good,' he said. Finally, he released her throat and stepped back. 'Now, I want you to go out and enjoy the festival tonight. I want everyone to see my prize being happy and grateful. The parade promises to be a most entertaining event.' He straightened his jacket before walking to the door. His sudden jovial mood swing left her as dizzy as his suffocation had. He actually wanted her to go out when he had just threatened her to "behave" herself. It felt like a trap. 'I sadly cannot attend, since I have some other business regarding your Captain Rogan to see to.' He opened the door where his two men were waiting. 'But I will make sure that you are well protected. I wouldn't want you to get lost in the crowd,' he said over his shoulder just to make sure she was still listening to his not-so-hidden threats.

'No,' she smiled mockingly, 'We wouldn't want that.'

There was a twinkle in Haych's eye just before he turned and headed out the door. Malia wanted to kick herself. She just showed him that she had a spirit that he was going to enjoy breaking.

As soon as she heard the echoing bang of the front door closing, Malia checked on Brandt. He was buried under a mountain of papers and torn books by her father's desk. Uncovering him, Malia could smell the rum. Brandt groaned as she gently turned him from his good shoulder onto his back. Other than a swollen eye, he appeared to be unharmed. He held a bottle of rum in the crook of his arm like he would a child and kept sleeping.

He was fine. Malia shoved off her knees and stood, tears of pure anger and fear blurring her sight. A slice of pain on the heel of her foot reminded her that she was stepping on glass. Tears were streaming down her cheeks, her chest felt tight in panic by the time she made it to her room. Claustrophobia closed in. Haych's hold on her throat, the pressure in her chest, the smell of her father in the study, it had all triggered something, and now that the adrenaline was gone, she was falling. She vaguely understood that she was on the floor when she saw Cora come into the room. She asked her something, but it was too late, Malia was already lost to the memory.

'Malia, sit back,' Brandt said.

'Why?'

'Because I don't want to have to catch you when you fall out the door,' he said jokingly.

'That wouldn't happen,' she said, ignoring him and keeping her face to the window.

'What? Me catching you, or the door coming open?'

'The door coming open. I know you would catch me,' she said, turning to give her big brother an ornery smile. It was their first ride in the new carriage, the only one on the island, and Malia couldn't hold back her excitement.

Brandt smiled back.

'Seriously, Bug. You are too reckless and you're making me nervous.'

Malia felt Brandt's warm hand on her shoulder to gently pull her back when they heard the horse neigh, followed by a "whoa, whoa" from their father. The carriage went back a few feet before the demand from their father became more urgent. Brandt's hand held her to the back of the seat.

'Do you think Moses is spooked?' Malia asked about their old, most trustworthy horse, who had traveled the cliff road thousands of times, just never with a carriage. But, their father had driven a carriage many times before moving to Blisse. He had been confident in his skill to drive them around the island. Brandt's arm still held Malia in place and she let him. Brandt's nervousness made Malia anxious.

'Maybe,' he said, looking around the ceiling, his eyes wide, like the carriage might be a trap instead of a luxury.

All was still for a moment. Then, 'NO! MOSES!'

Malia heard the horse neigh again, her mother gave a terrified scream beside her father, and the carriage lurched, first forward then back. The cliff path was wide enough for a carriage to travel along it without any danger, but something was wrong, something Malia and Brandt couldn't see through the glass windows.

The floor underneath Malia lurched and she vaguely noticed that the wheel beside her was flying down to the sea below them before she felt herself falling sideways.

'Brandt!' she yelled, smashing against the side of the carriage.

What came next was the sensation of being weightless before the deafening slam of steel and wood breaking. Malia hit the side of her head with such force she saw stars behind her closed eyes. There was a combination of screams that sounded like both her father and mother followed by rocks falling.

The carriage stopped with a hard crash that bounced Malia up before slamming her back down on her side, the seat of the carriage now above her. Disoriented, she blinked her eyes and saw the lush red velvet seats were hanging above her, and there was something hard sticking into her back. It took her a moment to understand that it was a fold in the steel roof that had bent itself around a boulder.

'Brandt,' Malia gasped, shoving her older brother's shoulder as he lay beside her. She felt the tears coming down her cheeks.

Brandt moaned, his nose was bleeding and so was a cut on his cheek, but as he came to, he didn't look to be hurt anywhere else. Malia's ribs and the back of her head hurt, but she also seemed to have fared mostly unscathed.

'You alright?' he asked, pushing himself up on his elbows beside her.

'No,' she sobbed.

'I mean, are you hurt?' He asked, moving slowly as he looked her over.

She just sobbed more as she shook her head. What had just happened? How had they fallen off the cliff path? What about their mother and father?

Both the windows in front and behind them now were broken, explaining Brandt's cuts. Malia's long hair was wildly strung around, but as she shook glass out of it she realized her hair had acted like a blanket and protected her from being cut.

As the pair sat up, Brandt froze, quieting Malia's hiccupping sobs. A second later, Malia heard it too.

There was rumbling and it was getting louder. Brandt looked out the broken window at their feet, up towards the cliff.

Malia didn't have time to ask what was happening before Brandt was on top of her, crushing her body to the floor. A split second later the roof, or rather the bottom of the carriage that was now above them, caved in. Malia's eyes were just above Brandt's shoulder, allowing her the perfect view of the rock avalanche that came to bury them alive.

'Don't move!' Brandt yelled in her ear.

Had she moved?

She buried her face in her brother's once-crisp white shirt, but was now covered in dust and his blood.

She felt the carriage underneath her give another inch as the last of the huge boulders hit the wreckage of metal. The steel screeched and groaned, covering Malia's own terrified scream. It broke through the last of the holding wood and metal frame, landing directly on Brandt's shoulder that was protecting Malia's face.

Brandt's scream curdled in her ear, making her freeze. She had never heard her brother make that sound. Not even when he fell off his pony and broke his leg the year before.

The scream stopped as Brandt's full weight crushed her beneath him, knocking the breath from her. The rocks stopped falling. It was dark, airless. Malia first squirmed, trying to breathe. Surely Brandt would wake up soon. But he didn't. Every time she moved, it felt like the newfound space was filled with dirt and rock.

That's when she began to scream for her father. And when he didn't come, she screamed for her mother. When she didn't come, and Brandt was still unconscious on top of her, she just screamed.

They were found in the morning. A fisherman spotted the carriage wreckage and rowed ashore to tell the village where their employer and his family had gone. It took the villagers until midday to carefully remove the fallen rocks. Brandt still hadn't woken up by the time the rocks were pulled away. His left arm dangled at an unnatural angle as they loaded him onto a boat and rowed him away. She heard the fishermen gasp at his arm and the villagers whisper in pitying horror at how Brandt, the great island musician, would never play his violin again. The bottom of the cliff had just enough ledge space to keep them away from the tide, otherwise they would have drowned. By the time they pulled Malia from the wreckage, she was blissfully unconscious too, but in one piece, which was more than could be said of her parents and Moses.

'Miss! Malia! Malia!' Cora's voice was as frantic as her shaking of Malia's shoulders. She gasped awake.

Cora was asking questions, her hands now fretting above Malia's shoulder's, but Malia couldn't make her mouth form any other words other than the same thing she kept saying over and over as she was lifted off her brother and the wreckage, 'I'm alright. I'm alright.' The statement was just as false now as it was a year ago. Nothing was alright.

Chapter Twenty

Malia

An hour before the parade began, the islanders flooded the streets. Rolling heat and flames soared through the air as the fire breathers awed and delighted their audience. Jugglers were impressing crowds as they threw up balls and daggers and a few of the village girls were doing acrobatics with ribboned batons while coins were thrown at their feet.

Red confetti littered the air and the cobblestone streets; every patron was dressed in red and black, making the streets appear to be drowning in spilled blood.

Malia stood at the edge of a circle watching a pair of fire performers with their bare chests and palm tree leaf bottoms, throwing their spinning torches at each other so fast that onlookers couldn't understand how the sticks stayed lit, the flames billowing dangerously with each toss. Embers floated through the air and flittered to the ground only inches from the men, but the threat of possible burns was worth the coins being tossed at their feet.

The bright red dress with its full skirt and deep neckline that Malia wore was another one of her mother's. It was incredibly tight, so she tried to remain still to avoid busting out of it. Her hair was in a side braid that was tied with a black ribbon. It hung over her shoulder and fell down to her waist. Her dress, like the black one of her mother's that she wore for the dinner, was too short at the hem and too tight at the bust, but she had spent all her time and resources on making the blue one from the night before special with its off-the-shoulder alterations and black lace. There wasn't any money for material left to alter the red satin. It had too many ruffles and not enough fabric in the front.

The only benefit was that she didn't think Rogan would complain about that detail. Cora had helped her squeeze into it. If she didn't have plans to meet Rogan, she wouldn't have been caught dead in it. She didn't need Haych's eyes roaming over her more than they already did. The feeling of his wet tongue on her skin had been enough to send her scrubbing her neck with a coarse rag for several hours afterward, leaving her skin raw and as red as her dress under her braided hair.

With such a large crowd all wearing the same color, locating anyone, especially Captain Dixon of the *Serenity*, felt nearly impossible. They were all just pieces of blood confetti, which she hoped to work to her advantage when she would find Dixon and talk to him discreetly.

Malia hadn't seen Cora since she had helped her get dressed. She was supposed to rendezvous with the Captain at the parade, but since Malia hadn't been able to talk to her, and she knew she was being watched, her only hope was to lose her guards for a minute and talk to him herself.

Finding the right moment to do so was proving difficult. She elbowed her way to one of the larger crowds in the square watching a street performance, hoping to find him there since it was where most tourists lingered until the parade started and the streets were cleared.

Straining her neck, she tried to see past the fiery haze and smoke the breathers were creating, but there was still no sign of Cora, Captain Dixon, or her Captain of Souls for that matter.

It was after sunset, so where was Rogan? She missed him. She was starting to worry that maybe he had left that morning. Something tugged in her gut when she acknowledged the fear of never seeing him again. She wanted to kiss him again and run her hands down his corded muscled arms and shoulders. Malia didn't really care what Haych had threatened her with. She knew what kind of future awaited her if she failed. It would be the same as Haych's previous two wives. If, in the end, she couldn't escape her fate, she would fill her final days with Rogan. Haych could slap her around all he wanted afterward, and she would fight back.

Haych's threats and her impending doom only strengthened her resolve. Malia always pushed back. Maybe it wasn't smart to be so reckless, but Haych couldn't hurt Rogan. In fact, she would enjoy seeing him try. And if her attempts to escape the island failed, Cora would succeed, and that left her with nothing to lose. She would fight and the memories the Captain had provided her over the last few days would be enough to keep her fighting until they met again.

Drums started to pound, signaling the start of the parade. Malia grew agitated, having failed to spot either Rogan or Captain Dixon. The chances of escape on the *Serenity* were slim now that her engagement was official, but she had to try something. If nothing else, Cora's safe passage needed to be set in stone. Malia might end up stuck on the island forever, but she wouldn't allow the same twisted fate for Cora. Seeing that Dixon wasn't anywhere up front, Malia moved back to make her way through the crowd when she stepped on someone's foot.

'I'm sorry,' she rushed, looking up to see that it was Captain Dixon. Cora's doctor, Duncan, had described his captain in great detail the night before. Older man, short, with a short crisp white beard and hair, and always in his old navy uniform of black and gold. 'Captain Dixon, I apologize,' she stammered hastily. 'I was just looking for you.'

'And I you, Miss. May we talk?' he asked with a smile that didn't reach his eyes. He held out his arm and gestured to the edge of the crowd near the alley on the far side of the village square, by Samora's bakery, where they had talked the previous night.

'Absolutely,' she encouraged, ignoring the unease building inside her as the Captain kept his eyes averted from looking directly at her.

The mouth of the alley was only slightly quieter, but they could talk without shouting or getting pushed around. The drums beat harder, announcing the clearing of the streets and the start of the parade. The crowd grew louder with excitement. People were beginning to line the streets to watch the parade of fire breathers, dancers, and snake charmers that was sure to be a good show.

The elderly captain and Malia fit comfortably between the two stone walls. He looked around a little nervously before he started to speak.

'Miss Malia,' he hesitated, and she knew from the regret on his wrinkled brow exactly what he would say. Haych and his men must have already sent the word out to the visiting captains and their crews. She wasn't to board any vessel. 'I'm afraid that I can't provide you and your friend passage off the island in a few days as we had agreed.'

'I can offer you more money,' she tried in vain to bargain. For once, she wished her intuition were wrong.

The Captain held up his tan, calloused hand to politely stop her. 'It's not that, Miss. I'm afraid that word has reached me about your fiancé and I can't risk Sir Eldon Haych's wrath. You see, my ship and I come into this island's port several times a year, not just during the festival, and I can't lose business or my employers' business. You understand.'

She nodded numbly. She understood perfectly. She wasn't escaping. Not on that ship. Malia fought through the fog of panic to think reasonably.

'What about my friend?' she blurted, as the Captain was turning to leave.

He paused, looking at her in confusion.

'Can you still take her? The order is just that I can't board, right?' she asked, fighting the urge to take the Captain by the collar and shake him. Dixon looked kind enough. She hoped that maybe either she or Cora reminded him of a daughter or granddaughter somewhere. Anything for some empathy.

When he didn't answer, Malia desperately pushed, 'I'll pay you whatever you want. Can you still take her?'

The Captain nodded grimly. 'But,' he said, 'there is no reason to pay more. Just enough for her passage will do. Dr. Duncan will be most pleased she will still be joining the voyage.'

She sighed and sagged a little against the stone wall beside her in relief. Cora would be free. 'Thank you, sir. She'll be there on Sunday morning.'

'Have her be on the deck of my ship by sunrise on Sunday and we will take her.'

Malia nodded again, suddenly feeling both more relieved and alone than she ever had in her entire life.

The Captain, undoubtedly feeling awkward, nodded his head and left to go watch the parade. The thought of being Haych's next dead wife made Malia shudder. She backed further into the alley, put her face in her hands and wept. The crowd's cheers and the parade music drowned out the sound of wracking sobs. Leaning her back against the stone wall, she slid to the ground and put her face to her knees, making herself as small as possible. Maybe she would just stay there forever.

Suddenly, the hairs on the back of her neck began to prickle. She was being watched.

Lifting her face from the folds of her dress, she wiped her eyes and searched up and down the alley. Looking into the crowd at the mouth of the alley she noticed several men, strangers, pretending to watch the parade procession, but their eyes constantly shifted to where she was backed into the shadows. Haych's newly added watchmen, no doubt. She had no control over the goosebumps that ran up her arm. She quickly pulled back the remainder of tears that wanted to fall. She wished for some water to wash her face, but she would have to make do with wiping the residue of tears away with the hem of her dress. She stood and straightened the red folds of her skirt. She would not have these men report back to Haych that she was crying in despair.

'Who are you looking for, love?' Rogan's voice spoke right behind her ear.

Letting out a surprised yelp, she bumped into the refuge barral.

'You scared me!' she said, slapping a hand to her forehead, trying to calm down.

Rogan looked rather amused with himself. His smile was wide as he sidled up beside her, but as Malia continued to glare at him, he put his hands up in surrender.

'Alright, alright, I'm sorry.' His eyes danced with mischief. The drums were starting to send vibrations through the soles of her feet. With Rogan now in the narrow alleyway, there wasn't much room to move about. His back was to the men that were watching her through the crowd. Instead of feeling closed in, she felt protected from the watchful eyes in the street, like she had just wrapped herself in a favorite blanket, comfortable and safe.

A large crash of drums pounded. Malia knew it was the entrance of the fire dancers into the parade. A split second of distraction for Haych's watchmen was all she needed. She grabbed Rogan's hand and dashed into a small alcove, on the opposite side of Samora's bakery where the back door of Noah's butcher shop received livestock. They were hidden now, at least for a few moments.

She had planned on warning him about the men watching her and what Haych had threatened her with that morning, but she didn't have the chance before his lips were devouring her own. Malia inhaled in surprise. He tasted salty. Her heart matched the thumping of the drums' deepening beat. He smelled of the strongest winds and something unknown. All the despair and barrenness she felt a moment ago was gone, replaced with Rogan, his tongue playing with hers. His fingers gripped the fabric of her red dress, making her long to never be let go. He was cold and sturdy as she felt the grooves of muscle press against the wrinkles of her dress, lifting her off her feet. She shivered and loved it. Rogan gave her some reprieve from the island that was always so hot. As he lifted and leaned Malia against the alcove wall, he unknowingly put pressure on the new bruises on her back. Malia unexpectedly groaned in pain. Rogan, mistaking it for pleasure, continued his kissing. She put her feet on the ground and shifted in his arms, taking his hands in hers. She pulled back smiling and face flushed.

She had never been wanted, especially not the way Rogan wanted her. Malia wasn't sure what to do with these feelings.

'Hello,' he whispered hoarsely with a smile. His fingers played with strands of Malia's hair near her waist, his other hand rested against the faded painted wall behind her head.

'Hello,' she said, just as breathless.

Rogan poked his head around the alcove wall. His black sleeves were rolled up and his collar open, the top points of his trident tattoo visible under his collar bone.

'Want to get out of here?' he asked, jerking his head with a smile she found herself melting for.

'Yes, please.' She glanced around nervously outside their little haven and saw that Haych's men were becoming shifty after losing sight of her. A few were closer than they had been before, and Ku, who had been keeping guard at the study door that morning, was pushing his way through the throng of people toward them.

'Let's go,' she said, anxiety leaking into her voice as she looked toward the end of the alley toward the jungle paths, their best way to escape. Rogan turned his eyes to the horde of people cheering and laughing. Streamers and banners flew through the air only feet from them. His brows netted in concentration as he studied the crowd. The drums were vibrating the stones around them. The parade was in full procession.

Two large shadows appeared, one on each end of the alley, blocking their escapes. Ku stood in front of them and Brom, with his neck scar, was stationed at their backs. Rogan took a small sidestep, placing himself in front of Malia, who he guided back into the alcove.

'Miss Malia,' Ku grumbled, choosing to ignore Rogan. 'I suggest you come with me now.'

Rogan's muscle in his jaw twitched. Malia wondered if he was hiding a smile or a sneer.

'Who are you?' he asked, sounding curious and annoyed that he was having to ask the most unimportant person in the world who he was.

Ku looked at Rogan for the first time, crossing his meaty arms over his chest. 'I'm Miss Malia's guard, and if I were you I'd move away from the lady and shove off.'

'Well, it's a good thing you're not me then, eh? For one, I'd be far less good-looking and about as charming as a chamber pot. But all that aside, why does Malia need a guard? How do I know you are a guard? How do I know you aren't some pirate hell-bent on kidnapping her?'

The man was not amused. He directed a threatening glare at Malia that she better speak up or else.

Rogan turned, gazing at Malia too.

'Do you know this man, Malia? Or is he a pirate intent on kidnapping you?'

She shrugged her shoulders. 'I don't know who he is. He must be a pirate. There surely can't be another explanation for that smell.'

The man's face deepened as scarlet as his shirt.

'Hey, not all pirates smell,' Rogan said, defending his mortal trade.

'Well, this one does.'

Rogan gave a wink and a corner of his perfect mouth rose before he turned casually back towards the seething guard.

'You see? I can't let her leave with you. If you were her body-guard, wouldn't she know you? Plus, she smells wonderful tonight and I would hate for that to change.'

'Her fiancé, Sir Eldon Haych, hired me. And she is to keep away from you.' He pointed a sausage finger at Rogan's chest. Malia noticed that Brom was still at the end of the alley. Keeping his distance.

'Now why,' Rogan questioned, using his own index finger to push away the other man's from his chest, 'would a fiancé hire six or more men to guard Miss Malia? Is he afraid of her fleeing?' Rogan looked over the man's shoulder and into the partying crowd.

A small bony man in a tattered sailor's uniform joined Ku's side.

'Sir Eldon Haych isn't afraid of anything,' the small newcomer said before spitting a wad of tobacco at their feet.

'Everybody is afraid of something,' Rogan said darkly. Suddenly, the lights from the street lanterns no longer penetrated the alley; a curtain of night had closed over the entryway. Malia stiffened. She wasn't sure what was happening, but adrenaline kicked in on instinct. Her chest froze and the air in her lungs squeezed from her like pieces of jagged ice, each breath as painful as the last.

'Rogan?' she whispered. The two men began to look unsure, their eyes shifting from Rogan to each other. The air felt charged as the temperature continued to drop in the alleyway. Malia had never felt the air that cold before or seen her breath puff out so far in front of her face. It was startling. Was Rogan doing this?

'Now, if you gentlemen still feel like Miss Malia should go with you, feel free to claim her.'

Malia stepped further into the alcove as Rogan took a threatening step forward. His shoulders were tight under his black shirt. Every muscle in his forearms were taut as his hands formed tight fists, waiting.

Two more men joined the others in the mouth of the alley. They were all squeezed together, leaving no room for a simultaneous attack– they would have to do it one at a time. Still, Rogan waited as darkness surrounded them. The drums had reached them, drowning out every other sound.

A smelly, bald man squeezed forward. How much damage could they really do to Rogan all squished together? What could Rogan do to them? Besides calling the souls, Malia hadn't seen Rogan display any power, it was so easy to forget how powerful he really was.

What Rogan was capable of was still a mystery to Malia. She was both excited and a little terrified at the prospect of seeing his potential.

The muscles in Rogan's back were tight, but his legs were loose, as though he was getting ready for a play fight with children. He bent his knees and waited to lunge, while Haych's men fought against being bottlenecked into the alley.

Smelly, having waited long enough for someone to make the

first move, darted forward. Rogan blocked his weak blow to his jaw with a bat of his hand, like swatting a gnat. Maybe that was how he saw them. Pests that were annoying, but not threatening. Rogan picked up the smaller man and threw him into the others with a strength that wouldn't be possible for a normal man, even a very strong one. The other two thugs caught their fellow attacker and fell hard to the ground, their eyes wide, momentarily awed before they shook off their fear and forged ahead.

Malia observed in fascination as Rogan only defended himself, never advancing. It was almost disturbing to watch him punch, elbow, and knee the ill-prepared men. As one went down, another stumbled over him to take his place. The dark alley assisted in disorienting the men and Rogan took full advantage. Malia saw how Rogan would disappear just as a man was about to plow into him, only for the stranger to tackle one of his friends. Rogan appeared on the opposite side of the crashing men and laughed over their furious cursing.

Another shadow appeared beside Brom at the other end of the alley. Malia noticed them, wondering if they were more of Haych's hired hands who would join in the fight by sneaking behind Rogan's back. But they remained motionless, simply looking content to stand and observe.

Why are they just watching?

Then the realization of what was happening struck. It was an ambush, a trap, but not a physical one like it had seemed. Haych had mentioned that he thought Rogan was the Captain of Souls. Now he would have witnesses that could attest to such suspicions. Malia had been the bait, the guards had set the trap, and Rogan had sprung into the fight without hesitation.

Ku was the last left standing when he whipped around swinging his meaty fists, only to hit the stone wall where Rogan had been. Malia heard the crack of broken bones in his hand before the bellow of pain and frustration roared from Ku. The rest of the men were in heaps on the cobbled ground.

Rogan ended the brawl with a resounding clunk against Ku's jaw that sent him to the ground in an unconscious heap.

Rogan, now completely solid, turned to look at Malia with triumph in his smile and power in his eyes. The air remained cold and charged.

The smile vanished from his face as he looked past her and saw the two fleeing shadows, instantly lost to the jungle.

'We need to move,' he ordered, grabbing her hand. He didn't have so much as a bruise on his knuckles. Malia sidestepped the moaning men on the ground. Rogan, however, chose to purposely aim and stomp on their limp limbs, crushing their already-fragile egos. As soon as they joined the crowds on the street, the chill that Rogan had created vanished. They were surrounded by bodies, humidity, and sweat.

Rogan led the way, easily pushing through the people and ignoring the fire breathers, jugglers, and masked court jesters that danced and tumbled in the street. The music sounded muddled in Malia's ears, like it was coming from a mile away rather than right beside her. They hurried across the street in between floats and performers as quickly as they could, but Malia saw some islanders pointing and taking notice of whom she was with. Word would get back to Haych within the hour, she was sure. They would have to lay low until the parade was over and the street dancing and drinking were well underway. People would be too drunk and busy to notice them then.

It didn't take Rogan long to get them through the crowd and out of the square.

'Wait! I want to make sure we aren't being followed,' she said after turning behind a small farming hut. They weren't far from the fruit fields.

'I'll take care of it. Wait here,' Rogan said, disappearing a second later.

In a few minutes, he reappeared.

'All clear.'

Malia figured hiding in plain sight would be best. Brandt knew she liked to go to the lighthouse to get away, so they might check there. She certainly wasn't going home. They fought their way through the mess of overgrown jasmine trees, and as the shrubs cleared away, they found their way back to her mother's forgotten garden.

Chapter Twenty-One

Rogan

The small ruined gazebo, with its open walls and iron work vines and flowers, didn't look quite as dangerous as it had the night before with all the rain and thunder. Although there were clouds dotting the night sky, the moon was bright and gave plenty of light inside the little overgrown garden.

The nagging suspicion that Malia had somehow set him up against those men wouldn't go away. Maybe she had made some sort of desperate bargain for her freedom?

Disappointment is hard to recover from, my dear, the Goddess had warned Rogan. Was that ambush what she meant? It had obviously been a sort of trap, but set up by whom? Rogan didn't want to believe it was Malia, but how well did he know her, really? He knew she was desperate for survival, and he of all people knew what a person could do when they were that desperate. Trust wasn't something he was used to giving freely, and he was finding it hard not to be paranoid. Rogan hadn't wanted to look at her and have her betrayal affirmed in her eyes. But she had pulled away when he kissed her in the alley.

'What was that?' Rogan asked as an unfamiliar feeling of rage swept over him. Enraged at whom, he wasn't sure. Malia? Haych? Angelos? Himself? One minute he had been kissing Malia and enjoying himself, as the drums beat in rhythm with his pulse. The next, he was doubting everything that he thought he learned about Malia during his time on the island that week.

'Did you set me up? Did Angelos put you up to it?' Rogan asked, pointing an accusing finger from the other side of the gazebo where the tree branch had broken the glass ceiling.

Malia gave him a wide-eyed stare, like he had lost his mind. Maybe he was. 'No,' she said, shortly. When he didn't reply, but continued to stand there awaiting an explanation, Malia exploded.

'What? You cannot be serious.' Her voice rose just short of shrill. 'Those were obviously Haych's men,' she retorted.

The longer Rogan stood there silent, the whiter Malia's knuckles grew in her fist. He was already feeling on edge with Angelos' words playing with his mind. He wasn't supposed to interfere with the lives of mortals, but he had just blooded a pile of men and left them in the alley. The Goddess' rules felt impossible to keep the longer he stayed.

He was also having a hard time processing the sudden constant onset of emotions. All. The. Time. He missed the bliss of his apathetic numbness. It was comfortable. Now? He knew he wasn't being fair, or rational, accusing Malia of such betrayal, but he was coming to understand that rationality and his emotions didn't keep company with one another.

Why am I sounding so critical? You don't know anything yet. Pull yourself together, Rogan.

'Yes, because I thought, "If I can get Rogan to start a random fight with half a dozen men, my life will be so much better."' She put her hand on her curved hip expecting him to back down after hearing the ridiculousness of his claim. But he just waited for her to deny it, he needed to hear her say it.

'No, you idiot.' She responded to his silence. 'You found me in the alley, remember? I didn't lure you there. Besides, you seem to be Haych's new obsession. He suspects that something about you is different. How or why, I don't know. Probably because no one knows anything about you, including himself, and he knows about everyone and everything on this island.'

When Rogan still didn't say anything she asked, 'Have you ever trusted another person, ever?' He didn't know how to fully trust another person, and the vulnerability of doing so made him rethink how good of an idea this current relationship was.

'No,' he finally answered. 'People only disappoint and betray you. There is only one person you can count on and that is yourself.

'Well, if that is the case, think of it this way. *I'm* going to be the one that pays for what you just did. Why would I do that to myself?'

'What are you talking about; you'll have to pay for it? Haych obviously wants me. He probably wants to know who I really am. Maybe you bargained a deal with him to save your own skin.'

'Wow...you are unbelievable. Do you know that? Yes, he suspects who you really are. He has always been devout with his beliefs, but since he was appointed Governor six months ago, he has become finatical about our island's festival, and just as zealous for power. He put himself in charge of all the festivities, and made it his business to know who and what ships are visiting. But when he asked me, I denied it. Then, you go and display supernatural power in that fight against his band of goons. He will be even more determined to find out who you really are now. Besides, does *this* look like I'm on Haych's good side right now?' She lowered the cloth at her shoulder, showing him in the moonlight the purple bruise that ran across her shoulder blades.

After a moment, Rogan realized what he was looking at and how it would have gotten there. He had seen and experienced countless bruises from being tossed around. A memory of being thrown into shelves by a workhouse forman affirmed Rogan's suspicion as to where Malia got the narrow bruise crossing her shoulders. Now the way she squirmed when he had kissed her made sense. She wasn't pulling away because she felt guilty like he had started to think. She pulled away, because he had hurt her.

He had hurt her. Haych had put his hands on her. Touched her.

He had felt anger plenty when he was alive, but rarely since his curse. This was more than that. This was an all-consuming, life-ending heat that tingled and burned from Rogan's chest to his head, and spread clear down his arms and legs. His vision tinged as red as Malia's dress. She pulled up the fabric. Finally, when Rogan found his way through the haze enough to use his voice he asked, 'He did that?'

'Haych doesn't like to be told no.' She walked over to the doorway's edge, staring out into the dark trees. The parade could be heard just above the scratching of the palm tree leaves against the glass ceiling.

'What happened?' he demanded, gently. His eyes searched hers as he thought of all the different ways he was going to disembowel Haych. Rogan could feel his power amplifying as he sucked in the energy around him. His emotions began to overwhelm all rational thought again. The air turned cold.

'He did this to you for information about me?'

'Well, not entirely, it was to hurt me too. He likes strong women. It's all the more satisfying and rewarding to the sick bastard when he breaks them.'

Rogan wanted to grovel at her feet for being so petty and distrusting before. Only, he knew Malia wouldn't want him groveling, she would want strength, a solution. Coming up behind her, he gingerly wrapped his arms around her shoulders, turning her to face him.

'Did he do anything else?' Rogan's hands were shaking with every ounce of self-control his immortality had taught him and it still didn't feel like enough. If she said yes, only the power of a god could keep him from ripping the man's thick throat out with his bare hands.

'No,' Malia said, meeting his eyes with her teary ones. 'He only wanted to scare me into giving up information, into being submissive. He said he wouldn't touch me *that way* until we were married on Sunday. The anticipation is half the game.'

'Married on Sunday? This Sunday?' Rogan asked, barely able to comprehend everything that was happening. His anger and jealousy were making it hard to focus. The red tinges that had moved to the edge of his vision were back to full force and it was all he could see.

She looked at him with years of disappointment in her eyes. Malia knew true betrayal, one that ran deep and unforgiving. Seeing her, Rogan understood that he knew nothing of it. He hated that she had been hurt. And not just by Haych, but had been hurt by the people that should have been looking out for her, helping her. The part he hated the most was knowing he would be the one that ended up hurting her the most when he left, leaving her to fend for herself in a cruel and unjust world.

A stray tear leaked from her eye before she hurriedly wiped it away.

'Tell me everything,' Rogan said.

Malia took a deep breath of the frigid air, and filled Rogan in on that morning's happenings.

'He wanted to know about you, and I wouldn't tell him.' She stepped back, looking suddenly embarrassed by her outburst of loyalty. Malia's breath was now visible when she exhaled. He needed to calm down. The heat around them was being absorbed into his anger. Frost covered the gazebo's iron flowers.

He let go of her shoulders that had goosebumps running along them. He took a few steps back in an effort to pull it together. Angelos would notice if the Captain she tortured that morning was about to misbehave. And she would certainly take notice if he killed Haych, but he would deal with those repercussions later.

As Rogan took a step to find Haych and teach him the meaning of immortal wrath, his feet froze. He could not move. Not until he calmed down. He could not kill a mortal, no matter how deserving they were or how angry he was.

'What's wrong?' Malia asked, looking at Rogan's pained face.

'Nothing is wrong, I just have to calm down. My curse as Captain won't let me hurt mortals outright.'

'You beat all those men, before?'

'Yes,' Rogan gave another frustrated jerk of his leg– it didn't move an inch. He curled his hands into fists and bent at the waist in frustration. 'But that was in self-defense. What I want to do to Haych is pure hateful revenge, so it looks like I'm stuck right here until I calm down.' Rogan stood back up straight, resigned to his position until his curse released him. He took heavy, deep breaths and ran his hands through his hair. He had never been stopped by his cursed power before. He was finding the taking of his free will to exact his justice on Haych even more infuriating than all the years he had been marooned on his ship by himself.

After a few minutes, while Malia waited patiently, Rogan was released and free to move around the gazebo.

'He already suspected you,' she said. 'He told me as much this morning when he was demanding answers. You are the only sea captain that he doesn't know everything about, or have in his pocket. It has made him suspicious. He also knows about your ship anchored in Cliff's Teeth. I'm assuming when he couldn't find any leverage or information about you, he put two and two together and made a good guess. That must be the real reason why he insisted that I leave the house to join the parade. He knew you would find me. He knew, if provoked, you would either get hurt and show him you are a normal human, or show your true colors, and you did. It was all a setup to keep me trapped and discover who you really are.'

'What would that crazy old man want with me anyway?' Rogan asked, completely baffled.

'Well,' Malia said after some thought. 'Stories of the Captain of Souls are legendary. Speculation of your powers have made you look more like the God of Death and less like a servant. Many believe that you can't be killed,' Rogan shrugged. That part was true. 'And that you can wield power over life and death. And after what his men saw tonight, they will probably be more prone to believe that. Can't you see why a man like Haych would be interested in you?'

'Yes, but being the Captain of Souls isn't some all-powerful position to feel envious of. I'm a slave. Bound to the ship and Goddess of Death. Until a few days ago, I had the same emotional depth as a sack of rocks.'

'Yes, but Haych doesn't know that. He only knows what legend has told him. And if you were to tell him differently now, he wouldn't believe you. He wants the power he thinks you have.'

'Well, he is in for quite a disappointment. The Captain is a position given only to those that the Goddess is interested in, feels like playing with, or who she thinks might have a soul worth saving. Haych doesn't fit those descriptions. In fact, she mentioned last night that she knows of Haych, and he isn't on her good side.'

'Probably because of what we all know but can't prove, that he killed his two previous wives by "accident". In addition, there has been a larger than normal amount of disappearances and deaths on the island, even travelers are disappearing more since my parents died,' she said.

'Well, that makes sense why when I collected all the souls last night, it was a rather large number for such a small area. Some weren't even in the cemetery, but had been called from somewhere else on the island. Including that missing sailor you danced with on the beach. He stumbled in from the jungle.

'Angelos knows of him, but she won't do anything about him, and reminded me that I can't either. Not unless he poses a danger to the souls in some way. It is that rule that is keeping me bound from going and hunting him down right now.'

'Wait, haven't you taken mortals before?'

'Yes,' Rogan said carefully, 'But that is only when they find out with ill intent, on their own, who I really am. I take their souls early to keep the integrity of others in tact. By rights, according to the Goddess' rules, that puts you on the chopping block more than Haych.'

Rogan could see the growing hopelessness in Malia's eyes as they darted around in the moonlight. She looked around like maybe the gazebo would hold the answer. But she only found him, and he had none.

A new emotion bubbled up in him– helplessness. It was a feeling he hated more than Haych or Angelos or the ship he was bound to. It was the same feeling he'd had right before Angelos cursed him. Before the festival, he had never cared enough to feel such a strong emotion as hate. But he recognized the old feeling while he looked at Malia's desperate gaze.

The negative emotions of hate and helplessness made his stomach churn and palms itch to hit something. Hate was a turbulent cycle, and he wanted out of that tempestuous sea. He wrestled for control over himself. He finally found that his feelings for Malia were stronger than his hatred for Haych, his fear of Angelos and even the feeling of helplessness in their situation. Is that what love was? This overwhelming and all-consuming sensation that would make a person do anything they could to keep another safe and, if possible, happy? Rogan knew he could never do either, but he loved her anyway. At this realization, the next emotion that came was— failure. Heartbreaking failure that felt like an endless weight that had just been placed on his shoulders. Why was love proving to be harder than hate?

Well, failure wasn't going to win. He determined then and there in that cold broken building that something would change. He would not leave Malia, who he had grown devoted to, to be broken, even if it cost him his soul. His resolve lightened the crushing weight of failure. He could do something. He would do something.

'Malia,' his voice sounded hoarse and rough in his own ears. She looked at him with surprise in her round eyes just before he kissed her. He felt her soft curves of skin pressed against his hard lines. It left him wanting. His fingers found the back of her dress and danced along the curve of her skin against the fabric. This broken gazebo, their secret place, was the best he could do, and that still wasn't good enough.

He pulled back his lips from hers to trace down her neck as she held tight to him.

'I don't know how to save you, Malia. But I will,' he whispered in her ear, feeling his chest burn as he vowed it.

Her embrace tightened, holding onto the hope as she nodded.

'You already are, Rogan,' she said into his neck. 'You're giving me something to remember and hold onto when the nights become long and the days painful. I'll have you in this place, always.'

'Always,' he agreed, their foreheads resting on each other. 'I have two more days, I'll figure it out.'

'Who said I need you to save me? Maybe it's the other way around?' she teased with a raised brow and a smile.

'I won't argue with that.' Rogan gave her his most roguish grin.

Malia quirked her head to the side as she studied him, like she was trying to think of something, anything, to help their situation. The moonlight shone in her dark eyes. They promised excitement.

'There might be one thing you can do for me,' she said.

'Oh yeah?' Rogan said, wiggling his eyebrows.

'Alright, two things.'

'Name it.'

'Teach me how to defend myself.'

'What?'

'Well, you were a pirate, and I saw you fight just now. Teach me.'

'Alright,' Rogan agreed easily, moving them outside the building to the small grassy clearing.

He placed Malia in front of him and took a step back.

'First, since this Haych is a coward, but wants the façade of perfection, he will probably avoid your face. But don't avoid his. You have nails, use them. Do what you can to his face or skin to show that he was in a recent struggle. Remember he wants fear to rule, and it only helps him when there is no evidence.'

They practiced several moves that Rogan had learned over the years. Most of them were to help her escape a grasp or dodge a blow.

Rogan had just wrestled Malia to the ground when fireworks shot off, distracting both of them as they watched sparks of light rain down. Blinding one moment and gone the next. More fireworks shot and exploded above them, brightening Malia's smile underneath him as her hand rested against the skin of his collar bone. Rogan angled her chin up and kissed her. Slowly at first, like he was drinking her in. But soon, the softness of her mouth and curves against him as she pulled him tighter against her turned their kisses to fire. More explosions went off in the sky around them, but they ignored everything but each other. It didn't take long before both were gasping and out of breath. As Rogan's mouth traced the curve of her neck, his body froze, just like it had in the gazebo. Rogan's face pulled back and away on its own, like someone had turned his lips forcefully away from Malia's. He swore. A large wave of magic hit the garden and the grass no longer smelled of earth, but salt. Malia's hold on his neck where she was pulling him down to her softened.

'What's wrong?' she asked, her voice breathless against his ear.

Rogan felt heat flame his neck and cheeks. Sweat prickled the back of his neck. He was... embarrassed.

'It seems,' Rogan said, then cleared his throat. His body had calmed enough, it would seem, and he was able to move his neck to face Malia. A line of worry creased her brows. Maybe it was his embarrassment, or the irony that Malia was worried about him that caused a bark of laughter to escape his throat. Malia laughed back, still confused, her hands now on his red face. 'What?' she insisted.

'It would seem,' he tried again. His body became more languid with every passing second. His hands now played with Malia's sprawled hair in the grass. 'That intimacy,' he said, clearing his throat again and tapping his fingers against the cool grass, 'Is apparently something I can't perform,' he said, laughing so hard on the last word that tears formed in his eyes. He tried to think back to the last time he was ever embarrassed. He couldn't. Not as Captain or a mortal. Apparently, embarrassment caused him to laugh, along with sweat and flushing.

'What?' Malia asked while she laughed into his shoulder as he ducked his head, his body shaking in laughter above her. 'Are you serious?'

Rogan couldn't answer from the laughing. He just nodded. Malia was laugh-moaning as she said, 'What? Why?'

'I don't know.' he managed to say as he wheezed. But his

neck and face no longer felt hot. 'The Goddess must really hate me.' He took several more deep breaths. Malia was laughing too, if only because his laugh was causing her to respond in kind. He looked down at Malia's resigned smile, her eyes full of humor and understanding and gave her a chaste kiss before rolling off and settling beside her. The cool humid grass tickled the back of his neck, making him shiver.

'Well, there seems to be another circle of Hell I was unaware of until now,' he said, his face sore from laughing. More fireworks in colors of red and white lit up the sky.

Malia gave a resigned, but happy sigh, her hair still wild around her before taking Rogan's hand. They were quiet for a moment, both needing time to reconcile themselves to the loss of what they both wanted from each other but was unattainable.

'I'm sorry, love,' Rogan said in almost a whisper, the disappointment finally catching up with him.

Malia rotated to her side to face him. She waited to say something until Rogan would meet her eyes.

'Do I look sorry?' she asked him. Rogan gave her a "stop patronizing me look". 'I'm serious, Rogan. I'm not sorry. Not for any of it. Besides, it was probably for the best.' Rogan's eyebrows shot up, unsure if he should be insulted or not. Malia gave him a mischievous smile. 'I've only known you a few days after all.' She poked him in the ribs, making him squirm. Apparently, he was ticklish too. 'Now that you have given me the gift of passion, something as big as that, it can wait. I only want it to be with you.'

'What if we don't have time for— waiting?' Rogan asked, giving her slender hand a squeeze.

Her eyes turned serious as another round of fireworks reflected off her dark irises.

'I'd wait forever, Rogan. It will either be you first, or no one at all.'

Rogan's voice caught in his throat at Malia's familiar stubborn set of her jaw. He didn't deserve her and knew it.

Unexpectedly, Rogan jumped to his feet. Night was escaping from their grasp. He didn't want to spend anymore of their night worrying about Haych, or lamenting what they couldn't do together. He wanted to enjoy it. To relish the touch of each other as much as possible. Malia took Rogan's outstretched hand, shooting to her feet. She crushed Rogan's mouth to hers.

He smiled through their kiss and said, 'Let's go dance.'

Chapter Twenty-Two

FRIDAY

Malia

As Rogan and Malia danced the night away in the streets, Haych's men failed to make a reappearance. She guessed that since they had gathered their evidence against the couple, they were off enjoying the festival, which left Malia wondering how Haych had spent the night. He wasn't at the parade or street dances, and she had been watching out for him. Rogan had too. She noticed that, despite the fun they were having, every now and then his gaze would shift to scan the crowd.

As the sky turned from a deep violet to a sweet, pastel flush, the people in the streets began to dwindle and Rogan walked Malia home.

'That room is mine,' she said, pointing to her open terrace visible through the jasmine flowers that bloomed beneath.

'That explains why you always smell like jasmine,' Rogan

smiled, leaning in close to her hair that had turned wild during the night.

'They were my mother's favorite flower,' she said, feeling that familiar ache in her chest of missing her parents that even Rogan's magic hadn't been able to fully take away.

Rogan looked up at the sky and he gave her a sad smile.

'Back to my day-prison I must go,' he said.

'Why only during the day?' Malia had always wanted to ask.

'The Goddess told me that the daytime during this week was a time for me to reflect and think about my future. She said she wanted time to mean something to me again.'

'And does it now?'

Rogan nodded. 'It means everything.' The intimacy in his gaze made Malia's stomach burn and her legs shake.

'I'll see you tonight,' he promised. Tonight was the Mourning Observance and would take place on the docks and harbor. It was an opportunity for anyone who had lost a family member over the past year to bid them farewell by placing flowers or other tokens into small sail boats in the water. Luckily, she didn't have anyone to honor that year. But almost everyone else on the island did. There were a lot of accidents on the island over the past year, her parents only being the first. Accidents like holes in fishing boats, drownings, and unexplained illnesses that never seemed to be contagious. Almost as if people were poisoned. People that had ties to Haych. She wasn't the only one that suspected Haych, she was sure of it, but he had done a fine job of scaring anyone that would point a finger at him into silence. After all, many of those finger-pointers had been the ones that ended up missing or dead.

She planned on possibly exploring her theory more about Haych's involvement, but for that night, the pair planned to meet on the beach, and sneak away while most of the island was distracted.

Malia nodded, already anticipating what they would do with another full night ahead of them.

He kissed her hand gently, then, as the sun rose over the crest of the ocean, he disappeared.

Sighing, while her hand still tingled from his touch, she made her way into the house of horrors to suffer for another day.

Walking into the house, Malia knew something was wrong.

It was quiet. Dead quiet. Even the morning calls of seagulls outside were muffled. Like all the windows and doors of the house were shut. They were never all shut.

Everything still looked to be in its place. Dust and cobwebs still lined the shelves and chandeliers, but not a sound or echo of voices could be heard across the old marble floor and walls. The only sound was from the small clock in the corner, ticking dimly in the chilled room. Usually, in the morning, Cora would be buzzing around, her pounding footsteps announcing her entry into the room. Not this morning. The silence was heavy. A cloak of mourning had settled in it, encouraging Malia to tiptoe her way in.

Where was Brandt? He had skipped the parade and merriment last night to nurse his wounds inflicted by Haych that morning, but even he should've been shuffling about the house somewhere. Even with the outside noises gone, the empty house echoed every sound within it. There was no echoing. Nothing.

She tiptoed up the stairs and all the way to her room. The door was shut. As she approached, there was hushed whimpering from the other side of the door. Malia froze. Who was in there?

As quietly as possible, she turned the knob. Once opened a few inches she peered into the room. She wasn't sure what to expect, but it wasn't what she saw.

Everything in the room looked the same as it had when she had left, just like downstairs. The furniture was there and all her scant possessions. But she would never be able to look into the room again without seeing Cora's bloody, broken face laying limply against the bed pillows as she whimpered in pain. Cora hadn't just been beaten. She was so bludgeoned Malia only recognized her by the wisps of wild black curls that hung limply down her face. Her clothes were torn and ripped, revealing purple bloodied skin beneath.

Brandt, who knelt beside her, was also bruised and swollen, but his wounds were from the beating the night before, not new ones. Malia's chest burned. She couldn't breathe. Air failed her. Finally, her body acted on instinct and inhaled sharply. The gasp notified Brandt of her entrance. Tears welled and nausea swarmed in Malia's belly. She was going to be sick.

'Malia,' Brandt breathed out in relief.

'What happened?' Malia ran to Cora's bedside, her legs collapsing beneath her. Tears blinded her vision as she tried to find someplace on Cora that wasn't bruised, restraining the need to physically touch her to ensure her friend was still alive. Had the ship doctor done this? Malia didn't recall seeing either one of them all night. She assumed they were together in secret somewhere, like she and Rogan had been.

Brandt looked down at her with both pity and anger. Both emotions churned in Malia's throat, making it hard to talk, hard to breathe.

'What happened?' Malia choked out. 'Brandt!' she nearly screamed when her brother didn't answer.

'Haych,' was Brandt's reply before rising to his feet.

'What happened, Brandt? Why would Haych do this to Cora? What did you do?' Malia stood up pushing her brother's shoulders. He had to have had something to do with this, but he looked just as confused and upset as Malia felt.

'This wasn't my fault. This was yours,' Brandt said.

'Excuse me?'

'What did you think was going to happen after Sir Haych claimed you, only to have you run off with that sea captain last night, again? He warned you not to embarrass him. Did you think Haych wouldn't retaliate? Did you think you didn't have anything left to lose?'

Malia looked down in horror at her dearest and only friend and felt dizzy with sickness. As sick as she had felt when she realized that both her parents were dead and Brandt's arm was shattered from protecting her. She was to blame for more tragedy.

Cora moaned again but didn't move.

'Haych found something out about you,' Brandt blustered, 'Last night when you were gone. Something about you and that captain. He was at the house this morning before sunrise, waiting. I found him in our father's study. He said that he had left Cora with a message. I found her just now. The last time I saw her was last night, before the parade.'

Kneeling beside the bed once more, Malia sobbed. This had been her fault. Haych knew who Rogan was now. He had known she was with him all night, and this was his retribution. Brandt was right. What had she been thinking? Why had she thought she could do whatever she wanted? Malia knew the answer of course; she had fooled herself into believing that there was nothing left to lose. Clearly, she did. Haych had her figured out. Malia would do whatever she wanted, if the consequences only affected her, but now he had involved Cora. She cried harder for her poor dear friend that had been beaten within an inch of death while she danced, kissed, and touched Rogan. First Brandt's arm, now her friend. The guilt threatened to swallow her whole. She was a curse. It was suffocating and she found she couldn't breathe. If she hadn't been selfish and naive, thinking that for the night Haych couldn't touch her, Cora would be smiling at her right now. He had just proven that he could do enough damage by not touching her at all.

'You're getting out of here,' she whispered into Cora's ear. 'I won't let this happen to you again. This is my fault. I'm so sorry. I should have just let Haych take me.'

'No,' Brandt said above her. 'This never should have happened to either of you.' Brandt knelt beside his sister with tears swarming in his eyes. They looked so clear, so hazel. For the first time in months he didn't look pathetic, but humble. He looked so much like their father and Malia's heart ached all the more. She wondered when the last time he had a drink was. 'I caused all of this. I am so sorry, Malia.'

For a moment, all the hate and resentment that had built up cracked. She saw for a moment who Brandt was and who he should have become. Such wasted potential.

Malia's hand acted of its own accord and reached up to grasp his dark hair and she found herself hugging him. Hugging the young man that also lost his parents and his world. Yes, some of that loss was of his own making but other parts were not. Rogan had taken Malia's grief the year before, allowing her to function, move along with her life. Brandt had to continue in his grief, alone. What he had done still wasn't right, but it was more understandable.

Cora's hand moved weakly as she gave a small whimper, pulling them apart.

'Has the doctor been here yet?' Malia asked, collecting herself.

Brandt stood up, sniffing loudly.

'No, we don't have money to pay him,' he answered simply, rubbing his shoulder. Had he carried her in here despite being sober and in pain?

'Go to the ship *Serenity,* get that ship's doctor and no other, Brandt. I don't doubt that Haych has already threatened Dr. Murdoch not to help us. We need to make sure Cora doesn't have any permanent injuries. And if it would be possible for her to travel soon.'

Brandt bolted from the room. After he left, she filled a basin with cold water mixed with her tears and started dabbing Cora's injuries, unsure of what else to do.

As Malia looked her over closely, she hoped her injuries weren't as bad as they appeared. Her hands and limbs didn't appear to be broken, which was good. But she couldn't account for her ribs, face or any other bones not visible to her immediate gaze. She had dried blood on her lips, nose, and a small cut on her forehead but no other open wounds. Her head, beyond her face, looked to be uninjured.

The tears wouldn't stop as Malia wiped away the blood and sweat from Cora's skin. She continued muttering how sorry she was and hoped that someday it would mean something. The cool rags throughout the day helped with the swelling of Cora's face. The chore helped distract Malia from the clock as she waited for the doctor to arrive and report the extent of Cora's injuries.

Malia had just dipped the blood-soaked rag back into the basin and placed it upon Cora's brow when her friend gasped.

'Malia,' was all Cora could muster. Her voice cracked in a painful whisper and she blinked her swollen eyes, trying to focus.

'Shhhh. I'm here, Cora. Don't speak; don't move, Brandt has gone for Duncan.'

Just then, Brandt burst into the room with the doctor on his heels. He looked so young in her bedroom, shocked by what he saw there.

'She is right there,' Brandt said, gesturing to the semi-conscious Cora on the bed.

Malia quickly got out of the way.

Duncan's face changed from shock to professional as he came to the side of the bed and ascertained Cora's injuries.

'Will she be alright?' Malia asked as the doctor applied pressure to Cora's ribs. Cora gave a gasp of surprise in response, but the doctor didn't seem surprised.

'Yes. I have seen these kinds of injuries before, after the usual fights and beatings, but never on a woman. How did this happen?' he asked with lines of concentration on his face. They wrinkled his forehead as he carefully placed different bottles and instruments on the bedside table that he was pulling from a black leather bag.

Malia hesitated, not knowing what or how much to explain. How had Haych acquired so much power over the people of the island? Once there had been a time, when her parents were alive, that Sir Eldon Haych had been a modest fisherman. How had he gained control over everything?

'A former suitor,' Malia muttered. It was the only logical lie she could think of that wouldn't scare off the Captain of the *Serenity* when he would eventually hear about his beaten passenger. The doctor looked away briefly to meet her gaze. 'She was leaving the island on your ship to go start fresh somewhere. He got wind of it, and well ...we found her in this state this morning.' Malia swallowed the lump building in her throat that threatened to strangle her.

The doctor nodded in understanding, his jaw tightening and releasing, then continued his examination.

Cora continued to moan and mutter "Miss" in a weakened voice but the doctor gave her something from his little bag, and she quickly calmed down and fell back asleep. She had to give the young man credit. He looked professional, like he might actually know what he was doing.

'She'll live,' he confirmed as he began to put his things back into his little black bag. 'She has some bruised ribs but nothing's broken as far as I can tell. She might have some fractures to her face, but she will recover, however painfully. Face and head injuries usually look worse than they are,' he said as to provide Malia with some comfort. 'Give her this.' The doctor placed a small vial on the bedside table. 'Only a few drops for the pain as needed.'

'Will she be able to travel by Sunday?' Malia asked in a rush, just as Brandt was ushering him out.

'If she is desperate enough, yes,' the doctor said, again looking sadly at Cora's sleeping form.

'How much for your services?'

'No payment needed. Consider this part of her passenger care she would receive on the ship. I'll be back to check on her as often as I can.' The doctor, now that he was finished, had turned a pale shade of ash.

'Thank you,' she muttered as he and Brandt left.

After they were gone, Malia continued her vigil at her friend's side. She hadn't noticed how quickly time had passed until Brandt had returned; the sun was already high in the afternoon sky.

'What did you mean by Cora traveling? She can't leave,' he said like Malia had suggested Cora joined a band of pirates.

'All you need to know, Brandt,' she said as patiently as possible while standing to face him, 'is that arrangements have been made for Cora to leave the island. I will not have her stay here where she can be used against me and tortured for a sick man's pleasure.'

Just then, the front hall door slammed against the resistant marble wall. Since Haych now owned the house, knocking or pretending to have the slightest sense of decorum was ignored.

Knowing it was him, Malia bolted towards the door, her claws out and ready to scratch out the old man's eyes. Brandt grabbed her arm, stopping her before she reached the door.

'Let go of me, Brandt,' she demanded, struggling against him. He was much harder to bypass when he was sober.

'No, Malia. Don't you realize that this is what he wants? He wants you to fight, to be outraged. If you go down there and confront him, he will only make things worse for you. Do you want to end up like Cora?' Brandt warned.

'I don't care,' she said irrationally. Guilt no longer plagued Malia, it was an all-consuming rage. 'What am I supposed to do instead? Roll over and take it?' Brandt's eye's lowered in shame.

That was exactly what he was doing. She pushed herself away from him. 'Well I can't, I won't. He wants to break me; I will die first. He thinks he can beat and kill without consequence, well he is wrong! I will die before I'm intimidated by him. I would rather die than submit.' The thought almost made her feel a kind of peace, to die determined to be herself with no apologies. Unbroken and alive, standing up to a monster was one of the best causes to die for that she could think of. Besides, if she died, Rogan would call her up one day. She didn't have that nagging doubt of what would happen after she died, what laid beyond, as so many others. She knew there was something else, and that gave her more peace in her resolution to fight until the end. If she died, or when she died, Rogan would call her forward, wait for her, and maybe his soul could go with her in the end?

'What about Cora? Think of her.'

'I am,' she argued. 'Cora will be on that ship, and she will leave. After that, he will have nothing left to use against me.'

'What about me?' Brandt asked.

'Do you think Haych will stop his reign of terror if I act subdued? No. He will know it's an act and will still do what he wants. He wants to fight, and right now so do I.'

Twisting away from Brandt's attempted hold, just like Rogan had shown her, she ran from the room. Haych was waiting at the bottom, his bushy eyebrows raised and bruised hands settled at his waist. Hands that were bruised by hurting her friend.

'Miss Malia,' he called cordially. Malia slowed and began to take slower, more calculated steps. 'How was your night enjoying the festival? Worth it, I hope.'

'What are you doing here?' she asked, staying on the high steps.

'Seeing as I now own this house and all its contents, I can come, go, and do as I please.'

'Does that include the beating of innocent women?' she

asked, her voice as strong as the grip she held on the railing. It began to shake under her grip. Not with fear but with rage.

'Ahh, so you received my little message. Good.' He said it so nonchalantly, like a list of chores had been left on a pillow instead of a comatose friend. He turned and started to walk away, as though all matters were closed and taken care of.

'No, I didn't,' she said, making her way down the last remaining steps. Haych stopped, his back still facing her. 'What was the message?' Haych swiveled slowly. 'That you are one sick bastard? I already knew that. That you are willing to go to monsterous lengths to get your way and prove your point? Fine. That's noted.' Haych was facing her now, the large veins in his neck and forehead pulsing. 'Or was your message lost by the men that followed me last night and whom Rogan beat to bloody pulps? What were you trying to say there? That you are as obvious as you are stupid.'

Even though she had expected it, it was still a surprise when Haych grabbed her shoulders and slammed them against the wall near the dining room door. Rogan's teaching from the night before came back to her, but she waited. She didn't want to enlighten Haych of her newfound knowledge of self-defense until the most opportune moment.

'What do you know about him?' Haych asked through gritted yellow teeth. She gave a tight grin. Two could play at that game. She had something he wanted.

'Whatever I know, I won't be telling you,' she answered patiently, enjoying the power she held.

Haych brought up his right hand and slapped her face, just enough to sting.

Malia gritted her teeth and balled up a fist. Every attack from him made her resolve all the more stronger. Malia forced herself to wait.

'Go ahead and hit me again!' she challenged. 'Beat me until

I'm black and blue, dead even! But you will not touch my friend again! You will not break me!'

'How do you plan on stopping me?' Haych laughed.

'I wouldn't tell you that,' she bluffed, 'I thought you knew the rules of the game, Haych.' Haych smirked.

'But I will give you one clue.' A brilliant idea had begun to form in Malia's brain. 'You want to be the Captain of Souls?' she asked. The smirk vanished from his face, lustful greed replacing it. 'Then you get on Captain Rogan's ship and ask him your questions yourself,' she challenged, hoping that he would take the bait. If Haych got on Rogan's ship somehow, Rogan could pulverize him and be completely justified. Or better yet, maybe the Goddess of Death would handle it.

Malia thought her shoulders might start to form indents in the wall behind her from the force of Haych's grasp. However, something she said clicked, and Haych seemed to relax and his eyes briefly wandered. Maybe she didn't have to escape the island, maybe all she needed to do was get Haych off of it and onto Rogan's ship. If she could get Haych on the ship, her problems would be solved. It probably wouldn't even be that hard. Haych looked greedy enough to do anything. Malia decided to tell Rogan about her plan that night.

'Why would you want me on the death ship?' he asked suspiciously, then brought her shoulders forward to slam them against the wall, again.

'What sort of trick is this?' he seethed, spit flying onto her face and the wall beside her. He gripped her throat and began to squeeze.

Malia fought down the panic Rogan warned her about when Brandt's frame came flying down the stairs.

'Malia!' he yelled, distracting Haych.

Taking advantage of Brandt's distraction, Malia threw up her knee, nailing the older man in the groin. Haych's eyes grew wide with shock and pain as his hands dropped from her skin.

His body crumpled to the floor. Just like what Rogan said would happen, completely unexpected and totally worth the slap she received earlier. He wasn't so tough when he didn't have half a dozen bodyguards protecting him.

Brandt took Haych by the shoulders and dragged him with his good arm to the door. He didn't utter a word as he opened the front door and handed the nearly-crying Haych over to the men standing outside.

Without another look, Brandt slammed the doors shut and locked them.

'You go upstairs, Malia, and look after Cora. I'll stand guard. He'll be back, eventually. You better think of a plan. This is legally his house, so he isn't going to stay out for long,' Brandt said.

Upstairs, Cora slept peacefully, thanks to the doctor's medicine. Her condition was unchanged throughout the day. She moaned a lot and, whenever she did, Malia would administer more of the medicine the young doctor had left.

Brandt was like a ghost wandering the house. He hadn't come back to the bedroom or spoken a word since throwing Haych out of the house, but just paced in and out of the barren rooms. If he had been this way the night before, Malia would have thought that he was working on some sort of apology to Haych, but something about his restlessness said that it was something different. Malia could hear the remains of the furniture being moved around and drapes being ripped. She was too concerned with Cora's state of health to worry about whatever plan Brandt thought would work to keep Haych out.

Malia drifted in and out of sleep on the settee beside Cora. Haych hadn't come back, and he hadn't even tried, as far as she knew, to regain access to where they hid. But, Malia saw that his men were patrolling the outside of the house. If they left, Haych would know.

She wasn't sure how the plan to have Haych climb aboard

the *Calypso's Voyage* would go over with its current Captain. She hadn't revealed who Rogan really was, she only encouraged Haych to find out for himself, which technically, wasn't breaking any rules. She wasn't even sure she could talk to him tonight with the house under observation and Cora unable to move. But at least the possible plan was proving to be a distraction, and that would work for her.

As nightfall arrived, Duncan stopped by to check on his patient. He was satisfied that Cora hadn't gotten worse and that no new injuries had been discovered. And, thanks to Malia's efforts, some swelling had gone down.

Cora became more coherent after the doctor left. Malia was half-dozing on the settee, her feet almost hanging over the side.

'Malia,' Cora muttered. Jerking awake from her doze, she looked down and saw that one of Cora's eyes could slightly open.

'Cora, are you alright? What do you need?' she asked, alert. She dipped and rang out a rag soaked in tepid water.

Cora shook her head. 'Malia.' The injured woman was more aware than she had been all day.

'Shhh, Cora, you shouldn't speak.'

'Your palm,' she whispered. Looking down at her hand, Malia couldn't see anything wrong with it. Maybe Cora was hallucinating. She wasn't sure what the side effects of the medicine would be.

'My hand is fine.'

'Let me see it,' her hoarse voice ordered kindly.

'You're not going to read it, are you?' she asked, somewhat reluctant, somewhat teasing. Malia lowered her hand to her friend's face anyway.

Cora gave a small shrug of her shoulder, making her wince, but she persisted, 'I'm bored.'

'Fine.' Malia doubted her puffy eyes could make out the

little lines on her hand anyway, and she wasn't about to deny her friend anything.

Cora was silent for several minutes as she studied the palm in question. Malia indulged her friend's request, but really, she knew what the future held. She didn't need Cora to reinforce it. A salty breeze washed through the room.

'Interesting,' she said after a few minutes of contemplative silence.

'Yeah?' she asked, playing along, 'Does my hand say that Haych will suddenly die of a heart attack tomorrow?'

'No,' Cora said like a serious teacher not wanting to be interrupted. 'Your lifeline is short before it splinters into different paths. I've never seen that before. Like I said, interesting. But I think you will, eventually, be happy.' Malia could see her eyebrows draw together in deep concentration before she declared, 'Just maybe not in the way or timing you thought.'

'Well that's specific,' she said, teasing.

'*Seeing*, isn't really an exact science, you know? Too many variables and choices affect it. But the lines in your palm are easier, more set, it is just the understanding of it that might come later, or too late. Can I have some water?'

Malia reached for the cup on the side table. As she sat on the edge of the bed, cup in hand, she couldn't help but ask, 'My palm didn't happen to mention Rogan, did it?' Now that was the kind of revelation that would interest her.

Cora took a sip of water while Malia cupped her head.

'Thank you,' Cora said deeply, relaxing again. 'No,' she answered, sounding exhausted. 'I still feel your fate is tied in with his, but maybe just not in the way I thought before. The splintering cuts through your love line suggest a shifting of some sort. I'm not sure what it means, yet.'

Malia looked down at her hand, it looked the same as it always had.

'It's not all written on your hand,' Cora chuckled, causing

her to finish in a grimace. 'I told you I know things other than just palms,' Cora said, closing her eyes, the conversation over-taxing her. 'And I know death follows Rogan.'

'That's enough talk for now. It's time for you to rest,' Malia insisted, ignoring the flesh bumps that appeared on her arms despite the heat of the day.

Cora sighed again, already falling back to sleep. The length and coherency of the conversation gave Malia hope that maybe her friend would be better by Sunday and able to get off this wretched island.

The room had grown dark, twilight having long passed. The curtains leading to the open terrace rustled. She squinted past the lace and saw Rogan standing outside.

Chapter Twenty-Three

Rogan

Most of the island's inhabitants were standing on the wood planks of the harbor docks to pay tribute to the dead. Little sailboats bobbed in the water, carrying a trinket back to their rightful owners. A token to help the souls remember their loved ones during their voyage. Malia wasn't there. Haych was. He spotted the old man's beady eyes scanning the crowd. But Malia was nowhere to be seen. Rogan went over the whole island's sandy beaches and couldn't spot her anywhere. She had said she would meet him where the beach met the harbor.

What happened? Where is she?

As he turned to leave, he spotted Haych staring at him.

The ceremony had just started. The only sounds were the crashing waves and the gentle sniffles of mourners as boats were released into the water. Rogan stayed near the line of trees at the edge of the crowd while Haych discreetly made his way toward him until he stood still beside him. Silent, with his hands casually behind his back. Waiting.

The sight of the old man, knowing that he had hurt Malia, sent him into a rage. He felt his hands grow hot, like blood boiled within them, but he was restrained by something beyond his control. Angelos. Like someone tying his hands together, reminding him that he was just a visitor to the living. He was only allowed so deeply into Malia's life because it entertained the Goddess. The Captain couldn't do a thing unless Haych acted first.

As Haych settled himself beside Rogan, it felt like the tying had moved from just his hands to a cord wrapped around his body, keeping him from choking the life out of the evil man right there on the beach. The most Rogan could do was twist his waist back and forth, his arms folded over his chest.

Rogan did the best he could to calm down and look bored as he watched the ceremony. He leaned against a palm tree, hoping he looked casual and not like a half-fallen statue. Haych rocked on the balls of his feet, expectancy on his face.

'I know who you are,' Haych finally said. His eyes stayed on the crowd.

'Really?' Rogan said, unconcerned. He was bluffing. If the man knew his real identity, Rogan would be able to move and take his life to protect his identity. Let him make a move. Rogan realized that he was itching for an excuse, anything, to completely pulverize this man. Or better yet, let Angelos have a go at him. The thought of what the Goddess could do to a man like him, had him fighting a grin. Let Angelos restrain him now, so long as he got to watch her wrath later.

'Is there something funny, Captain?' Haych asked in a clipped tone. He looked over to Rogan briefly. Although the islanders pretended to pay attention to the ceremony, way too many shoulders were slightly turned in their direction, their backs straight, listening intently for the latest gossip to spread.

'Indeed,' Rogan agreed, turning to face him fully, his feet working. He was calm enough now that the restraint had lifted. He felt his muscles relax at the release. He exhaled. 'So, you know who I am. And?'

Haych looked at the younger man. His eyes were squinted and calculating, his mouth grim and determined. He was a bull waiting to charge.

'And you should know that a man like me wouldn't let that kind of knowledge pass without using it to his advantage,' Haych idly threatened.

'Right,' Rogan said unfazed. If the man wanted the cursed position of Captain, he could have it. Unfortunately, it wasn't his to give away. 'Well, you just keep on plotting along; in the meantime, I have an important matter to attend to.' Rogan slapped him on the shoulder in the best condescending, good-natured way he could muster and turned to leave.

'Would that important matter involve my fiancée?' Haych asked, bringing his hands from behind his back for the first time to examine his nails. Through the dimming light, Rogan saw that his knuckles and hands were covered in fresh bruises. The kind you get after spending hours punching a piece of meat without gloves. Or someone's ribs.

Malia wasn't on the beach, and Haych was making sure Rogan got a good look at his hands. Rogan faced him, without commenting. He had to stay calm. He had known men like Haych forever. Cowards that liked to play games. Malia was probably fine, Rogan convinced himself. Haych just wanted Rogan to act out. Countless years of immortal patience kept Rogan still. He waited for Haych to finish his threat.

'Like I said before, Captain Rogan.' Haych looked up from his purple and red knuckles to meet Rogan's steely blue gaze. 'I am the kind of man that uses knowledge to his advantage. And I have no problem taking advantage of certain ... liberties to gain that knowledge, if you understand my meaning, to get what I want. And I always get what I want.' He looked up at the Captain since Rogan nearly towered over Haych's shorter stocky frame.

'Liberties?' Rogan asked. As reluctant as Rogan was to give into Haych's pettiness, his wording had caught his interest. Whatever had happened, he knew that the bruises on his hands were related to Malia somehow, otherwise he probably wouldn't still be talking to him on the beach. Sir Haych thought he had leverage to threaten Rogan with, which piqued Rogan's interest, despite himself. The cords that bound him to amity began to strangle tighter again, in an effort to keep him restrained.

Haych seemed to either ignore or not notice the Captain's discomfort as he struggled with the power that held him captive to the details of his curse.

'Oh certainly. A self-made man in my position doesn't have to play by a humble man's rules. Not anymore. If I want something, I take it. That is the only way to play the game of this world.'

'So, you play by your own rules?' Rogan asked, loving where this conversation was about to go. Haych thought the Captain of Souls was all-powerful. He didn't know the restrictions, and the old man wanted to play. Rogan could *play*. He decided since he couldn't beat this man to a bloody stump, he would do the next best thing to scare him— bluff. Angelos didn't have any clear rules about scaring mortals. They were only ever implied. It was a gray area, and Rogan liked this gray area.

'Certainly. Particular morals and shall we say – human codes, do not always apply to someone of power.'

'You are someone of great power?' Rogan asked, laughing outright.

Haych's voice lost its light tone and became angry, 'I've worked too long and too hard to let opportunities pass me by. On this island, I rule.'

The pompous claim made Rogan laugh harder, earning

dirty looks and stares from the hushed people on the docks. Here was a man that had the one thing Rogan wanted, and Rogan, himself, was the one person this insane man wanted out of the way. He laughed quietly at first, but it quickly grew loud and boisterous. Haych stood beside him trying to hide his annoyance at Rogan's attitude while still trying to look threatening.

'Oh, you mortals.' Rogan sighed cheerfully. 'You really think you are something special, don't you?' Rogan kept chuckling as Haych's vein forehead began to pulse.

'My apologies. You want me to take you seriously? Go ahead,' Rogan said, gaining control of himself.

'You know, you are just one more person in a long line of people that haven't taken me seriously. Malia's father didn't. I guarantee you, if he were still alive, he would have regretted it. Miss Malia didn't take me seriously either. But after last night,' he paused to look down at his swollen purple hands, 'I think she will. Malia won't be so disobedient to my wishes again. She might be headstrong, but I don't think she is stupid. After all, do you see her here?'

Without warning, all Rogan's pent up anger and frustration burst, and the invisible bands held him back. The scent of magic was strong and biting, and only went unnoticed because of their proximity to the sea.

'You like to play by your own rules to keep people on their knees?'

Concentrating on Malia's face and how he was wasting time with the vermin in front of him rather than being with her helped to bring him back to the present. She was somewhere, possibly hurt because of the swine in front of him, and he needed to find her.

He took another step back, with something dripping down the middle of his back. Sweat? 'You better stick with your island, old man. The rest of the world is too dangerous for someone as small as you.' Rogan warned.

He didn't wait for Haych to respond before turning and walking away, disappearing after he was in the trees.

There were two dim lights in the windows of Malia's house. One was downstairs, and the other came from her open terrace windows. Rogan spotted guards making a lazy patrol around the house.

Steeling himself, he peered inside through the lace curtains.

Malia sat, unharmed. She hadn't noticed he was there yet as she sat by someone on the bed. No new bruises marked her skin that he could see. She did, however, have dark circles and heavy bags under her eyes, making her look years older and haggard. Her cheekbones, which last night had been round and smile-ready, were gaunt and shallow, like maybe she hadn't eaten that day.

Her hair was even more unruly than usual like each strand was fighting for space with the one next to it. He couldn't see who was in her bed, because of its placement against the same wall. For a panicked second, Rogan feared it might be a man, but quickly banished such a stupid jealous thought. But the nagging had started. She was going to have to share another man's bed someday and if she didn't get off the island it might very well be Haych's. He swallowed down a bitter taste covering his tongue and concentrated on Malia in the moment. He couldn't think clearly when his gut got all twisted.

She sat there in the same red dress that she had worn the night before, only now it was wrinkled. Rogan moved into the glowing lamplight.

She instantly noticed his shadow. Recognizing him, she ran into his arms, sagging against him. Rogan held her up as her knees gave out, no longer able to hold herself up. Wrapping his arms around her too-slender body, he squeezed her close, supporting her. He didn't even notice how far up the terrace was.

'I didn't know if I would see you tonight,' she said, her voice muffled into his shoulder.

Rogan squeezed her tighter now that he knew she was safe and in his arms. He thought back to only an hour ago. The conversation he had with Haych on the beach made Rogan never want to let her go.

'When I ran into Haych instead of you at the harbor I came as soon as I could.' He put her back on her feet, but Rogan's hands refused to let go of her waist completely.

'What did Haych have to say?'

Rogan's eyes darkened at the memory.

'It doesn't matter,' he said, not wanting to spend any more mental energy or time on Haych. 'Are you alright?'

'I'm fine. I couldn't leave Cora,' Malia said, her voice cracking as she pulled back with a look of guilt into the bedroom.

'What's wrong with her?' he asked soothingly. 'What did he do?'

Tears brimmed on the edges of her dark brown eyes. She became too emotional to speak. Whatever was wrong with Cora had to be serious. From what he knew of Malia, emotion usually made her louder, stronger, and more defiant or enthralled in whatever she was feeling. Cora was also her own loud force of determination, which made the silence of the bedroom ominous to the point that Rogan felt the hair on his arms stand on end.

'What's going on?' he asked as she backed away, further wrapping her arms around herself, guilt drowning her eyes in tears.

'Go see,' she choked out, looking inside the room as tears wetted her face.

Taking several cautious steps into the room, gently moving

the white lace curtains, he saw through the lamplight what she meant.

Sturdy little Cora was almost impossible to recognize. Her eyes were puffy, dry blood still crusted the drier part of her lips.

'Haych did that?'

'Yes,' Malia choked out, 'While we were together last night. He said it was a message. A message that I received loud and clear.'

'He did this just to intimidate you?' If he did this to Cora without a blink, what would he do to Malia?

Rogan felt sick, like the first time he was at sea, and stumbled his way outside for some fresh, salty air. For the first time, he noticed how high up the terrace was and stayed close to the house wall as his palms itched. Whether from fear of heights or the impulse to punch something, he wasn't sure.

'She is leaving on Sunday morning,' Malia explained. 'It's been arranged. Haych can't do this to her again.'

'And what about you?'

He looked away to the lighthouse in the not-too-far distance, frustrated and discouraged. They had to figure something out.

'I have an idea,' Malia said slowly, like she had given whatever plan she had a lot of thought.

Gesturing for her to go on, she began to pace the small area of the terrace.

'I'm not sure how this could work, or if you are even willing, but. . .' she hesitated.

'What is it?' he asked, trying to be patient. He was willing to do whatever she asked.

'We, somehow, get Haych on your ship,' she rushed out and it was like the world around them went still. The trees stopped brushing the wind, the distant waves hushed like the island had gasped in surprise at her plan.

'I can't allow him on the ship, and you cannot tell him who I really am,' Rogan said, wondering where she was heading with this.

'I would never tell him who you really are. And I know you can't "let" him, but what if he got on? Wouldn't you be in your full right as Captain of Souls to do what was needed in order to protect your ship and its cargo?'

He stood still, contemplating, when he noticed the man named Ku turned the corner on the lawn. Rogan put a finger to his lips to silence Malia until Ku left their side of the house.

'Think about it,' she rushed on in a whisper. 'He knows where your ship is. Neither of us have actually told him who you really are. You don't have to let him on, just don't stop him. You said the Goddess requires payment for any mortal that gets on the ship, right?'

'Theoretically. As far as I know it's never been done before, it's just what she has said as a warning.'

'Well, if for some reason you can't take care of him; let the Goddess take her price. Either way, he gets more than he bargained for.'

He nodded, already devising how this could work.

He could tell she was trying to hide a smile at the brilliance of her plan. It really was obvious. Don't stop an evil man from getting onto the ship; take care of him, which is within his full right as Captain. Or, better yet, have the Goddess take care of him. And he'll see Malia alive in another year. And if he never did see her again and didn't call her soul from the grave, he would know that she had escaped the island and might have actually made a life for herself somewhere. Maybe even a happy one. A life she deserved.

Chapter Twenty-Four

Malia

Half an hour after Rogan appeared on the terrace, he was gone, their plan firmly set in motion.

Since they hadn't met up at the harbor as planned, Malia was sure Haych would show up sometime soon. So she waited for him, ready to lure him onto the soul ship, where Rogan would be waiting, poised and ready to attack.

Cora hadn't woken up since before Rogan showed up. Since she was resting comfortably and probably asleep for the night, Malia slipped out and went downstairs to wait for Haych.

The house was dark, the village quiet as they observed the last night to mourn their loved ones. The island was a cemetery.

Brandt had barricaded the front doors sometime during the day to keep Haych out. She began removing the chairs and junk to free up the entryway.

The study door opened wide.

'What are you doing?' came Brandt's shocked voice.

'Don't worry. Rogan and I have a plan. Besides, we can't stay holed up here forever, Brandt,' she said as she lifted and moved a small chair from the pile. Brandt's gesture of brotherly protection warmed her. He had shown some resemblance of a backbone that morning by dragging Haych out and attempting to keep them safe.

Malia stopped her work. 'I have a proposal for Haych, and when he shows back up tonight, which I'm sure he will, I have to be able to let him in. And I don't want him coming in the back way and trying to sneak up on me.'

Brandt took hurried steps, stopping beside her. 'Don't do any deals with him. Trust me, I know the man and how his bargains work,' Brandt warned.

'This is different,' she said, looking at her brother in the weak lamp light. His features were shrouded in shadows, but his earnest anxiety leaked through his voice.

'How?' he demanded.

'I can't tell you,' she said simply, resuming her work. She didn't want Brandt involved in the plan if it could be avoided.

'You can't tell me your plan?' he asked suspiciously, like maybe she was the one preparing to sell him off instead.

Malia sighed, trying to calm her annoyance. 'Look, Brandt, Haych is easy to understand. He is greedy and power-hungry. Rogan and I know some things he desperately wants. I hint at some things that he wants to know in exchange for him leaving us alone and forgiving your debts,' she explained as evasively as possible.

'Just like that?' Brandt asked in disbelief as if he was talking to a delusional person. 'You think Haych will give up everything he has taken, including you, for something your sea captain just made up?'

'Not just something. A ship. A special ship.'

'The man owns nearly a dozen as it is. What makes this one so special?'

Through gritted teeth, she gave a carefully worded answer. 'Does it matter what's so special about this ship, or how I know about it? Just know that there is something Haych wants. I know what it is, and I'm going to use that knowledge to my utmost advantage. He wants this ship desperately. Desperate people can do all kinds of foolish things,' she said the last bit hoping it would be simple for Brandt to understand. She knew the feeling of true desperation and so did he. She had moved another chair out of the way when Brandt decided to help. Another gesture.

It only took another few moments before the doorway was clear.

As they stood there, side by side, staring at the scratched closed door, Brandt sighed and said, 'I hope you know what you're doing.'

Malia remained silent, standing there, waiting, like Haych would show up the instant the doors were free.

After a minute, when nothing happened, she said, 'Maybe you should go and sit with Cora while I'm down here. Just to make sure she doesn't wake up or need anything. I don't want her to be alone.' This much was true, but she also didn't want Brandt around for the conversation she needed to have with Haych.

Brandt hesitated, studying his sister, but he didn't say a word as he turned, lit a candle, and trudged his way up the stairs.

Since she had no clue as to when Haych would arrive, she went to her father's former study. The room was surprisingly clean. Brandt must have swept out all the broken glass. A large haphazard pile of papers were now in the fireplace and no longer strewn all over the floor. The shelves that used to hold the books, ledgers, and keepsakes of their father were gone. Malia's quiet footsteps echoed back to her from the now-bare walls and ceiling. The study once warm and inviting was now like a mausoleum, like the rest of the house. Cold and full of dead memories. The only thing remaining of her father was his chair and large wooden desk he had ordered from Starzea when she was little.

Malia sat on the mutilated cushion of the once overstuffed chair, afraid that any movement or weight on it would send herself and the remains of the chair tumbling. Once the chair was sure to hold her, she relaxed and waited. The dark wood of the desk told the story of her childhood in that room. It had so many chips and nicks along the corners. If she bent to look underneath, she knew she would see where Brandt had carved hers and his names into the wood. She couldn't bear to look at the remnants of the happy memory now. Instead, she sat, and waited.

Sitting there, with light coming from the only oil lamp they had left, Malia replayed hers and Rogan's plan over and over again until her head spun.

Brandt's words had made her nervous. What if it didn't work? What if somehow Haych did find out she was trying to trick him, what then? What if Haych couldn't get on Rogan's ship by sunrise before the ship disappeared? What if Angelos prevented their plan?

The plan had to work; Rogan wouldn't let her down. He wouldn't stop Haych from boarding, so he could do what was needed and destroy Eldon Haych for good, setting her and the islanders free. Was it murder if someone set up another's actions in order for them to die? Did the fact that she considered her actions self-defense matter? Would this plan keep her from going to Paradise in the end?

Malia jerked in her chair, having dozed off in her fretting. To keep herself awake, she began biting her nails, listening to the silence of the house. It was all-encompassing, like a tomb. Barely anything left in it that had once made the house a home. The silence set her on edge like a person holding their breath before being plunged into water. She opened some windows, letting the cooler night air in the stuffy house. The sound of close jungle frogs croaking and the palm tree branches swaying helped to fill the dead silence of the house. The familiar sounds of her home soothed her nerves.

She went to flip hair from her face and was reminded of how stiff and sore she was. Stretching her neck and sore muscles did nothing to lighten the weight she felt. The bruising, sleeplessness, and stress of the last few days were catching up with her body, even as she chose to ignore it. The tension and pain were finding ways to sneak into her notice in the quiet moments. The bruises across her shoulders and on her neck were sore and sensitive, but it was the cuts along her foot from the broken glass that hurt the most. Dancing in the streets last night probably hadn't helped either, but she refused to limp. Refused to show weakness when Haych arrived.

Her thoughts were going around in circles. If the plan did work and Rogan sailed away Sunday morning with his souls, and she woke up a free woman, would she see him again? Now that the seed of adventure and exploration was planted in her mind would Malia even want to stay, if it were possible? Without Haych there to ruin her life, would the island still feel like a prison, or would it feel like home again? Would there be a way to make a life for herself on the island? She realized then that she didn't want to; she wanted to leave. A headache was starting to form behind her eyes. Malia absentmindedly rubbed circles on her temples in an effort to ease the building anxiety.

The one thing that made her hesitate was if she left, there would be no more Rogan, perhaps ever. The thought made Malia's chest constrict like someone was crouching over her, crushing her airwaves so she couldn't breathe. She had been so focused on survival and escape that she hadn't given much thought to what would happen after. But if their plan did work and Malia was free, could she accept never seeing Rogan again? Could she come back to the island every year to see him? A lot could happen in one year. It was plenty of time for her life to take on many changes, not to mention Rogan's own fate.

Maybe he could earn back his soul and live? Live with her?

A swoosh of air suddenly sent the stack of papers in the corner dancing in Malia's face.

The front doors rattled against the walls as if they had been opened with a battering ram. Malia jumped, nearly falling out of her chair.

Haych had arrived.

She could see from the doorway leading into the entryway that even in the dim light from the moon behind him and the lamp, he was frazzled. His silver hair was wind-blown and tossed, his suit was dirty, and he was completely alone.

'Sir Haych,' she addressed him formally like he hadn't bruised her back and threatened her life hours ago. She stayed seated.

'Where is he?' Haych bellowed as he stumbled into the study and leaned against the large desk. Was he drunk? He didn't smell like alcohol, just cigars and sand.

'Who? Brandt?' She couldn't be sure who he meant.

Haych whirled. 'No, you idiot, that Captain of yours.'

'I can only assume you mean Captain Rogan.' Haych came to stand in front of her, the desk now between them. Malia stayed where she was, her fingers interlaced with one another, resting on top of the warm wood, and looked like she possessed all the patience that a business transaction would take.

'Yes, yes, of course,' he said impatiently, waving his hand before putting both on top of the desk and leaned forward. 'You're his slut, aren't you? Surely you know where he is.'

Inwardly cringing at the rudeness, she ignored the temptation to rise to his bait. His insult presented the perfect opportunity to set up their plan.

'I don't know where he is,' she said, anger rising as she stood. His own hands slammed on top of the desk. The anger wasn't hard to let out, he didn't need to know that Rogan wasn't the actual source - he was. Haych just had to believe that Rogan was.

Haych stared at her, disbelief evident on his bitter face. He stood there waiting for a further explanation. 'And I'm not his slut anymore, either.' She could feel the fake tears coming and hoped they looked real enough for Haych in the dim light.

Haych cocked his head curiously like a bird that found an interesting worm at its feet.

'I was a fool,' Malia muttered through clenched teeth, 'Thinking that he loved me and would take me with him. But he doesn't. He doesn't care about anything. Especially not about me, and now he's got what he wanted,' she swallowed, hoping she looked embarrassed and ashamed as she hunched her shoulders and looked down at her hands. 'He is just going to take his ship and sail away.'

Haych turned away and began to pace.

'I hate him. I'd love to see him rot,' she declared. Rogan and Malia had decided that weeping tears wasn't the best plan to get Haych to fall into their trap, but anger and shared revenge would work better.

He stopped pacing and turned to face her. His face had suddenly gone sympathetic, almost fatherly. Even indebtedness, a business deal would be the perfect trap. They were right.

'My dear,' he came around the desk and put his arm around her shoulders as if to give her wise comforting advice, but he was stiff and awkward. She doubted he knew how to touch someone without being aggressive. His false niceness put her on edge, like someone trusting a poisonous snake not to bite them just because it let them get close. The tight lines around his eyes revealed how straining it was for him to act so far out of character. 'Maybe we can help each other?'

She looked up at him distrusting, exactly how he would expect her to act.

'Really? she asked.

If I ever get off this island, maybe I will go into acting.

'Why don't you sit down,' he said, gently guiding her to the chair she had just recently jumped out of, 'and tell me all you know about him.'

'Oh, I don't know,' she said, suspicion deep in her voice.

'I know we have had our recent disagreements,' Haych said with a wave of his hand, like throwing her up against a wall was simply a misunderstanding. 'But think of how he hurt you. How he betrayed you. Don't you deserve some revenge? I can help you with that, my dear.' Haych's teeth were gritted in impatience. It looked like he was about to give her hand a reassuring pat, but changed his mind and withdrew his hand.

'Well, alright. But I'm not a complete fool.' Haych looked like he believed otherwise, but he quickly recovered as he, again, moved to the far side of the desk, waiting for her to continue. 'Rogan warned me that if I told anyone about him, I could be in big danger. So, if you want to know more about him, I need some assurance first.' Malia sat in the chair, feeling powerful and in charge. It was amazing to have this horrid man eating out of the palm of her hand, and he didn't even realize it. It was a sort of high that only Rogan had been able to elicit in her before.

Haych opened his hands like it was his pleasure to negotiate terms for her protection.

'First,' she stated, 'a little agreement.'

Haych looked annoyed but waved his hand, gesturing for her to continue.

'If I tell you Rogan's secrets and you get what you want from the information I give you, then you have to leave me and my brother alone, forever. That means forgiving all debt and there is to be no marriage deal, do you accept?'

She sat, praying she appeared calm and businesslike. Malia restrained from fidgeting with her fingers, but the clinching in her stomach had her leaning forward slightly. Haych contemplated, stroking his grizzly chin.

'I will need a guarantee of my own. If you are lying to me, I refuse to come out of this deal empty handed.'

Malia swallowed down her terror at the gleam in his smile.

'What kind of guarantee? You already have or will have everything.'

'Not everything,' Haych said, his smile disappearing as he approached her with a predatory hunch to his shoulders. Malia felt herself being backed into a corner as he licked his lips and flexed his hands.

Nausea swam its way up from her stomach and into her throat as Haych leaned in and smelled her hair. Malia stayed perfectly rigid, her shoulders pressed against a corner of the wall. She tried to stay calm, but her breathing had turned erratic. Haych looked down at her heaving chest. A callused finger ran across her collar bone and started working its way down when Malia snatched his finger in her hand and twisted, grabbing his wrist with her other hand she brought his wrist up, forcing Haych to take a step away to ease the pressure on his upturned wrist. A huff of shock followed as Malia said through gritted teeth, 'Fine. If you don't get everything from the Captain that you desire, I will be yours, without a fight. I'll submit. But not,' she pulled his finger back further bringing his wrist higher. Malia smiled as Haych gave a wince of pain, 'a minute before. Deal?'

His brown eyes burned with hatred and a promise of what was to come should they fail. But, he nodded and she released his wrist.

'You are awfully accommodating. Why?' he rubbed his wrist as he studied her.

Malia thought fast. 'I'm hardly accommodating to this bargain. I'm just confident and vengeful. Which you will learn, sir, is a dangerous combination for me.'

There was a moment's pause where Malia was sure he wouldn't take the bait as he turned and paced. She kept her chin high as she held her breath.

'If I get what I want, then it's a deal, and if I don't, I get you to do what I want, when I want,' he agreed and stuck out his hand. They shook hands once, knowing he wouldn't keep his word, but if everything went according to plan it wouldn't matter. He had to believe the deal was real and that she believed him, that this was not a trick. If he didn't, any hope she still had would be gone forever.

'Well,' she started. She had practiced over and over just the right wording to trap him, but not herself. 'You already suspect who he really is,' she whispered the last part as if she was revealing the latest gossip to a close friend. Haych nodded impatiently. 'A pirate.' Haych looked at her confused. Clearly he wasn't expecting such a common confession. 'Only he would never tell me what his cargo was. Although, he would say unusual things like, his cargo is the stuff that people sell their souls for.'

As she spoke, the greed grew larger in Haych's dark eyes. She could practically see him salivating. 'He told me that it is his ship anchored off Cliff's Teeth. He put it there so no one could get to his ship. He was so dramatic about it too. Always bragging about how priceless his cargo was, and how he was the only person to man the ship. When I told him that was impossible, he boasted that his skills weren't like any other sailor I had ever met, but were goddess-blessed. Whatever that means? Cocky bastard.'

'Really?' Haych's eyes were dancing before he straightened and began to pace casually.

'Oh, yes. He says he moves the ship during the day, but at night he always takes it back to Cliff's Teeth.'

Malia waited a moment as Haych stood back up, pacing fast. He was falling into her trap perfectly. 'Can you get to it?'

Haych looked frustrated as he admitted, 'I have not tried yet. To brave the Teeth...I wanted undeniable evidence of what that ship held.'

'Well, that ship is definitely Rogan's. If you have any hope of boarding it, it would be at night when he is on the island.'

'So, I can't get on the ship in daylight because he moves it. The only way to gain access is at night, whilst he is away, correct?'

She nodded encouragingly. He had fallen into their trap so perfectly.

'So, do you think ... this Captain Rogan has already returned to his ship tonight?'

'I doubt it,' she scoffed, 'He said he wanted to enjoy the rest of the festival and stop wasting his time with me. So, I would assume he is out enjoying himself with someone new.' She pretended to wipe a tear. The gesture was lost on Haych as he looked out the window in the direction of the cliffs, plotting.

'Brilliant,' Haych muttered. 'And he just told you all this?' Haych still sounded unconvinced, but Malia expected it.

'We all have different powers of persuasion. Mine happens to be—perkier than others.'

Haych took in her implication by scanning her body. She was still wearing the too-tight red dress from the night before. Malia was going to have to scrub her skin raw for a week.

'However,' she said, hoping to correct his attention before he got too distracted, 'He did say he was leaving tomorrow night. So, tonight would be your last chance to try and board his ship without him knowing.'

That piece of information stopped Haych's pacing as he looked at her. She couldn't read him. Was he going to take the bait?

'It is only eleven, you have nearly six hours until sunrise. His ship is by Cliff's Teeth, just sitting there, with all his loot easy for the taking. Just like it always is.'

Haych's bushy eyebrows shot up, having just caught on to what she was saying. Without a word, he ran out the front door.

Chapter Twenty-Five

Rogan

He was going to meet Malia in the gazebo, just as soon as it was finished. Rogan found himself fighting a smile when he appeared on the deck of the ship. He was going to give the woman that he was in love with what she wanted most – her freedom. She was going to be happy and live a good life. If there was anyone that could understand the importance of such a gift, it was the Captain of Souls.

Looking around the ship in the dark, he waved his hand and lit the deck's lanterns – something he hadn't done since arriving almost a week ago. The deck glowed in yellow light and shadows, making the cliffs in the distance hard to see clearly.

Once the deck was lit, he went below to check on the cargo.

The spirits hadn't moved from their sitting positions, their stares still blank. Some would occasionally flinch as they watched in their minds something horrible they had witnessed or done in their life. They looked like what Rogan imagined opium addicts looked like. They wouldn't move much until the ship was on its way. Then, they slowly became more aware of themselves and where they were going. By the time they reached Paradise or Hell, they would be acting practically human. But for right now, they were irritated. He wasn't sure why. They never were before, but seeing their dull faces and glassy eyes had him missing Malia's vibrancy. He hadn't known he missed life and the living until he got a break from the dead.

Once Rogan saw that all the souls were there and accounted for, he flew up the stairs back on the deck, where he almost ran head-first into Angelos.

'Rogan, Pet,' she said sweetly. 'How are things this evening?' Her sail dress dipped dangerously low in both the front and back. He couldn't help comparing Angelos' body to Malia's, and found it lacking. Malia was all color and soft curves. Angelos was blank and bone. He looked away, not wanting to see any other woman dressed that way unless it was Malia.

He slowly moved around her, pretending that he was busy.

'Fine, Goddess,' he answered. If Malia convinced Haych to get on the ship, then he would be arriving soon and he wasn't sure if having the Goddess around was a good thing or a bad thing.

'Where are my souls?' she asked, a smile to her voice. She looked around the ship like she would find them playing a hiding game.

'Down below,' he said coolly and began to tie knots in some rope. 'Safe. Just like always, Goddess.'

She shrugged her shoulders as she leaned against the railing. 'I guess that is as good a place as any.' Her posture said it didn't really matter, but Rogan saw the sly look on her face that revealed she knew the souls were making him uncomfortable.

'You are awfully restless tonight. Is there a particular reason why you are onboard the ship?' She bounced up to sit on the railing, looking very comfortable on the hardwood. Her legs crossed under her sail-like gown.

'I'm the Captain of Souls, aren't I?' he asked with a charming smile, hoping this interrogation wouldn't go too far.

Angelos gave a smile back. He knew that she had always liked his wit. He guessed that was one of the reasons he got away with so much.

'Yes, but you haven't been on this ship at night all week. The night is young, nowhere near dawn yet, but here you are trying to look busy tying pointless knots.'

'I wanted to make sure I was back in time,' he answered, which had her smile widening. He didn't know what else to say, so he kept fiddling with the coarse rope in his hands.

'Where is your little sweetheart, Malia? Why aren't you enjoying nighttime pleasures with her? That is why you are still here, isn't it?' A tinge of jealousy tainted her voice.

He shrugged again. 'It was.'

'Was?'

Rogan nodded. 'Sure, Malia and I had our fun, but there's no point in leading the poor girl on anymore. I'm not big into tears and *emotions*. It is what it is.' He said all this without once looking at the Goddess. He knew, even in the dim light of the ship, that she would see the lie in his eyes.

Angelos' beautiful laugh trickled over to him where he was making himself busy with the mast rigging.

'Oh, Rogan, you do not fool me.' She got off her perch like a stalking jungle cat and made her way beside him. 'Even if you did what you just told me, it would still be a lie.' Her finger began to trace a line on his shoulder and arm. A gentle caress.

'Is that so?' Rogan asked, finally turning to look curiously into her burning gold eyes.

She nodded, her eyes big and eager. She knew something.

'How?' he challenged. He was never going to learn to keep his mouth shut and let things go.

The Goddess got right up in front of him then like she was floating on air, a hand found its way into his shirt while she wrapped her legs around Rogan's hips and whispered in his ear. 'Because you love her.'

He gave her a dubious look and ignored his racing pulse. As she wrapped herself around him, weighing nothing, it only reminded him of when Malia was wrapped around him. Her weight, her warmth, her *realness*. Angelos was empty. A phantom.

'Don't be ridiculous, Goddess. I don't know how to love, remember?' he said, playing it off as Angelos started tracing invisible patterns on his chest with her finger.

She laughed again, throwing her head back and exposing her shoulders and most of her chest, but her legs stayed firmly around Rogan's hips. Rogan felt a flush against his cheeks. She was sure to notice that.

'Whatever you say, Rogan, but we both know the truth.' She looked at him, holding his gaze. When she saw his blush and his averted gaze, all traces of humor were gone. 'And the truth is, it doesn't matter if you love her.' She gripped the back of Rogan's neck, forcing him to look at her. 'You are mine,' her legs tightened around Rogan's hips. Her hold on him could have been mistaken for intimacy if she wasn't causing Rogan to lose feeling below the waist. 'And I will keep you. She will lose you soon enough. I can have you for eternity.'

Rogan looked at her, trying as hard as he could to keep the emotion off his face, searching deep inside himself for his old indifferent mask.

Something behind Rogan caught the Goddess' attention, 'What is that?'

She released Rogan, her legs flowed to the deck. He turned toward the rocky cliff shore to see what he had hoped to see only a few minutes ago. A small rowboat had just come around the beach side of the island, heading in their direction. It was Haych. Malia had done it.

'A small fishing boat,' he commented, looking away, unaffected, but he felt a tremor of anxiety in his hands. After the discussion he just had with Angelos, Rogan would have preferred her gone by the time Haych reached the ship.

'Rogan,' Angelos' voice had gone icy. She already knew the answer to the question she was about to ask him. 'Who is in that boat?'

Rogan gave a little chuckle. 'How should I know?' He turned back to where the lone man was rowing vigorously toward the ship, fighting the water that wanted to push him back toward the cliffs.

'He doesn't look familiar to you?'

Rogan shrugged.

'That is Sir Eldon Haych, your bonnie lass' future husband,' she clarified.

He looked back over his shoulder, feigning surprise. 'Oh, so it is.'

Rogan had to give the older man credit, the way he was rowing would have put many younger men to shame, such was his eagerness to get to the ship.

'What do you think he is doing?' she asked, looking closer out at the dark waters.

'Fishing?' Rogan added, as though he found the old man entertaining. Only, Angelos didn't look the least bit amused.

They watched and waited until Haych was only fifty yards away from the ship. He kept hoping Angelos would leave, but she seemed to be waiting for Rogan to do his job. Only he didn't hide or redirect the boat. This was his one and only chance to help save Malia. He would deal with Angelos' wrath after the job was done. Based on their conversation in the square, he knew that she had no love for Haych, so maybe she would let Haych cross the threshold and obliterate him. Rogan decided that playing at nonchalance was best. He just stood with his arms resting on the railing, looking bored, as Haych got closer. He was getting close enough that Rogan heard his labored breathing.

'Stubborn, old goat,' Rogan conceded, but he wasn't about to completely stop the man's chances of getting on board. Since Angelos was there, and to make it look like Rogan put in an effort to stop him, he sent up a wall of invisibility like a curtain falling from the sky, but he didn't move the ship.

Rogan watched, with not entirely fake amusement, as Haych turned around suddenly and saw that the ship that he had been working so hard to get to had, without explanation, disappeared from sight. He whirled around confused like maybe he had been rowing in the wrong direction the whole time. From Rogan's position on the deck, he could almost see Haych's vein on his forehead bulge as he sputtered and began to yell obscenities. But, to the old man's credit, he picked back up the oars and rowed toward the ship.

'Rogan,' Angelos said in her terrifyingly calm voice. He turned, almost lazily, still playing the arrogant nonchalant card. 'Do I need to do your job? Haych is getting closer to the ship.'

Rogan clenched his jaw and balled up his fists. An abrupt wave of anger seized Rogan's muscles. Haych had to get on the ship. Angelos was ruining everything.

'Are you actually going to let that man, that mortal, board my ship?' she asked, fighting to keep a gritted smile on her face.

Rogan straightened from off the railing and lifted his chin.

'So what if he does? I'll just do what I've done before. I'll take his soul early and he'll be on his way to Hell.'

No point in completely denying it, but he wasn't ready to tell her the full truth either. Haych was close enough to the ship that Rogan could spit on him.

'I had some business to discuss with him. I wasn't going to *let* him on the ship, I simply just wasn't going to *stop* him if he found his way on board.'

'Business?' she asked, looking confused. Confused was better than furious. 'You do not have *business*' she said the word like it was foul, 'With mortals Rogan. You do not interfere with mortal lives. Remember?'

Her eyes were starting to brighten and the veins under her skin darkened.

Rogan felt something inside him snap like a rope pulled too tight. 'You've had no problem letting me interfere with Malia's life. And why is that? Because it amused you. But when I could do some good, do the world a favor, you stop me? What I could do to Haych would save Malia and her family. He deserves it! He deserves worse!'

'YOU ARE NOT THEIR JUDGE!' The Goddess' voice had gone deep and echoed off the cliff sides like thunder. She was always calm, even when she tortured. But this, this was terrifying. Her feet rose off the deck of the ship and wind swirled around them, flapping her dress against her legs. She flung her arm out and Haych flew from his dingy and skidded along the top of the water, like a stone skipping on top of a pond.

Angelos dumped him on the rocks.

When she turned back to Rogan, her hair began to float, like she was swimming in water, but her voice was calmer, like usual. 'Mortals must be allowed to make their choices. You have been allowed in Malia's life for this week because it will not change her fate. You, however, had already chosen what you did with your life. This is the consequence! Malia and Haych will have their consequences, rewards and penalties for themselves! The power of life and death is not up to you, slave.' Rogan's feet gave out from him as she flipped him over, upside down. 'You have forgotten your place.' Angelos raised Rogan in the air as she followed. Terror gripped him. He was so high. 'And your purpose is to serve me and perform your task. You were going to let an evil being such as him on this ship. Do you not comprehend the precious cargo you hold? You fool!'

His entire body felt like it was strapped to ropes that were being pulled in different directions by horses. He hung so high upside down, his ship began to look like a toy. His ears rang. There were black spots spreading in his vision. His lungs felt punched out, keeping him from shouting out. He was suffocating, without being given the release of unconsciousness from sheer panic. Horror choked him as she dropped him. He landed hard, hard enough to break every bone in his body if his bones were capable of breaking against the deck of the ship.

He felt the blood again leaking out of his ears, nose and mouth. He hadn't been lying against the rough wood of the deck long when his ears popped and he could breathe. He gasped for air again and again.

There was no other sound around them but Rogan's gasping coughs. No waves from the sea, no air in the sails. Everything was – still.

Angelos grasped his hair, twisting his face upward to look at her calming eyes. She whispered in his ear, 'No mortal steps on this ship without paying a price. He is an infection, a disease, a hole in the stern. I DO NOT want Haych's payment...not yet. .' Angelos released her grip and started to walk away to the starboard railing. Over her shoulder, she said, 'Time's up. You have until sunrise to leave with my souls.'

Like the wind, she had just driven the ship with, she whooshed into the air. Rogan looked up at the night sky and saw it was turning gray. Sunrise would be within the hour. The night was almost over, and it had only felt like minutes. That damned soul ship and its clashing perception of time had stolen the night from him. Malia would be waiting for him. And he would have to tell her that he had failed. Out of all the emotions he had felt that week, failure was the most unfamiliar, the harshest.

Rogan's feelings of frustrating failure boiled inside him, turning to hate. He hated the ship. He hated being a puppet. He hated that time passed like water through his fingers.

Rogan tore at the ship's sails. He cut the ropes. He threw empty barrels and rowing oars overboard only to have everything return undamaged and in its place. Nothing changed, except him. He cursed his existence as screams echoed out of his throat. As the last scream left him, a tear of frustration slid down his cheek. He didn't even know that a person could cry from anger and frustration.

The astonishment of that realization, as his hands shook and tears fell, gave him pause enough to think clearly. He only had a short amount of time left with Malia and he was wasting it. A part of him wondered, as he sat there on the deck of the spotless ship, if being with Malia had been worth the awakening of his emotions, of his humanity that he was just realizing he had lost and was regaining. He needed Malia if only to remind him that all the agony he went through and the agony to come was worth it. Even if the remainder of his time was going to be filled with heartbreak and disappointment.

Chapter Twenty-Six

Malia

Malia was wearing a hole into the floor across the small enclosed space of her terrace as she paced. Haych's guards patrolled below. It was almost time to meet Rogan at the gazebo.

She wished she knew what was happening. Had Haych gotten on Rogan's ship? Had Rogan really dealt with Haych? Could she dare to hope that the nightmare that was her potential future was over?

Brandt was sitting in a chair beside Cora's sleeping body. Cora hadn't moved or talked most of the night and neither had Brandt. Malia had spent most of her time watching the two men circling the house and knew that in about a minute there would be a thirty-second gap where her way would be clear to escape to the gazebo.

The second guard turned away. She had half a minute to clear the trees and get out of sight.

'Watch over Cora, I'll be right back,' she said, briefly sticking her head back into the room. Brandt gave a confused shrug, but didn't say anything before she climbed off the terrace and down the strong vines. The vines were how she had snuck out of the house the year before when she met Rogan for the first time.

The night was quiet. So quiet even the waves sounded muted. This wasn't a night for partying, but mourning for the families that had paid tribute to their lost loved ones. Tomorrow night would be the last big party, ending on the beach wishing the Captain of Souls goodbye. Then, the Festival of the Dead would be over. The ships and travelers would leave, taking Rogan and Cora with them. And, maybe, she hoped, herself.

She pushed such thoughts away as she made her way through the overgrown garden.

One step at a time, Malia reminded herself.

She needed to focus on the present. The night sky had begun to turn into violet morning. She could make out the forming rain clouds above her. Birds were starting to announce the morning with their song.

Breathless, Malia pushed the last lot of overgrown vines out of her path. The wet grass was slick on her bare feet as she found herself in the small clearing, the broken gazebo there looking mournful and forgotten. Or maybe it seemed that way because of the man standing beside it. Rogan stood outside the gazebo by the fountain. He looked like he was afraid to come closer, but she couldn't be certain due to the soft morning light.

'Rogan.' She had never felt as happy and relieved as she did at that moment. He was there. The morning dawn gave just enough light for her to see the blue of his eyes and the cut of his cheeks. She ran straight to him, her lips colliding with his as she wrapped her arms around his strong neck and shoulders, her hands grazing the ponytail at his nape. Rogan's arms lifted her up and held her tight. She felt her body relax against his, exhaling a long breath.

Her smile broke their kiss. A smile she reserved only for him and a giggle escaped. He was there; he had done it!

Rogan's hold didn't loosen, his tight arms squeezed and his fingers tightened against her ribs, reluctant to loosen their grip. He sighed into her neck, tickling her skin. Her lips found his again. He kissed her long and soft, but as their kiss grew longer, his lips began crushing hers. A desperation she hadn't felt from him before.

When they were both breathless, he finally placed Malia on her feet and took a step back, giving her the first really good look at his face. She had to blink and then blink again, hoping she was reading him wrong.

'What's wrong?' she asked with lips that felt plump and pleasantly swollen from their kiss. His jaw was gritted; his cheeks tight. His eyes were scarlet with bloodshot. He looked— inconsolable.

'Our plan didn't work, did it?' Malia asked, terrified of the answer she already knew was coming. Her heart sank into her stomach.

Rogan struggled to find words as he licked his lips, like his tongue was sewn to the roof of his mouth. The crease between his brows grew deeper.

'Rogan?' she asked gently, gripping his forearms tightly as her stomach knotted. 'What happened?'

He was silent for another torturous moment before his hoarse voice spoke quietly, almost in disbelief of the news he had to present to her.

'The Goddess arrived on the ship minutes after I did. When she saw Haych approaching the ship on his rowboat,' he paused and shook his head as if to clear it. 'The Goddess would not let Haych on the ship.' She felt the sting of tears threatening to spill over before she had even fully comprehended what Rogan meant. 'Haych never made it...and I'm leaving at sunrise.'

'Leaving?' she asked as her lungs gasped. Malia took a shaky step back. Haych was alive and angry. He would take it out on her, no doubt, very shortly. But even more horrifying and heartbreaking was that she had only minutes left with him. He was becoming easier to see in the growing light. She thought she would have at least one more night, one more free night to be with him. That had just been taken from her too.

She shook her head in denial. There had to be something else. There had to be.

'Alright, so that failed. What about this price the Goddess requires?' Rogan was shaking his head before she finished her question. 'What?' she asked, nearly yelling in frustration. 'Do you even know what it is? I'll pay whatever she wants. . .'

'Don't say that,' Rogan said, cutting her off. 'You have no idea the cost the Goddess will demand of you. Believe me, even in your most desperate situation it wouldn't be worth it.' He tried to grab her arm, but she flung it away from him.

Her chin quivered as she fought for composure. 'If I don't escape now,' she choked on the reality of it but swallowed hard, 'The next time I see you will be when you call my soul from the grave! So, I will be dead anyway.'

Rogan gave her a look that clearly emphasized how badly he didn't want to believe it. 'There are fates worse than death, Malia.'

'I know! Haych has had two wives and several mistresses, none of them lived over the age of twenty-five. I will be no different. In fact, I will probably die sooner because I won't let him break me first. Once you leave, it will either be me, or him,' she cried and shook her head, unable to finish her thought. Her breathing was sharp and fast. 'Without you, what would my life be anyway?'

Rogan gripped her face in his rough hands. Tired lines creased around his eyes and mouth, tired and helpless— mortal. She gripped his hands tighter as a lone raindrop fell and bounced off his wrist.

'You were a fighter before I got here, Malia. You will be a fighter after I leave.'

Rogan's statement stirred something in her. A fierce determination. Nodding, she decided she would fight, as she always had. And if fate had decided that she was going to die, well, she would take Eldon Haych down with her. If worse came to worse and Haych killed her, no way would she leave him standing to kill Brandt or anyone else. Dying by her own hand first had never been an option, and it still wasn't. Rogan was right, she was a fighter, and that meant fighting for her own life too.

'I'll see you in Paradise, then?' Malia didn't know what to say, but her face must have been filled with doubt.

'I will,' he vowed. 'I will earn my soul and I will meet you there! If we can't be together now in this time and place, we *will* be together later. I will make it there.' His eyes burned with his words that she so desperately wanted to believe. Even if in the end, it was an empty promise, it would give her something to hold onto.

'Promise?' she whispered.

He nodded, gritting his teeth so hard she thought his jaw would break. 'I promise.'

'What if I don't make it to Paradise?' she asked.

'Then, I'll follow you to Hell and you'll be in good company.'

He kissed her then, his lips still warm from earlier. The realization that this might be their last kiss forced Malia's heart to lurch into her throat and she pressed harder against him until a moan erupted from him and a gasp escaped her. No matter how tightly she held onto him, she couldn't go with him, neither could she hold him there, any more than she could stop the rising sun.

He pulled back with the sky growing brighter by the second. 'In another year, I'll be back. Stay alive until then and maybe I can work out something with the Goddess.' She realized then, just like he had promised to meet her in Paradise, she needed to promise to live, no matter how doubtful she was that she could keep it.

'Promise,' she said. They kissed again, and she wasn't sure that when the sun came up she'd be able to let him go. The seconds were going too fast.

When he pulled back slightly, he whispered, his forehead resting against hers, 'I love you.'

Those words. She hadn't heard those words for a long time. It was those three small words that burst the large dam wall she had built inside her. She had forgotten what it felt like to be told something so simple, yet powerful. To have her own feelings affirmed and echoed back to her was intoxicating. Even if she couldn't keep him, she would keep those feelings. Forever. No one, not even the Goddess of Death, could take them away. They were hers to keep. Rogan was hers to keep. She didn't care where they were or the distance between them.

'I love you too.'

'I'm so sorry,' he said, the words catching in his throat.

Rogan drew back like he was in pain and Malia realized the sun was up, casting his usual midnight hair into hews of warm brown. Without saying another word, he disappeared out of her arms and into nothing.

She looked around her, with morning birds chirping and the wet grass sticking to her feet, having never felt more alone in her life.

'No,' she whispered her denial to no one.

A sob escaped her throat, and then another, until she couldn't stand or speak. She lost track of time, not that it meant anything as she cried into the wet grass. She would have been content to stay where she was for eternity until she remembered Cora. Her friend was counting on her. She knew she had been gone from the house for too long and Haych was sure to be back in a rage. She couldn't let him take it out on Cora again.

She climbed to her knees, and once there she inhaled deeply, in and out, until she could stand steady on her feet and slowly walked back to her prison.

She heard Haych's growling yells from the outside court-yard. Straightening her shoulders, she steeled herself for the fight that was to come.

Chapter Twenty-Seven

SATURDAY

Rogan

R ogan landed in a crumpled heap on the dry, hard deck of his ship. His chest felt crushed and he wasn't sure if the pain came from Angelos, who was glaring at him from across the deck, or the fact that he had just left Malia, possibly forever. Rogan didn't try to get up. He just stayed where he was.

'Tsk, tsk,' Angelos clicked her tongue. 'Rogan, Rogan, you are late.'

'Does it matter?' he croaked out, rolling onto his back to look up at the morning gray sky. Clouds had come in. It would be raining all over the island and coast before long. A bird flew overhead, seeking shelter. He envied the creature.

Angelos ignored the question. 'You have been very defiant this week, Pet.'

'This is what you wanted, wasn't it? Something to shake me out of my apathy?'

'When I wanted you to learn about empathy and permitted you to take part in the Festival of the Dead, I had no idea you would become so extreme,' she said in a soft, curious voice. 'Most wouldn't be so disobedient of a god's orders.'

Rogan tried to sit up, but his chest felt too heavy. He had no muscle or will to lift himself. Maybe hearts didn't actually break or shatter. Maybe they grew too heavy to carry, to move, to care.

'So morose, Rogan, truly? Can you really care so much for a girl you've known less than a week?'

'What's the price?' he asked, desperate at the memory of Malia's inconsolable eyes when she realized he had failed. He sat up, his heavy chest lifting at the possibility that he might still be able to do something.

'I beg your pardon?' she asked, looking away from the rocky coast to meet his gaze, as though she hadn't been fully listening.

'What is the price for a mortal to get on the ship?' he asked carefully as she continued to stare down at him. She paused, her face going from shocked to pleased. 'You said once that I couldn't afford it, but the way I see it now, I have nothing to lose and Malia has everything to gain by me asking you. You know how I feel. You know the situation and what I could do for her if I pay. You didn't want Haych's payment. So, what would the Goddess of Death want? What's the price?'

The Goddess smiled wide and she placed a hand on her bony hip, strumming her fingers against it. She approached him, stopping within inches of his face. He could see no blemish or flaw as her eyes searched his.

'Are you sure? Would you pay anything to save Malia from her fate?'

'Anything,' he answered and meant it.

'The price is a soul, Rogan. A soul that would be mine for eternity.'

He sighed, 'Well,' he said, almost smiling, 'You already have that from me.'

'You don't understand, love.'

He waited for her to explain.

'I have your soul in a kind of limbo, shall we say. It is technically still yours. I borrowed it, giving you the chance to earn it back or throw it away. Allowing you to either end up in Paradise or Hell, depending on what you did with the time I gave you. But, if you *give* me your soul, the very thing that makes humans what they are, there will be no Paradise or Hell for you. Understand? If you give it to me freely, your eternity will be this ship, always this ship with the souls of those that will eventually move on somewhere else. You will have no Malia, no end, and no continuation. You will have an eternity of nothing but collecting souls and sailing them to their destination. Before this week, you wouldn't have cared, but can you say the same now?' She had begun to circle him. 'Now that you have spent time among the living, has that changed? You have felt things, experienced things. It has opened you up to the possibility of all that you missed while alive and all you could have later.' She finally stopped in front of him, his eyes meeting hers. 'You also made a promise to Malia that you would earn your soul and make it to Paradise. Are you willing to break it? Are you willing to stay on this piece of wood forever with me and blank-staring souls being your only companions?'

'If you buy Malia's passage,' she continued as Rogan contemplated what she said, 'so she doesn't have to pay with her own soul, yours will be forfeited.' She paused as he tried to imagine what this would mean for him and for Malia. 'I would keep you forever.'

He would have to break his promise of meeting Malia in Paradise. But it would give her a chance to live and be happy with someone else, someone worthy. She could spend Paradise with someone that deserved her. Rogan hoped that she would forgive him for not being there, if she remembered him at all by then. He hoped his sacrifice would give her something else, something better. He swallowed the painful bile that had risen in his throat as the sacrifice of not having her forever settled in his gut. Giving up Paradise with Malia for her to have it with someone else. Every jealous part of him yelled "No" before he silenced it. She deserved better than him, and he could give that chance to her.

'Can you see why I wouldn't allow you to let Eldon Haych on this ship? I do not want his vile presence near my souls. I want him judged and put where he belongs when the time comes. There are no second chances for mortals like him.'

Rogan looked down at the deck, the floor he would spend forever staring at.

'Do you really think this sweetheart of yours is worth it?' she asked, cynically.

'Done,' he said, looking her straight in the eyes. The Goddess' eyes widened with disbelief.

'Take it, it's yours.' he shrugged. Angelos stood there stunned and speechless. 'I can live with spending forever knowing that I was able to give Malia her freedom. I can give her a chance to live and love, even if it isn't with me. I couldn't stand forever if I allowed her to live in pain and misery only for her to end up in Paradise without me anyway. Because let's face it, Goddess,' he said, slowly rising to his feet, 'My soul isn't worth saving, but Malia's life is.'

'You do not want time to consider this? This isn't something you can take back, Rogan, or change once it's done. Once you sacrifice your soul to me to do as I will, it is permanent.'

He stood in front of Angelos, waiting for her acceptance of the deal. The longer he stood there the more it looked like she was about to cry. Probably tears of joy at having her favorite plaything forever. Finally, she shook her head, clearing her face of emotion, straightened her shoulders and gave him a firm nod.

'Done. Payment...' she hesitated, giving him his last chance to take back what he had promised. Rogan stood rigid and kept his mouth firmly shut. He wasn't taking this back.

'...Accepted.'

He didn't feel any different as Angelos turned her back and began to walk the starboard side toward the bow.

She turned back on her heels like an afterthought just came to her. The sky darkened with rain clouds and the Goddess' power. 'Collect your sweetheart after sunset and before sunrise, Captain. You sail at sunrise with or without your prized cargo. But there are a few stipulations that even I cannot break. You cannot just transport her here. You cannot bring her to the ship, she must get here herself or the deal is off. She must willingly be the one that steps foot on the ship. She must be the only mortal to get on, otherwise your payment will not be sufficient, and I will take whomever else's soul comes aboard to do with what I will. And the last term... even if she does make it on the ship, but not off of it, the payment is the same and cannot be taken back. Your soul is still mine forever. Do you understand the terms? She gets on the ship, you sail, she is dropped off at a destination, and you will spend forever on this ship, with only other souls and myself as company.'

He nodded firmly. It was better than he thought. He would have time with Malia, exclusively on the ship until they reached where she wanted to go. He understood that he had just made the best decision of his existence. He would take Malia anywhere and she would live her life and be happy forever.

Angelos slowly approached Rogan and kissed him. Rogan felt a pulling sensation in his chest, right over the head of the trident tattoo. It didn't hurt, but it left him breathless. It was only for a few seconds, then it was over. He felt strangely cold and empty, like something was missing that he hadn't noticed was there before. But he felt satisfied, happy even.

Can you feel happy without a soul?

That didn't seem right, but he wasn't going to question it.

'I'll see you tomorrow morning,' was all Angelos said with a sort of excitement in her tone before she disappeared and rain poured on the world.

Chapter Twenty-Eight

Malia

M alia readied herself for a fight but was surprised when Haych simply ordered her to her room, telling her she would learn her lesson after tomorrow's wedding. He wouldn't have his new bride spoiled before her time and he didn't have the time to do it properly at the moment.

'Bride?' Malia asked.

'Tomorrow morning,' he barked. 'You will be there, and you will act and be treated as my wife. Now, get out of my sight.' He pushed her up the stairs with so much force that her palms met the marble stairs moments before her face, saving her nose from a sure break.

Yanking her back to her feet, he marched Malia to her room. Cora was awake when Haych practically threw Malia into the room at Cora's feet. Brandt jumped up from the settee and caught his sister before she collided with the floor. A gesture that surprised Malia as much as the soberness in his eyes.

Haych left with a promise that her full punishment would come tomorrow. Once she was his wife and everything was official, he could legally do whatever he wanted with her.

'I guess your deal with Haych didn't work?' Brandt asked quietly, steadying her shoulders before helping her onto the bed beside Cora.

She shook her head. No, nothing had gone according to plan.

A cool rainy breeze invaded the room from the open terrace doors. Humidity brushed her arms and face, feeling as familiar as Cora's light pat on her hand and the smell of jasmine flowers that blew in on the breeze. She knew at that moment that she would always think of Rogan when it rained. Memories of Rogan alone in a cemetery, his kiss in a gazebo and him vanishing from her arms. All were memories surrounded with the trickling of rain in the background, the smell of wet grass and the hot feel of humidity on her skin.

'Malia?' Cora asked in concern. She kept her watering eyes on the blankets that covered her friend's mostly-bruised body, still unable to look her in the eye. There should have been happiness bubbling out of her with the knowledge that Cora was doing so well, but at that moment she was too exhausted. There was only guilt and sorrow swirling in her stomach. Hot and acidic. Cora's face and eyes were still swollen and bruised, but her friend was alert and sitting up now, able to move a piece of wet matted hair away from Malia's face. Cora would be able to leave tomorrow morning and escape this horrible place, leaving Malia. Maybe forever. The realization that Malia might never see her best friend again hit her between the eyes almost as hard as Rogan's news had. She was losing everything. Fast. Malia would figure something else out, she had to. She would be the victor in the upcoming fight against Haych. She had to believe that. She had to hold onto the seed of hope of seeing Cora and Rogan again. Of a better existence. Or, why even try?

Cora was speaking to her, but all Malia could hear was the pitter-patter of rain and rolling thunder.

'He'll come for you,' Cora said loudly this time, 'Your Captain will come.' With a little shake of Malia's shoulders, her friend forced her to turn, holding her gaze with warm promising eyes. Again, Malia wondered how much Cora really knew about Rogan and who he really was.

She couldn't tell her friend how wrong her words were. Instead, she simply snuggled into Cora's bony shoulder without offering a response. He wasn't coming, but they would meet again in Paradise. The Captain had promised. Malia grabbed a hold of hope and squeezed. She gripped the bedsheets until her hands ached and Cora slowly unclenched each individual finger to hold them in her own. Malia broke down in tears on Cora's shoulder, and Cora let her.

The rain continued to dance outside, while the three captives waited in anxious silence for the day to go by until it was time to smuggle Cora aboard the *Serenity*. Malia drifted in and out of sleep, only waking when the nearby roll of thunder woke her.

They received meals by a new grumpy-looking cook that came from Starzea, who Haych had employed for his household when he bought a market square house a year ago. She trudged in, dumped the plates onto the table and departed without saying a word. The understanding deepened that they were now prisoners in their own home. As evening drew closer, Brandt cleared his throat.

'Malia,' he said. She lifted her head from where it was resting beside Cora's on the mattress. 'There is something I need to say to you and I should have said it a long time ago, but I'm a coward and could never bring myself to.' His sincerity and red-tipped ears, like he was embarrassed, caught her attention. Brandt cleared his throat, uncomfortably, before he started again, 'I'm sorry, Bug. I have done nothing but resent you for the past year because of what happened to my arm in the accident.' He took a moment and looked at his arm that rested on his thigh, like he was collecting his emotions. 'What kind of brother resents his sister because he saved her? What kind of human does that? A selfish one. Malia, I have been the most selfish human being in the world. But, I want you to know that I wouldn't change a thing. If it came to my shoulder getting crushed or your body, I would choose my shoulder, everytime. I took for granted that you were still around to clean up after me. I have wallowed too much in my own self-pity to realize what my patheticness was costing you. I'm just sorry that it took me losing everything, losing you, to wake up and try to make things right. I know I can't replace or fix everything I've cost you, but if there is anything I can do now, please let me know.' Brandt had remained nearly silent all day. Malia wondered if sobriety had done that or if the realization of all his mistakes had finally accumulated, bringing a guilty silence upon him. Either way, it was nice to see that he was still capable of remorse.

Malia was too emotional to say anything. Instead, she launched herself into Brandt's chest and hugged him as tight as she had when the carriage was crushing them both. Brandt hugged her back, awkwardly stiff at first, but eventually his hold tightened and Malia pulled away.

'Actually, there is something I need you to do.' Brandt nodded his head both in encouragement and agreement to whatever she needed. 'I need you to go and confirm Cora's sailing departure with the *Serenity*. I can't leave this room until my marriage with Haych tomorrow morning. You will also have to be the one that takes her to the ship. Make sure you deliver her to the young doctor that came yesterday. He is waiting for you to arrive with her. She isn't going to want to leave without me,' Malia looked over her shoulder at her sleeping friend and whispered the rest. 'So we are going to have to lie or something. But you have to do this. We owe her as much.'

He nodded and without a word went into the sprinkling rain through the terrace doors. Cora shifted in her sleep, guiding Malia's attention back to the matter at hand. She couldn't imagine the ship leaving without her by mistake. She had to be on it in a few hours and she had to leave. Cora would escape.

Malia licked her dry lips. She couldn't believe what she was going to tell him next. 'Brandt, you should also get on the ship. Leave this place.' Brandt's eyes rounded, then creased in anger. Malia hurried along before he could interrupt, 'Really, Brandt. There is no reason why you should have to...' she didn't want to say die too, because she was still clinging to that hope that she wouldn't. 'Be here anymore.'

'I know I have been a shitty brother this past year, Malia, but if you think I'm going to leave you to suffer the consequences of my actions, all alone on this island, you are sorely mistaken. It's not as if anyone would take me either. Haych gave orders that I wasn't to leave, not that I would. If I thought it was possible, I would sneak you onto the ship with Cora and take care of Haych myself. Maybe I still will.'

Malia gave her brother a pleading look.

'No, Malia. I will fix this. End of discussion.'

Malia let it go, but a small part of her wondered if he really would sneak on the *Serenity* with Cora, now that the idea had been brought to light.

Evening came, turning the dim sky darker. Brandt still hadn't returned. Malia couldn't help the nagging voice that said he might have jumped onboard a ship himself. She shook off her paranoia with logic. Surely, if the word had gotten around that Malia couldn't board a ship, word had spread about Brandt too. Moreover, she hoped and despaired that her brother wouldn't leave her to face this life completely alone.

The sky turned from gray to black. The last night of the festival was supposed to be a farewell party on the beach, much like the welcoming festivities on Monday. Only instead of welcoming the Captain, they were sending him and their loved ones off. Malia could hear the crowd's laughter and merriment as they broke free of their houses and hotels for the last night of the festival. Just like how the festival started on the beach, it would end there. The beach would be full; the sand roughed by the flurry of dancers.

The inevitability of Malia's reality sank in as the sounds of revelry started, even in the rain. She would never see Rogan again; not whilst alive. Only now, sadness had turned to anger. During the day she could still pretend Rogan was around but was unable to see him. Now, with the day over, it brought with it the feeling of finality. Things had happened so fast that morning that Malia hadn't had time to feel cheated out of time with Rogan. Now, however, her indignant anger swirled in her belly. Instead of enjoying the last night of the festival, dancing in the rain, she was a prisoner in her own room waiting for her dreaded wedding day that was going to be as cheerful as a funeral.

Needing some air, Malia shoved the lace curtains aside and went out onto the terrace, her torn-up feet screaming at her to sit back down. She ignored it. The pain helped center her. The cold puddles hit her feet, helping to clear her head and soothe the inflamed cuts, making room in her head to find different means of escape. Looking out over the property, she noticed Haych had doubled his guards, none of them moving or rotating. Not one man would move from his post that night, making it harder to smuggle Cora out.

Malia groaned in frustration and threw her head back to look up at the arriving stars through the parting clouds, like she might find some help there. The aching in her chest felt like her heart was heaving in an effort just to beat. As if her very soul was crying.

Rogan was somewhere navigating by the same night sky, far away from the island. The heaving in her chest grew heavier; she missed him. She missed him so much that she didn't even try to stop the rolling tears. But Malia had made him a promise. It was truly all she had left. After a few moments of overwhelming self-pity, she took a few deep breaths to gather control over herself. A shaky sigh fell from her lips as she gave the stars one last glance.

"Love is in the stars," she had once told Rogan. Looking at them now made her feel closer to him. Turning to go back inside, she stopped short. There were footsteps against the stone pathway below.

'Who's there?' she called, peering over the side of the terrace and seeing no one. Not that it mattered– it was probably one of Haych's men.

The bushes below, where a man stood guard, shook violently as swearing grunts echoed up the side of the house before collapsing into silence.

'Malia,' a man whispered and for a moment her heart leaped and hands shook. She almost called out his name, but Brandt crawled up the side of the railing of the terrace.

Both disappointed and elated she asked, 'Brandt? You're back? What did the Captain say? Is Cora still good to leave tonight?'

Brandt didn't answer before the ship's young doctor pulled himself up and over the railing himself. Duncan had a smile plastered to his face, looking proud of himself for managing to climb onto the terrace without breaking his neck or ripping his shirt.

'Yes, Miss Malia,' he answered for her brother. 'Cora is still granted safe passage aboard the *Serenity*. I've come to check her condition and help her onboard.'

'Of course,' she said, indicating for him to go inside.

The doctor quickly, but gently, awoke Cora. A smile broke across her face when she recognized who had roused her. His returning smile was equally as warm. He was smitten with her as much as she was with him.

'I'm leaving?' she questioned, looking between the two men then to Malia with furrowed brows.

The men nodded then and she looked at Malia, waiting for her explanation.

Kneeling beside the bed, Cora studied her friend with a hurt, pained expression.

'Cora, it isn't safe for you here. I can't have you stay for me only for something worse to happen to you. I won't allow it.'

'Malia...' She began to protest, but Malia cut her off.

'Cora, listen to me,' she paused, building courage for what she was about to admit for the first time aloud. 'I cannot leave this place, at least not yet. You know this. I will have to figure out another way. My fate is different than yours. There is no getting around it. But you, you can have something better: a life, a family. You are like my sister,' Malia loosened her grip on Cora's fingers, not wanting to hurt her further. 'Leave here and live for both of us, please,' she pleaded.

'Malia, I can't just leave you here to face that man alone.'

'She won't be alone,' the most familiar voice said from the terrace doors. Malia whirled, not daring to believe it. But there he was. His hair fell down to his shoulders in black damp waves and his dark clothes were soaked, like he had been for a recent swim. The top spikes of his trident tattoo peeked from behind the collar of his shirt. Rogan. His piercing eyes cut straight to her core, freezing her in place. 'Hello, Love,' Rogan said.

Malia put a hand to her mouth, trying to breathe past the sob that was stuck in her throat. The Captain of Souls swooped in and pulled her up in his arms, crushing his lips to hers. His chest beat as wild as Malia's.

'Cora's cousin?' Brandt asked, confused.

'I told you he would come for you,' Cora said with a satisfied and relieved smile.

'You're here?' Malia questioned, her surprise evident as his lips just eased away from hers. Malia was starting to seriously question her sanity, but if crazy meant Rogan, she would take it.

'I'm here,' he reassured. His strong hands gripped her waist, settling around her ribs before his lips were on hers again and she forgot about all the other people in the room. He tasted like he had that morning; wind and salt.

'What's going on?' Brandt whispered to Cora.

'Well, it's obvious isn't it? Her Captain has come to rescue her,' Cora said with her old fire.

Malia's smile matched Rogan's, but smiling didn't stop them from kissing.

Loud laughter came from somewhere downstairs, forcing them all back to reality. The room fell dead silent. They listened. After a few moments, when it was clear that no one was coming to check on them, everyone exhaled.

'What are you doing here?' Malia asked breathlessly, her face still wet from happy tears. 'I thought the Goddess was making you leave this morning?' she asked, before remembering that they weren't alone.

'She was,' he said. He was warmer than she had ever felt him. 'But she and I made a deal.'

His words caused Malia's stomach to clench. 'What kind of a deal? Weren't you the one that told me, forbade me even, from making deals with Angelos?'

'Wait a minute,' Cora interrupted, still sitting on the bed. 'Goddess?'

'Angelos?' Brandt asked. The doctor remained poised at the corner of the bed looking thoroughly confused and fascinated at the same time. Like they were in some kind of play or extra stage show that he got to privately experience on his last night on the island.

'The Goddess of Death?' Cora's voice nearly shrieked. 'You made a deal with the Goddess of Death?' she asked, her eyes as round as teacups.

'It's not as crazy as it sounds being who I am,' Rogan tried explaining vaguely.

'And just who are you exactly?' Brandt asked, suddenly becoming the protective older brother he was supposed to be.

'It's a little too late to be the protective older brother now, isn't it?' Malia couldn't help saying. Brandt ignored her and waited for Rogan to explain himself.

'I'm Rogan, Captain of Souls.' He shifted Malia to one arm and held out his hand as if he were simply a suitor calling on her, wanting to shake Brandt's hand in formality. Brandt just stared at his hand like it was a skeleton.

'*The* Captain of Souls?' Cora asked. Leave it to her not to be intimidated by such a confession.

Malia was speechless. Could he do that? Just confess who he was? He looked the happiest she had ever seen him, like a man free of burdens. Something else was going on.

Rogan smiled at her questioning stare, then turned his head to answer Cora's question. 'Yes, Ma'am. The collector of Souls, the captain of the Judgment Voyage,' he pointed his thumb to his chest like it was the best job in the world.

Rogan's humor was lost on Cora, who appeared deep in thought. Her eyes briefly went to Malia's hands, like she was remembering when she had read her palms. Malia curled them into fists.

'Well, that makes sense then,' Cora said. Malia was about to question her but Brandt intervened.

'This makes sense? The Captain of Souls is your cousin?' Brandt asked, growing frustrated. Cora laughed aloud, and Malia and Rogan quickly joined her in hushed snickers.

'Trust me, Brandt, you have nothing to fear with Rogan,' Malia provided after she had regained her composure. Brandt continued to stand, baffled, as the doctor looked over Cora's injuries. Malia was still in Rogan's arms when she asked, 'So when you say I won't be alone, are you staying here? Are we leaving? What exactly is this deal?'

'No, I can't stay,' he said, his eyes darting around as if

searching for a clock to tell him the time, 'But you are coming with me.'

Malia's lips split into a smile so wide she thought her cheeks would burst. He returned it with one of equal joy. A genuine smile. A smile that she hadn't witnessed before, an authentic wide grin that bore no worries or regrets underneath it.

'Really?' she asked, almost feeling silly in her brewing hope.

'Really,' he answered before he briefly kissed her again. 'Listen,' he said urgently while holding her face in his hands. 'I don't have much time and I'll explain more about everything once you're on the ship.'

'Rogan, I have to know. What was the price? If you... '

He cut her off, 'The price was time. I just have to give the Goddess more time as Captain. But what is time when eternity awaits, right?' Rogan answered so fast, deliberately sounding like he wanted the subject dropped.

Malia, about to question him further, was prevented from doing so as a loud crash came from downstairs followed by boisterous laughter.

'We need to hurry,' the doctor said. 'That man below the balcony won't be out all night. If we are going to move her, we need to do it now while the rest of them are distracted downstairs.'

Brandt and the doctor gently guided Cora to her feet.

'I have to move my ship, so you can get on. I will be in the harbor before sunrise. You, and only you, can meet me on the ship, and you have to do it before sunrise. Understand? I cannot take you or even transport you from the shore. You have to come on your own and by yourself. Once you are on the ship ,we will leave and never look back.' He grinned and kissed her again.

'So, Cora, you can leave with the young doctor here,' Rogan ordered kindly. 'I've got your friend taken care of.'

Cora smiled, although Malia could tell by the way she was

now fidgeting with her fingers that she was nervous. For herself or for her friend, Malia wasn't sure.

'I have to go,' he said, remorse tight in his voice as he considered the inky night sky outside the windows.

'What?' Malia grasped onto his shirt tightened.

'I have to move my ship, and the harbor is full of ships leaving or getting ready to leave by tomorrow morning. It's going to take some time and skill to get the ship into place for you to board. Plus, you have a friend that needs you right now,' he explained, moving hair off her shoulder. It was a bit distracting to see him so fully content, but she enjoyed it.

'Alright,' she agreed reluctantly. Helping Cora escape was the only thing that could break her grip from Rogan.

'I'll see you soon,' he vowed, giving her chin a nudge.

She followed him back to the terrace doors as Brandt and the doctor ignored them in preparing Cora for her voyage.

'Before sunrise,' he warned one last time.

'I'll be there.' There was no way on Earth she wouldn't be.

They kissed again, and he smiled before stepping out of her terrace doors and disappearing.

Chapter Twenty-Nine

SUNDAY

Malia

C ome on, Cora. We need to get you out of here,' Malia insisted as the young doctor and Brandt helped get Cora to her feet. She was slow, but steady. They were going to have to time Cora's escape just right, so that by the time they were checked again, the room would be long-empty.

Malia hadn't asked Brandt what he was going to do; if she was being honest with herself, she was afraid to.

'And you? You will just go off into the sunset with the Captain of Souls?' Cora asked, trying not to wince as she stood, clutching the doctor's hand tightly. Malia grabbed Cora's single bag of belongings that she had packed for her earlier in the day.

'Yes.' Malia felt her smile falter when she remembered that the only reason this was happening was because of a price Rogan paid. A price he was vague, but very happy about. A price he wouldn't discuss until she was already on the ship.

The house was considerably quieter as the night passed. After drinking all the liquor left in the house, Haych's men must have gone out for the party, leaving them mostly alone, besides the guards, Ku and Brom, to plan their escapes. Something about the silence of the house and the mysterious price Rogan had paid left Malia with an ominous feeling – she didn't like it.

'Oh,' Malia said, rushing over to her secret cabinet and plucking out her mother's jewels. 'I almost forgot. You have to be able to pay for your passage and new life somehow.'

'Where did those come from?' Brandt asked, astonished.

'Mother left them to me. We were able to nab them before you discovered and gambled them away, along with everything else.' Brandt looked spiteful and angry. Malia wondered if he was going to try and take them by force. The doctor's mouth dropped open as he supported Cora.

'Don't you think Cora deserves them? After all, if it hadn't been for us, she wouldn't be in the condition she is in. She is also being forced to leave her home and will need a way to support herself,' she said, challenging Brandt to make a move. It really didn't matter what Brandt thought or wanted; Cora was taking the jewels. When Malia kept her eyebrows raised, refusing to drop her challenge, he eventually diverted his eyes to the ground in shame.

'Oh, I can't take everything. What will you use?' she asked, pulling back her hand, refusing to accept the gift. The doctor was patiently supporting her at her elbow.

'Here,' Malia insisted, pulling out the teardrop diamond necklace on a simple silver chain. It had been her favorite of her mother's. She was glad not to have to part with it...yet. 'I'll take this one.' Maybe she wouldn't lose everything from her parents. Putting the necklace on, the stone felt like a cold fingertip touching her chest, just like Rogan.

'This will be enough to get me what I need to start my life. Consider the rest of these as your back pay with interest. Go with Brandt and the doctor. They will get you to the ship and hopefully, someday, I will see you again.' Malia's eyes stung and her voice caught in her throat as she relinquished Cora's hand with the last remnants of her family's legacy. 'With Rogan, I'll be fine,' she assured when Cora stood there looking torn. 'I won't need anything else. Hurry before we are checked on. I still need to plan how I'm getting to the harbor.'

'Thank you, Malia,' Cora said, pulling her into a hug.

'Thank you, Cora,' she whispered in her ear before pulling away. 'Now go, quickly,' Malia urged.

Cora had tears streaming down her puffy face as the doctor draped an arm around her shoulders and led her out the terrace doors.

Duncan slung down first, eager to help Cora. Malia hoped he would look out for her. He hadn't said much since Rogan had shown up and left, but Malia imagined something like that would shock a practical man into silence for a while.

Brandt had tied a harness made of rope around Cora and gently lowered her to the gardens below. Malia watched and helped Brandt with the rope until she felt the cord relax and Cora's weight release.

'Get her to the ship, Brandt,' she ordered as he was about to hop over the railing and make his climb down.

'I will,' he promised. Malia handed him Cora's bag. He slung it over his shoulder and headed down into the dark gardens. Malia gave her friend a little wave and as much of a smile as she could muster when she saw Cora look back. Light from a window glistened off the tears running down Cora's cheeks as Malia cried her own. She believed she would see her again someday, even if that day was in Paradise.

Once the shadowy figures were gone, Malia went back inside to get ready for her own flight into the darkness.

She had just changed into a simple white beach dress and pulled out a bag when the bedroom doors flew open.

Haych burst in, looking drunk and malicious in the dim lamplight. His brow was sweaty and his face red either from drinking, exertion, or rage – probably all three.

'What's going on here?' he demanded as he stood straighter, looking around the previously-crowded bedroom.

'Brandt took Cora to get some fresh air,' she lied, gripping the bedpost behind her back. Haych stumbled around a little, like the pieces of furniture intentionally moved to trip him.

'What is this?' he asked, stumbling so close that his shoulder collided with Malia's. She smelled the familiar stink of brandy and cigars coming from every pore of his body. He was pointing to the necklace.

'It was my mother's,' she said unapologetically. 'I figured I would wear it during the wedding ceremony.'

'It is mine,' Haych said like he was some big toddler and made a swipe for it.

Malia saw his hand coming with enough force to knock her over, but he was slow and clumsy. She ducked out of the way and hurried toward the open door. Haych's nose rammed into the bedpost when he missed. He cursed, reaching for his face. She raced out the door.

Thunderous footsteps pounded behind her as Haych gave chase. Malia sped faster to beat him down the stairs, hoping that his drunkenness would slow him down, or if she was lucky, result in a life-altering fall. The last thing she wanted was to get caught at the top of the stairs and have him push her down them, making her death look like another convenient accident.

The house was dark and shadowy with only a few candles lit. The night was still showing its stars outside.

Haych was on the stairs behind her. She leapt off the last one as he lunged with a growl.

Her knees hit the marble floor of the foyer with Haych's

weight crushing her back. Her wrist snapped underneath her against the marble floor. A useless scream escaped her throat. No one would hear.

As Haych grappled with the material of her dress and legs, Malia turned and kicked her bare feet until the heel met teeth. Haych let go and rolled off. Scrambling up, Malia cradled her broken wrist to her chest. Black spots danced in her vision. She ran blindly towards the front door. Haych reached out and snatched a large piece of the fabric, but it gave way when she twisted from his grasp. She ran.

She would lose him outside and make her way to Rogan's ship. She felt certain Haych wouldn't attack her in public and there would still be people all around the island. She wrapped her good hand around the cool iron of the handle and pulled. Haych's swearing echoed closer. The doors didn't move. They were locked. It was the split-second delay that Haych needed. Crushing arms encircled her chest, lifting her off her feet. Malia screamed and kicked and flailed, but he dragged her back further into the house. All she felt was clouded panic. All she could think of was getting out to Rogan's ship. She was so close to escaping.

Screaming and kicking only caused Haych to tighten his grip around her ribs until she found it hard to breathe.

'Where do you think you are going? You are mine,' he said through gritted teeth before tossing her like an old rag doll to the cold marble floor. Malia screeched out in pain as her wrist slammed down on the ground. Black spots had formed a tunnel in her vision.

'Did you think after all these years of planning and work that I would just let you go? Oh no, my dear.' He wiped the spit from his chin as he crouched down. Slowly, he unsheathed a dagger from his boot. He held it to her jaw. The cool steel froze her. If she moved the blade would knick her skin. 'I need everything to be legal, with no loose ends. You will marry me in a few hours, even if I have to tie you up and drag you there.'

He began laughing, his eyes wide and face sweaty, looking completely mad. He sheathed his dagger, the handle just sticking up over the top of his boot.

She stayed where she was on the floor, calculating how long it would take to break one of the long windows by the door and get out. Too long. Could she make it to the back kitchen door?

'No one will argue with me if you show up in ropes and you know why? Because I own them! I own everything and everyone on this wretched island. I own the bank, the ships, the fish. You are the last piece to conquering your family empire just like I swore I would.' His eyes grew distant as he became distracted by his thoughts. He began to pace. 'Imagine a lowly fisherman, the son of the island whore, becoming the lord of this island. I learned early on that if you want something, you take it. Now, I'll take this island.' Haych paced and preached like he was giving a political speech. It almost felt like he had forgotten she was even there.

'Your father,' he pointed an accusing finger at her, but still without looking at her. 'An outsider. Came to my island and demanded change. He was giving people decent jobs, giving them hope. Hope for better lives and pay. If they didn't work for me, if they went to him, they would be happier. Then, there was your mother,' he said, stopping and looking down at Malia for the first time since he had started his rant. 'The most beautiful creature I had ever seen, and he took her too! I knew her first. I loved her first! And I couldn't have her. Then, he denied me you! And I was humiliated, again.' His fist closed dangerously. 'But I am a man that gets what he wants. Always.' He began to pace again. His words were slurred as he spoke faster, his pacing picking up speed. 'The people of Blisse only care about what is happening on Blisse. No one knew about what I had done on Starzea, to that Nomadic village. But your father, he was the only one on this island who knew about those charges. He could have ruined everything. He had to be dealt with.'

Realization dawned. 'You killed them,' she whispered. The accident that had destroyed hers and Brandt's lives hadn't been an accident at all. She felt sick with rage and pain. 'The wheel on the new carriage; Moses getting spooked. You did that.'

'Of course I did!' he yelled. 'Do you think I would just let your father come here to my island and take over everything? NO! Accidents happen easily and all the time, stupid girl. Horses get spooked and wheels come off carriages. Your father really should have been more careful about showing off his wealth. It wasn't enough to have them gone, oh no. Everything had been left to his little brats and you both inconveniently survived! Your brother took time, but he was easy enough to deal with. But when I couldn't turn up any of your family heirlooms, I knew that they must have been left to you. Brandt had only lost a few small trinkets to me, so I knew there were more. Those jewels are worth a fortune by themselves. Precious stones are worth way more than selling fish and rum,' he said greedily. 'With them I could expand trade. Pay off old debts. Bribes. You aren't your brother. You are smart, resourceful even. You are the heir to the jewels, which means you have kept them hidden somewhere, haven't you?' When Malia didn't answer, it was confirmation enough. She inwardly smiled. The jewels were with Cora, and Cora was gone.

Haych paused and studied her for a moment. 'You are as beautiful as your mother. Same fighting spirit too and there is nothing I like better than to break in something wild. You are mine and when you are my wife, the jewels will be too.'

She felt light-headed from her wrist and nauseous from Haych's revelations.

'Now,' he said conversationally, 'I'm only going to ask you once. Where are the rest of the jewels?' Haych squatted in front of her. She noticed the tip of a knife handle holstered at the top of his boot just above his calf.

'I don't have them,' she answered honestly. The glint of the knife jutting from his boot caught her eye.

He came within inches of her face. His face was so red it was almost purple in the weak light. But Malia didn't back away. The knife at his boot was almost within reach. This monster had killed her parents, plotted their downfall and schemed her life away.

'Don't lie to me,' Haych warned, his palms curling into fists.

Her relief that Cora now had all the jewels except for the necklace was indescribable. She would be rich and hopefully happy. And Haych, at least in part, would lose.

Lifting her chin, she smiled right before spitting in his face.

His meaty fist flew faster than she could dodge, slamming into her ribs. Falling back, all air was sucked from her lungs, threatening to pull her under. Desperation helped her breathe. She had to make it to Rogan's ship and she couldn't let Haych know that the jewels were on a ship that hadn't left port yet.

Haych crouched in front of her again, but not close enough. He needed to come closer. His leg and knife were nearly in snatching distance if the room would just stop spinning; the sharp pain in her ribs made it impossible to gain a decent breath.

Haych continued to mutter obscenities before grabbing a handful of hair and pulling it back forcing her face up. It was just the few inches she needed.

As one hand pulled chunks of hair and the other closed around her throat, she put a hand on his booted ankle, like she was trying to support herself. His bloodshot eyes were crazed and Malia felt his hand begin to squeeze. Zeroing in on her goal of the knife kept her panic at bay just long enough. Her hand closed over the hilt of the knife. She jerked it from his boot and slashed at his thigh.

Surprised, he let go of her throat, roaring more in anger than in pain. He looked down at his shallow wound, distracted, but he still had a good hold of Malia's hair. She reached up and stabbed his forearm. The impact caused her sweaty palms to drop the knife, but he dropped her hair too. She scrambled to her feet. She reached the door latch when a deep, white-hot pain stabbed between her back ribs. Haych's hot sour breath was on her neck. Malia tried to cry out but found getting enough air to scream was impossible. Her lungs wouldn't fill with air. The steel of the knife prevented her from breathing.

'I guess there won't be a wedding after all,' Haych said in Malia's ear. He pulled the knife out, finally giving her lungs room to scream. She clung to the door handle to keep herself upright as it turned open. She just had to get to Rogan's ship. She looked over her shoulder as Haych pulled his arm back for another stab. As Haych's arm arched, he was tackled from the side.

Malia turned around, astonished and confused at the sudden help. A man got to his feet, hunched and ready for a fight. A flash of dark hair caught the morning light along with a set of familiar hazel eyes. Brandt.

'Go, Malia!' he ordered just before Haych charged at him, knife in hand.

'GO!' he screamed again, as Haych slammed him to the floor.

She unlatched the lock. The door swung open. Malia ran.

The stars were disappearing. Morning was on its way.

She ran out the door, nearly falling off the front step. Brandt and Haych's struggle was as loud as a hurricane behind her. Where were Haych's hired guards? It didn't matter, so long as they weren't in front of her. She had to make it to Rogan. She tried to catch her breath but only a rasp made it to her lungs.

She stumbled past the yard and straight down the road, taking the most direct way to the harbor.

Rogan will be there by now. He will see me.

Malia's legs became far too tired, too fast. Black spots danced in her vision, but she pushed on. Her heart pumped as blood soaked her back, traveling down the side of her dress and legs.

A few people were still on the streets, making their way home. She ducked behind a jungle brush when she saw someone coming. Anyone that saw her would stop her from making it to Rogan's ship either to help her, or worse – send her back to Haych. With no shoes, covered in blood, she half-ran, half-stumbled in the mud toward the coast.

Finally, the harbor was in sight. Malia stopped and tried again to catch her breath. She leaned over a forgotten barrel and coughed. A splatter of blood on the barrel and her hand surprised her. Her shortness of breath wasn't going away. Her chest heaved, but her lungs still burned.

The sky was getting brighter. Time was running out. Something deep and desperate inside demanded that she push on. Stumbling down the small hill toward the board planks of the docks in the harbor, she looked for Rogan's ship.

She knew which one was his as soon as she saw it. The wood, almost black, the sails, white and crisp. A beacon calling to her. The *Calypso's Voyage* was anchored and ready, only fifty yards from where she stood.

'Rogan!' she tried to scream, only for it to come out a hoarse shout. She made her way down the dock, stumbling for his ship. He was there. She would make it.

She spat out more blood. Terrified that he wouldn't hear her and would think she hadn't come to him, she screamed again in desperation. 'Rogan!' Her legs were heavy with mud, sand, and fatigue.

She was almost there when Rogan's bewildered face appeared over the railing of the deck looking for her.

'Rogan!' her voice cracked as she waved. A smile appeared on his face before being replaced with terror. He disappeared from her view as she limped down to his dock, struggling to stay on her feet and not fall into the water. She remembered what he said, he wouldn't be able to help her onto the ship. Falling on her knees, the wood pierced and splintered her flesh as she reached the side of his ship. A gangplank lowered, almost hitting her in the shoulder. Looking up, Malia saw Rogan's agonized face as he watched and waited for her to get on board.

'Get up, Malia!'

Laughing and crying, she crawled up the plank, across the threshold, and fell into Rogan's waiting arms.

'I made it. I made it,' was all she could think to say.

'Malia,' Rogan's horrified voice broke, 'What happened?'

He gently lowered her onto the deck floor, cradling her in his arms.

'It doesn't matter, I made it! We are free.'

Malia sighed in relief, but it only made her splutter and cough. Blood splattered on her hand and Rogan's shirt at his chest.

Rogan looked all over her body. Tears swelled in his eyes as he looked lost and helpless.

'Haych tried to stop me...Brandt saved me...I got away,' she wheezed.

'Brandt saved you?' a terrifying yet beautiful voice asked. Malia recognized the Goddess of Death, Angelos, standing not too far behind Rogan. A crown of finger bones and pearls decorated her head.

She nodded. Rogan ignored the Goddess, never taking his eyes off the girl in his arms.

Malia was surprised to realize how tired she felt. Weak. She wanted to get up and tell him she was fine and to start sailing, but couldn't find the strength. She loved being in his arms. There was no better place.

Rogan's arms were Malia's paradise. Only it was growing uncomfortably wet. Looking down, she realized it was her blood soaking Rogan, her, and the deck. By the amount of blood and terror in Rogan's eyes, she knew she was losing too much.

'Rogan?' she asked, tears stinging her eyes, a coppery taste coating her mouth and throat. The panic of realization was starting to set in.

Rogan held her tighter. She was dying. She knew it and Rogan did too.

'Shhh, Love,' he whispered, his arms encircling her tightened. 'Can't you do something?' she heard him ask the only other being on the ship.

'I'm sorry, Rogan. I cannot.' Angelos' voice sounded gruff like she was holding back her own emotions.

'Rogan...I'm so sorry,' Malia said. A tear streaked down into her hair.

He pulled her face back. A tear escaped his eyes, hitting near her lips as he kissed her.

'Salt,' she whispered when he pulled back. He gave her a curious look.

'You always taste like the sea: salt and freedom.' She smiled weakly as she started to feel cold.

'Malia!' Someone was calling her name in the harbor. That outraged voice could only come from one person. Haych.

'Rogan,' she said, a last flutter of panic resonating in her chest. 'We have to leave.'

Rogan looked around the ship and up to Angelos, as though maybe she would help.

Angelos gave him a little nod. 'Don't you worry about Haych.'

She disappeared from sight.

Malia felt her body start to relax, but Rogan's grip tightened. Rogan's heartbeat under his trident against Malia's cheek, was creating a sort of lull, pulling her to sleep.

'Is it awful? Being dead?' Malia asked, a little scared as she looked up at him.

Another tear ran down her Captain's handsome face.

'No, Love,' he said softly. 'It's as gentle as a kiss.'

Malia smiled. 'That doesn't sound so bad.'

'No,' he reassured and brushed the hair from her face. 'It doesn't.'

'You'll be there? When my soul is...called? You'll be the one to do it, right?' She gasped. It was getting harder to breathe. Harder to focus. Rogan was blurry, but his blue eyes stayed steady.

Rogan looked like he couldn't speak as he gritted his teeth. Nodding was all he could do.

'And I'll remember you?' she wheezed. Rogan felt hot next to her. She was so tired.

He swallowed.

'Yes. You couldn't forget about me,' he said, braving his old arrogance, making her smile.

'Never. This face saved me. And we'll dance?' she asked, her eyes feeling heavy.

'Oh yeah. We'll dance forever.' She was confused. Why did he look so tormented?

'I'll see you soon then?'

'Yes.' His tears flowed freely.

If we are going to meet and spend Paradise together, why is he so sad? Malia wondered but couldn't find the energy to ask.

'Kiss me,' she sighed.

Malia's eyes closed as she smiled and felt him kiss her lips. His warm mouths pressed to hers and she couldn't imagine paradise being any better. Then, just like he had said, her eyes closed, and death came as gentle as his kiss.

Chapter Thirty

Rogan

Malia's body became limp, encased in Rogan's arms. How could this happen? He looked over her again, brushing her hair aside with a crimson bloody hand. She was gray, her only other coloring being that of the blood dripping from her lips.

She was still, her chest no longer rising, her heart no longer beating. The simple dress she was wearing might have been white at one point, but was now covered in brown mud and red blood, telling just how hard she had fought to get to him. Her hair was free and to her waist, soaked in her blood and sweat. She looked beautiful and tragic. Her feet were bare. Seeing her bare feet finalized it. She never wore shoes. It was something so characteristic of Malia that it made reality impossible to block. She would have started her new life with bare feet. This was her body that he clutched in his arms, and life would no longer flow through it. He knew if he returned to the island, her soul would call to him, the trident would burn white hot, begging to collect her. As the Captain of Souls, he could feel her spirit waiting peacefully, slumbering almost, simply asleep.

Fury began to quiver in Rogan's hands. This one person, with so much life in her possession, was no longer living and he couldn't bear it. It felt so wrong. It couldn't be true, but it was.

The echo of her screaming his name as she searched desperately for the ship in the docks still rang in his ears. Her sweet voice echoing in his head crushed his ability to think. He couldn't breathe as he remembered how he was frozen in place on the ship and couldn't go to her, couldn't help her as she staggered onto the ship and died in his arms. Tears blurred his vision.

She was gone. The price had been worthless. Rogan gnashed his teeth and a snarling groan wrenched his throat. The only thought penetrating his mind was that he had caused this, and he deserved his eternal purgatory for causing Malia's death. He was enslaved on the ship forever. Rogan had lied to her in those last moments because he couldn't bear to tell her the truth – that she would go on and he would not. A chance at a good life with a family would never be hers, and Paradise would never be his.

Rogan was gripping the fabric on her shoulders so tight seams ripped as he buried his head in her hair. Jasmine, she still smelled like jasmine...and blood.

'So, she's dead then?' a masculine voice stated more than asked. The voice caused a flurry of rage through Rogan so strong he couldn't see straight. Eldon Haych had boarded the deck of the ship. The sky behind him was faintly rosy, but the sun wasn't yet over the horizon. There was triumph on his face. He had the look of a man drunk on his own gloating.

Rogan gently laid Malia's body down. Her broken wrist made a sickening thunk on the deck as it slapped the puddle of gore that surrounded her. Rogan took a long breath to keep the bile from rising.

Haych stepped further onto the deck, now undeniably on

the ship. He glanced around, inspecting the piece of property he thought he had just earned. But Rogan would have his justice. Haych was on his ship, and Rogan could feel his unrestrained power and fury pumping through his veins. This vicious man would pay.

Rogan rose to his feet. His whole attire was soaked with Malia's cooling blood. He looked down at the never-ending red. It was all Rogan could see.

He took a crazed step toward the murderer and froze. Like walking straight into an ice wall. Rogan became frozen there – just like when he had wanted to tear him apart a few nights ago when Malia had said he had hurt her. He didn't understand what was happening, until Angelos appeared beside him. Her dress flowing, hair still, the bones in her crown flashing promises of pain. She looked as beautiful and docile as a lamb. Only Rogan saw her eyes were no longer gold, but glowing green. He struggled against his infuriating invisible barrier and chains that bound him but to no avail.

Haych had walked around the main mast, inspecting ropes, and had missed Angelos' arrival until he retraced his steps. When he caught sight of the Goddess, he froze, but with shock and awe at the creature he was seeing. Not with the horror that he should have felt.

'Sir Eldon Haych,' Angelos said his name like they were old enemies.

Haych was speechless and practically drooling as he stood there gazing, mesmerized by the Goddess. Finally, he answered in a wondrous voice filled with greedy anticipation. 'Yes?'

'You are mortal, are you not?' she asked, circling him. She was the perfect image of a hunter examining its prey. Haych turned with her, his eyes seeing nothing but beauty, clouded with lust and greed. Now that his most recent female conquest was dead, Rogan knew he would want a new one. Once Haych knew who she was, he would want her power as well. If Rogan hadn't been in such a rage and straining against the Goddess who blocked his power, he would have found the present conversation, and Haych's impending fate, satisfying and amusing.

'Yes, my lady,' he answered, unable to take his eyes off of her. 'And you *aren't* mortal, are you?' he whispered in wonder.

'Are you aware then, Eldon Haych, that any mortal that steps foot on this ship must pay a price?' she asked, ignoring his tone of wonder.

'That's why I'm here, my lady,' he explained, licking his lips, his eyes wide and eager. 'I want the power of the Captain. Give it to me?'

Angelos clicked her tongue. 'I'm afraid that is not how things work,' her voice grew with authority, like a teacher giving a lesson to a particularly stupid student. 'You see, Rogan is my Captain, my servant, my work manifest,' she offered him a warm smile. If Rogan could have, he would have spat in her face too. This was her doing. She had the power to stop it but hadn't. He hated her almost as much as he despised Haych. 'You see, there is no power given to him that I do not first bestow. And I only bestow my powers on those I like, on those I choose. On those souls with potential. Ones I think deserve a second chance to redeem themselves or at least to those I enjoy the company of. And you, Haych, do not have any of these qualities.' She stood there staring at him, waiting for her words to sink in, for a response. It took Haych a moment to realize that Angelos did not particularly enjoy his company, his presence was a mere inconvenience to her day.

Haych stood there confused, but the Goddess ignored this and continued. 'You see, Haych. When the Goddess of Death and Judgment doesn't like you and you're on her ship, you now owe her a debt, and things can get a little. . .messy,' her voice now sunk low and dark, as it often did when a victim was about to experience her unrestrained wrath.

Haych's eyes went from wide with admiration to round with horror. The Goddess reached out a hand and curled her fist. Haych's face went purple.

He looked to Rogan briefly, as if pleading for an explanation, but all Rogan could do was glare and wait for Angelos to hand out her justice. Haych looked back up at the Goddess again. Her sailing dress rippled in the air.

'But, my lady,' Haych began to beg, choking on his words. Angelos cut him off.

'Silence, mortal!' and with a swipe of her hand, Haych's tongue flew from his mouth, like she had taken a dagger to it. 'You are on my death ship, my *judgment* ship now. And you will be weighed!'

Blood ran out of his mouth and down his exposed neck. If he could scream, he would have. Angelos made another fist, preventing any sound from escaping from his throat. His eyes were so wide, Rogan waited to see if they would pop out and roll on the deck. His hands clutched his neck and face, painful, confused terror painting his features. His feet rose a foot above the deck.

'Isn't this what you wanted?' Angelos asked from above his writhing form. 'To be a part of Rogan's world? Of mine? You wanted to beat him and thus, by doing so, beat me? Stupid child. You can't escape death. You've killed enough; you should know that.'

A fountain of blood dripped down his chin and chest as he withered in the open air.

'But, Haych, you don't seem to know the rules of the game, and have therefore lost. The deepest circle of Hell is reserved especially for men like you. My father will immensely enjoy your company in the Underworld.' She began to list off his offenses and struck him with a piercing glare with every crime. 'Mortals that like to hurt and kill others for sport are sent there.' The Goddess' voice remained calm and it was only the blaze of her eyes and ripple of her dress that told of her emanating power. She made another slice with her hand and Haych's hands that gripped his throat were covered in blood. 'Humans with blood on their hands spend eternity bathing in it,' she continued. Haych looked down at his blood-soaked hands and back at the Goddess pleadingly. 'Mortals that like to hurt children, the gods take particular enjoyment in watching their souls shrivel and burn— slowly in the Underworld.' She knew of all his cruelties.

'You have destroyed and harmed numerous lives. I, unable to interfere with human decisions and fates, could do nothing but watch. However, since you are now on my ship, interfering with my work, you are mine. Welcome aboard the *Calypso's Voyage*.'

Haych's body lifted higher off the deck as he fought weakly, screaming silently, and waving his arms like he could swim back to the deck from the air. Angelos rose with him. The wind swirled and water sprayed like they were out at sea, not in the harbor. A depthless whirlpool forming in the shallow water.

'This is for your greed,' she roared. Haych's arm detached and flew into the air, disappearing inside the whirlpool. Haych flung his other limbs around in sheer panic. He was a fish on a hook.

'This is for your brutality.' His other arm and both legs were ripped from his body and flung into the same watery hole. 'For your horrors.' His eyes were next. 'For their screams.' His ears.

What was left of Haych hung there in the air. His head was limp against his rotund chest, but his face was contorted into a soulless agony. He was still alive, his blood cascading down into the whirling hole to hell. Angelos was sending him there, piece by piece.

'And this is for my Rogan, and his sweet Malia,' Haych's body dropped, swallowed by the whirling and bubbling tunnel of water, his head still suspended in the air staring at the Goddess. 'Say hello to my father,' she said with finality as his head finally fell into the whirling water.

Angelos floated back down to the ship. Once her feet touched down, she released Rogan from his bonds. He fell to his knees beside Malia.

'That was my affair to settle, Rogan,' she explained as she came to stand beside him. 'A mortal stepped onto my ship; he couldn't pay the price with his soul because his was worthless.'

Rogan seethed. She had robbed him of his vengeance. She answered his glare with a patient answer. 'He wronged more than just you and Malia. Justice needed to be served. That also is my job.' Fury still burned in her eyes like she wished parts of Haych were still around to rip off.

Now that Haych was no longer distracting him, the full weight of his loss pounded down on his shoulders. His hands fell to the deck, catching him before he fell into Malia's blood. It was more than unfair; it was cruel.

'You,' he accused through gritted teeth. The fact that Rogan had witnessed her tear a man limb from limb had not dampened his rage. Malia was still gone; his soul still lost. 'How could you let this happen? You-you could have let him on the ship and killed him days ago,' he yelled.

'You, collector, could not be a part of that mortal's choices. The timing was not right. This time, it was, and I could not stop it, Rogan. Stopping a mortal's agency is not within my power. Consequences of those choices, however, are up to me.' she explained gently, holding out her hands as though she were helpless.

'How could you let this happen?' Rogan asked again, his face crumpled in agony and tears. 'Not just to Malia, but to me!' he yelled, struggling to his feet. 'You set me up. You know the fates of mortals. You knew Malia would die all along, didn't you? You knew Haych would kill her. You said, when we made this bargain, that my being in Malia's life would not change or inter-fere with her fate, which means she was always going to die! So, why make me watch? Why make me finally feel? Why make me care if I was only going to lose her?' Rogan's voice was hoarse and strangled.

For the second time over the centuries, since Rogan knew Angelos, she broke her calm exterior and shouted back, 'Because I am the only one that does what is needed to save the souls of mortals! There is so much more at stake than *feelings,* Rogan. The ends justify the means! Without me, Hell would be fit to burst and the cosmic balance of good and evil would be tipped. Trust me, you do not want that to happen. A power war with my sisters isn't a fight where humans win, even if they are lucky enough to survive. I have been the one tasked with keeping the power of energy in check and the scales of justice balanced. I'm not kind, Pet. I can't afford to be. Nor do I have to be in order to see my responsibilities met. I do what has to be done.'

Both stood there, eyes locked in their individual rage. Rogan didn't care what her excuses were.

'You told me once,' he said through gritted teeth, 'that the affairs of the gods aren't my concern. How could something that clearly affected mine and Malia's eternity not be my concern?'

Finally, she shook her head and rolled her eyes, like a sad parent who had a child that would never understand the problems they caused their parents. 'Rogan,' she spoke softly, 'I'll answer all your questions if you answer these last ones. Was it worth it?'

Rogan looked at her like she was losing her mind. He wanted to strangle her.

She asked slowly, 'Was knowing Malia, even though it was only for a week, worth it? The love you feel for her, the fun, joy, and happiness she brought you, wasn't that worth the sacrifice of your happiness right now? Her peace and freedom were worth your soul yesterday,' she reminded him. 'Has that changed? Is she not free and at peace? Would you really exchange those nights, her caresses and kisses, for anything else? Would you give up that love, simply so you wouldn't feel the loss?'

He didn't want to listen to a word she said, but the word "worth" stuck in his mind. Rogan thought back over the past week they had spent together. He remembered Malia dancing in the moonlight and firelight on the beach with sand kicking up around her, hair flying. He could see her smile and glare at the boy that thought she was easy to get. He saw her crying in the gazebo from fear and sorrow when he told her he had to leave yesterday. He felt her lips on his with the cracked marble floor beneath them. He could feel the cool rain on her skin, the flesh, the curves, the hunger beneath his hands. He remembered the way they danced together and how it changed everything in him.

'Would you rather go back to who you were? A being that felt nothing, that had nothing?'

'No,' he finally muttered miserably, looking at Malia's peaceful face. 'No, I wouldn't give that up to go back to who I was.'

Angelos sighed in what he thought was relief.

'Finally, Rogan,' she whispered.

'Finally, what?' he asked sharply.

'You have finally been shaken out of your apathy. You have finally found your humanity.'

'What? This was just a game? So I could learn a lesson?' Rogan's hand curled into a fist, ready to strike her delicate face.

'No,' she answered sternly. 'I told you, Malia's fate would not change. This was always going to be the result. But remember when I also told you I would not share you. Let me amend my former claim of "I will not share you" to "I cannot share you." This was your last chance, because Malia, who is your soul's match, would no longer be a mortal to teach you after this week. It was either Malia, or my servant for eternity. Sharing you was no longer an option. You had a lesson to learn. You needed to learn how to feel; you needed to find your humanity, Rogan. You needed to save your soul! I needed you to save your soul to help with the cosmic balance. Do you understand now? Your emotions were stolen from you when you were alive. Now you have them back. And sacrifice, love, loss, joy, even heartbreak, they are all a part of being human. Love is the very essence of one's soul. Love, the greatest weapon a mortal can possess. To love is to be human. You learned that. How could I expect you to earn your soul back if you didn't want it? If you didn't see the worth of it? If you didn't know what it meant to have it, how would you know what it meant to lose it? Or in your case, give it away to save someone else? How else would you learn the true worth of a soul? The true worth of humanity? The true worth of Malia?'

'You did all this, to what? Save me?' he asked dubiously. It sure didn't feel that way.

'A soul's well-being is my job, Rogan,' she reminded him. Then she urgently leaned forward, 'Your soul is worth saving and you have earned it.'

'Are you giving me back my soul?' he asked, still untrusting and unsure of what game she was playing. She was implying that there was a chance to be with Malia, forever. He wasn't going to let her laugh at him over believing that.

'Why do you think I've been so cruel to you since you arrived here? You are one of my favorites, Pet.'

'Because you were jealous?' he answered.

She laughed. 'I like you, Rogan, but don't flatter yourself. I have much bigger plans.'

'Then why did you torture me? Why the threats and deals?'

She waved her hand like what she had put him through that week was nothing to bother with now. 'For one thing, you were late with my souls that morning. Every soul counts on my scale. The loss of just one, let alone an entire collection, could have had catastrophic consequences. I was cruel that morning, because you deserved a punishment.' She spoke without any hint of regret for what she had done to him. The remnants of her wrath were still clear in her tight mouth. 'But don't forget your body was physically dying when you were made Captain. It is the curse, as you call it, that is keeping it alive. Once you are relieved of the curse, your body will die. The only place and time you can be with Malia is in Paradise. So, she would have to be dead in order to be with you. But aside from that, how else was I going to get you to make a sacrifice? To take a risk and then do something despite that risk? Not everyone would defy a god, Rogan, and not everyone would make a deal with one to save the woman he loves. Trust me, I know. I've been around for a long time. By sacrificing your soul and losing your prize, but not regretting it, you have earned it back. Do you see now? You are free.'

Rogan was prevented from saying anything as a man stumbled onto the deck from the gangplank.

'Malia?' Brandt, bleeding from his chest, stumbled towards them. By the blood he had cascading down his front, and the amount still leaking between his fingers, there was an obvious knife wound from Haych. He tripped over the threshold of the deck, just as the sun rose and the ship would be disappearing from mortal eyes. The call of seagulls and lapping of water against the haul were loud in shocked silence.

'Brandt?' Rogan asked, surprised as he caught Malia's brother just as his knees buckled.

Brandt saw his dead sister and shoved Rogan aside. He crawled to her body.

'Brandt?' Angelos piped up with interest. He continued to ignore everyone as he moaned and mourned over his sister.

'What happened? What happened to my sister?' Brandt asked, his physical agony and emotional pain coming through his gnashed teeth.

'Don't worry about your sister,' Angelos comforted, kneeling beside him. 'She is at peace and will be with her Captain soon.' She gave Rogan a wink and it hit him. He would be with Malia after all. By loving her, he had earned his soul and would be spending eternity not on a ship, but with Malia in Paradise.

Brandt looked up then, as though he were just realizing someone else was beside him.

'Who are you?' he asked, his face growing white, his voice weak.

'I am Angelos, Goddess of Death,' she purred.

Brandt's eyes were confused and a little vacant.

'And you are on my ship, mortal. Payment must be made.'

Chapter Thirty-One

Malia

What is that noise? Is that whistling?

She turned her head, discovering that she was laying down.

The whistling was getting louder. It sounded familiar.

Wherever she had ended up was shrouded in darkness. Malia realized that her eyes were shut and she felt like she was floating, but she brought herself to a standing position. Opening her eyes, she looked around in confusion.

What is going on? The last I knew, I was dying in Rogan's arms, and now I'm floating to music? Where am I?

Looking around, she found herself in the island's cemetery with the familiar lighthouse guarding over her. She vaguely understood that only a few other souls were there and they all looked as confused as she felt.

Suddenly, it hit her. If she were breathing, she would have gasped.

I died. I'm a spirit that is being called by the Captain of Souls. My Captain.

Where was he? She looked around in search of Rogan, eager to see him. He had to be near. He had promised. She heard the pipe. No, not a pipe. A violin?

She remembered the souls before had appeared to glide, but she felt solid.

I don't feel any less human, any less alive. I'm missing a heartbeat. If I still had a heartbeat it would be thundering right now. I no longer need to breathe the salty air, but I am...

Malia weaved around headstones, away from where her parents laid beside her, in search of him. He was here. He had to be.

Flashes of lightning shone from behind the lighthouse and swept across the cemetery. And she saw him.

There he was. Rogan. Standing looking expectant and impatient in the graveyard. But he had his shirt on. He wasn't calling the dead. She saw another person there – Brandt. He was now shirtless, a spade tattoo glowing on his chest as souls approached him. He was the one playing the music, the violin. His left arm worked like it had never been hurt. Malia saw the corner of his lip lift into a smile when he saw her, but kept playing.

When Rogan spotted her, his lips widened into the most beautiful smile he had ever blessed her with. Brandt continued to play his tune, but he didn't call to her soul. Rogan did. Her Captain was there. He too was like her, she noticed. No frail human body, just a radiant soul.

Finally, she reached him. His strong, warm arms encircled her, lifting her weightless body and crushing them together. His deep voice chuckled as he squeezed her. He drew back, caressing her face, moving her still-wild hair out of the way to give her a fierce kiss.

'Paradise.' he said.

Epilogue

Brandt

Sailing away with Paradise at his back, Brandt felt both free and lonely. Like being on a floating deserted island. He was free of the burden that mortality heaves onto you. He no longer had to worry about money, drinking, physical pain, or how he was failing all the time. But the lightness was its own kind of burden when there was no one to share it with. Angelos wasn't exactly the type of woman he could see himself opening up to. And if he let himself, he would find himself spiraling into an abyss of shame, guilt, and an all-consuming bereavement that alcohol would no longer be available to dull.

Having just dropped off his sister and her Captain to their eternal paradise, unknowing if he would ever see her again, made Brandt feel more alone than ever. Before leaving the ship, Malia had given him a hug and threatened that he better find his way there someday. After all, Paradise wouldn't be perfect without all of her family there to enjoy it. Brandt had been too full of shame to commit to anything. He knew he had failed her, their parents, and himself.

'Don't worry, Pet,' the Goddess said while she ran a hand through his thick brown hair. The horizon was changing, the sea ahead was rougher, the night darker. They would be across the mortal barrier soon. 'You'll have the opportunity to make things right, I'll make sure of that.'

'Make it right for whom? Malia is already in Paradise,' he said.

'Not for your sister, silly. For yourself. As soon as we cross back into the mortal realm, I have a new assignment for you.'

'I'm not going to be a collector?'

'Oh, no, you are. You just won't be a Ship Captain. I have somewhere else in mind for you.'

Brandt was confused, how else was he going to collect souls? 'I don't understand, Goddess.'

Angelos gave a wide smile and a loud laugh that showed all of her white teeth.

'Time is a funny thing for a collector,' she said. 'While it feels we have only been gone from Blisse for a few days, by mortal time you have been gone much longer. And, by the time you reach your new station on Starzea, even more time will have elapsed. There have been changes— advancements in transportation that I would like for you to procure while under my services.'

'What kind of advancements?' he asked.

'It's called a train, and you are to be its conductor. Another kind of soul collector.'

Acknowledgments

I want to give a huge thank you to the publishing team at SmashBear Publishing. They believed in this story and were willing to work tirelessly to get it where it is today. Lore, Bianca and all my other editors, you are amazing and it's been humbling to work with you.

I want to thank my best friend, Kimberly Climer. Kim, we both know this book would not have happened without you. You have helped in numerous ways, not just with critique and support, but in keeping me sane and listening to my endless neurotic rants. You are the kind of friend that everyone should want to be when they grow up.

A huge thank you to my husband, who never doubted that I would get this story published one day and has supported all the sacrifices made it do it. And my three kids, Kimberlyn, Clark, and Zander who have taught me what it means to live for something bigger than myself.

The support of my sister, Nikki, and parents and friends who have encouraged me over the past decade to follow my dreams has been immeasurable, thank you.

Thank you for supporting SmashBear Publishing and our authors.

For more information about our authors, upcoming releases and what we publish, you can check out our website

www.smashbearpublishing.com

Or find us on: